TH
KILLER
SHADOW
THIEVES

A DI Tom Blake Thriller

J.F. Burgess

To Shiva
Best wishes
J F Burgess

Printed in the United Kingdom

First Printing, 2018

You can visit the author's website at:

www.jfburgess.co.uk

Dedication

Thanks to my family for their unconditional love and support, especially my wife Rachel.

About the author

My name is J.F. Burgess and I live with my wife and two children in Stoke-on-Trent, England.

"I write tense, gripping, crime fiction thrillers with a twist – or urban cross breed, as I call it. My dramas take you deep inside the criminal mind."

After spending many years doing less than ideal jobs in and around the Potteries five towns, I finally took the plunge and quit work to follow my creative side; starting off initially in 2007 publishing horse racing guides and how-to manuals.

Inspired by the success of local author Mel Sherratt, and in need of a new challenge I decided to try my hand at writing fiction.

CHAPTER 1

Detective Inspector Tom Blake sat drumming his fingers on the wheel of the white Astra pool car parked on Victoria Road, a main artery that fed the city of Stoke-on-Trent. His stomach rumbled in expectation of the return of his partner DS John Murphy with breakfast: hot bacon and cheese oatcakes, a Staffordshire delicacy, enjoyed all over the county.

He turned down Radio Stoke, but Sam Cooke's soulful tones were suddenly replaced with the unmistakable rumble of a high-performance car rapidly approaching from behind. In anticipation of a pursuit he reached for his seat belt and fired up the engine.

Returning to the Astra, DS Murphy glared at the speeding vehicle as it screeched past them doing at least fifty in the thirty zone. Hastily opening the passenger door, he jumped in, dropped two greasy paper bags onto his lap, before wrestling with his seat belt.

'You see that?

'Yeah.'

'I'd put money on it being nicked. Twenty grand's worth driven by a maniac in a red cap,' Blake said, tracing the black Audi TT as it cut straight across the path of an oncoming van and carved through the traffic heading up Lichfield Street.

'Could be a boy racer,' Murphy said as his boss hit the siren, then the accelerator and flew towards the busy Joiners Square roundabout. They swerved around a flatbed pickup, avoiding collision with a red Nissan Duke by the tightest of margins. Blake glanced in the rear-view mirror at the chaos he'd caused: cars screeching to a halt, horns blasting, bringing the roundabout to a standstill.

'Shitting hell, Tom! You trying to kill us before breakfast?'

Focusing on the road ahead he didn't reply. The back end of the car drifted as he headed up the incline, slamming through the gears, adrenaline pumping through him like an electrical surge.

Murphy radioed in the shout. 'In pursuit of a black Audi TT registration NT43 USD. Heading up Lichfield Street, requesting assistance from traffic. Possible stolen vehicle driven at excessive speed?'

Further up the road they closed to within fifty yards of the Audi. It slowed down behind a Citroën people carrier, air brakes hissing, before the driver slammed on the gas and flew dangerously past several other cars on the wrong side of the road. It was ten a.m. and, the commuter traffic had cleared. Thank god, Blake thought, manoeuvring with caution past the line of cars that had eased to the curb.

A gap of around two hundred yards had now opened between them. The Audi swerved around a tight left-hand bend and disappeared down Regent Road.

Blake pumped the brakes and the back end of the Astra drifted to the right as it swerved round after him. Keeping control he eased off, then, as the road straightened, he put his foot down and slammed through the gears, mindful of a sharp left-hand turn leading onto College Road six hundred yards ahead.

'You're losing him, Tom!'

'Don't worry, he's got to slow down before joining College Road because after that there's speed humps. God forbid he gets that far… there'll be loads of students milling about!'

Cleveland Road eased to the right before straightening again, and the Audi came back in view.

'Shit, he's not slowing.' Blake clenched the wheel; taking his foot off the gas he jammed onto the brake and winced. Murphy pushed hard into the footwell, hands clenching the sides of his seat. Both men prepared for impact with gritted teeth as the Astra swerved and screeched to a grinding halt across the middle of the road, leaving an arc of rubber burns on the tarmac.

'Shit, he's losing it,' Murphy said in disbelief.

They watched in horror. The Audi's brake lights flashed. The car skidded, mounted a tarmac island partitioning the bend, locked and swerved before slamming into a solid six-foot high wall on the opposite side of the road. The bonnet crumpled, like a soda can being stamped on, spraying shards of glass and plastic over the pavement as the windscreen imploded. Its back end bounced, flashing a glimpse of the chassis before crashing hard onto the pavement.

Blake froze in his seat, sweating, his heart pounding; a disturbing flashback of the devastating hit-and-run incident that had killed his young son and wife ten years ago flooded his mind. The side impact of the vehicle had spun their car a hundred and eighty degrees into a dry stone wall. His colleagues never caught the driver, and he found himself subconsciously looking for the perpetrator every time the force apprehended a joyrider.

Rooted to their seats they expected the worst. In a moment of deadly silence they watched steam dissipate from the destroyed Audi's radiator. A blue Volvo stood stationary in the right hand lane of College Road; its driver had exited and stood behind the vehicle warning oncoming traffic. Residents from nearby houses stood rubbernecking behind the safety of their front gates. Time froze for a few seconds while the two detectives processed the carnage.

Without warning the crushed driver's door was forced open and a young man no more than twenty, nursing what looked like a broken arm, ran frantically across the road and disappeared through the Victorian entrance gates of Hanley Park. Murphy flung his door open and dived out of the Astra in pursuit of the fleeing joyrider.

Blake shook himself out of paralysis and hit the radio. 'DI Blake, vehicle crashed and abandoned at the junction between College Road and Cleveland Road, requesting immediate ambulance and traffic presence. Suspect left the scene. DS Murphy pursuing on foot.'

Puffing like an old codger DS Murphy gave pursuit, but he was embarrassingly out of shape; too many takeaways and pints after work had increased his waistline enough to handicap him. Sweat ran down his spine. He brushed his fringe out of his eyes and cantered, zigzagging over low flowerbeds and new cut grass, levelling pansies like a portly Jack Russell first time off its lead for a week.

An elderly gent plodding along with his Labrador just about managed to dodge the fifteen stone Sergeant in full pelt. Considering his arm was broken, and he may be suffering the effects of concussion, the kid had some guts to attempt outrunning the cops, Murphy thought.

Flighting three steps at a time down towards the bandstand, Murphy saw his prey was quickly losing pace as he tried to escape through a cluster of ash trees like a pigeon with a clipped wing.

Whilst attempting to rejoin the winding concrete path that meandered through the park, he stumbled over a loose edging stone and crashed to the ground. Seeing him writhe in agony, Murphy decided to spare him the full force of the law. He walked cautiously towards him, knelt and handcuffed his unbroken arm to a belt loop above his backside.

'Ah! Ger off me, you fucking pig!' he screeched, flapping on the path like a captured fish.

Totally spent, Murphy bent, hands on his knees, catching his breath. He paused for another few gulps of air. 'I'm... arresting you... on suspicion of vehicle theft... and dangerous driving.'

The kid struggled for a few seconds before capitulating, as the out-of-breath DS finished reading his rights, his knee rooted in the lad's back. Up on their feet, the DS jostled the reluctant captive the few hundred yards back towards the park entrance where Blake stood waiting with two paramedics who'd just arrived at the scene.

Blake shouted once they were within earshot. 'Did he give you much grief, John?'

'Nothing I can't handle,' he said, still suffering from his exertions.

One of the paramedics motioned the kid towards the nearest bench. 'Let's get you checked over, son.'

'Check my sarge over afterwards, will you? He looks like he's burst a blood vessel,' Blake asked, smirking.

'Sod off, Tom!' Murphy said, unimpressed.

Although in pain, the kid looked more annoyed at being arrested than anything else. It never ceased to amaze Blake how arrogant these little bastards could be. Joyriding had decreased across the city in recent years. Better education and stringent sentencing deterred teenage potheads from the Estates, but there was still a minority who were difficult to reach, often from dysfunctional families.

The paramedic lifted the lad's eyelids and flashed a torch over his pupils, then asked him some basic cognitive questions. Apart from the arm and a few facial scratches, he appeared unscathed, which both detectives thought was a bloody miracle considering the Audi was a complete wreck.

'What's your name, son?' Blake probed.

The lad stared, into space.

'Can't this wait until the doctors have seen him? He needs that arm plastering,' protested the paramedic, walking their patient back to the ambulance parked in front of the park gates.

'Once we get the all clear from A&E we'll come and collect him for an interview,' Blake responded.

The cheeky sod shot them a juvenile smirk.

Murphy glared at him. 'Don't worry, son, you'll keep till later.'

The two detectives strode back to the Astra in a heightened state of alert. Unbelievably Murphy stood salivating like a ravenous dog at the limp paper bags on his seat.

'Seriously, you're still hungry after that?'

'A man's got to eat,' Murphy protested, feeling cheated after his exertions. 'Did you see that? Pisses me off! Little bastard totals a twenty-grand motor, tries to leg it and he's frigging laughing at us.'

Blake reassured him. 'Don't worry, John. We'll get him on car theft and dangerous driving. He'll be looking at twelve months plus and a driving ban.'

'Some poor bugger's looking at an insurance nightmare, though,' Murphy moaned. 'Those bastards always try to wriggle out of paying.'

'Suppose. Total write-off that one.'

'Yep. Premium through the roof next time. I'm just going to check the vehicle,' he said, making his way towards the abandoned wreck as Murphy dragged his aching carcass behind.

'Careful, Tom, it could blow!'

Blake ignored his concerns. Peering through the window he spotted a cream manbag lying in the passenger foot well. 'Any ideas how we'll get that?' he asked, tapping the glass.

Murphy was still puffing like he'd done ten rounds in the ring with a heavyweight. 'Just… give us a minute, will you, Tom?'

'You OK?' he asked staring at the moons of sweat under Murphy's arms.

'Knackered! Too old for this game; without the broken arm I wouldn't have caught him. My suspect chasing days are numbered.'

'After that performance I was thinking of entering you into the Potteries Marathon,' Blake teased.

'Yeah, right, good one, Tom. Traffic will be here any minute. Let's get back and slap the oatcakes in the microwave. I'm bloody starving!'

'Not until we've fished out that bag.'

'How? The door's demolished!' he said, annoyed the joyriding little shit had delayed his breakfast.

Blake had an idea. 'Hang fire a minute while I fetch my baton from the car.'

Minutes later he'd caved the window in and fished out the bag like hooking a duck at the fair. He unzipped it and retrieved a package.

'Shit, there's thousands-worth here,' he said, holding a bag of brown powder the size of a regular sugar pack, strengthened at each end with parcel tape.

'You're not kidding. Major league quantity?'

'Could be a mule for a dealer? We'll know more after questioning him.'

'Doubt he'll give us a name,' Murphy said, his normal pale colour gradually returning. What's with the logo?' He pointed to a bottle kiln printed in brown ink on the side of the bag.

Blake turned to face him, oblivious to a thin stream of smoke rising from under the bonnet of the Audi.

'Your guess is as good as mine. Must be some sick branding for the local market?'

'Tom, get back! It's on fire.'

Blake darted towards his partner who'd retreated to a safe distance. They both stood behind the park gates and watched in disbelief as flames lapped around the edges of the crumpled bonnet. Within seconds the car was burning intensely, engulfed in red heat, bellowing black smoke as the plastic and foam interior fed the fire.

The residents of Cleveland Road stood motionless as the muted sound of sirens echoed in the distance. That silence was shattered by a deafening explosion. A huge ball of orange flames erupted into the air, showering fragments of glass and plastic onto the road. An electrical cable trailed from the smashed base of the traffic island, which the joyrider had flattened in his insane trajectory into six foot of bricks and mortar. Incendiary blue sparks of electricity arced under the burning remains of what was once a top-of-the-range motor.

CHAPTER 2

The duty doctor in A&E gave the joyrider the all-clear around lunchtime; apart from a broken arm, his injuries were superficial. No concussion, not even a stiff neck. DS Murphy glanced in the rear-view mirror at the agitated youth, handcuffed to PC Haynes in the back of the patrol car.

'Unbelievable! You're lucky to be alive after the mental stunt you pulled earlier. That Audi you totalled caught fire and exploded. It could have killed someone. Best if you cooperate with us. What's your name?' he asked, indicating to turn into the station car park.

The kid hesitated. 'Dean.'

'Dean what?'

'Taylor.'

'Well, Dean let's get you booked in at the desk,' Murphy said, slotting next to Blake's Jag, mindful of knocking his boss's pride and joy. Climbing out of the patrol car. Murphy led the way to the reception with the PC towing the reluctant kid.

'Sarge, this is Dean Taylor.'

Lowering his specs the sergeant studied him. 'Back again, lad? I thought you might have learned your lesson by now. What is it this time, Dean?'

Taylor shrugged his shoulders nonchalantly. His face reddened as the desk sergeant typed his name into the database. He'd got previous form.

'You know him then, Sarge?' Murphy asked.

''Fraid so. Dean's visited us a few times in the last couple of years.'

The kid's record showed several convictions for drug dealing on the Heath Hayes Estate. After his mother died from cancer he'd been left in the care of his alcoholic father whose parenting skills were non-existent. Social services had intervened, and placed him in care. By the age of fourteen he was a full-time drug mule, distributing cannabis across the Heath Hayes Estate on a BMX before eventually doing six months in Werrington Young Offenders Institute for possession with intent to supply ecstasy. The drug squad came close to prosecuting his supplier, Yusuf Benzar, a local Turkish wide boy. But a search of his property produced nothing; subsequent surveillance also drew a blank, and the case against him fell apart through lack of evidence. At no point did Dean ever shop him.

The sergeant frowned. 'You've excelled yourself today, Dean; joyriding and possession of a large quantity of a Class A. Not looking good.

'Sarge,' Murphy said, 'can you get someone to put him in interview room two? I need a word with DI Blake.'

Half an hour later Blake kicked off proceedings. The overwhelming amount of evidence against Taylor left his solicitor with little to do except observe and take notes regarding his plea.

'Whose gear is it? You might as well tell us because we're well aware of your associates.'

Taylor sat with a scowl on his face, and clearly had no intention of revealing his supplier.

'It's mine.'

'Come on, Dean, we've tested the one-kilo bag found in the Audi, and it's ninety per cent pure; that's rare in this county. Its estimated street value is around eighty grand. We can appreciate you're scared of what your dealer might do to you if you give him up. I can assure you we'll keep you safe.'

Frustrated, he said, 'Yeah, right! Will you be sharing a cell with me?'

'Given your age and circumstances, we can ask the CPS to place you in a prison where known associates of the dealer aren't serving sentences? We know the gear isn't yours. Our records show that only a handful of people in Stoke-on-Trent deal in the quantity found in your possession. I'm going to say a few names, and you just give me the nod? Azeed Akhtar, Barry Chamberlain, Yusuf Benzar.'

To his annoyance Taylor refused to play ball. So he changed approach.

'Where did you nick the car from?'

'Car park.'

'Which one?'

'In Fenton.'

'Funny that. The owner says he left it parked on Mill Street car park in Longton.

The teenager sat there, seemingly oblivious to the severity of his situation.

'Cooperate with us and the judge will take that into consideration when sentencing you. Anyway, we have a few enquiries to make and will have proper chat soon. In the meantime PC Haynes will get you settled in a comfy cell. Should give you time to consider how much trouble you're in?'

Dean Taylor's foolish reluctance to cough up his dealer's name would cost him an extra twelve months' jail. Thankfully, recent raids put the most serious players away for a long time. Nemesis was a massive coordinated drugs operation, which swept across the whole city, leaving just two dealers who fitted the profile in terms of financial clout. It didn't take the biggest leap of faith to decide who to bring in first. Turkish wide-boy Yusuf Benzar was a prime suspect.

Taking the initiative, Blake picked up the phone and called DS Jack Landman, his colleague in the drug squad.

'Jack, how are you?'

'Good, yourself?'

'Not too shabby. Listen, we've hauled in a joyrider named Dean Taylor. According to PNC records you did him for possession with intent to supply ecstasy, a couple of years ago. He ended up in Werrington for six months.'

'Taylor?' Landman paused. Oh, yeah, I remember we did a month's surveillance on his suspected supplier. Clever bastard shut his entire operation down though. Went to ground and he's not been on our radar since. Why, has something come up?'

'Apart from slamming a twenty-six grand Audi into a wall, we caught him in possession of one kilo of ninety per cent pure heroin.'

'Shit! Ninety per cent? That's virtually unheard of outside London. Is that definite?' he asked, surprised.

'Had it confirmed by forensics earlier; the report should be on the database soon.'

'So you're wondering if Yusuf Benzar is back in business?'

'Exactly. Taylor's a known associate and we want to pull Benzar in for questioning. Obviously we don't want to step on any toes and compromise ops you've got going on with him?'

Landman glanced at a sheet of A4 next to his monitor, with dealers' names on it. 'Hard to say, really. Nemesis put most of the known faces inside, but there's one or two small-timers still peddling weed. Ninety per cent pure is in a different league though. Turkish transit from Afghanistan probably, which means there could be larger quantities waiting to hit the streets.'

Blake pressed. 'Are you working him at present?

'No. Like I said, he dropped off the radar.'

'OK. We'll bring him in for questioning then?'

'Let me speak to Clive first. We don't want to jeopardise missing out on a significant haul. Benzar's a clever bastard… keeps his distance from distribution by using self-sufficient criminal cells. Dean Taylor is just collateral. Gimme five minutes and I'll get back to you?'

Twenty minutes later Blake's office phone rang.

'DI Blake?' DI Moore said. 'DS Landman's put me in the picture about Yusuf Benzar.'

'What do you think?' DC Moore's father, Clive headed up the drug squad and had the first say on tactical decisions concerning drug-related suspects.

'It's a tough call. I've had no intel from Customs or SOCA on Benzar. Problem is pulling him now; would spook him. Based on the kilogram alone I'll push for surveillance, if Coleman will sanction it, with all these bloody government cuts,' Moore warned.

'You're not kidding; we did bloody stationery inventories last week!'

'Unbelievable! Counting the pens! Bureaucratic arseholes!' He groaned. 'Anyway I'll put it to him and call you before the end of play. Appreciate the heads up on this one, Tom.'

'No problem,' he lied. He wanted to nail Benzar himself, not hand him to the drug squad on a plate.

Yusuf Benzar currently lived in a modest terraced house in the shadow of three 1970's tower blocks at the top of Limekiln, a long winding hill leading up to the city centre. To the dismay of law-abiding locals, the area was known for heroin users.

A three-man surveillance team hid behind the net curtains of number thirty-two Carson Street. A camera fitted with a field lens sat on its tripod, pointing directly at Benzar's house. Their task was to watch his movements. DI Clive Moore practically had to beg Chief Inspector Coleman to sanction the operation.

On day two of surveillance the three officers were bored rigid. There was only so much poker and online porn you could absorb. Benzar had only left the property to fetch bottles of lager and fags from a nearby off-licence. He'd had two visitors: the postman who'd delivered a small parcel; and a woman they'd assumed was a prostitute, judging by her garish six-inch pink heels, short skirt, and skimpy top.

'Does this tosser ever go anywhere?' moaned the bald officer.

The camera tech scoffed. 'God knows? It's as if he knows we're here.'

Wiping beads of sweat from his shiny dome, his colleague speculated. 'Thing is, he's not your average dumb ganja dealer; he knows the score. Clive reckons there's another large consignment on its way.

'Yeah, I know,' the camera tech countered. 'He reckons it's straight from Afghanistan, which means organised.'

'What's the world coming too?' The bald officer added. 'It's so much easier staking out skanks, selling weed and monkey dust.'

'You're not kidding. If we sent a team in there now they'd find diddly,' the tech speculated, 'apart from a few wraps of personal. I'd put a fiver on it.'

'A fiver! You tight twat,' the bald officer remonstrated. 'It's got worse since the EU's open-border policy. That bastard will have multiple identities and funds scattered over Europe.'

'Yep. I bet most of his mullah's stashed in small East European countries with antiquated laws and corrupt officials.'

'Definitely. Pay monkey nuts you get monkey work.'

'You're not kidding. That's why half the Eastern block is clambering to get here. Seven quid an hour looks a bloody good deal.'

'Honestly, you pair are fantasists,' said the third cop.

CHAPTER 3

Barry Gibson sat in the White Horse pub, Hanley; resisting the urge not to buy another pint before his dealer arrived. The skinhead had been receiving gear on the tab for a few months, and he surprised even himself at how he'd managed to pay back what he owed each month and make a profit. But it was getting harder. His heavy drinking was costing more each week and he'd developed a taste for the pills; they blotted out the troubling memories and depression. Because he'd established a level of trust with the dealer, he'd decided to go for broke: ordered a hundred Kilnee's, thirty wraps of Charlie, and an ounce of Afghani black. Those skanks on the Heath Hayes Estate would lap it up. Only this time, he had no intention of paying any of it back.

The dealer known only as Stomper to third parties went straight to the bar and ordered two pints for him and Gibson, before sitting down opposite him.

'All right?'

'Yeah, have you got the gear?' Gibson said, lowering his voice.

'What's with the big increase in quantities?'

'Demand! There's loads of revival rave nights from back in the day going on.'

'Fair enough.'

'So?'

'Usual deal?'

They entered the men's and Gibson slid a shot bolt on the back of the door. He had an arrangement with the landlord: a free quarter of black for his wife's back pain in exchange for fifteen minutes of uninterrupted time. Gibson called him an hour before he was coming in the pub, and he whizzed the bolt on with his battery driver, then took it off after they'd gone.

'There's no sale or return on this. You know the fucking consequences of not paying in full.'

'Yeah, yeah I know.'

Stomper fished an eight inch long block of Afghani black resin out of his cagoule. Gibson stood back as he placed it on the marble surrounding the basin. The dealer retrieved a small razor-sharp knife from his coat. He held it in his right hand and ignited a cheap lighter in the other. Once the blade was glowing hot, he sliced through the resin and passed the off-cut to Gibson. Gibson put it in his pocket along with a freezer bag containing the wraps and pills. All he had to do now was shift the gear, before he necked half the profits. Maybe just one pill to calm his nerves, he thought to himself.

CHAPTER 4

Ibrahim Benzar – the man known as the Ghost by local criminals – stood on the leaded roof of Hanley's Victorian Town Hall gazing with purpose across the city skyline, his attention focused on one building in particular. But, until the right people were on board, he'd keep the target under wraps. Just the thought of it excited him.

The logistics of a job such as this carried huge risk, as Stoke-on-Trent's police headquarters were located close by. The whole event could be locked down within minutes, leaving the crew to fight out their exit in the cop's backyard.

He'd collaborated on months of meticulous planning with the Collector: one of the world's richest, most reclusive thieves. And everything needed checking and rechecking before finalising with the team he planned to execute the job: a group of experienced professionals in various fields, who he trusted to pull it off.

The muscle end of things was straightforward to arrange; the ruthless Simbala brothers, ex-members of the Kenyan Mafia, would deal with anybody who stepped out of line. Although naturally brains were considerably more important.

With the next phase rooted in his mind, he delved into the pocket of his Ralph Lauren jacket and retrieved the secure mobile the Collector provided. The cunning bastard always used crypto phone technology to communicate with his operatives, including Ibrahim. The two-way encryption and decryption conversations, once in session code, couldn't be eavesdropped on by anyone. Ultimately, they were far less traceable than amateurish burners.

It was 7.30 a.m. in Miami and the reclusive Collector sat sipping iced grapefruit juice, shading from the blinding morning Florida sun. Gazing over his office balcony he watched the endless cycle of pacific waves crashing on the glorious white sands in front of his forty million dollar beach mansion on the Miami coast.

They'd met eight years ago in what the Turkish classed as hell on earth – Diyarbakir Prison in south-eastern Turkey, where overcrowding and torture were rife. The obscenely rich American was incarcerated for attempting to smuggle stolen artefacts from the Turkish National gallery to America. Ibrahim was in for racketeering. Fearful for his life amongst the murderers and drug lords, the Collector paid him shedloads for protection during his four-year sentence. This was the one and only time he'd been caught and he didn't plan to repeat the nightmare ordeal.

'Richard! Just a quick call to inform you I'm putting the team together for our venture.'

'Excellent! Just choose your people wisely. No amateurs or squealers,' he said in the familiar Texan drawl Ibrahim was accustomed to.

'Don't worry, I'll only use the best people.'

'OK, let me know when y'all ready to move.'

'I'll call when we have something more solid.'

'OK. Y'all take care.'

Ending the conversation, Ibrahim retrieved a small diary from his inside pocket and flicked through the contacts. He made a series of calls, starting with his brother Yusuf to arrange an evening meeting at the Genting Casino, Hanley. He gloated; life was sweet when you controlled your own destiny.

CHAPTER 5

Ibrahim Benzar sat beside Charlie Bullard in the mock Mead hall of the Potteries Museum & Art Gallery, gazing at a glowing orange fire, imagining a fierce Saxon King perched on his throne draped in boar skin, receiving gifts and surveying his stunning gold. They watched a Saxon docu-drama on a large wall-mounted TV. The narrator told the Hoard story.

'Lichfield seven hundred AD. Two huge shires laboured a two-wheeled cart through meadow grass, daisies and white clover as a gentle breeze carried the subtle smell of summer across the violet skies of Anglo Saxon Staffordshire. In silence seven Saxon warriors followed their esteemed leader – Athelred the Mercian Overlord – as he edged through the grass towards a mound overlooking the ancient Roman road known as Watling Street.

'Their eyes adjusted to the blue enveloping darkness surrounding the meadows and forests. Mindful no one was watching they strode towards the proposed burial ground. After a guarded glance across the field he signalled to the colossal warrior Abrican to join him with a drawn finger pointing towards a grassy mound.

'The battle-hardened warrior unclasped his Tri-bird brooch, allowing his wool cape to fall onto the dry summer earth. Then raising his sword-scarred arms, he heaved his hefty chainmail tunic over his head, laying it on the earth beside the cape.

'"Fetch me the Iron Hoe," he uttered under his breath at the other six expectant warriors waiting in anticipation by the cart.

'The small but fearless warrior known as Beadurof lifted a long shaft iron hoe from the pile of digging tools stacked on top of a hessian drape, disguising the Hoard from prying eyes. They'd passed through many villages on their arduous journey to find a burial site. Suddenly, the silent anticipation of the gathering was disturbed by a flock of late summer larks swathing west across the violet skies. The King spoke with clarity.

'"Balder came to me in slumber two nights past, pointing to this place; we must act now. The wolves prowl over yonder forest and we must heed attack. Pray for his watchful blessing on this morn as we commit our Hoard to the ground, lest into our enemy's hands it shall fall."

'Abrican's veins strained against his muscles as he swung the iron hoe with raw power. It struck the sun-dried earth with a deep thud, dispersing dust onto the turn shoes of the encircled warriors clasping iron hoes, in readiness to join the dig. Patiently they

waited to bury: filigreed gold sword fittings, pommel caps, hilt collars and the twisted cross of their pillaged Hoard, stolen from the slain corpses of their enemies on the Northumbria and East Anglia battlefields.

'As the iron hoes pummelled the ground, thud after thud, Athelred raised his arms, outstretched his palms skyward and proclaimed to Balder…

"Rise, Lord, and may thy enemies be dispersed and those who hate thee be driven from thy face."'

The pair spent the next half an hour discreetly surveying the room and surrounding area, looking for exit and entry points, cameras, alarms and assessing the locks on the Hoard display cabinets, keeping in mind the Collector's ten-point blueprint for museum heists: a plan used in several successful robberies from the world's richest museums. He'd even included video footage of an infamous painting haul, captured by one of his operatives wearing a body-cam.

This was their third visit in two months, but to avoid suspicion Ibrahim sent his cousin Stellio to take discreet tourist photographs on his phone. That, combined with a floor plan and architectural plans downloaded from the Internet, and now with the caretaker onside, they'd just about got the measure of the place.

Charlie itched his silver, eighties style moustache. 'You reckon we can do it then?'

'Why not? Imagine what you could do with a million quid?' Ibrahim enthused.

'That's a lot of poke!' Charlie said, not wanting to consider the prospect of going back inside if it went tits up.

'As long as we stick to the plan everything will be OK. Anyway, don't worry about that now; the others aren't on board yet and there's still shit loads to organize.'

Charlie gave him a suspicious agreeing look. 'OK.'

'The main thing is we need to be ready by the nineteenth of June, because the other half of the Hoard is being transferred from Birmingham Museum, for a three-week exhibition here. That's the only time the collection will be complete. All three-point-three million of it.'

'So, this is only half?'

'Yeah.'

'Phew! This might sound a stupid question, but how can we get a million each if it's only worth three-point-three?'

'Best if you don't ask too many questions. Safe to say our benefactor is minted.'

On the way back out of the museum, Ibrahim veered into the visitors' shop, which stocked a curious mix of handmade pottery, nineteenth-century black-and-white postcards of industrial Stoke, reissue Arnold Bennett books, Spitfire memorabilia and an entire stand dedicated to the Staffordshire Hoard, including replicas of the key pieces. In the end he purchased the official Hoard guide for a fiver.

He winked at Charlie as they parted outside on the block paved bridge way. 'Bedtime homework.'

CHAPTER 6

Ibrahim's mobile rang; it was his brother Yusuf.

'You won't fucking believe this. That dumb bastard Dean Taylor's been arrested and lost our shipment. Pig scum!'

'How many times? Not over the phone!'

'We need to meet now.'

'In an hour. I'm busy.'

'Are you crazy, bro?'

'Think, before you say another word? One hour, I'll call you,' he said, stabbing the call end button.

Yusuf was such a bloody liability. His coke habit had escalated over the last twelve months and it was cutting into the profits. He was only still breathing because they were brothers, otherwise he'd have eradicated him months ago.

Regaining his composure, he continued climbing the winding slate staircases leading to the second floor of City Central Library.

Inside the Reference Library he sat at a large table circled by floor-to-ceiling shelves of telephone directories, trade directories and local maps. The windows above the bookshelves were narrow slots, designed to maximize storage space. Being a muggy summer's day several were open. Peering out he saw the massive roofs of the newly completed council buildings stretch out behind the Library.

A helpful librarian provided him with three map resources, including an A4 Street Atlas of Staffordshire, which looked the most promising with its comprehensive coverage, but more importantly large text street and road names of the city centre and surrounding areas. The main buildings were colour-coded. Having lived in Stoke-on-Trent most of his adult life, he recognized the street names, but this map of the city gave him an entirely new perspective.

CHAPTER 7

Nathan Dukes had been buying gear from his supplier Yusuf Benzar for a couple of years. The brickie's labourer and part-time bouncer had developed an unhealthy weekend coke addiction. Unfortunately, due to work drying up he was laid off-site for two months, leaving him four weeks adrift on his rent money, and owing Benzar four hundred quid. The money he got from working the door at the White Horse paid for the shopping, and his missus' part-time hours at the *Bargains Galore* discount store in town just about covered the bills, but they struggled. Their landline had been cut off, and his car tax was due in a week; leaving him no option but to do some debt collecting for the dealer.

People who owed money were usually scared by big guys turning up on their doorstep unannounced. And, if he was honest he enjoyed intimidating them. It was the only time he was in control. Besides, Benzar promised him a couple of grand to settle outstanding debts, and he wasn't fussy how he collected the money.

Dukes had already come down heavily on a middle-aged bloke who owed five hundred quid, battered a youth who borrowed money to buy a moped, and confiscated a woman's new TV.

Today, he was off around the Heath Hayes estate with a telescopic police baton in his combat trouser pocket. He was pissed off at visiting the same people more than three times and someone was having it. If any one really needed scaring he'd flash his blade.

He sat in his car fired up; eagerly waiting for the addresses to be texted through to him. After five minutes he had his first house call, a couple living in flat 23 in the row of maisonettes on Creswell Road. He recognised the address, a pair of scruffy twats in dirty tracksuits he remembered from his last call two weeks ago. They'd better have at least three hundred quid, or there'd be mither.

Dukes parked his BMW in the street just behind Creswell Road. He didn't want to alert them. He knocked on number 23 lightly, within a few seconds he heard a man's voice, 'Hang on I'm coming.' Great, they were expecting someone. A scrawny thin youth in his late twenties eased the door open about twelve inches and peered through the gap with a fag hanging out of his mouth. The moment he saw Dukes he panicked and tried to slam it shut. Dukes jammed his boot in the gap and barged in, knocking his fag out of his mouth.

'What do you want?'

'Don't play the stupid twat. You know what I want, at least three hundred today, or I'm taking stuff.'

'Is Dave back with the draw, I'm dying for a spliff,' a female voice shouted from another room.

'Babe get here! It's that debt collector! He's threatening to take stuff if we don't give him three hundred today.'

'For fucks sake! I told him last time, come at the end of the month, when the housing benefit comes through,' she moaned standing in the hallway looking at her partner on his arse.

'I tell you what, how about I take your new TV and stereo and a hundred quid?' Dukes said giving them the chance to avoid the inevitable.'

'No chance! We only just got them about a month ago.'

'You won't miss them then, will you?' Dukes replied.

The youth reared up into his face. 'Piss off!'

Dukes belted him hard on the side of the head. Disorientated, he stumbled and fell back onto the carpet.

Realising they had to pay something, the woman grabbed her partner by the neck of his hoody and dragged him into the living room. She shut the door on her way back into the hallway to confront Dukes.

'Listen, come in here,' she motioned Dukes towards another door. It was a small bedroom with the wallpaper stripped off.

'Sit down Mr; I'm sure we can come to some arrangement?' she said, rubbing his crotch.

'You filthy bitch.'

'I'll suck you off if you'd accept forty quid today? That's all I've got.'

Dukes stared at her. Thinking – yeah and you'd bite my dick off as well you mad cow; although, she wasn't bad looking. 'Make it a shag and fifty quid, and the stereo to call the dogs off?' The young woman thought about it for a few minutes, then stripped down to her knickers and lay provocatively across the bed. Dukes undid his belt and dropped his trousers to his ankles, as she reached under the mattress and pulled out a condom.

Shagging her, he looked around the barren room realising these poor sods hadn't got a pot to piss in.

CHAPTER 8

'Carl, what the bloody hell are you doing?' screamed Katrina Osborne down the stairs of her boyfriend's terraced house in Cooper Street, Milton. At once she realised there'd be consequences for her outburst. Their relationship was toxic at the best of times, an addictive communion neither of them had the guts to break apart.

Without warning Carl burst out of the kitchen, flew through the sparse living room, and launched his fist into the nicotine-stained door leading to the stairs. Hand throbbing, he stormed up the steps, and grabbed her chiffon blouse, pulling them face-to-face.

'Piss off, you're hurting me! What you banging at?' she grimaced.

'I'll bang you in a minute, bitch. I've told you not to interrupt me when I'm working on me scooter.'

'OK! It's my night out. Just don't start, please; I'm begging you?'

With reluctance he let go of her and retreated downstairs without another word. She padded back into their bedroom. He loved that frigging scooter more than her, she thought, putting the finishing touches to her blusher.

Turning to the side she studied herself in the full-length mirror on the wardrobe door. Considering she was forty-two, she still had it. A nice set of pins, a great arse, a blonde bob with no grey roots, and pert breasts that had yet to droop south.

She glanced at her outrageously high cork wedges, and felt horny. Hitching up her knee-length leather skirt, she thought, sod him, I'll go commando, and wriggled her tiny G-string knickers over the shoes. She slipped them into her shoulder bag next to a loaded coke bullet and a joint she'd nicked earlier from Carl's secret stash in the bottom of his bedside cabinet drawer. Tonight she needed to forget the arrogant bastard.

Suddenly, her phone vibrated on the bed.

'Hello.'

'Hi, babe.' It was Luna, her best friend and drinking buddy. 'I'll pick you up at half past seven.'

'See you then,' Kat said sharply.

'What's the matter? You OK?' Luna asked, detecting despondency in her friend's voice.

'Just had a row with that bastard.'

'You'll be OK with a few glasses of wine inside you. Did you get that gear?'

'Yeah.'

'Forget him. He's not worth it. Let's party?'

'Ta ra.'

'Ta ra.'

She took a last look in the mirror before tackling the steep stairs, gripping onto the flaking handrail as she waddled down.

In the living room she perched on the tired, black, leather sofa, and balled through to the kitchen, 'Carl, can you lend me twenty quid for the taxi? I'll pay you back tomorrow, promise.'

He poked his head through the kitchen doorframe and ranted, 'Are you taking the piss?

'I need to get home. Can't walk very far in these shoes.'

'Wear your pumps then,' he mocked.

'Real sexy, don't be stupid.'

'How you going to pay for drinks with no money?' he snapped. 'You daft cow.'

'I'm going to the cashpoint.'

With a surprise change of attitude he said, 'There's eighty quid in my coat on the back of the chair. Take one of the twenty notes, but I want it back in the morning.'

'Thanks, will do.' What had come over him; generosity, without questions? She fished in the pockets of his black coat locating his mobile first. Standing with it in her hand, curiosity got the better of her. Tapping the screen she saw two new text messages. One from his mate, and another from his boss.

Meet us at the Millrace at 8.00.
Pick me up at the Slipware Tankard 12pm tomorrow.

She fumbled it back inside his pocket and then found the eighty quid in the other inside pocket. Why was he lending her cash? Seriously out of character, she thought. But, it was Friday night so she ignored it. The twenty quid would do for taxis, but the credit card she'd taken from his drawer earlier would pay for drinks.

She was about to sit when the taxi's horn beeped. She trotted into the front room, opened the door, grabbed the tarnished brass knocker and slammed the tatty green door of number twenty Cooper Street.

Katrina had met Luna at Club Golden in the mid-nineteen nineties. She looked stunning in her new Primarni PU leather dress, with daringly low cleavage and waistline peep holes.

'You look hot!' she pouted, closing the taxi door behind her. 'Are those new heels?' She stared at Luna's black vamp cut-out platforms as the taxi turned right heading along Leek Road towards the city.

'Got them today.'

'They're lush.'

'So, what you been rowing about?'

'Not in here, babe, I'll tell you in the pub.

They left the taxi in Old Hall Street at 7.45 p.m., and crossed the road linking arms. Heading for the nearest cashpoint, they passed the Reginald Mitchell pub across the pedestrianised space opposite McDonald's, to a chorus of wolf whistles from a group of young blokes sat smoking on the granite street furniture.

Kat lit the joint and inhaled. Glancing at each other they giggled like teenagers. Shit, that felt good, she thought, exhaling the warm ganja smoke.

'We're old enough to be their mothers.'

'Nice to know you can still turn heads though, Kat.'

'I know,' she said, passing the spliff over to Luna.'

'How much you brought out? Kat asked her.'

'Seventy quid.'

'You won't need that.'

'Depends, if we latch onto any blokes.'

'I'd better get the same.'

'Whose card you using? Carl's? Does he know you've got it?

'What do you think?'

'He'll go sodding ballistic!'

Kat sniggered as she passed over the spliff. 'To be honest, Lune, I couldn't give a shit any more. He never buys me anything or takes me anywhere. This is payback.

'Where we going first?'

'Auctioneers, OK?'

'Fine by me, babe.'

She knelt and ground the spliff out under her wedge.

'You dirty cow,' Luna said, surprised. 'I've just seen your arse!'

'Let's hope there's no wind tonight then!'

'Where're your knickers?'

'In my bag.'

They turned onto Percy Street and hobbled towards the pub. Two chubby bouncers stood on the stone steps leading up to the Auctioneers, one of the oldest pubs in Hanley.

Like so many of the city's pubs, it was a chameleon, attracting different age groups depending on which day of the week it was. Monday to Friday cheap ale and wall-to-wall horse racing attracted the punters. Fortunately, the Friday night clientele was a mixed-age party crowd. And it filled up with a more discerning crowd later; revellers into Northern Soul and Disco.

'What you drinking, Lune? I'll get these, Carl's treat.' She laughed as the effects of the spliff mellowed her.

'Get me a double Jack Daniels and Coke.'

'Ice?'

'Please.'

'I'll have the same.'

The lanky greasy-haired student behind the bar was so fixated with Luna's breasts he almost tripped over himself.

They sat on the comfy settees under the front windows, away from the high chairs near the bar. Although they both liked male attention, they could do without pervy stares from beer-bellied middle-aged blokes with too many tats.

Katrina downed her first JD and Coke in one gulp, her cheeks flushed, and Luna could see the tension begin to drain from her.

'Slow down, you mad cow. We've got all night. You'll be pissed within the hour knocking it back like that?'

'Don't worry, duck, I'm feeling much better,' she said with a warm glow.'

'What's that bastard done now?'

'The usual crap: he explodes like a pissing bomb, for no reason. He's a bloody nutter. Grabbed me on the stairs, just because I asked him what he was banging at in the kitchen.'

'Why do you put up with him?'

'Got nowhere else to go; he owns the house.'

'You can stay with me until you find somewhere else, but it's not ideal, with just one bedroom. It'd be like the old days when we shared that flat in Shelton.'

'That's good of you, Lune, but I can't afford to live on my own,' she said, disheartened. 'I suppose he has good points. The bills are paid, and there's always food in. Besides, we'd end up falling out. No offence, babe, friendship is one thing but living together, you know we'd argue.'

'Remember that big scrap we had because you gave my ex a blow job in the old flat?'

'Embarrassing wrestling on that shitty lino like kids. You bit a chunk of my hair out.'

'Yeah. It cost me forty quid to get that filling fixed.'

They both laughed at how ridiculous and immature they had been back then.

'If I had a decent job I'd consider it, but not at the moment.'

'OK, the offer's there if you need it.'

'Where are we going next? There's not enough talent in here. Fancy the Slipware Tankard?'

'Bit of a hike in these shoes.' Luna glanced at her heels with a smirk.

Feeling a touch stoned and up for anything, Kat grinned. 'I know, babe, but they've got an outside terrace, and it's a lovely night. We can sink a bottle of Pinot G?'

Luna downed her drink. 'OK, you've convinced me. Let's go.'

She pushed through a group of leering blokes who'd be single to the grave, Kat thought, by the looks of them.

CHAPTER 9

To the rest of the world Carl Bentley seemed a popular bloke, but like most people he had secrets, and a reputation in Milton, a village three and half miles from the city centre.

He sat opposite the wall-mounted jukebox in the pub with his two best mates, John McKnight and Terry Clarke, necking lager like there'd be a drought within the hour. His leg bounced under the table to the Northern Soul classic 'The Snake', by Al Wilson.

'Fucking love this tune, man!' he said nodding to the beat.

The Millrace was a traditional two-room bar and lounge gaffe set back off Maunders Road leading toward the busy Leek New Road. A sixteen-mile stretch linking Stoke-on-Trent to the rolling Staffordshire moorlands countryside. Like plenty of other locals in the city it had gone through hard times during the recession, but thrived under the present landlady.

Bentley and his mates were waiting for a taxi to ferry them to the city centre. Most Friday nights they crawled round the local pubs. For a village of moderate size, Milton had more than its fair share of boozers; five in total and Bentley used them all. Everyone who frequented the pubs knew him. Although, apart from his circle of close friends, no one knew what he did for a living, the general rumours were that he worked for a local businessman. Most suspected he was involved in organised crime, but none dared confront him to clarify his job description, which was wise, considering his reputation as a notorious football hooligan during the late eighties and early nineties.

He slammed his second empty pint glass onto the table and reached inside his pocket for his fags. 'I'm going for a tab after I've had a piss and check on the taxi.' Passing the pool table on his way to the gents he bumped into a couple of locals. 'Out on the piss, boys?' he asked.

'Yeah,' said the colossus Grant Bolton. 'We're off up town, about twelve of us. Got a minibus coming.'

'We might bump into you later then? What pubs you going to?' Bentley asked.

''Spoons, White Horse… the usual. A few of us have got tickets for the All-Nighter at King's Hall. Brilliant last time. You going?'

'Nice one. Got mine last week. Bought it off Richie for a tenner 'cause he can't go. If I don't bump into you uptown, I'll see you down there.'

'Yeah, sound, mate. I'll give you a bell. Still the same mobile?'

'Yeah.'

'Nice one. See you later.'

Minutes later, Bentley stood to the left of the main entrance doorway, and lit up whilst gazing down the road trying to spot their cab through a plume of rising smoke. Whilst stubbing his fag out, he heard a taxi horn blast from lower down the road. Without checking he cocked his head back through the door into the lounge and signalled to his mates with a hooked thumb: 'Taxi!'

Before they could join him Grant Bolton heckled his mates. A sudden rush of lads shoved their way past the bar over to the entrance. Bentley watched the rowdy group of twelve dive into a silver transit van, which he'd mistakenly thought was for them.

Ten minutes later, Bentley and Clarke jumped onto the back seat of their taxi, leaving McKnight the unenviable task of riding shotgun and picking up the bill in the front. It was a juvenile prank they played when sharing a cab.

He knew as soon as the cab hit the city centre those tossers would jump out like Batman and Robin, pissing themselves laughing while he coughed up.

CHAPTER 10

Across town, Kat and Luna hobbled towards Piccadilly and cut down the bank through Brunswick Street, past Liquid and the Sugar Mill nightclubs, all the while taking care not to turn an ankle. The hundred-foot Telecoms Tower rose above the buildings like a seventies concrete draughtboard with its thousands of embossed squares.

'Stop a min, babe. I need a fag!' Kat said, fishing in her bag.

They crossed Marsh Street, North, heading towards the bar. The Slipware Tankard was the former home of the Staffordshire pottery firm George Ashworth, on Etruria Road, Hanley, and was built in 1807. The sixteen-bay-long factory had two stories, separated by a string course. Above the arched entrance, a tympanum with Venetian-style windows finished off the mixed architectural styles typical of the period on the front façade. The whole place looked like the stable block of a country manor house.

Two of the four original bottle kilns remained standing in the central courtyard; their curvaceous form gave them the appearance of female hips squeezed by a tight corset.

The regular crowd were a mix of hip and trendy eighteen to thirties; into fashion, bands, EDM and weekend partying.

Two doormen greeted Kat and Luna as they entered through the side doors leading into the main bar area.

'It's quiet, Kat.' Luna said, glancing around the huge interior at dozens of empty seats framed by four brick-bonded industrial tiled walls.

'Don't worry, it soon fills up. It's still early yet. Besides, we get to pick the best seats in the courtyard.'

Kat ordered a bottle of Pinot Grigio on ice.

'Seventeen quid!' Luna said, giving her friend a shocked stare.

'I know, but that's the price you pay not to be surrounded by Neanderthals.'

'Suppose so, Let's get a seat outside?'

'In a min, babe. I need a pee!' she said.

'Yeah, now you mention it, I need to go.'

With that they asked the barman to hold the wine until they came back from the ladies, up a short flight of steps, to the left of the bar.

Leaving the cubicle, Luna spun in a wild circle proclaiming she wanted to dance and shag all night in that order. They hobbled back down the steps, collected the wine and drifted outside into the courtyard. It was a muggy summer evening and they were both salivating at the prospect of ice-cold Pinot Grigio.

'Where should we sit, Kat?' she asked, making eyes at the well-groomed fella in mirror shades, lounging across a pile of sumptuous cushions covering one of the sofas perched on the block paved courtyard. 'I spotted him first!' she insisted, staking her claim on passing his table.

'Calm down, girl.' Kat smirked jealously.

The man glanced at them with a wry smile.

'You don't think he heard me, do you?'

'What do you think? He's sitting about ten feet away from us.'

Kat poured, almost draining the bottle since the glasses were more like goldfish bowls than wine glasses.

'Shit, that works out almost eight-fifty a glass,' Luna moaned.

'Sod it, we're out for a good time tonight. I don't give a shit, it's only money, and it's not mine!'

The man sitting opposite, texting, was in his late thirties, six feet, with dark-brown hair styled short back and sides, swept over to the right. He looked Italian, sporting facial stubble, and wore a black Ralph Lauren polo shirt, jeans and loafers. Very dashing, they thought.

He observed them coolly through his shades, smiled again, then continued checking his messages.

After about twenty minutes they'd demolished the wine over girlie chit-chat and cigarettes.

Where the fuck was Yusuf, he wondered. Although he made allowances because they were brothers, his lack of punctuality enraged him. Bored with waiting, Ibrahim Benzar offered the girls a drink to amuse his curiosity. Confidently he called over, 'Would you ladies like to join me for a drink?'

'Yeah!' they voiced simultaneously, with unblinking eyes, and a slight air of desperation.

His arrogant approach worked and within minutes they sat eagerly awaiting another bottle of wine. Like a gentleman, he moved to the opposite side of the table, giving up the cushions.

'Please have a seat. What do you want to drink?' he asked with a slightly foreign accent, 'More Pinot, or perhaps champagne?'

He didn't have to ask again. Without hesitation they opted for champagne.

Kat and Luna watched him get up and go to the bar.

'Shit girl, he's cute. Even better, he's got money,' she said, cosying up to the cushions.

'Haven't had champers in ages.'

'We've only been in here half an hour. What a catch: champagne in the sun.'

'Not quite, babe; he's just after a shag like most blokes.'

'I'll shag him as long as he keeps us topped up with drinks.' They faced each other and laughed.

Ibrahim returned, and within five minutes the Moët Chandon was sitting in an ice bucket in front of them and they were sipping from tall flutes, bubbles tickling their noses as the straw-coloured liquid slid down to the background sound of Classic Soul.

'What are your names?'

'I'm Katrina and this is Luna,' she said, tugging her skirt down crossing her legs.

'And you are?' Luna butted in.

'Ibrahim.'

'Unusual name.'

'It's Turkish.'

'Ah! That explains your accent. A mix of Potteries with a hint of eastern European?'

'I lived in Turkey with my parents until I was sixteen, but that was over twenty-five years ago. I came over here with my brother to get an education. After college I went to Staffs University to do an English language degree.'

'Where do you work?' Kat probed.

Luna nudged her with a subtle elbow.

'I have one or two businesses in Hanley.'

'What type of business?'

'You ask a lot of questions?'

'She's a right nosy cow,' Luna said.

Kat felt awkward. 'Charming, that is, babe.'

He paused and rubbed a hand over his stubble. 'I own a bar, and a martial arts gym, amongst other things.'

'What's the bar called?' Luna asked unashamed.

'You're sitting in it.'

Both their faces animated and in a sudden moment of clarity it dawned on Kat. They were talking to Carl's boss. He'd mentioned him a few times in conversation but never divulged more than his name, and that he owned the Slipware Tankard and shouldn't be crossed. At that point she knew the smart thing to do would be to make excuses and politely leave, but against her better judgement, she decided to stay; after all, she wasn't doing anything wrong, having a drink with her friend and her bastard partner's boss, even though she did fancy the pants off him. Kat needed a release, a way to forget her mundane life and loveless relationship for a few hours.

'What do you two do?' he asked.

'I work in a call centre,' Luna said.

'I'm just in-between jobs at the minute,' Kat said, chewing her bottom lip with a blush of embarrassment. She fumbled for a cigarette to boost her confidence.

As the conversation progressed, he appeared to have more eye contact with Kat, building a better rapport with her.

After thirty minutes of small talk, he offered them cocktails. The blonde was so hot, he thought, noticing that she didn't appear to be wearing any knickers, which made him lust after her even more. Although he knew coming on to virtual strangers was a touch lecherous, he could tell by their flirtatious body language that at least one of them would be game, and he'd be in with a chance of screwing one of them in the bridal suite at the Willow Room Hotel in town before the night was out.

'If you want to follow me, my barman will bring the mojitos in to us.' He led them across the courtyard to the bottle kiln on the left. Both kilns had been beautifully restored and the glass walkway that joined them was a stunning architectural talking point. The thirty-foot-long frameless structure doubled up as a dance floor; flashing coloured LEDs were fitted seamlessly into the stone-slabbed floor.

Ibrahim opened the large coffin-shaped steel entrance door leading into the uniquely circular space.

'Take a seat,' Ibrahim said, pointing towards two vanilla leather Chesterfield sofas facing a coffee table in the centre of the two-hundred-year-old kiln.

They glanced nervously up at the early evening sky peeking through the narrow neck of the kiln high above, as Ibrahim removed a large framed photograph of the bar from the heavily sandblasted curved brickwork, revealing a safe. He tapped in the code, opened the door and extracted a wad of notes. He came back over and to Kat's delight sat next to her.

'This place is unreal; it's like a cave,' Kat said, looking around curiously at the interior; subtle up-lighters cast strange shadows across the brickwork. 'Must have cost a fortune to do,' she said, addressing Luna.

'You not been inside a renovated kiln before, babe?'

'No. Seen a few from the outside.' She gave Luna a puzzled look.

'I'll have to take you to the Dudson Centre in Hope Street for a coffee. They've got one just like this, but it's a mini pottery museum inside with a spiral staircase up to a mezzanine level.'

Kat was about to reply when the barman entered, carrying the drinks on a tray. He set them down on the table and nodded to his boss before leaving.

Ibrahim stirred the crushed ice, mint and lime in Kat's tumbler with the straw. She took a slurp, the sweet and sour rum tasted divine. 'Not bad.'

Luna gave Ibrahim a slow sexy smile. 'We don't normally do this sort of thing, you know,' she said, trying to sound coy as if being the centre of attention was a new experience to them.

'I understand the need for escapism as much as anyone else,' he said.

'You not having one?' Kat asked.

'Maybe later. I have a business meeting tonight and need to keep a clear head.'

His phone rang. Glancing at his watch, he lifted it from his pocket and tapped the green answer button. 'Yusuf! Excuse me a moment, I have to take this,' Ibrahim said, edging back towards the entrance.

Practising martial arts had taught him controlled emotion, especially in front of other people. Ranting and displays of anger in public were impolite and a sign of weakness in Japanese culture. Make no mistake; he'd bollock Yusuf properly for the no-show later behind closed doors.

He hated having to involve family in his business, but had promised his mother and father twenty years ago to look after Yusuf, although for how much longer he couldn't say, as the arrogant bastard pissed him off. Yusuf was becoming a real liability.

'Sorry, I have to be at a business meeting now. But if you call me on this number –' he passed over a business card to Kat '– we can meet later for drinks. Both of you are welcome to join me and my associates at the casino after we've finished.'

With that Ibrahim ushered the girls back out into the fading sunlight of the courtyard, which was filling up with weekend revellers. He kissed them both on the cheek, said goodbye and exited into the bar in front of a few gawping onlookers sipping pints of iced cider.

They both stood in amazement, bemused at what just happened.

'He won't answer his phone later,' Kat declared cynically, with a leery look on her face. 'Players like him never do.'

'Probably not. Call it female intuition but he was definitely giving you more attention than me. He fancies the pants off you, babe.'

'They're already off.' She laughed with a mischievous wit in her blue eyes.

'You dirty cow.'

'Keep it down, those two over there heard you,' Luna said, referring to two chubby women in garish floral dresses, seated to the left of where they were standing, fat legs red from sunbathing.

They looked at each other and burst out laughing, then disappeared back towards the loos, bladders bursting with champagne and mojito.

CHAPTER 11

The Genting Casino was situated around a hundred and fifty yards from the Slipware Tankard bar on the same side of Etruria Road. The converted nightclub, formally known as Valentino's, looked fairly anonymous in the daytime, but, when darkness fell, this state-of-the-art bronze clad structure came alive. Spectacular roof lighting cascaded waterfall effects in hues of blue down the front and sides of it, casting a shimmering pool of blue upon the concrete driveway leading up to the entrance. The Vegas-style portal provided a late-night playground for tourists, gamblers and high rollers.

Ibrahim smiled at the receptionist as he strolled with confidence past the curved mirrored reception desk, through the sliding glass doors into the huge casino room, split up into five distinctive zones.

God, I love this place, he thought, gazing around the room at the spectacular, glass pendant shades and illuminated ceiling edge. On passing the touchscreen slot machines he scanned the bar.

Unlike his brother Yusuf, he expected the summoned crew members to be on time for the meeting. He spotted Charlie and Leonard unwittingly propping up the illuminated glass fronted bar four stools apart, whilst Malcolm sat hunched over his mobile at a high table behind the glass petition separating the formal bar area from the casino floor. None of these guys had met before, the common thread being they'd worked for Ibrahim in the past. This was an introduction to assess their interaction. A meeting of minds.

He'd known Charlie Bullard for several years. They'd met at Ibrahim's uncle's restaurant in London where he'd worked for twelve months during the early nineties. Charlie dined there with a Cypriot crime firm who he'd pulled jobs with. Charlie claimed he'd retired after his last stint inside in ninety-four, which had cost him ten years of his life. Although judging by his dingy council flat in Hanley, and his seventy-three quid a week pittance of benefit payments, Ibrahim was convinced he'd get him on board. Besides, after already discussing the heist, he was in far too deep to refuse.

Loner Leonard Vale didn't find it easy to mix with new people, especially women, who avoided him because of his repugnant appearance. The 35-year-old's greasy shoulder-length ginger hair, wispy ginger goatee and shitty-looking fag-stained teeth, made him a pariah. The unemployed tech geek had zero ambition, and previous convictions for hacking in America, and was always looking to supplement his job seeker's allowance. Most importantly, he was a freaking genius when it came to computers; his specialisms were hacking into financial institutions and illegal surveillance.

Malcolm Preston was Ibrahim's accountant. The 45-year-old bespectacled weasel, who had a weakness for classy escort girls, had followed HMRC tax laws religiously for years when Ibrahim acquired his services five years ago. But due to the economic downturn of the pottery industry all of his biggest long-term clients went into administration, virtually wiping out his business in the process.

Teetering on financial insolvency, against his better judgement, he set up the usual legitimate tax avoidance schemes for Ibrahim's businesses, until Ibrahim reeled him in with an introduction to the lucrative business of money-laundering, although he remained frightened shitless that his association with the Turk would be discovered by the authorities.

To avoid being overheard, Ibrahim ushered them to one of the private booths clustered around the sound stage. Whilst waiting for Yusuf to arrive, he introduced them.

'Charlie, this is Malcolm Preston, my accountant.' Charlie offered a welcoming hand over the table.

'Malcolm, this is Leonard; he's a computer whizz who does my tech. You all know my brother Yusuf who'll be here soon if I don't have him assassinated before he arrives,' he joked with a dissatisfied grin. That bastard brother of his was an embarrassment.

'What can I get you to drink?' he asked the unlikely cohorts.

'Guinness please,' Charlie said.

'Stella for me,' Leonard muffled, barely audible.

'My usual please.'

'I'll join you Malcolm. Chardonnay, bottle OK?' he nodded. Apart from worshipping cash, one of the few things the accountant and Ibrahim had in common was their enthusiasm for half decent wine, which they quaffed during monthly accounts lunches.

He drifted over to the empty bar; most of the punters were busy splashing cash on the casino floor, an ideal situation considering the highly illegal proposal he was about to discuss with the gathering of career criminals.

A tap on the shoulder startled him; he turned to find Yusuf grinning. Just like Ibrahim, his 37-year-old brother was a suave Mediterranean type. Surprisingly, he was in good shape, considering the lazy bastard smoked, ate like a pig, and didn't rise from his bed until around eleven most mornings.

Ibrahim scanned his brother, shaking his head in disgust.

'Selam,' Yusuf said, trying to thaw his brother's reproachful stare.

'What time do you call this?' Order a drink, sit down, and keep quiet.'

'Nice manners, bro.'

'Gentlemen!' Ibrahim announced returning to the booth, rubbing his hands. 'I'm sure you're wondering why I've called this meeting. You're invited because I value your professional opinions about certain aspects of a very lucrative job that's come my way. In fact, the person bankrolling the job is prepared to pay large sums of cash to each of you in return for your specialist help. I'll tell you the finer details later, but as always information leakage would fuck things up. Not that I'm implying any of you would blab about this… I can't emphasise enough the need for strict confidentiality. Even if you decide not to join us in this venture.'

'How much are we talking?' Malcolm asked.

'I'll tell you when I get back from taking a piss,' Ibrahim said, keeping them dangling.

CHAPTER 12

'One million pounds,' Ibrahim said with a deadpan look.

'Shit!' Leonard said, scratching his goatee.

Malcolm pitched in. 'That's a shedload of cash to keep quiet about.'

'Chill, a smart accountant like you knows how to avoid detection. It'll be two million in used notes, split five ways, and the rest will be an untraceable bank deposit, leaving no paper trail.'

'Used notes?' Malcolm screeched gulping air. 'What the hell are we supposed to do with four hundred grand in cash each?'

'Shh! Malc, keep the volume down,' insisted Ibrahim, ticking him off. 'Chill out, they'll be laundered,' he asserted. 'But one thing is for sure, you can't pay those notes into a UK bank, buy fuck-off big, cars, yachts, houses, or anything else that looks beyond your current financial status. More a case of retiring early with some serious mullah under your mattress.'

'Count me in,' Leonard spluttered without hesitation.

'Don't be too hasty,' Ibrahim cautioned. 'You need to know the facts before deciding.' He leaned closer into the table, scanned around the bar area. double-checking they couldn't be overheard. 'The bounty is gold,' he whispered.

Leonard grinned like a court jester. 'What, you mean treasure?'

Yusuf looked at the group smugly. 'Is he for real, like pirates and all that shit?'

Shaking his head in annoyance, Ibrahim shot him a dissatisfied look.

'For once Leonard, you're spot on, it's treasure.'

Yusuf shuffled his chair in, looking bewildered. 'Is this a wind-up?'

'Deadly serious, bro. A cool three-point-three million in gold right on our doorstep.'

'And it's not a security transit blag, or a bank?' asked Charlie.

'Nope. Nothing like that.'

Charlie took a slurp of his Guinness, Leonard sat there beaming at his empty pint glass, and Yusuf kept his mouth shut.

Nervously pushing his specs onto the bridge of his nose, the accountant broke the momentary silence. 'If we've finished playing Cluedo,

I'll put you out of your misery. He wants to knock off the Staffordshire Hoard from the Potteries Museum,' he said, breaking the tension.

'Correct, Malc,' Ibrahim interrupted. 'Seventh-century Saxon gold… all three and half thousand pieces of it. Kind of ironic, since the Saxons plundered most of it from invading tribes and enemies during their battles. The best part is they're mostly tiny pieces, which makes it easier to steal. The bulk of the Hoard is sword fittings, but there are also several brooches and some decent-sized crosses encrusted with rubies.'

'Someone's done their homework,' Yusuf said sarcastically, annoyed that he'd not been informed before the others.

'What did you think we were going to do? Stroll in the place waving shooters, smash the glass with hammers, and meet up in the pub for lunch?'

Yusuf slid down in his chair like a scolded child.

Shifting from casual conversation to more pointed questions, Bullard probed Ibrahim. 'I hate to state the obvious, but Hanley Police headquarters is down the road from the Museum. It would be like trying to slip the police commissioner's Rolex off his wrist, during his afternoon nap. We wouldn't get three hundred yards before being pinned to the tarmac by an armed response team.'

'Good point, Charl. All depends on how we plan to get out the building. After discussing our options at length with the buyer, who's turned over plenty of museums and galleries. I think we've found the perfect exit strategy borrowed from the lucrative world of art theft. Just bear with me a minute and I'll explain the concept we're considering, then you can give me your opinions.'

Ibrahim reached inside his jacket pocket and fished out a large android mobile with a six-inch screen. Tapping the device he located the picture gallery. His three co-conspirators shuffled their chairs closer. The slide show began with an opening shot of the entrance to the Potteries Museum followed by consecutive images, leading into a room decked out in the style of a Saxon Mead hall where the Staffordshire Hoard was on display to the public.

Finally, he whetted their appetites with close-up shots of some of the key pieces of the Hoard; garnet-set sword pyramids, garnet inlaid buttons, a folded cross, the eagle mount and, his personal favourite, a decorative strip of gold bearing an inscription from the Vulgate version of the Latin Bible.

Leonard piped up. 'Looks like a load of old brass tat!' Then he added, 'Seriously, this gold is worth three-point-three million?'

'Listen, I know it doesn't look like it's worth much but you've got to understand the significance of this collection. It's the largest Anglo-Saxon Hoard in the world. To an egotistical collector it's priceless.'

'If it's worth three-point-three million,' Malcolm quizzed him, 'paying out a million each doesn't make good business sense? The buyer is taking a hit of one-point-seven.'

'Profit is irrelevant to him.'

'Must have money to burn?' the accountant added.

Ibrahim shrugged. 'That's not our problem. We still get five million split between us all.'

'OK, we get the gist of it, but how do you plan to steal the gold from the Museum undetected?' Charlie asked.

'That's the clever part.' Ibrahim grinned. 'As I said earlier we're going to borrow a strategy used by forgers. Basically, we get replicas made of the main pieces on display and do a switch. The idea being only a Hoard expert will notice the difference. The average museum visitor and Dad's army security guards will be none the wiser. By the time they discover the gold's gone, it will have disappeared without a trace.'

'Sounds risky,' Malcolm said.

'All scams are risky, but as they say in the movies, it's all in the planning. If we get that spot on then we should be able to pull it off.'

'Any more questions?'

'Yeah! When do we get the mullah?' Yusuf asked.

'What a surprise Yusuf's asking about the mullah already. Listen bro, we'll get an advance for expenses and equipment upfront followed by the balance on delivery of the goods. I'll personally make sure everyone gets paid. In order for this to work we must trust each other. If you decide you're in, then we're buying your silence and your expertise. Remember at this stage I'm just sounding you guys out and there's no obligation. Although once you're in, you're in, no backing out. We're not turning over the jewellery cabinets at Argos, these are ancient artefacts,' he said emphasising the point.

Malcolm swept his hand through the few strands of hair left on his head. With a concerned expression he asked Ibrahim. 'When do you need to know if we're in?'

'Soon as, by Monday at the latest. That gives you a whole weekend to think about it. I'll carry on working on the logistics with Charlie and Leonard over the next week or so, but that will depend on their decision to join us or not. What you thinking, guys?'

'Definitely a million each?' Yusuf asked.

'Yeah. Four-hundred grand cash, the rest in an offshore bank.'

'As long as we can develop a workable plan that covers all bases then I'm in,' Charlie said. 'But it would have to be rock solid before I'll commit. Any slip ups and we'll all go down.'

'I take your point. Leonard, how about you?' Ibrahim could tell he was bricking it.

Vale fidgeted in his chair. Clearing his throat, he said, 'Erm, what would I have to do?'

'Don't worry, your involvement will be technical, computer surveillance, and stuff like that.'

The tech geek felt relieved knowing he wouldn't be directly involved in nicking the gold, although this didn't ease the empty feeling in the pit of his stomach. 'OK, I'm in,' he murmured.

'Good man,' Ibrahim said, patting him on the shoulder.

'What's my role in this?' Malcolm asked, aware that it would be difficult to avoid sharp-end involvement, considering Ibrahim virtually paid his mortgage.

'Same goes for you, Malc. You wouldn't be involved in the heist, just setting up the best ways we can each splice a million into our lives without detection.'

The accountant closed his eyes and sighed.

'Yusuf?'

'Do I have a choice?'

'Do I ever make you do anything?' Ibrahim said knowing his brother couldn't refuse.

'OK, I'm in,' he surrendered, with a half-hearted shrug, knowing he owed his brother far too much to refuse.

'Don't worry guys; we'll have several meetings during the planning stages,' raising his wine glass, Ibrahim proposed a toast 'One-million each! OK, now that's out of the way, let's hit the casino floor.'

CHAPTER 13

Barry Gibson leaned his heavily tattooed forearms on the packed bar of the White Horse pub in the city centre. His highly polished oxblood Doc Martin boots with red laces, and blue Fred Perry polo defined him as an ageing skinhead with attitude; a throwback from a bygone era. He'd been out since seven and was bladdered, meaning he could kick off at any moment.

Grant Bolton and his mates had finished their pints and it was his turn to get a round in. Pushing through the three deep throng at the bar, the stocky Miltoner accidentally nudged Gibson in the back; stumbling forward he spilt a mouthful of lager down the front of his polo.

'Watch it!'

'Sorry, Bud, it's all these pushing in,' Bolton said. It was then he realised it was that tattooed bastard who gave his younger brother a kicking last Christmas in the Burton Stores, but he didn't let on. Eighteen year old Liam Bolton never reported it to the police, because he knew his big bro would sort it. Grant vowed when his suspended sentence for theft was up, he'd take Gibson out, but this wasn't the right time: too many witnesses.

'Clumsy twat!' Gibson uttered stretching his top from the bottom, to stop it clinging to his chest.

'What did you call me?' Bolton demanded, staring at him whilst easing into an available slot at the bar.

'A clumsy twat!'

'You're fucking lucky I'm in a good mood tonight, or I'd do you!' Bolton said.

The burly landlord Darryl Connor overheard the altercation whilst pulling a pint of Titanic. 'Come on now, no trouble,' he said.

'This tit spilt my beer!

'Fuck off you eighties retard,' Bolton taunted, thinking Gibson would keep until later.

'Any more of that shit,' Connor asserted, 'and you'll both be out!'

Turning to face the bar, Bolton said, 'Yeah, OK, do us seven pints of Stella, and five Kopparbergs, Strawberry and Lime flavour?'

Gibson was seething, judging by his face, which looked like a smacked arse. Taking another gulp of lager, he tried to keep a lid on his temper.

Arthur Cumberbatch, a regular sitting opposite the bar, also overheard. The 70-year-old alcoholic knew Gibson and squeezed through the tight knit throng in an attempt to stop a major fracas.

Seeing the old man in the line of fire, the landlord stopped serving and called one of his bouncers to defuse the situation.

Nathan Dukes faced off with Gibson. 'Not you again – fucking pervert. Any more mither and we'll sling you out.'

'Whatever,' Gibson said, far too pissed to care.

Dukes glared at him. He then made his way into the back room, slipped his cagoule on and nipped outside for a fag.

A broad man edged through swathes of drinkers and made his way over to the gents in the White Horse pub. Upon entering he noticed his target hunched over the trough taking a pee. Barry Gibson leaned his head on the tiles as he took aim in a pissed stupor. Whilst emptying his bladder the stocky man glanced sideways at him.

'What you looking at?' spewed the skinhead.

'Not you.' The man didn't want to put Gibson into defence mode: that would just make it harder.

'Yeah, right, you're giving me the big eye,' he slurred.

'I'd keep your mouth shut, if I was you, or you'll be drinking your own piss in a minute,' the man retorted.

'Yeah, fucking come on then,' the skinhead said, spinning round with his knob still hanging out, dribbling over his boots and onto the floor.

'I'll kill you, you scummy twat,' the man said staring face-to-face. He was supposed to take him out somewhere remote, stab him and let him bleed out, but this was it, his window.

The skinhead spat in his face: putrid stinking fag and beer saliva.

Steaming with anger, red mist enveloped the man. Without hesitation he flung his head back and butted the skinhead hard on the bridge of the nose, breaking it on contact. In one fell swoop he slipped in his own urine, crashed backwards violently, smashing his head on the sharp edge of the stainless steel trough, before landing in a heap on the floor. The man leaned over him, his blade drawn ready to finish him off. Getting closer still he noticed the skinhead was still breathing and blood was gushing down the front of the trough from a gaping wound in the back of his skull, pooling onto the tiles behind him. If the bastard somehow survived, he'd be able to identify him.

Hands on head with indecision, he paced the gents frantically trying to think what to do. Adrenaline rushed through his veins. He darted towards a wastebasket in the corner, which was double-bagged with clear bin liners. Whipping them out, he emptied used hand towels onto the floor, then placed them over each hand.

As he yanked his victims head forward, blood transferred onto the bags. Without hesitation he carefully pushed the tip of the blade into the wound: forcing it until at least an inch had penetrated his brain. Blood gushed from the wound like water from a cracked pipe. He withdrew the blade, and wiped it clean on his victim's polo shirt. The skinhead's skull banged against the edge of the trough.

How the hell was he going to get out unnoticed? Looking around the gents he spotted a wooden door wedge sitting on the windowsill behind the door. He slammed it under the door and kicked it hard to stop anyone entering the gents. 'Fuck, fuck,' he uttered under his breath. Think, think.'

Impulsively he grabbed the skinhead around the ankles of his docks and dragged him across the terrazzo floor level with the second cubicle door, desperately trying not to get blood on his clothes. 'Oh, fucking hell,' he gulped, looking at the stream of blood across the tiles. It was carnage.

Trying not to leave any fingerprints, he scrunched the bag on his right hand into a fist and banged the cubicle door open. Spiking adrenaline gave him a massive burst of strength as he heaved his victim up on the toilet. Rushing, he got the angle wrong and gravity took over as the skinhead slumped forward, arms dangling limp down his sides. Luckily for him the cubicle was narrow. In haste he leaned the body cross-legged against the graffiti-covered Formica side, and exited, shutting the door behind him.

One of the ceiling strip lights flickered eerily and popped.

In partial light, with the sound of his heartbeat thrashing in his ears, he agonised. 'How am I going to get out of here?'

Looking round the piss stinking magnolia box, he remembered the window at the opposite end of the room; a small, white, double-glazed unit, which opened sideways. It looked about two feet high, just tall enough to climb through. He dashed towards it, grabbed the handle and yanked it up, thanking his lucky stars that some careless cleaner had left it unlocked.

He clambered through, hands first and dropped four feet onto the concrete below. Up on his feet he spun around but stumbled into a pile of black refuge sacks. Scanning around he realised he was looking onto Old

Lane, a courtyard at the back of several premises in the city centre. He slipped his hood up and exited stealthily. This was messy, very messy. He should have bladed him straight away: no questions asked. That vile bastard Gibson had been a dead man walking, but now it looked like an accident, a fight; maybe that would work to his advantage.

CHAPTER 14

An hour went by and the dance floor at the Slipware Tankard had filled up with revellers.

'Shit, what time is it?' Kat said, pointing to her wrist.

'Twenty to eleven.'

'Bollocks, bloody forgot we were supposed to call that bloke around ten.'

'You can try, but you won't get a signal in here.'

'Let's go back out to the courtyard? It's much quieter out there.'

'OK, I could do with some fresh air.'

They swiped the full glasses from the table, leaving the empty bottle behind and made their way through the busy bar, wine sloshing onto their shoes.

Exiting the bar area, they experienced sensory overload as their eyes and ears adjusted from the darker, louder atmosphere to the courtyard, which was now packed.

'Soon filled up out here. How long we been dancing for? I've lost track of time,' she said with heavily dilated pupils. Luna checked her mobile.

'God, that's gone quick. We've been in there over an hour.'

They inched through the throng of people, trying not to spill too much wine. Surprisingly, there was still one sofa available next to the bottle kilns. Perching their bums on the edge of the cushion, Kat pulled out the card Ibrahim had given her earlier from her purse.

'Lend me your phone, please, Lune? Mine's out of credit,' she said, sounding apologetic. She was always skint after losing her job as an accountant's secretary months earlier. Carl slipped her the odd tenner here and there but he was a real selfish bastard and didn't give her an allowance. Her Jobseeker's money rarely went further than a new outfit and the odd night out.

Luna could tell by Kat's sullen expression she hated not having her own money. 'What are you like?' she said, passing her phone over.

Kat tapped in the number, fidgeting with her skirt whilst waiting for an answer. The phone seemed to ring for ages. She was about to hang up when Ibrahim answered.

'Hello, who's that?'

'It's Katrina from earlier, you said to call later.'

'Oh, hi. You okay?'

'Yes, thanks. Can we meet up? 'Do you know where the Genting Casino is?'

'Yes, it's down from your bar.'

'Great, come to the main entrance in forty-five minutes? I'll meet you both there.'

'Okay, bye.'

'See you,' she said, intrigued.

CHAPTER 15

The White Horse was still heaving when a punter reported to Dave Millburn, one of the bouncers, that the gents was inaccessible because the door was jammed. After taking a brief look he went to fetch the other doorman , but couldn't find him. Must have nipped out for a fag, he thought. He pushed, shoved and kicked the door but it refused to budge. He stood staring at the boot scrunched remains of a Northern Soul All-nighter poster hanging from the door.

Heading over to the bar he scanned for the landlord. 'Where's Darryl?' he shouted to Tabatha, the barmaid; attempting to be heard over the landlord's soul compilation cd.

'Don't know. He was serving before going to the loo.'

'If you see him, tell him the gents' door is blocked. God knows how.'

A few minutes later, a sweaty Nathan Dukes joined him.' What's up, Dave?'

'Gents' bog door is jammed.'

'Jammed?'

'Yeah, completely stuck. Won't bastard budge. I've been kicking it.'

'Let's have a gander. Shit, it's well stuck.'

After a few minutes of taking it in turns kicking, the door squeezed open a couple of feet. Cautiously Dave Millburn squeezed his head through the gap. He scanned around the gents, weighing up the situation. 'Oh shit! There's blood all over the floor, Nath!'

'You're kidding me!' Dukes sounded worried.

'Take a look?'

'Shit!' he said, retracting. 'That looks serious, man.'

'Where the bloody hell is Darryl?' he moaned gawping at the terrazzo tiles they'd unwittingly cracked.

A few tense moments passed before the fifty one year old landlord joined his bouncers. He looked flustered and out of breath. 'What's this about the gents' door being jammed?'

'Looks like there's been a fight to me. There's blood all over the floor. I reckon some nob has blocked the door and climbed out of the window.

Just about sums up the mentality of this lot,' Dukes said, offering his opinion.

With a look of dread on his face, Connor squeezed his head through the gap. 'Shit! That's a lot of blood.' His eyes followed the damp red trail, which snaked across the floor and disappeared under the first cubicle. 'You pair stay here and don't let anyone in.' He slithered his burly torso sideways through the gap and stepped carefully over into the corner. He dropped to his knees, turned his head and glanced straight under the cubicles. 'My god!' There's someone still in there. There's a pool of blood around the toilet. Shitting hell, it's not looking good. Dave, get an ambulance and the cops on your radio now! Nathan, keep all the punters in.' The colour drained from his face as he considered the disturbing possibility of a dead body on his premises.

With the radio noticeably shaking in his hand, Millburn said, 'Three-two-nine White Horse requesting urgent police assistance, major incident in the pub, potential fatal wounding in the toilets. Send an ambulance.'

Dukes entered the pub and covertly locked both exit doors and made the announcement. 'Listen up, everybody? We need you all to remain calmly in the pub until the police arrive.'

A group of lads moving towards the exit at the end of the bar became rowdy.

'You can't do that; we're meeting someone in a minute.'

Connor approached them for a quiet word. 'I'm really sorry about this but there's been a major incident in the pub and the police have told us not to let anyone leave until they arrive.'

'What pissing incident? Look around you, mate, there's no bother in here.' said one of the lads.

'It's in the toilets. That's all I can say at the minute.

Others in the crowd became restless.

'Open the doors or you'll have a riot on your hands!' a tall, bearded bloke at the back shouted insightfully.

Another chipped in. 'Yeah, this ain't right. We want free beer if we can't leave.'

Dukes knew the situation was likely to get out of hand quickly if the cops didn't arrive soon.

Within minutes sirens could be heard, gradually getting louder until the blue flashing lights of the emergency services reflected off the windows of the White Horse.

CHAPTER 16

A team of uniformed officers cordoned off the area, setting out a manned entry and exit corridor to the White Horse crime scene. Several CID officers entered the pub followed by Tom Blake. To calm the situation the Detective Inspector delegated DS Murphy to address the punters, while he made his way apprehensively to the gents.

'I can appreciate not being able to leave the pub is inconvenient, but if you could just bear with us while we take statements, I will let you all know when you can leave. Please remain calmly in your seats? Thank you for your cooperation. Are you the landlord?' Murphy said, addressing Darryl Connor who was standing next to him with a look of horror on his face.

'Yeah.'

'We received a call about a fatal wounding in the toilets. What time did you discover this?'

'Around twenty minutes ago. One of our regulars reported the gents' door was jammed. My door staff forced it open and took a quick look inside. There's tons of blood across the floor and someone locked inside one of the cubicles. It's deadly silent in there.'

'Have you been here all evening?'

'Yeah.'

'And, you've not left the pub at any stage?'

'No, apart from standing on the steps to have a smoke.'

'How about you pair?' Murphy said addressing the doormen.

'Been here all night,' said Nathan Dukes, speaking for both of them.

'OK, thanks,' Murphy said. 'Take a seat for us over there. It's imperative we establish if the victim is still alive. The boss will have called the Divisional Surgeon by now.' Murphy slipped on a protection suit, silicone gloves, and joined his DI. Inside the gents a SOCO officer was passing the last foot-plate to Blake, through the gap in the doorway. The common approach path towards the victim staggered either side of the sinister looking blood trail. A shiver ran through him as he stepped closer towards the cubicle.

'What do you reckon, Tom? Looks real nasty.'

'Very.' Blake said sliding the cubicle door catch. Slowly he edged it open, knowing the chances of the victim being alive were slim: he'd lost too much blood.

He stood in front of the body, which was that of a tattooed white male he'd estimate to be late forties. The distribution of blood down the wall tiles and pooling around the toilet suggested his injuries came from a major trauma to the back of the skull. Leaning close to the victim he placed his fingers on his neck to check for a pulse. There was nothing. He could see no rise and fall in the upper chest. In his opinion he was dead.

Five minutes later the Divisional Surgeon declared life extinct, making it a potential murder enquiry. Blake glanced around the room, but saw only one other exit apart from the door; a window at the far end. He moved closer and noticed the handle left in the open position, meaning it had been shut from the outside.

Pointing to the frame, Blake offered his opinion to the doctor. 'Whoever did this legged it through the window. He jammed the door to delay anyone discovering the body, buying himself enough time to get away. My gut instinct tells me this is an alcohol-fuelled dispute that escalated into a fight. If so, chances are the victim's death was accidental. Any idea of the time of death?'

'Judging by his temperature and slight rigor mortis in the eyelids, neck and jaw, my best guess, based on what we have so far is he died within the last hour or so. His body's cooled to the ambient room temperature. Algor mortis, Inspector. It's normally two degrees in the first hour. The blood trail shows the body's been moved in a crude attempt to hide it.'

'Cause of death?'

'We'll know more after the PM, but there's massive blood loss. The fatal wound that caused this is at the back of the skull, where there appears to be a nasty fracture. The initial blow to the head would have rendered him unconscious. He's bled out sitting there unceremoniously on the throne.'

Blake was accustomed to the doctor's gallows humour. They both exited the toilets and Blake briefed the crime scene photographer.

CHAPTER 17

Fifteen minutes later, a three-man SOCO team entered the gents, whilst uniformed officers interviewed the pub clientele. After an hour it became clear that the crime scene had been exposed to tons of contamination since lots of blokes had used the gents, making the gathering of elimination prints difficult.

To get a feel for the atmosphere Tom Blake joined one of his officers who was interviewing three lads in their early twenties. He flashed his warrant card.

'Lads, I'm Detective Inspector Blake. I'll be taking over from PC Haynes. What time did you enter the pub?'

'About eight,' said a fair-haired lad wearing a checked shirt.

'Have any of you used the gents?'

They looked at each other hesitantly, worried they might be implicated if admitting to taking a pee.

'Don't worry, we're just trying to establish people's movements between the time they arrived and when the incident was called in?'

'Yeah. Three of us went earlier.'

'And you saw nothing suspicious?'

'Like what?'

'A fight, or someone injured?'

'Not really.'

'You either did, or you didn't?' Blake stressed.

'There was a bloke stumbling talking to himself, but he came out before us and went back to the bar,' said the tallest of the three.

'What did he look like?' asked Blake.

'Shaved head, loads of tats on his arms. Like a mad skinhead.'

'How old do you reckon he was?'

'Dunno, about forty-five or older.'

'And you definitely saw him leave the toilets and make his way back to the bar?'

'Yeah. I remember 'cause me and Nick were laughing at the red laces in his doc boots, weren't we?'

His mate agreed.

'Did you see him in the pub later?' Blake continued.

'Can't remember… we were all talking, so didn't notice.'

'Has something happened to this bloke?' the lad in the checked shirt asked.

'I'm afraid I can't give you details. All I can say is there's been a suspicious death. That's why it's so important you guys remember as much as you can. Anything, even the slightest little detail could be significant?'

'Bloody hell! That's bad.' The dark-haired lad gazed mournfully at his mates who looked numb with shock.

'When can we go?' the fair-haired lad mumbled nervously.

'Yeah, I'm bursting for a piss.'

'I need one as well.'

'I'm afraid you'll have to go somewhere else. We shouldn't be too long now. One of the forensic team will come to you in the next ten minutes with his laptop and take witness elimination prints. We need to get fingerprints from everyone here tonight.'

'Prints! What for, we've done nothing?' the fair-haired lad said anxiously.

'Once your prints are eliminated from the enquiry, they'll be destroyed.' Blake thanked them for their cooperation and left the three lads sitting pale-faced. He stepped outside where his uniformed officers were managing the cordoned-off area.

'Everything OK out here, PC Evans?'

'Under control, sir. Apart from shifting the odd drunk from under the tapes.'

'OK. It's going to be a long night. The SOCO team are in there now. Make sure no one enters Old Lane. We could do without questioning more drunks, considering we're still processing that lot.'

Blake went back into the pub. The worried-looking landlord approached him with a large brandy noticeably shaking in his right hand. 'How long will it be before you remove the body? It's giving me the bloody creeps. Me and the missus live upstairs; I doubt we'll get any sleep tonight.'

'Do you have family or friends you can stay with?'

'We could probably stay at my wife's daughter's.'

'Good.' You won't get your pub back until tomorrow. Although I need a statement from you and your door staff, so take a seat and I'll be over in a minute.'

After a quick word with his sergeant about the witness statements, DI Blake joined the shaken landlord and his two doormen, and opened his notepad. 'We've got a preliminary ID of the victim from his driving licence. A Mr Barry Gibson. Do you know the name? Is he a regular?'

Connor paused for a moment before answering. 'No, doesn't sound familiar.

'Perhaps you'd recognise the victim?'

The colour drained from his face. Clearly the thought of identifying the body put the fear of God into him. 'What, you mean see the body?'

'No, just a forensics photo. It's unpleasant, but would help us to build a better picture of the victim if you recognise him.'

'Can't you describe him?'

Blake could see he was fragile, so decided against exposing him to the pictures of the bludgeoned skinhead's corpse.

'OK. White male, forty-nine years old, with a shaved head, both arms covered in tattoos. Dressed like a skinhead, red Doc Martin boots with red laces. Does this description fit any of your regulars?'

'No, but I've seen him in the pub before. He's been in a few times in the last couple of weeks. Normally talks to one or two of our regulars.'

'That's very helpful.' Blake looked at Nathan Dukes and asked, 'Do you know the victim?'

'Seen him a few times around town. Can't miss him, if you know what I mean?'

'How long have you worked the doors?'

'About four years.'

Looking at the ID strapped to his arm, Blake asked him. 'What's the company you work for?'

'M8 Security.'

'Is this your regular gig?'

'Sometimes do the Burton Stores and the Auctioneers, but usually I'm on here Fridays.'

'In your capacity as a doorman have you ever had to deal with Mr Gibson?'

'No.'

'Are you sure? One of the regulars told us Mr Gibson could be violent when he was pissed and the Burton Stores was his local haunt. Think carefully, Mr Dukes? We'll be contacting M8 to check company records. We keep accurate records of incidents in town. If I find out you're lying to us, you'll lose your registration with the Security Industry Authority.'

'OK, I only know him from the Stores, but that's it. He's just another pisshead.'

'We'll leave it at that for now, but may want to speak to you again at some point.'

Dukes looked worried. 'Why?'

'Standard police procedure, Mr Dukes. And you are?' Blake quizzed the other doorman.

'Dave Millburn.'

'Did you know the deceased?'

'Seen him around town from a distance, but that's all.'

'Just refresh my memory. Which of you, apart from the landlord, entered the gents?'

'Just Nath,' Millburn blurted, attempting to absolve himself of any blame. Dukes shot him a disapproving glare.

'OK. Mr Connor, how many regulars are still in the pub?'

The landlord glanced around and spotted Arthur Cumberbatch's familiar trilby. He was perched in his usual spot in the front window, with his son. The regulars nicknamed his son Wazza because he pissed his trousers last Christmas.

'If you three could wait here? One of our SOCO team will take your prints, footprints and DNA for elimination,' Blake said, leaving them to accompany PC Haynes in interviewing the old man.

'Mr Cumberbatch, I'm Detective Inspector Blake and this is PC Haynes. He'll be making a few notes whilst we talk.' He flashed his warrant card to a small greasy-looking bloke in tweed, whose gaunt face and eye bags gave him the demeanour of a heavy drinker. Judging by his unkempt scruffy appearance Wazza was also a pub waster.

'We anna done nowt, have we, son?'

'Been here all night, Pops, supping, minding our own business. Darryl will tell you,' he said, clearing his conscience.

'What time did you enter the pub this evening?' Blake asked.

'What's this, the pissing third-degree?' The old man glanced at his son and sniggered, flashing nicotine-stained teeth.

'Mr Cumberbatch, I'll remind you this is an informal witness interview, but we're dealing with a very serious incident. That could easily turn into an arrest, so we'd appreciate your full cooperation.'

'What bloody incident?'

'I can't give you full details yet, but a body's been found in the gents.'

'Sodding hell! Who's been murdered?'

Blake gave him a suspicious look. 'I didn't mention anyone being murdered. The victim is a forty-nine-year-old skinhead with heavily tattooed forearms. Does that description fit anyone you know?'

'Oh, bollocks, it's big Gibbo. What happened?'

'We're not sure yet but it's possible he got into a fight. The forensics team are still processing the scene so we'll know more later.'

The old guy sat up soldier-straight, his anti-law enforcement resolve in tatters. 'Knock us a roll-up out, Wazza, would ya? I need a tab to calm me nerves.'

'You can have a smoke when we're finished.'

'We've known big Gibbo for a few years,' Cumberbatch spilled. 'He normally drinks in the Stores; he's a bit of a lad.'

'In what way?' Blake asked, probing the old man for details.

'He's calmed down a bit since we first met him. Likes a bloody good row, that one. Nice as pie until he's had a skinful, then you had to be on your guard. He could turn real nasty.'

'What, physical violence?'

'I've never seen him in a scrap. Most shit a brick when Gibbo reared up. He offered plenty of 'em outside, but they usually backed down.'

'Why's that then?'

'People thought he was a nutter… didn't want the mither, I suppose.'

'Looks like he met his match this time.'

'Thinking about it, he had words with a big youth earlier on. I stepped in to calm him down.'

'Why didn't you mention this sooner?'

'Forgot. I'm in bloody shock.'

'Look, around the room, Mr Cumberbatch? Can you see him now? It's very important.'

The old man scanned the pub. 'Can't see him.'

'Are you sure?' Blake said, rising to his feet. 'Come with me; we'll take a tour to be certain.'

Stiff as a cane, he eased out of his seat and shuffled around the room, nervously glancing at the witnesses. 'No. He's not in here.'

'Positive?'

'Yeah.'

'Was he with anyone?'

'Ar, there was loads of 'em. But it was packed so I couldn't see faces.'

'How many would you say?'

'Dunno, more than a handful.'

'What did he look like?' Blake asked, glancing at PC Haynes who was still taking notes as they sat back down.

'Oh, I can't remember. Me memory's no good these days.'

Not surprising, Blake thought. 'Did you see him, Raymond?'

Raymond glanced at his empty glass. 'A top-up would jog me mind?'

Blake glared at him. 'Should we arrest him for wasting police time, PC Haynes?'

'I reckon so, boss,' he replied, retrieving handcuffs from his belt.

'Hang on a bit, it's coming back to me. Broad youth about five ten-ish, short greying hair, wearing a top and trousers,' Raymond spluttered.

'Don't mess me about! Understand?'

'Loud and clear, boss!' he said, fidgeting nervously.

'What time was this incident?'

'At a guess I'd say around nine.'

'Can you describe what happened between Mr Gibson and this bloke?'

'He knocked into Gibbo, spilt his beer on his top.'

'How did he respond?'

'Oh! He was fuming. Started mouthing off, but he was a big lad, broad like. Gave as good as he got. The landlord told 'em to pack it in, or they'd be out.'

'What happened then?'

'The youth ordered a load of pints, passed them over to his mates, and sat over there,' he said pointing to empty seats opposite the bar.

'So, it was just the beer talking, nothing physical.'

'Yeah.'

'Thank you for your cooperation. PC Haynes has your details. We'll be in touch if we need to speak to you again.'

Blake and PC Haynes moved over to the table across the room set up as a makeshift police desk. DS Murphy was sitting discussing witness statements with DS Roger Jamieson.

'Anything, boss?'

'According to that greasy old alco, Mr Cumberbatch and his witless son over there, the victim was involved in a minor altercation in the pub around nine o'clock. He says the landlord threatened to have Barry Gibson and the bloke he was arguing with thrown out, which is strange because he never mentioned it when we first spoke to him.'

'You'd have thought he'd remember something like that?' DS Jamieson said.

'Exactly. We'll speak to him again in a minute. Either he's drinking too much of his own ale or, he's hiding something. That bouncer Nathan Dukes was also vague when I asked him about the victim. He couldn't wait to leave.'

CHAPTER 18

When Ibrahim mentioned to the group they were soon to be joined by two beautiful ladies Malcolm's eyes lit up. The accountant had a thing for good-looking women and Ibrahim exploited this weakness by indulging him with the occasional call girl. The downside being he knew the Turk had taken voyeuristic pictures of him satisfying his deviant fantasies, and was fearful he'd e-mail them to his wife Susan, who was a librarian.

'No perving, Malc; play nice. These two are hot with big tits, but their asses aren't for sale.' Ibrahim gave Charlie and Leonard a mischievous wink as Malcolm's cheeks flushed with embarrassment.

Piss-taking bastard, the spectacled number cruncher thought to himself. If only the wife'd oblige him with more than the missionary position, he wouldn't have to stray. Blow jobs, bondage or anything resembling kink to get his rocks off was definitely off the menu. He'd married an intellectual stiff!

Ibrahim glanced at his Rolex; it was 11.35 p.m. He left the three of them perched on high stools focusing their expectations on the bright red roulette table.

Yusuf drummed on the leathered edge of the table. 'Get in, twenty quid, first spin.'

'Lucky bastard!' Charlie said as the dealer placed a marker on the winning chips, cleared up the losing ones, then slid Yusuf his winnings.

'Who are these birds, Yusuf?' Charlie asked.

'God knows, he's said nothing to me.'

'I get the impression he's pissed off with you.'

Yusuf ordered another round of drinks from the waitress. 'A few more wines will chill him.' Their relationship had been strained recently. Ibrahim was old school in his approach towards both family and business, something their father had ingrained into their core values from an early age. He could almost hear him now: '*Your word is your honour boys.*' So what he was late, hardly a big deal, he thought.

Ibrahim greeted the girls at reception with kisses on the cheeks, signed them in, then ushered them onto the casino floor, like an overlord's concubines, with the palms of his outstretched hands resting above their bums. Heads turned as they entered.

Kat winked at Luna feeling a rush of excitement. The glow of slot machines filled the room. As they moved toward the roulette table, the sounds of gambling rushed around their heads.

Luna giggled. 'These places always remind me of a Bond movie.'

'I know what you mean, glamorous and sexy.'

'Yeah, but without the good-looking men in tuxedos,' she said, eyeing the clientele.

'Oh, I don't know, what's-his-name is gorgeous.'

Kat winked. 'Ibrahim, you mean?'

'Yeah, he floats my boat, babe.'

With a confident swagger, Ibrahim asked. 'What are you ladies drinking? The Lanson Rosé Champagne is nice.'

'It's out of our price range,' Luna said, embarrassing the pair of them.

'You don't have to buy any drinks,' he said catching the eye of a passing waitress. 'Can you send a bottle of the Lanson Rosé, a pint of Guinness and a pint of Stella over to roulette table number three, please?'

'How many champagne flutes would you like, sir?'

He dropped a gold casino membership card onto her tray full of empties. 'Four, thank you. Stick it on this.'

Kat and Luna exchanged a glance.

'Come on, let me introduce you both to my associates.'

Malcolm had already spotted them, and his eyes nearly popped out as he cast a pervy glance at Luna's revealing dress.

Yusuf continued playing roulette, but was now sixty quid adrift and trying not to show his displeasure at losing. But the glare he gave the dealer wasn't fooling anyone.

Surprisingly, Leonard seemed more interested in roulette and the fact he was thirty quid up pissed Yusuf off even more.

'Fellas, meet Katrina and Luna, friends of mine,' Ibrahim interrupted with a self-assured look. This drew Yusuf's attention away from the roulette wheel. Although Ibrahim could tell by the scowl on his face he was losing again.

'Hi, I'm Yusuf,' he said, jumping off his stool, frivolously kissing Luna's hand like a medieval muppet.

Laughing, she wobbled and feigned a curtsy. 'So, you're his brother?' she asked, thinking he was good looking.

'Where did you meet Ibrahim?'

'Earlier in the Slipware Tankard.'

Glancing between the two of them he asked, 'Was he a gentleman?'

'Definitely, he bought us champagne.'

'Shit, he *is* being generous tonight. Rounds of drinks and bottles of champagne,' he scoffed, realising how jealous and insecure he sounded.

'Let's see if we can win Yusuf his money back,' Ibrahim interrupted, ushering the girls onto vacant high stools at the roulette table. He could do without the hassle of falling out with him, considering they would be working on the heist together. For all his faults Ibrahim knew his brother was the only person he could really trust. 'Let's have some fun, girls, you can play roulette for me.'

They gave each other a worried look. 'What if we lose your money?' Kat said, flicking her hair from her face.

'Don't worry, they're only tenner chips. Besides, unlike my brother, I always play to a stop loss. If we're not up after a few bets we'll walk away,' he reassured them. He could well afford to waste a few quid indulging his male ego in front of them.

Charlie and Leonard looked at the croupier watching with anticipation as the girls hesitated, then chose red numbers between 13 and 24.

'Good first bet,' Ibrahim praised. 'Safe and simple, paying out at even money.' The croupier dropped the ball into the spinning wheel. Kat clasped her hands together whilst Luna clutched the edge of the table as the wheel ground to a halt and the ball dropped into red 17.

'We've won, babe!' Kat screeched with excitement, offering her right hand up for a high five from her friend. Ibrahim congratulated them with a group hug, and he felt Kat's breasts rub against his chest. God, she smelled edible, he thought.

Noticing Ibrahim seemed to have developed chemistry with Kat, Yusuf made his move, sidling up within touching distance of Luna to see if she would respond. She stayed put and at that moment the champagne and pints arrived.

Leonard moved round the table staking his claim to his second free pint of Stella.

Charlie removed his pint of Guinness and took a slurp whilst eyeing up Kat's bum perched on the black leather high stool. It had been almost six months since his last oil change and the sexy pair made him realise how much he needed a good servicing.

Positioning the iced champagne bucket on the table's drinks Caddie, the waitress, poured out four flutes of Lanson Rosé.

Ibrahim offered the first two glasses to the girls, passing a third to Yusuf. He raised his glass and proposed a toast to the group.

'To beautiful girls, winning and *antik altin,* ' he resounded, then gave Yusuf a conspiratorial wink, the only one of the group who could translate the last few words – ancient gold.

'Cheers, cheers!'

Chinking glasses Kat gazed into Ibrahim's brown eyes giving him the signal to make a move on her. She felt herself electrified and turned on by their chance meeting. Champagne bubbles tickled her nose as she drained the flute in one shot.

'More roulette!' he said.

This time they opted to go for black numbers. Bets placed, the wheel spun, but the ball dropped into red 34. The dealer cleared the losing chips from the table. After allowing the girls to place five more bets, Ibrahim was sixty quid down. He could see the girls felt dejected.

Pulling Kat seductively closer towards him, Ibrahim whispered, 'One last spin, stick fifty quid down on the white line between two and five. It's a split bet.'

The croupier gave them a bewildered look. 'Any more bets? Place your bets now?'

With Ibrahim's guidance, Kat slid the teetering pile of £5 and £10 chips onto the white line. The dealer gave them a wry smile.

Although this was harmless fun to Ibrahim, he loved the childlike way in which Katrina and Luna were so excited by the game. Holding hands, their faces lit up in anticipation as the dealer released the ball with velocity. The girls stared, hypnotised by the white dot as it raced around the wheel, before descending then bobbling between 10 and 0, eventually landing in the black 6 slot.

'We've won!' Kat screamed, grabbing the sides of her head. Luna jumped around. Yusuf punched the air with a clenched fist.

Like three monkeys, Leonard, Malcolm and Charlie stood gawping in amazement across the roulette table at the lucky win.

Malcolm moaned. 'You could spend all night betting in this bloody neon palace, and still go home shirtless, yet the eye candy landed a 17/1 win within forty minutes. Bloody unbelievable!'

'How much have we won?' Kat asked?

'Nine hundred quid,' Ibrahim replied, smiling.

'Bloody hell,' she said in amazement. 'I've never won before.'

'Technically you've won nothing. My brother told you where to place the bet,' Yusuf butted in with a hint of sarcasm.

'Come on, bro, we wouldn't have won at all without this gorgeous pair helping us. They brought lady luck with them tonight.' Ibrahim heaped praise onto them. 'Just because you've spunked your mullah, there's no need to give them grief. How much are you down?'

'Sixty quid.'

Ibrahim tapped his palm onto Yusuf's face to show they were mates again, then counted out a hundred quid and slipped it his brother's suit pocket.

'Sweet, bro, OK?'

'OK.'

'Excuse me, ladies, I'm off to get these chips weighed in, back in five. Yusuf take Kat and Luna over to the booths by the sound stage, get more champagne in?'

'Are we in?' Yusuf blurted in front of them, like a Neanderthal.

'Manners!' Ibrahim shouted.

Luna looked back at him as they skirted through the upmarket Restaurant.

Understanding they were surplus to requirements. Leonard, Malcolm and Charlie bid their goodbyes and left the brothers to the enviable task of seducing the eye candy, as Malcolm put it.

'I'll call you both tomorrow,' Ibrahim said, addressing Charlie and Leonard. 'I'll see you Monday, Malc. Remember what I said, not a word?' He glanced at them placing a silent finger on his lips.

CHAPTER 19

Ibrahim returned from the cash desk and nudged in next to Kat in the booth, which, by design, gave its occupants privacy due to its high back curved shape. Judging by the brazen position of Luna's hand on Yusuf's thigh, they appeared to have wasted no time getting acquainted, which didn't surprise Ibrahim in the least. Yusuf wasn't big on small talk, more a man of action.

Leaning seductively closer to Kat, he said, 'Now we can talk without interruptions?'

'Who were those other blokes with you?' she asked.

'Business associates of mine.'

'What, they work for you?' she pestered him.

'You ask a lot of questions.'

'Just making conversation.'

'It was my accountant and two guys who work for me sometimes. Forget them, tell me about you?'

As the champagne flowed Kat and Luna escaped deeper into the fantasy of being swept away, blissfully unaware they were cavorting with two career criminals.

Ibrahim knew by Kat's body language that she was ripe for the taking. He'd plied her with enough alcohol and charm to break down her defences. If he left it any longer to make his move she'd be too hammered and fall asleep.

A glance at his watch confirmed it was 12.30 a.m. Making excuses, he made his way to the gents to set the next stage of his charm offensive in place. He fished his mobile out of his jacket pocket and called Jerry, the late-night receptionist at the Willow Room Hotel in the centre of town.

He returned five minutes later and asked Kat to spend the night with him. Surprising herself, she agreed. She stood up, hugged her friend, 'I'll call you tomorrow, take care?' Luna gave her a mischievous grin.

Ibrahim signalled to his brother for a brief chat. 'Make sure Luna gets home okay, pay for her taxis? I'll call you later.'

CHAPTER 20

The Willow Room boutique Hotel was in the heart of the city's Cultural Quarter. The five-storey late-Victorian building painted county cream, was originally built in 1889 and combined original features with shabby chic interiors.

They entered discreetly through the side entrance of the hotel, taking the lift to first-floor reception. Ibrahim pushed Kat against the mirrored back panel. Their eyes met, they held each other's gaze and kissed until the lift juddered to a halt on the first floor.

Ibrahim told her to take a seat in the reception lounge, while he sorted out the paperwork for their room with Jerry. She dropped into a black velvet wingback chair in the corner.

'You OK, Jerry?' Ibrahim offered a guarded handshake, containing the cash.

Jerry nodded and slid the paperwork onto the granite counter top. Going through the motions, he asked, 'Will you be paying for the room by card or cash, Sir?'

'Cash.'

'That's a hundred pounds, please. Do you have a vehicle to register for our secure parking?'

'No.'

The receptionist smiled and winked at Ibrahim, before passing his key card. With the formalities over, they took the lift to the third floor Bridal Suite and exited onto a narrow landing. Not wanting to alert Kat to the fact he'd had sleazy liaisons in the Bridal Suite before Ibrahim pretended not to know where room 12 was. Briefly he studied the tall vintage decals sign written on the wall displaying the room numbers for that floor.

Feeling the effects of the champagne, she tottered just in front of him along the corridor on the oak floor boards. Ibrahim stared at her backside and scanned down her legs to her wedges. Her curves aroused him.

He inserted the key card, opened the door and held it for Kat to enter, then slotted it in the holder behind the door and the lights came on. She gasped at the beautiful vintage interior. Light sparkled from the large ornate glass chandelier in the centre of the ceiling. A breath-taking architectural sepia mural of the town in the 1800s acted as a feature wall behind a king-sized Vignette upholstered bed laden with throw cushions

Curious, she stepped into the bathroom. 'Shit, look at this! It's gorgeous!' she said, running her fingers over the huge copper roll-top bath with side taps.

Ibrahim switched on the bedside lamps trying to create an ambiance. Sat on the edge of the bed, he glanced around the room keeping up the pretence he'd not been there before. 'Yeah, it's very nice. Do you want a drink from the minibar?'

'What is there?'

'Beer, wine, vodka, Coke, water, whatever you want.'

'Just water for now, please,' she said, wanting to enjoy the sex without the room spinning.

She sat on the bed beside him, opened her bag and rummaged through looking for her compact mirror. Surprisingly her make-up still looked OK. Turning to look at him with smouldering blue eyes, she leaned seductively close and kissed him, whilst placing her hand on his inner thigh.

'You're a bad girl!' he said.

'Champagne always makes me horny. Not that I do this often.'

'I'm not complaining.' He sat up before moving over to the minibar to pour a glass of wine as Kat popped the lid off the water and took a swig.

He placed the wine on the mahogany dresser and sat on the bed. Kat perched on his knee, kissed him and then pushed his shoulders down forcing him to lie back. Ibrahim kicked his loafers off. She undid his belt and teased his jeans down. The bulge in his boxers showed his arousal. Straddling him, she lifted her dress, pulling it over her head in one tantalising move, displaying her bra and shaved flower with its diamond droplet. She tried to kid herself that not all one-night stands were meaningless, but overheated passion. It was lust pure and simple.

They continued kissing as she tore off his polo shirt. His upper torso was ripped tight, like a Greek God. She dragged his boxers down, moving her head towards his iron-hard erection.

Tilting forward, her hair brushed his groin. She combed her fringe behind her ear with her free hand provocatively exposing her blowing him. He gasped and groaned with pleasure as she teased him. He unclasped her bra, and discarded it onto the floor, exposing her pert breasts. He pinched her nipples, sending sensual shock waves through her entire body.

They were both naked apart from her wedges, which she left on adding to the kink of wanton sex. He rolled her over on the bed. She responded by raising and parting her knees. They continued kissing as he entered her. Arching his back, he placed his hands on her breasts.

Kat groaned as her breathing became faster. Dominantly he rolled her sideways resting her long leg upon his shoulder, he spanked her backside. He felt much bigger than Carl, not that she could remember that well as it had been months since they'd shagged. He was always too wasted or tired to perform. She thrilled with excitement and pleasure.

'God, yeah!' she cried.

Ibrahim groaned. They gyrated for a further five minutes before he turned her face down. He placed both hands on her hips and she instinctively rose up on her elbows and knees into the doggy position. Her bum cheeks tingled as he spanked them again with the palm of his hand, intensifying the pleasure. She felt dirty and submissive experiencing forbidden fruit.

Leaning forward he placed his hands on her shoulders and kissed her neck. His tongue traced the side of her neck; it felt divine. She didn't know how much longer she could hold out. As if reading her mind he withdrew, and stood over her, then taking her hand, led her into the lounge part of the suite, dropped on the leather sofa and pulled her onto his lap.

Wedges rooted on the floor she eased onto him, facing a large gilt-framed mirror. His strong hands rested on her hips and she rode him as they both watched in the mirror. It was so erotic. The erogenous zones in her brain ignited to a point of intensity. She could hold no further.

They both panted hard.

Catching her breath, she couldn't decide whether she'd experienced her first multiple orgasm, or alcohol- and drug-induced euphoria. It had blown her mind, and, like an addict, left her wanting more.

For the first time in months she felt wanted.

CHAPTER 21

Kat woke at six a.m. feeling pretty rough. Ibrahim stirred and lay dosing. She showered, brushed her hair, made a quick cup of tea and wrote her mobile number with the hotel stationery, then kissed his forehead and left a note by the bed.

Call me later. Kat X

She let the room door slip to, and sneaked barefoot down the corridor to the lift, wedges swinging in her right hand by their ankle straps, praying no guests would be around at this ridiculous hour. It was obvious what she'd been up to, still dressed in last night's party gear, panda eyed with no make-up.

Ibrahim had ordered the taxi to pick her up from the side entrance of the hotel before dropping back off to sleep. She climbed in the back of the cab, slid down in the seat clutching her bag and gazed out of the window with a banging headache.

What have I done, shagging Carl's boss! she asked herself. She sighed in disbelief.

The cab sat at the crossroads opposite the the Slipware Tankard waiting for the lights to change, then turned left and cruised up Marsh Street North past Mind and the huge Go Outdoors camping centre heading towards the ring road roundabout. It turned right, then left towards Sneyd Green, past Central Forest Park. As they reached the top of Milton Road, a steep mile stretch leading to Milton, she gazed across the valley at the rolling hills and trees of Bagnall Woods on the horizon, worried about the consequences if Carl found out.

She told the Asian cabdriver to swing a sharp right just before the humpback bridge. 'Stop here, mate, on the left?' 'How much is it please?'

'No charge, cab already paid for.'

'OK, thanks.'

Ibrahim must have an account with the cab firm she thought, but more importantly, what bullshit could she feed Carl about last night?

The safest option would be to tell him she'd slept at Luna's. He'd have no reason to think otherwise. She often stayed there when they went out. Then she remembered he'd lent her twenty quid for taxi fares. He'd definitely want it back. Luck would have it she'd only bought one round of drinks so there was plenty left to pay him back. Sod him! she thought, smoothing her dress in a feeble attempt to look more presentable, before opening the front door.

On entering the living room she noticed the absence of beer cans and overflowing ashtrays on the coffee table in front of the fireplace. Often when she went out with Luna, Carl crawled the local pubs and staggered back home for spliffs with his loser mates.

She crept upstairs to check if he was still asleep. Easing the bedroom door open, she saw the bed still made. So he hadn't come home either? Aware he could enter the house anytime, she rustled the covers and pillows to make it look slept in. Slipping off her shoes, she put her dress in the wash basket, changed into her comfy jogging bottoms and a vest top.

Where the bloody hell was he last night, she wondered, not really giving a shit. She suspected he'd cheated on her in the past, although he always denied it, claiming he'd crashed on one of his mates sofas far too wasted to make it home. But that was back in the nineties when he was a wide boy in the heady days of Hanley's club scene.

These days the potbellied 48-year-old rarely strayed from the local Milton pubs. That crowd wouldn't give the middle-aged stoner a second look; he was well past his sell by date.

Her stomach rumbled; it'd been twelve hours since she last ate and then it was only a bag of mangy chips from the kebab house she shared with Luna. She made her way downstairs, heading for the kitchen.

On entering the galley kitchen she got a whiff of stale Chinese. Glancing around the hi-gloss cupboards she'd bribed Carl to get installed a couple years ago when she was working, she zoomed in on plates littered amongst used Chinese takeaway cartons strewn on the hardwood worktop by the sink. Carl was a greedy bastard but there was more food than one person could manage. John McKnight, his best mate, must've helped him scoff this lot when they got back from the pubs. Pair of lazy bastards couldn't even slide the rubbish in the bin, before buggering off to his flat.

'Disgusting!' She grimaced looking at the spare ribs chewed to the bone like stray dogs had ravaged them.

She brewed a pot of fresh tea and then opened the fridge looking for breakfast. Unopened packs of bacon, tomatoes and mushrooms stared back at her. She salivated at the thought of a full English. After twenty minutes of grill watching, she transferred the plateful to the dining table in the living room.

Turning on the TV, a bloody annoying reality show star minced around, reading out viewers Tweets and Facebook comments on cheating partners; how ironic. She blushed. She'd almost finished her breakfast when the front door swung open and Carl swaggered in looking like shit.

Bold as brass he announced he was effing starving. 'Smells well nice. Do me a fry up, babe?' the chauvinistic tosser said, expecting her to comply.

Glaring at him, she pointed to the kitchen.

'Ah, come on, babe?' he protested.

'No chance!'

'Bollocks to ya, I'm off up the Oatcake shop.' He rummaged through his pockets, pulling out a tenner and some roll-up papers. The remnants of last night's binge.

She didn't want to ask but knew he'd be suspicious if she didn't give him grief for not coming home. Pretending to be annoyed she remarked, 'Where were you last night?'

He hesitated. 'Er… Me, Johno and Macker went local, then ended up back at Macker's playing cards.'

'What about all that shit in the kitchen?'

'Oh yeah, sorry babe, got a takeaway before going John's. We were starving.'

Keeping up the pretence, she added, 'And you didn't think to call me?'

'Soz, you know what it's like. We were yapping, listening to tunes in the pub and I forgot.'

'You don't give a shit about us. Do you?'

He shrugged his shoulders, disinterested, then buggered off through the front door.

She sat wondering why she felt guilty. Disappointed with the way Carl had turned into a typical bored middle-aged bloke with no kids and no ambition, who treated her like one of his useless mates. The fact he got pissed every weekend only made matters worse.

She desperately needed a job to claw back her self-respect and dependence from this prick who took it for granted she'd cook and clean like a good wifey, even though they weren't married, and were barely even together.

She leaned back in the chair, closed her eyes and touched herself, conjuring images and feelings from the hotel room in her mind. Like flower petals opening in the summer sun, something inside her had awoken.

For the first time in years she felt alive.

CHAPTER 22

A searing ray of daylight entered the room through the left side of the roller blind, waking DI Blake after only three and half hours sleep. The day's tasks slowly emerged in his mind as he sat on the edge of the bed stretching his arms towards the ceiling to loosen the tight scalene muscles in his neck.

The whiplash pain burned like hell, but paled in comparison to the emotional trauma of losing his wife and young son in the hit-and-run ten years ago. Grief counselling and cognitive behavioural therapy helped him bury those feelings of despair, but the crash on Friday had acted as a stimulus. After taking several deep breaths, he stood, rolled up the blind and gazed out of the window at the cloudless sky, filled with early-morning jet streams. He sauntered into the bathroom, climbed into the glass cubicle, and immersed his head under the powerful jets of the large rainfall showerhead. The steaming water washed away the morning cobwebs and eased his neck pain.

After drying, Blake slipped on his pressed Oxford shirt and fastened the trousers of his grey three-piece, noticing they felt tighter: a middle-age spread developing. Too many late nights and beers after work, he thought. He brushed down his jacket before taking the stairs.

Entering the kitchen he spotted an orange Post-it note from his daughter, on the toaster:

Dad, I'm going to college this afternoon, lying in. Will call you later love Izzy. X

Isabel was such a sweet, considerate kid. Removing the note, he slotted a slice of bread into the toaster, and then gathered his phone and car keys from the opposite end of the granite worktop.

Whilst bending to put on his brogues, the sudden ping of the toaster popping startled him. He scoffed it down; the salty butter moistened his lips.

After sitting for ten minutes, he exited the house at 7.30 a.m. The leather soles of his brogues crunched on the gravel driveway as he strode towards his prize possession, a Willow Green 1975 Jaguar Roadster. He climbed in, turned the V12 engine over and was pulling off when last night's murder was announced on Radio Stoke:

"A man in his late forties was found dead in the White Horse pub in the city centre at around eleven o'clock on Friday evening. Hanley police are treating the death as suspicious and informed Radio Stoke they will release a further statement on Monday."

He parked the vintage Jag at the station half an hour before clocking-on time, desperate for a morning coffee lift, so made his way past the Potteries Museum over to Marzipan Pig, a popular locally owned coffee outlet, to buy a takeout of what he considered the best coffee in the city.

Cup in hand he headed up Bethesda Road. At the top he climbed the steps onto the stone pedestrianised area in front of the Town Hall. Pausing for a moment to take a sip, he gazed at the buildings four-storey façade, which bizarrely looked like a French Chateaux. Above its two-column grand entrance, a decaying stone crest displayed the familiar Staffordshire shield, presumably smoke-stained during the pre-clean air act years.

He paced a further ten yards and sat on one of the granite seats in front of the building, removed the lid and drained the cup half empty.

Hot air blasting out of a council micro street cleaner disturbed his morning solitude; its brushes spun in an endless cycle, polishing the stone paving in a mirror of water. Then like a stereo's volume being turned slowly down, the cleaner dragged along Albion Square past the war memorial statue of Lady Britannia, past Radio Stoke, finally disappearing into the wide boulevard of Cheapside, which led to Piccadilly and the other London-named streets.

With a warm coffee buzz inside, Blake strode back to the station. The morning sun had risen, casting long shadows along the wide streets of the city centre. He considered what details would unfold in his first briefing, about Friday night's murder case.

His phone jolted into action with four bars of the cool jazz tune 'Kind of Blue' by Miles Davis. The caller display ID showed it was Nick Pemberton, his Don Juan office manager.

'Nick?'

'What time you in the office?'

'In five minutes. Needed a coffee kick start.'

'There's new developments in Friday's murder case.'

'Such as?'

'Evidence.'

'Anything useful?'
'I'll tell you once you get here.'
'OK, see you in a minute.'

CHAPTER 23

He knew it would only be a matter of time before the pathologist discovered the fatal knife wound in Barry Gibson's brain. The police would be looking to find the weapon, so he'd got rid of it. He considered himself a calm operator, but Barry Gibson's killing was a frenzied attack, and in a panic, he'd tossed the knife in some nettle shrouded bushes half a mile along the Caldon Canal towpath in Shelton, whilst on his way home on that fateful night. Problem was when he'd gone back to retrieve the weapon the next day, with plans of destroying it, it was gone.

Fearful he may be arrested this was the best he could do to cover his tracks, and although he'd wiped that scumbag's blood off the blade, there'd still be forensic traces all over it; what an idiot he'd been! In hindsight he should have been far more cautious with his liberty at stake.

The missing blade would have to remain in limbo. All he *could* do was pray that whoever found it wouldn't hand it in to the authorities: it was a poisoned chalice.

He'd always carried. There was no way he'd go out without protection. The world had become a much more dangerous place recently. At least he was prepared to go down fighting tooth and nail.

One night in the pub, his mate had told him about how Barry Gibson had tried to rape his 14-year-old daughter on a dark winter's night, while she was coming home from her karate class. Luckily the feisty 14-year-old kicked him in the bollocks before he could ruin her life. But, because the incident happened in an alleyway at the back of some derelict shops, and the bastard was wearing a hood and gloves, the police didn't have enough evidence to convict him. In fact, they couldn't even place him at the scene, and he walked scot-free.

The vile scum had it coming. Every time he heard his name mentioned a wave of anger rose in him. In the end justice had been served his way. He exited the house, climbed in his car and headed to work.

CHAPTER 24

Blake swiped his pass and entered the city's police headquarters situated opposite Crown Court. He trotted up the stairs to the first-floor incident room. Nick Pemberton, his office manager, had laid out case files around the briefing table. Several members of CID had weekend leave cancelled and their arrival was imminent. The SOCO team were processing the evidence, and Blake had established a line of enquiry in the community. Preliminary boxes ticked, it was time to brief the team, sift through the available evidence and pick the bones out of it.

'What have we got then?' he asked Pemberton.

'SOCO have just informed me they found traces of the victim's blood in the sink basin in the ladies toilets.'

Blake shook his head in disbelief. 'In the ladies…? How did that get there?'

'Looks as if someone has washed it off their hands, or clothing.'

'Any prints on the taps?'

'Afraid not.'

'Sounds significant. I'll call them, thanks Nick.'

Before he could access the number from his contact list, the majority of the murder investigation team entered the incident room, followed by Chief Inspector Robert Coleman, Blake's stuffy boss. He sported a grey Edwardian moustache, and behind his back the team referred to their lofty chief as Kernel Mustard. He was a stickler for details and punctuality.

Coleman kicked off proceedings. 'Morning, everyone. DI Blake was the duty officer attending last night's crime scene at the White Horse pub in town. Can you take the floor, Tom, and bring everyone up to speed with what we've got so far?'

'Last night at around eleven p.m., we were called out to the White Horse in town to investigate what the door staff described as a potential fatality. On arrival we entered the crime scene in the gents' toilets, and discovered the body of a forty-nine-year-old white male known as Gibbo by some regulars. We later identified the victim from his driving licence and debit card as a Mr Barry Gibson of Heath Hayes Estate. The pathologist estimated time of death between nine-thirty and eleven. Witness statements taken from the forty punters present provided no clear leads. Those are being looked at by DS Murphy. Persons of interest are Nathan Dukes, one of the bouncers, and Darryl Connor the landlord. We'll be bringing in that pair in for further questioning. Forensic evidence is being fast tracked so we may have something to work with today.' He nodded toward the exhibits officer. 'Over to you, Langford.'

Langford Gelder was the SOCO team's obsessive exhibits officer. To the displeasure of his wife he often worked around the clock with only cheese-door wedges and energy drinks for company. The balding 43-year-old had been a police scientist for twenty years, and this nit-picking compulsive always delivered the goods in Court.

'Because the floor was wet, SOCO recovered some good footprints. However, closer inspection of those shows they are smooth leather soles, which makes them more difficult to identify.'

Nick Pemberton, the stations trusty office manager, also ran a tight ship. The divorced 51-year-old had a taste for ladies much younger than him. Sexual conquests aside, Pemberton was an extremely officiant office manager.

'As you all know the next forty-eight hours are crucial; the suspect will be desperate to cover his tracks. The absence of informative witness statements makes things trickier. Some of the forensic evidence recovered from the scene shows that the victim either slipped or was pushed during an altercation, leading him to crack his skull on the corner of the stainless steel trough in the gents. The police surgeon has pointed to massive blood loss resulting from this fracture. The fact our man dragged the victim across the floor and then seated him on the toilet indicates he tried to callously hide the body and made no attempt to preserve life by contacting emergency services. With this in mind we are probably dealing with a non-premeditated murder. DI Blake is scheduled to meet the pathologist this afternoon and will reveal the post-mortem findings later. The forensics team have yet to identify any conclusive DNA pointing towards a clear suspect. There is limited fingerprint evidence due to there being far too many sets of elimination prints. What's interesting is the perpetrator emptied the bin onto the floor and removed two plastic bags. Placed them over his hands whilst moving the body. This is very significant, showing we are dealing with someone with previous, who is on the national fingerprint database. Ultimately, he's smart and didn't panic.

'The perpetrator exited the crime scene through a small window leading on to Old Lane behind it, but there were no cameras covering the gents, or outside,' Coleman said before passing the baton over to Blake.

'DS Murphy, I need *you* to go through all the surrounding-area CCTV footage for the last twenty-four hours. Langford and I will go through the forensic evidence with a fine-tooth comb, see if there's anything we've missed. See if we get a hit on the fingerprint database from the available prints. Sue, our family liaison officer, is heading up to Heath Hayes Estate this morning to see the victim's family. Luciano, if you could schedule a press conference for Monday morning and put together a media pack. Nick will track progress and liaise with you all to make sure everything is done by the book. We have an excellent record with this type of crime. So let's get to it.'

CHAPTER 25

DS John Murphy stood up and arched his spine like a cat working out the kinks. He'd spent the last few hours trawling through grainy CCTV footage from Friday evening and his back was killing him. This process often proved invaluable in tracing a victim's last movements, identifying witnesses and potential suspects.

Positives aside, it was still a ball ache sifting through hours of mind-numbingly uninteresting, jerky footage of pissed revellers wobbling around the city centre, puking up the odd kebab here and there.

Just as the screen's time-stamp displayed 10.20 p.m. he noticed someone emerge amongst the groups of Friday night drinkers: a shadowy hooded figure pacing up Stafford Street. The fact he was wearing a cagoule with the hood up was suspicious. Friday was a warm summer night, which made this appear odd behaviour. Closer inspection of the image showed a stocky guy wearing dark trousers, possibly jeans. Murphy zoomed in, froze the frame and fetched Blake for a second opinion.

'I think I've found something, Tom. Take a look at this bloke. Might just be a coincidence, but he's within the vicinity around the murder time frame. Body language looks suspicious with the hood up.'

'Rewind, John. Let's see it from the start.'

Murphy hit the keyboard, spinning the footage backwards to where the suspect was pacing up the street.

'Zoom closer. A touch more – stop! What's that badge on the arm of his coat?'

'Looks like a fist.'

'Do you reckon it could be some kind of brand?'

'Hang on, I'll search online.'

He typed 'fist logo' into the search engine, returning 25,000 results. Over the years, tons of organisations had used the symbol, everyone from the civil rights movements to the economic freedom fighters.

'Could be any of these?' Murphy said.

'Hang on… zoom in closer, closer. Stop! Look at the bottom of the circle. There's a slogan?' Blake said, squinting his eyes, drawing up closer to the screen.

'Is that a K, John?'

'Have a look, your eyesight's better.'

'Keep… the… Fa. "Keep The Faith." Well, bugger me, looks like our suspect is into Northern Soul music. My sister's boyfriend was mad for it in the seventies… used to go the Golden Torch in Tunstall and travel to Wigan Casino. It was a big movement, back then, similar to the rave scene in the nineties. Kids used to dance all night, off their heads on slimming pills. Mani Brown! He always used to bring a box of records round our house and play them on our Josie's little red turntable.'

'Just because he's wearing that doesn't mean he's into the music?'

'You joking? Northern Soul was a bloody religion round here; still is. Read in last night's *Sentinel* there was an all-nighter at King's Hall, Stoke. People came from all over the country; apparently the scene is going through a resurgence. People into the music wear the fist logo. You can get bags, T-shirts, key fobs and loads of other stuff with it on.'

'Still don't see how this could help us identify the perp?'

'Surely one of the witnesses must remember a stocky guy wearing a dark coat with a fist badge on the arm?'

'What if he wasn't wearing the coat in the pub; it was a warm night, he may have dumped it on a seat?'

'Oh, shit!'

'What is it?'

'The all-nighter on Friday. There'd have been dozens wearing that badge in one form or another.'

'Maybe, but that was in Stoke.'

'Yeah, but these gigs don't get going until late. I'd imagine locals would use a few pubs in town first, then taxi to Stoke later.'

'OK, brilliant spot, John. It's bizarre how something like this can trigger a memory from the past.'

'Can you check out online ticket sales? See what names come up. Our perpetrator looks local judging by how he's navigating the streets.'

'OK, I'll do it next.'

'Zoom back out again and let it play?' Blake pointed at the monitor. 'Suspicious! Look how he turns his head, obviously attempting to hide his face away from the camera angle. Why would you do that if you nipped up an alley for a quick piss in-between pubs?'

They both watched the hooded figure use a little-known blank spot in the camera's scope and disappeared down Old Hall Street.

'Definitely a local. Could be our man?'

'We can't rule out our mystery man who argued with Barry Gibson in the pub. Any further leads on him?'

'Nothing, yet.'

'Somebody must know him?'

'Get onto the ticket company, ask them for a list of males who purchased tickets with Stoke-on-Trent postcodes. Get DC Moore to search online for local and Internet stockists of those types of badges. See if that throws up any names.'

'Don't want to piss on your parade, boss, but there's thousands of them in circulation on eBay.'

'Point taken. Tell him to have a stab at the local stockists for an hour, covering sales in the last twelve months to see what he can find?'

'Capture and print images; we need to include this in tomorrow's press release. Someone knows who this guy is. Anything else worthy?'

'Nothing. Just the usual crap, drunks, and stuff. Great YouTube material,' he jested with a sarcastic smile. 'Girl changing a tampon, a lad barfing over his mate's shoes.'

Blake beamed. 'Ha, you think they'd learn. Weekend binge antics never cease to amaze. Oh, to be young! It's going to be difficult, though, without a face. We can't get sketches done. Great work though, Murph. I'll get back to you later, just off to meet the pathologist to find out if Barry Gibson's PM has revealed anything we can use.'

'Don't envy you on that one.'

CHAPTER 26

Blake arrived at the city mortuary just before lunch; he donned scrubs and a paper mask before entering the examination room. Unlike the state-of-the-art glass viewing platforms in BBC cop dramas, this was more down-to-earth. Officers had to observe PMs in the actual examination room: a clinical depressing theatre of death dominated by three huge stainless steel autopsy tables. To the left of the entrance seven cold storage units stood side by side. No doubt cadavers lay inside on stainless steel body trays, waiting to reveal their secrets.

Over the years Blake had endured many post-mortems, but he still hated this part of the job. Witnessing human organs being removed, weighed, dissected and probed left him with hard-to-bury mental images. It always amazed him how coroners could detach from the foul imagery and putrid stench of death.

Hoping to diagnose a problem, Felix Wimberley Smithson leaned over the peeled-open corpse of Barry Gibson, looking inside his chest cavity as if gazing under a car bonnet. Glancing up he addressed Blake in his usual detached cheery manner.

'Good of you to join us, DI Blake.'

'Sorry, Felix. I'm running late today.'

'Nothing new there then?'

'You know how it is. Cuts and demands on police time are getting worse. What's the verdict on the victim?'

'We've completed our preliminary post-mortem report, and initially I thought the cause of death was a fatal blow to the back of the skull, causing a massive haemorrhage in the brain, leading him to bleed out. That was until Sarah took a cast of the fracture. Not all the dimensions match those shown in the forensic photos of the corner of the stainless steel trough. In fact, the depth of the wound is around an inch, and closer examination revealed torn tissue; the kind of thing you'd see in a stabbing. It looks to me that your killer has forced a sharp instrument into his brain to accelerate blood loss, and death. It's quite possible, if the victim had been discovered, and paramedics stemmed the bleeding straight after the fall he may have survived. To back this up, blood has been wiped from a flat pointed instrument onto the victim's polo shirt. See how it's dispersed here?' He said showing Blake a photograph of the 49-year-old's blood-smeared Fred Perry.

'So, to be clear you're saying this is murder? And we should be looking for a knife?'

'I'm afraid so, Inspector. Because of its dimensions I would say the knife is possibly a small hunting weapon, the type that can be purchased from survival websites; blade no longer than a few inches, around an inch wide. Having encountered this type of stab wound before it could be what's known as a drop point type. Usually their stainless steel curved blades are about three to four inches in length, but only the inner edge is sharpened. The back edge is blunt so when used in a stabbing, or probing way it leaves a wound that appears to be clean cut on one side and swollen on the other. Because of their strength, drop point blades are popular survival knives.'

'So you're saying the murderer could be one of these survival types, or just a nutter who got his hands on one?'

'Problem is Inspector, anyone with a credit or debit card can buy one online, but if I was to stick my neck out I'd say it's mainly males who either collect weapons or have survival tendencies.'

'I think the recent knife amnesty proves how many nutters there are out there; leaving us with potentially a lot of suspects.'

'Unfortunately I have to agree. Ironically, further examination of his liver revealed serious damage. I know Mr Gibson has been killed but I don't think he would have lived much longer anyway, judging by the state of his liver, which shows clear signs of severe cirrhosis, the type associated with excessive alcohol consumption. At a push I'd say he would have had six more months propping the bar up. We've also had the blood toxicology tests back from the lab which shows a high strength MDMA compound in his system; ecstasy no doubt.

'Can't say I'm surprised; according to his wife he's been on a self-destruct mission ever since he lost his job.'

On a minor note his medical records show his right arm had been pinned in three places in February this year. I'll compile my report later today and have it sent over to the station. Then the body can be prepared and shrouded ready for the next of kin to view.'

'That's grim, although it looks like his untimely death has saved him from a lot of suffering later down the line.'

The pathologist arched a sly brow. 'I'd call it a sick blessing, Inspector. Any leads on the suspect yet?'

'DS Murphy has identified someone we're very keen to speak to. We're hoping that will help us identify a key suspect, but we've got very little to go on.'

CHAPTER 27

'Mr Dukes, when questioned about knowing Barry Gibson on Friday, the fifth of June, in your statement you said: "Look, I know him from the Stores, but that's it. He's just another pisshead.' Blake glanced at the report. 'That's not true, is it, Mr Dukes? One of my officers has contacted your employer, M8 security, and their records show that on the ninth of February you were manning the door of the Burton Stores. At ten forty-five p.m., you and Mr Craig Dobson, another doorman, used force to remove Mr Gibson for being drunk and disorderly. CCTV footage outside the pub shows Barry Gibson waded into you with a stream of punches. In your defence Craig Dobson knocked him to the floor, and in an act of sheer aggression, you retaliated by repeatedly stamping on his arm. Mr Dobson had to use brute force to stop you from continuing to kick Gibson.'

'Sadly, no one reported the incident to us and, so it's gone unnoticed until now. Being a conscientious citizen, Mr Dobson filled out a report with M8, who are on record saying: "This is Nathan Dukes' second and final warning for using unreasonable force against a member of the public. Any further incidents will result in instant dismissal."

'Furthermore Royal Stoke A&E Records show Mr Gibson was treated for multiple fractures to his arm around twelve forty-five a.m.: an injury sustained from a fight. Two days later you had an x-ray done at Royal Stoke, for a suspected broken nose. What do you have to say about this?'

'He was bang out of order. I had to do something. He's a maniac!'

'Whilst we can appreciate the deceased attacked you whilst doing your job, you completely lost it. Instead of restraining him and calling the police, you attacked him. He had to have reconstruction surgery and three metal pins in his arm.'

'That bastard broke my nose!'

'I get it, being a bouncer can be dangerous; especially when people are pissed. You need to protect yourself, so you carry a knife just in case?' Murphy tried to prise him open.

'Do you think I'm stupid? As if I'd carry a knife. I protect myself with self-defence,' Dukes said.

'Since when is stamping on someone's arm classed as self-defence?'

Dukes ignored the remark.

'Do you take steroids Mr Dukes? A lot of doormen do, they think being pumped up gives them an edge over the punters. Thing is, steroids mess with testosterone, and make you aggressive. We've seen it before; bouncers on the dreaded 'roids losing it big time.'

'You're clutching at straws with this. I don't take steroids, never have done. They make your dick limp.' Dukes responded.

'Here's what I think,' Murphy said. 'You had a grudge against Barry Gibson and he gave you grief on Friday. So, you waited until he went for a pee. Knowing he was drunk, you head-butted him, resulting in him slipping on a urine-soaked floor, and smashing his skull open. In a panic you blocked off the door, moved his body into the cubicle, and stabbed him to death; then climbed out of the window, before returning to the pub from a different entrance later. Nobody would have suspected you because you were present when Dave Millburn called emergency services.'

'That's total bollocks! I admit kicking him outside Burton Stores but he was asking for it. Gibson grabbed my missus in the women's toilets and got his dick out. God knows what would've happened if she hadn't managed to get out and fetch me and Craig.'

'Why wasn't this incident reported to us?'

'She didn't want the embarrassment or her name going public.'

'So, you're saying Barry Gibson exposed himself to your girlfriend on the night you put him in hospital?'

'Yeah.'

'And she'll verify this?'

'If need be, but I'd rather you didn't ask her. At the time, she didn't want her name mentioned in the papers if we reported the vile bastard to the police. She still doesn't.'

'I understand that, but we only have your word for this. Seems you had the opportunity and a strong motive to attack Gibson,' Blake continued.

Dukes raised his voice. 'Yeah, me and plenty of other blokes. That nutter was always winding someone up.'

'That's quite a temper you have, Nathan. This isn't the first time you've used violence to deal with punters, is it?' Blake said.

'What are you talking about?'

'You haven't been listening. M8 security also have you on record for using unreasonable force when breaking up a fight in the Slipware Tankard four years ago. On that occasion you broke a young lad's jaw. Again it went unreported to the police. Clearly M8 have some serious questions to answer.'

'These things happen. You should know; police are always in the news for battering people when it's kicking off. You do what you can to break it up. Most the stupid wankers are so hammered, they'd glass you given half a chance.'

'Public relations is not your strong point then?' Murphy mocked.

Dukes shot him a contemptuous look. 'Whatever!'

'We know you were working at the White Horse on Friday, but can you tell us exactly where you were between ten-twenty and eleven?'

'I was in the pub, obviously.'

'Don't get smart. You know what I mean. Did you visit the gents between those times?'

'Having a piss isn't something you'd make notes about, is it?'

'We can appreciate that, Mr Dukes but, to eliminate you as a suspect from this enquiry, it would help if you remember.'

'Obviously I used the gents during the night, but I can't remember the exact times.' He paused. 'Thinking about it, a lad asked me the time as I was going for a piss, around nine-twenty. I didn't go after that.'

'Sounds convenient.'

'Can you describe this lad to us?'

'Seriously? I didn't pay attention to him.'

'I'd rack my brain if I was you, Mr Dukes, because this lad could be a key witness?'

Murphy asked. 'Was he a regular? Someone you might have seen before?'

'No.'

'I thought you said you didn't pay attention to him. How can you say he wasn't a regular if you didn't look at him?'

'I don't know, you're messing my head up!' Dukes blurted, getting flustered.

'Furthermore, Dave Millburn told us in his statement he never entered the gents, just popped his head around the door. Whereas you and the landlord went into the toilets, and in the process got the victim's blood on the soles of your shoes whilst trouncing through the crime scene.'

'We were only trying to help; he could've still been alive.'

'That may be the case, but the crime scene report states your footprints only showed tiny traces of the victim's blood – which is strange considering you waded through pints of the stuff. Very suspicious, wouldn't you agree, DS Murphy?'

'Definitely.'

'Do you have anything to say regarding this, Mr Dukes?'

'No.'

'I'll tell you why, shall I? You washed your soles in the sink in the ladies' toilets. You might think you were being clever, but some of the leather from them transferred onto the taps.'

'That's bullshit. I stepped over the blood.'

'Well, it was you or the landlord, because as I mentioned earlier, Dave Millburn claims he never set foot in the gents. One of you is lying. Anyway we'll soon know when the forensics come back.

'That's not the only lie you told us, Mr Dukes. When asked if you'd stayed in the pub all night, you said yes. Under caution, Mr Millburn informed us when the blocked door was discovered he couldn't find you for around thirty minutes. So where were you?'

Dukes' lawyer glared at his client willing him not to answer. 'I think it's time to take a break, Inspector?'

But Blake wouldn't be interrupted in full swing. 'Furthermore your M8 time sheet for the fifth of June shows that, after we'd finished questioning you at the White Horse, you worked the doors at the Northern Soul All-nighter at the King's Hall, Stoke. Seems to me the trauma of discovering a body left little impression on you?'

'DI Blake, I demand to speak to my client?' insisted Dukes' lawyer.

Nathan Dukes' lawyer returned from consulting with him. 'My client has requested immediate release. You have no real evidence to charge him with, in relation to Barry Gibson's murder.'

'Well, that's where we beg to differ, Mr Collins. He had opportunity, motive, means and there's forensic evidence. Either your client or Darryl Connor washed the victim's blood from the soles of their shoes in the ladies' toilets. Considering Mr Dukes' history of violence with the victim, we have more than enough to detain him.'

Dukes' face turned crimson with fury. 'You can't be serious? For chrissake, I didn't bloody kill him!'

'Mr Dukes, until you can prove otherwise, we're detaining you on suspicion of murder.'

'This isn't right. I need to let the missus know; she'll be worried about where I am.'

'I'll get the desk sergeant to call her?'

'Whatever. What about my car on Glass Street car park? The ticket's only for three hours. It'll get clamped.

Blake sensed an opportunity for forensics to give it a once over. 'If you tell us the make, model, colour and registration, we can get that brought over to the compound for you.'

'BMW 840CI graphite grey, reg DUKE B16.'

'Interview with Nathan Dukes suspended for comfort break, at one-thirty p.m.'

As a classic car owner, Blake knew the market, and Nathan Dukes' BMW was over ten years old, with a book price of thirty thousand, which begged the question, where does a brickie's labourer and part-time bouncer get that kind of money?

He made his way out of the front entrance over to the compound facing the city's ring road. Glancing across the road he spotted Fia Reilly's white forensic suit perched behind the wheel of Dukes' immaculate BMW. She turned in through the galvanised spike-topped gates and popped it next to a row of recovered stolen motocross bikes, caked in mud.

'Any problems?' Blake asked her through the open driver's window.

'Gears are a bitch,' she said in a soft Edinburgh lilt.

'Lovely motor though, isn't it?'

'Aye if you're into retro,' she said, retrieving her silver case from the passenger seat before climbing out.

'Pop the boot first?'

'OK.'

Blake stood hands in pockets, speculating what secrets it would spill. He hoped to find the knife, but doubted anyone could be that stupid. Initially he was disappointed at the contents. An old cardboard box stuffed with shopping bags for life and another containing valeting products.

That was until Fia emptied the boxes onto the tarmac. Under the bags was a folded black cagoule. She held it up for Blake to scrutinise. Grabbing the right-hand sleeve he stretched the arm out, and there it was. A circular stitching mark left by a removed badge.

'Bag it up. I'll get this over to Langford straight away.'

'That important?'

'Looks very similar to the coat worn by our key suspect captured on CCTV. We definitely need to do more digging into Nathan Dukes' background. We're going to speak to his employer, and give his house a going over.'

CHAPTER 28

Disappointed the search of Nathan Dukes' house didn't uncover any new evidence linking him to Barry Gibson's murder. Blake decided it was time to pay an unannounced visit to the door security firm he worked for.

M8's upper floor premises in Gilbert Street, Hanley looked like they hadn't been refurbished since the 80s. The wood panelled waiting room with red carpet, and stackable gold conference chairs was a real blast from the past. A white melamine TV stand glared from the corner of the room; underneath several violent Xbox games; including Mortal Combat and Medal of Honour lay on top of it, four controllers were tossed on the carpet. On the wall there was a cork board with several flyers advertising local martial arts centres.

'It's all a bit macho,' DS Murphy commented to Blake, looking at the flyers.

Blake knocked on the office fire door with a faded M8 security sticker on it.

'Hello,' replied a male voice from inside.

Blake opened the door and entered followed by his sergeant. 'Mr Millburn we meet again.'

'What can I help you with?' Dave Millburn asked, slouching in a reclining office chair with a copy of the Sun laid out on his desk.

'Your sparring partner Nathan Dukes is currently helping us with our enquiries, and we'd like to have a look at your security records to clear up a few things.'

'He's not my partner, just works for us.' Do you have a warrant?' Millburn asked.

'Do we need one, to look at routine staff records?' He glanced at DS Murphy.'

'Probably not, but we can always sit here for the next couple of hours until one is issued, boss,' Murphy said.

Millburn's face reddened as they called his bluff.

'Is there any reason you didn't disclose that M8 security was your company, when we interviewed you in the White Horse?'

'You never asked,' Millburn said arrogantly.

'You should have told us.'

'Yeah right I think you'll find we cooperated fully with you on Friday.'

'Why were you working on the doors, surely you've got enough staff? You're not exactly a spring chicken any more.'

'Well, that's the problem of running a business Inspector; people let you down. One of my guys was taken ill, so I had to stand in.'

'I don't deny that, but if you'd told us it would have provided some context. Anyway Mr Millburn, we're not here to argue the minor details, can you dig out Nathan Dukes' time sheets and incident reports since he's been employed?'

'What do you want those for?' Millburn protested.

'Like I said he's helping us with our enquiries.'

He got up and moved over to a large grey filing cabinet in the corner. After a minute of rummaging he reluctantly dropped a pale green swing file onto the desk. DI Blake picked it up and had a quick browse. Millburn slid his chair back in front of the cabinet, and sat down almost as if guarding its contents. Blake had a suspicion they'd be back to look at the other files.

'Nathan's a decent doorman you know. We were there all night when that Gibson bloke got killed. None of us saw anything because the door was jammed. What's all this really about?'

'All you need to know is Nathan is helping us with our enquiries, if we need any further assistance from you, Mr Millburn, we've got your number.'

'What exactly are you looking for in his records; I may be able to help? They're real boring reading, just time sheets, venues, dates and any recorded incidents; which I think you'll find are very few and far between. Some punters can get real nasty when they've had too many. It can be really dangerous especially if a group kicks off and you're outnumbered.'

'Enlighten me? What normally happens in that type of situation then?' Blake asked him.

'All depends on manpower. If there's a full-scale brawl we can transfer staff from other doors onto the situation; after calling the police that is. Thing is, it doesn't always go as planned, sometimes people get caught in the crossfire.'

'So, what you're saying is if there's enough bouncers you dish out a kicking to anyone who gets in the way?' DS Murphy chipped in, rattling his cage.

'No sergeant, that's not at all what I'm saying. You should know; when you send out a Maria – things can get a bit nasty; especially when groups of young blokes are bladdered. If you don't restrain them properly they'll rearrange your face with a glass.'

'Do some of your guys practice martial arts?'

Millburn gave him a quizzical look. 'It's like any other line of work; piss poor preparation leads to piss poor performance. So yeah, some of the guys do martial arts and weights, but there's no law against that is there?'

'Just as long as they don't use it on the punters.'

'Your guys carry batons, cuffs and PAVA, but it doesn't mean at the first sign of trouble they'll dish it out.'

Blake ignored his derisory comments, 'Speaking of tools of the trade, have you ever dismissed a staff member for using any kind of weapon on punters; knuckle dusters, or perish the thought, a knife?'

'You can't be serious? Every one of my blokes has attended an SIA approved training course, and they've all passed the required SIA criminality checks.'

'We understand that, but you can't keep an eye on them all the time. If there's a bad incident it's possible they could take extra steps to frighten off their aggressors.

'Bloody unlikely, I'd say. The door security industry is heavily regulated,' Millburn explained.

'Well Mr Millburn, this is now a murder inquiry. Barry Gibson's killer stabbed him in the head with a knife. Do you understand what I'm saying?'

'Sounds like your implying one of my door staff killed him; if you are that's a serious accusation, Inspector.'

Blake ignored his bluster. 'Okay, that's all we need for now. We'll be in touch about returning Nathan Dukes' records.'

Indicating to pull out onto the main road Blake said, 'Something not quite right about that bloke. Reading between the lines, I'd say he likes getting stuck in when it kicks off. I think we'll be bringing that whole filing cabinet over for scrutiny, before he gets a chance the doctor anything.'

'Definitely Tom, it would be interesting to see how many of his thugs for hire have been involved in fracas. Judging by all the violent games knocking about in that room I reckon they thrive on it.'

CHAPTER 29

Dave Millburn nervously paced around his office. What was he supposed to do now? Those bastards would be coming for the rest of his files. His boss would go mental. He picked up his mobile and called him.

'Listen, we've got a serious problem; the frigging cops are sniffing around in our business, they're questioning Nathan Dukes about that murder in the White Horse on Friday night, and they've taken his records. What should I do?'

'Did he do it?'

'I don't think so, but I can't be sure. Nath's got a bad temper, and he did go missing for a while on the night, but so did the landlord.'

'Just keep your nerve. If you're arrested don't say anything without representation. So far they've got nothing on us; it's just a fishing trip.'

'What about the staff records? There's loads of fights. Once they start digging, they'll notice stuff is missing. We could lose contracts if they start pulling our blokes in.'

'They'll find nothing. Stay calm and get rid of anything incriminating.'

'Yeah, but what about—?'

'Shut up, now, you don't know who's listening?'

The line went dead. Millburn stared at his phone. He stood up, slipped it into his jacket pocket then headed out towards his car. He figured it would only be a matter of time before the cops would end up searching his house. He couldn't take the risk of them finding the other paperwork in his spare bedroom/office. He needed to get home as soon as, and incinerate a folder full.

On the way home he called in a newsagent to buy lighter fluid.

Luckily his missus was at work. The last thing he needed was more awkward questions about the need to have a sudden fire. As he turned into the street two uniformed coppers were climbing out of a patrol car outside his house.

'Fuck! They're already on to me,' he thought, pulling over to the curb and sliding down in his seat. He stared nervously through the windscreen as one of them raised the knocker on his front door. Suddenly his colleague shouted to him. He couldn't make out what was being said. Cold fear crept over him. He gave a massive sigh of relief as they walked away from his house and opened the gate of number forty-three across the road. This was the only time he was glad that little bastard Jason Weaver had been up to no good.

He watched them go in the house, before slowly reversing out of the street. He parked a couple of streets away then returned on foot, through the fields at the back. Forcing his way through a hole in his leylandii hedge he crossed the lawn and entered the house through the back door.

He darted up the stairs, burst into the back room office and tore up the carpet in the corner, and retrieved a blue document wallet.

With the lighter fluid and box of matches in his pocket he made his way out to the garden. He emptied the incriminating sheets of A4 into the galvanised sand bucket his missus used to stub out her fags. Doused them in fluid, then struck a match. With a glow of relief he watched the orange flames take hold.

Walking around the side of the house he peered through the latch hole in his wooden gate. Jason Weaver was being bundled into the back of the patrol car handcuffed. His poor mum stood at the end of her yard sobbing over that arsehole son of hers.

CHAPTER 30

Back at the station Darryl Connor was waiting in interview room three under the watchful eye of DS Jamieson, and his solicitor. Blake entered the room carrying his case files. He sat down next to Jamieson and kicked off the interview. 'Mr Connor, when I asked if you'd been in the pub all night you said yes, apart from standing on the steps for a smoke. According to Dave Millburn and Nathan Dukes, they couldn't find you after discovering the gents' door was blocked. Tabatha, your barmaid, says you disappeared around ten and she didn't see you until the incident was called in. That's a whole fifty minutes unaccounted for. Where were you?'

The muscles in his face tightened. 'Er… went out for a roll-up. It was bloody manic behind the bar all night.'

'What, for almost an hour? Seems a long time for a smoke.'

'I had a wander around town.'

'Was anybody with you?'

'No.'

'Did you tell anyone where you were going?'

'No.'

'Sounds strange. You left your staff in charge of the pub without letting them know your whereabouts.'

'Not really; I trust them.'

Blake gave him a disapproving look. 'So if we search CCTV footage of the surrounding area around that time you'll be on there?'

'Er… maybe… I don't know.'

'Which streets did you walk?'

'Stafford Street, I think. Past Wilco,' he said nervously.

'Where did you go then?'

'Mooched about, finishing my smoke.'

'What time did you get back into the pub?'

'I can't remember, just after half ten maybe; I didn't check.'

'And this is when you told the doorman to call us?'

'There about.'

'Our records show the call was logged at ten-fifty p.m.'

'Fair enough.'

'We noticed the pub licence is in your wife's name. Dominika. That's Polish, isn't it?'

'Yeah, so?'

'Why's it not in your name?'

Connor hesitated. 'Works out better for tax.'

'In what way?'

'My accountant says it's something to do with national insurance contributions. I don't fully understand it. He set us up as a limited company.'

Blake glanced at Jamieson. 'Sounds interesting. I take it all your books will be up-to-date and above board then?'

'Should be,' he said with a worried look.

'You don't sound too sure?'

'What's this got to do with the murder?'

'Come on, Mr Connor. We both know the licence is in her name because you've got previous. We've done a PNC check. You can't get one because of your criminal record. In ninety-nine you did twelve months in Featherstone for GBH. You beat up a customer in your old pub, the Sun Castle in Burslem. In the case notes it says he'd been having an affair with your ex-wife, Mrs Shelia Anderson. Michael Leese spent two weeks in hospital from the injuries inflicted by you. Eyewitness statements said you threatened him with a knife, before battering him unconscious. By all accounts very nasty. Do you possess a hunting knife, Mr Connor?'

'Don't be ridiculous. As if I'd have a knife!

'You threatened Michael Leese with one, and according to the statements from the time, no knife was ever found at the crime scene.'

Connor ignored Blake's accusations. 'I've done my time. Even apologised to Michael Leese. I'm a different man now.'

'Are you still on the wagon?'

Connor reared up. 'That's bang out of order. I haven't touched a drink since being on the recovery programme.'

'Sit down, Mr Connor,' Blake continued. 'Running a pub isn't exactly the best job for a recovering alcoholic. Must be difficult to stay away from the demon booze.'

'I don't work behind the bar. Dominika and my staff do.'

'That's strange because according to several witness statements you were working behind the bar on Friday.'

'That's just a one-off because a staff member let us down.'

'The courts forced abstinence on you. Part of the deal your lawyer arranged. So in answer to your earlier question, what's this got to do with Barry Gibson's murder? It's obvious. You're an alcoholic who's done time for GBH. Furthermore, your wife reported Barry Gibson to us, for making racist and lewd comments towards her when you first took over the pub five years ago?'

Connor looked frustrated at Blake's lack of empathy. 'Like I said, I'm a changed man. Gibson apologised for that. He even sent Dominika flowers. Prison taught me everyone is entitled to a second chance, especially addicts. I should know.'

'Here's what I think. You accepted his apology because he was sticking all his benefit payments behind the bar. So you swallowed your pride in the name of profit. But Gibson was a nasty pervert who couldn't help himself when he was pissed. What did he say to Dominika on Friday?'

'This is harassment!' he said, seething.

Sensing he was on the ropes. Blake attacked. 'I bet he insulted her again and when you confronted him in the gents he kicked off, so you slapped the nut on him. You didn't mean to kill him, just send the depraved fellow alcoholic a warning. When you realised he was dead, you panicked. The pub was full, so you blocked the door and jumped out of the window, then returned later acting surprised. Isn't that right, Mr Connor?'

'You can say what you like, but I never killed Barry Gibson,' Connor protested.

CHAPTER 31

Spending seven hours in a cell focused Nathan Dukes' priorities. The thought of being wrongfully charged with murder mortified him. He'd seen the big guy who'd argued with Barry Gibson in the pub before. But until now his name eluded him; that was until a deep memory recall from that fateful night dragged him into self-preservation mode. Most of the night was a blur, but around three the pill he'd dropped started to wear off so he took a break and got a drink from the King's Hall bar. He remembered bumping into two old school friends: Tracy Taylor and Cheryl Douglas. Cheryl, the prettier of the two, had just broken off snogging with a big guy who seemed familiar; he looked like a fella he'd briefly worked with in the late eighties. That's when he asked Tracy who he was. Grant Bolton; that was his name. He leaped off the mattress hastily and hit the panic alarm, desperate to tell DI Blake.

Within ten seconds the duty sergeant slid his cell door hatch and peered through. Seeing Dukes nervously pacing up and down, he moaned. 'The alarm's for emergencies only. What's the problem?'

'I need to speak to DI Blake now!'

'What about?'

'I've got information about Friday night's murder.'

'You had plenty of opportunity during your interview.'

'I've only just remembered.'

'Tell me and I'll pass the message to him?'

'I want to speak to him in person.'

'OK, but you'll have to wait while I check if he's available.'

'He bloody better be,' Dukes said still pacing back and forth.

Luckily the duty sergeant managed to catch Blake, who was heading out the station entrance to fetch coffee. He desperately needed caffeine.

'Sir! Prisoner by the name of Nathan Dukes is asking to see you. Says he's got new information about the Barry Gibson murder case?'

'Really? That's interesting. He was unhelpful during his interview.'

'Seems pretty wound up, sir; he's adamant he'll only speak to you.'

'OK, I'll come now. This had better be good to interrupt my break,' he moaned.

Blake followed the sergeant back into the station and headed towards the cell block. Minutes later Williams stood holding the door as Blake entered.

'Right, Mr Dukes, what have you got for me?'

'I could do with a drink first. My mouth's really dry; it's like a sauna in here.'

'Let's hear what you've got to say first.'

Dukes became hesitant. 'I… er… remembered the name of the bloke who argued with Barry Gibson in the Horse.'

'And that would be?'

'Grant Bolton.'

'And you're only just telling me now?'

'I couldn't remember before. Friday night was hectic, and with everything that happened my mind went blank.'

'You know this guy?'

'No.' he lied.

'So how do you know his name then?'

Dukes told Blake about his old school friend snogging the bloke who rowed with Gibson, on the dancefloor at the Kings Hall.

'And you're absolutely sure it's him?'

'Definitely. I remembered because he was built like a bloody power lifter and wearing the fist,' Dukes stressed.

'What's the fist?'

'Not sure if you know but people into Northern Soul sometimes wear the badge?' he said vaguely.

Blake acted dumb. 'You'll need to be a bit more specific, Nathan?' He wanted an accurate description.

'It's a fist inside a circle. Round the outside it normally says, "keep the faith". Or sometimes the name of the scooter club or county.'

Blake continued the charade. 'I see. And whereabouts was this badge?'

'About here on his arm,' Dukes said tapping his left triceps.

'Similar to the badge you've removed from your black cagoule?'

'What you on about?'

'The one I found in the boot of your car.'

Dukes became animated. 'You've got no right to search my motor.' I never signed any warrant.'

'Need I remind you, Mr Dukes, that this is a murder enquiry. I don't need a warrant to search your car. You removed the badge after realising it could identify you on CCTV. In fact, around the time you left the pub for a cigarette break, CCTV captured a bloke of your height and build pacing up Stafford Street wearing a black cagoule with the hood up. And guess what?' He paused for effect. 'The fist logo on the left arm.'

Dukes screwed up his face. 'That's bollocks. I ripped the badge off because it was hanging off. This is bang out of order. I'm trying to be helpful, and you're stitching me up. How many more times… I didn't kill Barry Gibson!'

'Calm down, Mr Dukes. We'll look into this new information straight away and if this mystery man does turn out to be Grant Bolton we'll have three suspects.'

Blake turned to the sergeant. 'Lock him back up, Williams?'

As the key turned, Nathan Dukes flung himself into the back of the door and bawled. 'I'll sue you bastards for wrongful arrest! Where's my drink?'

CHAPTER 32

There were fifty Stoke-on-Trent men who purchased tickets for the all-nighter at the King's Hall on the 5th of June. DS Murphy and DC Moore had run them all through the PNC in the hope of identifying anyone with previous for violence. They whittled it down to just ten names. Seven of those had nothing more serious than parking tickets. The three remaining men had all been arrested for various forms of violence.

Straight after leaving a distraught Nathan Dukes to sweat it out in his cell, Blake headed purposefully to his office. Sat at his computer, he quickly typed Grant Bolton into the PNC database.

Bingo! The 46-year-old had several convictions for affray and hooliganism up until 2013. One incident in particular seemed to fit the MO of the Barry Gibson murder case: a fracas with Derby fans in the Barn Pub, Stoke in 2012. Bolton head-butted two of the visiting fans; leaving one with serious head injuries. With remission he only served twelve months of a two year stretch. Currently, he was on a two year suspended sentence, for theft. They needed to bring him in.

He picked up the phone and called DS Murphy to arrange for two uniformed officers to join them in arresting Grant Bolton.

An hour later, a four man team led by DI Blake stood outside number seven, Market Street, a typically run-of-the-mill terraced house in Milton.

Blake instructed the two uniformed officers to man the rear exit. Once they were in position he rattled the lion-head knocker, whilst DS Murphy peered through the front window.

'There's no one in there, Tom. Could be at work?'

'There's no work address on the database.'

'Judging by how tidy this property is, he's got money coming from somewhere,' Murphy said.

Blake was just about to try the knocker again when Bolton's neighbour opened her front door and nosed in.

'He'll be at work. Is he in trouble?'

Blake addressed a large middle-aged woman with bleached hair in black leggings and flip-flops. 'We'd like to speak with Mr Bolton. What's your name, love?'

'Denise.'

'Do you know Mr Bolton well?'

'Not really. He's a bit of a bastard, if I'm honest. Hardly ever speaks to me. My Mick's had a few words with him about loud music and parties at the weekends. Waste of time, though… told him to F-off.'

'Has he ever been violent towards your partner?'

'There's been a couple of incidents. Mick told him about his mates leaving cars outside our house all weekend. He pinned Mick to the wall. You can't reason with him. I'm bloody sick off him.'

'I see,' Blake said, trying not to be drawn into her neighbour issues. 'Where does Mr Bolton work then?'

'He's a window fitter for a company called Warmer Windows. Parks their van outside, bloody big white thing… blocks out the light.'

No sooner had she spoken when Murphy found the company's address on his mobile. 'It's in Burslem Boss, down Blunt Lane.'

'OK, thanks, Denise…?' Blake paused.

'Sumner.'

After she'd gone in, Blake said, 'Let's head on over there now.'

CHAPTER 33

Warmer Windows were one of those UPVC companies that used aggressive cold calls to annoy thousands of homeowners. The fact they employed an ex-con with a history of violence left Blake wondering about the morals of the CEO.

Without prior warning, the two police cars came to a halt on the company's car park in front of World of Wicker; their new glass-fronted showroom was plastered in 'Everything must go 70% OFF!' banners.

Blake was first out of his vehicle and signalled to the uniformed officers to follow him and DS Murphy towards reception. Inside they were greeted by a young receptionist, Stacy Anderson. A large woman sat next to her looking disinterested, stuffing crisps into her mouth.

'DI Blake and DS Murphy from Staffordshire Police. We've been told Grant Bolton works here; is that correct?'

'Yeah, he's been with us two years now. Can I ask what this is about?' Stacey Anderson said with a rather worried look.

'Afraid I can't tell you at present but let's just say we need to speak to him urgently. Is he on the premises?'

'If you could just bear with me a minute, Detective, I'll find out.' She picked up the phone and dialled internally. 'Is Grant still here? The police want to speak to him in reception. OK, thanks. I'm afraid he's gone out on a job.'

'How long ago?' Blake asked.

'About an hour ago. He's on a fitting job in Tunstall. Sorry I can't be more help.'

'Can you provide us with an address?'

'Not sure… it's against company rules. I'll ask my dad; he's the boss.'

'You've been very helpful, but I'm afraid it's not negotiable. We need the address as soon as possible. Also I'm asking you not to warn Mr Bolton we are coming. We have a warrant for his arrest; anything that hinders that process will lead to further arrests.'

'Oh right, Sharon will get it for you,' she said, nervously turning to her assistant.

DS Murphy spotted a Warmer Windows van parked on Tunstall High Street. Assisted by a young lad, Grant Bolton was drilling fixing holes into a PVC window frame resting on the pavement. The two police cars pulled over onto double yellow lines behind his van. Full of concentration, Bolton carried on drilling – until he saw the four officers pacing towards him with intent. He tossed the drill and fled up the high street like a fox being chased by hounds.

'Go, go!' Blake ordered the two uniformed constables who were younger and faster than either he or DS Murphy.

Bolton disappeared around a sharp right-hand bend leading down towards the A5271 and the retail park. He hurdled the railings and suddenly dashed out in front of oncoming traffic, dodging and swerving through cars blasting their horns. The two uniformed officers stopped on the opposite pavement tracking him. As the lights changed they continued the pursuit. Bolton took a sharp left up the boulevard past the library into Green Gates Street.

Slightly breathless, PC Haynes signalled through his Airwave set. 'Suspect heading towards a derelict factory, over. Following on foot.'

By now PC Davis had caught Haynes up and overtaken him. Attempting to lose them, Bolton dived through the archway of the factory entrance. Davis was gaining on him. But as he entered the building, he stopped dead. Bolton seemingly disappeared without a trace into the cavernous dark of a three-storey turn-of-the-century pottery factory.

Davis hit his radio. 'Suspect disappeared into derelict factory on Green Gate Street. Requesting immediate assistance. Over.'

A minute later he was joined by PC Haynes, shortly followed by DI Blake and DS Murphy.

'Sir, I followed the suspect in here but he could be anywhere,' he said, retrieving a small torch from his belt.

'We'll need to split up into two groups, but this building looks dangerous so don't take any risks. No climbing or any other crazy moves? Clear?

'Yes, sir.'

'DS Murphy, you go with Davis and take the second floor while Haynes and I scan around this one.'

Haynes pointed the torch in front and swept it around the factory. The huge expanse of concrete was strewn with broken cups, saucers and plates with the famous Blue Willow pattern lithographed upon them. Under different circumstances it would be classed as an urban collage; modern art.

In the far corner a row of ancient pottery machinery stood rusting under a hazy shroud of almost a century of dust. A sudden movement startled them.

Blake's heart skipped a beat. He shouted into the darkness. 'Police, stop there!'

Haynes moved forward, cautiously zoning the torch beam onto a moving target, his extended baton clasped tightly in the other hand. Blake darted to his left. Together they stealthily moved closer to a frightened figure crouched against the far wall, its face hidden inside a hood. They were within a few yards, when without warning the dishevelled figure suddenly rushed them. Screeching like a madman, arms raised like a gorilla attacking. PC Haynes swiped his baton hard across their assailant's knees. He dropped, sending a cloud of dust into the air.

They stood over the figure of a young homeless man, no more than twenty-five years old. His piercing blue eyes reflected in the torch light like a wolves. His skin was taut over his skull like a skeletal creature from another world. His clothes were filthy from rough sleeping.

Blake looked concerned. 'Are you OK, son? What you doing in here?'

The man paused. 'I live here.'

Blake was saddened by his predicament. 'We may be able to get you into a hostel. But first, did you see a large bloke enter this factory about fifteen minutes ago?'

Rising to his feet he said, 'Yeah, he ran up to the second floor.'

'Thank you. Once we've arrested the suspect I'll see if we can get you sorted out,' Blake said compassionately.

The homeless man nodded and shuffled off towards the light emanating from the entrance.

Blake called after him. 'Is it safe?'

He shrugged his shoulders. 'Not really.'

Blake looked a PC Haynes. 'Get Davis on your Airwave. Find out what's happening up there.'

'Haynes, over. Have you located the suspect yet? Over.'

After a moment's silence Davis replied. 'Not yet, it's pitch black up here. We need more light. Over.'

The sudden sound of glass smashing prompted them to act. Blake grabbed Haynes' Airwave set. 'Davis, is everything OK? Over.'

'My foot's trapped. I think it's broken. Can't find DS Murphy, sir?' He groaned in obvious pain.

'We're coming up now! Over.' Without caution, Blake bolted towards an oak staircase fifty-feet to the left of the entrance. He bounded up the steps with PC Haynes at the rear.

'Sir, it's not safe!'

'Davis is injured and DS Murphy could be in danger.'

At the top of the steps there was a small landing leading into the darkness. At the back of the floor, daylight streamed through a smashed window, projecting an eerie corridor of light across the floorboards. They could hear PC Davis's radio set crackle somewhere in front.

Haynes passed Blake his torch. Rooted to the spot he scanned the dark. 'John, are you OK?' His voice echoed into the abyss. Haynes tried to locate his colleague but his radio had died. He'd forgotten to fully charge it.

Blake bawled into the darkness. 'Davis, Murphy, where are you?'

'Over here, sir! Davis's strained reply echoed. 'I think DS Murphy chased the suspect to the floor above.'

His foot was lodged in a hole left by a broken floorboard. He lay in agony, his first metatarsal bone protruding and pressing against his boot.

'Shit! Where are the stairs?'

'To your left, sir.'

Blake quickly spun the torch and located another set of oak steps leading to the next floor. 'Haynes is coming to you now!'

'I've already called for backup, sir.'

'Never mind that, get an ambulance!'

'On its way,' Davis said, pain resonating in his voice.

'Hang on in there.' Blake tried to keep him talking, but he didn't reply.

He must have passed out, thought Blake, wondering how the bloody hell a straightforward arrest could turn into this carnage.

At the top of the stairs, daylight streamed through dozens of smashed windows, illuminating the floor. Over in the far corner he spotted DS Murphy desperately grasping onto something attached to a rusty cage, spanning floor-to-ceiling.

'John, what's happening?'

'It's Bolton! He's jumped into an old lift trying to escape. Get over here now… I can't hold it much longer!'

Blake darted to him. His DS had jammed the chain mechanism, which lowered and raised the lift, with an old broom handle.

'It won't hold much longer; the crazy bastard keeps jumping on the platform so the lift will drop to the ground floor. He won't listen to me!'

Blake leaned on the rusty cage and shouted down to Grant Bolton, who'd started frantically jumping up and down again like a wild animal trying to escape its captor. His neighbour Denise Sumner was right: he was a bloody maniac.

Suddenly the strain on the broom handle became too much. Fearful of losing an arm, DS Murphy released his grip and dived onto the floor. The tension on the chain cut through the remaining quarter inch of the handle and the lift descended rapidly, but before it hit the bottom with an almighty thwack, a corroded link exploded. The chain snapped and was dragged into the lift shaft like a killer snake attacking. Grant Bolton let out a deathly scream.

Both detectives lay on the concrete, afraid to look. Blake edged towards the cage and peered down through dusty eyes. The lift was empty. They exchanged a look of astonishment. Blake shook his head in disbelief as sirens reverberated outside the derelict pottery, echoing through its crumbling walls.

CHAPTER 34

After they'd failed to arrest Grant Bolton, both DI Blake and DS Murphy received a bollocking from Coleman, which they just had to soak up. The Chief Inspector suggested Murphy needed to shift a few pounds. It was only a month since occupational health had referred him to his GP for a follow-up appointment for cholesterol management; which provided his colleagues in CID ammunition for regular piss-taking jibes such as 'Blobby Bobbie' and 'Who ate all the pies' regularly being directed at him and another portly duty sergeant.

The shoddy, white Astra pool car came to a halt outside the murder victim's house, on the notorious Heath Hayes Estate, three miles from the city centre. The detectives were permitted entrance into the seventies' council house on Bloodland Road by Audrey Cliff, Barry Gibson's mother-in-law. The flaky looking 70-year-old ushered them along the threadbare hallway carpet into Tracey Gibson's nicotine-stained artexed living room. The pungent mix of fag and dog odours was rather gag-inducing, thought Murphy.

Mrs Gibson sat on a tatty, green, leather sofa, glaring at a huge state-of-the-art wall-mounted TV, which looked at odds with the rest of the house. She slurped tea from a stained mug, whilst watching the popular TV show *Con-men & Crooks*. Oddly, she seemed put out by their presence and took longer than necessary to turn it off.

Five minutes into the interview, both detectives thought she didn't appear too shaken by the death of her husband, which seemed suspicious.

'Can't say I'm surprised; that bastard was always pissed!' she ranted as if talking about a complete stranger.

'What was your relationship like?' Murphy asked. Considering her first caustic comment it sounded a stupid question.

'Bazzer used to be a decent bloke, until Crown Porcelain in Burslem closed. He was never the same after losing his job. Bloody loved the place, he did. Years he give 'em. They paid him and three hundred others a grand before chucking 'em all on the scrapheap. Same happened in ninety-three when William Adams closed. That's when it started. I saw no money; he pissed the lot up the wall. Never trained do nothing else apart from kiln placing. Bloody good money and all.'

Blake put her anger down to grief, so continued probing. 'Did Barry have any enemies that you know of? Anyone with a grudge or someone he'd fallen out with recently. Maybe someone in the pubs?'

'He was always rowing with people,' Tracey Gibson moaned, 'especially after too much ale. Nice as pie until he'd had a skinful, then he was a real nasty bastard. Kicked off at anything. He's barred from most pubs in Hanley.'

'Apart from ranting off in the pubs, was there anyone specific he mentioned?' Blake continued.

She paused for a moment. 'Couple of weeks ago he turned up with that TV. Said he'd won it at the bingo in Hanley, which is bullshit. He'd never played bingo in his life; bloody hated it. A few days later this bloke came round looking for him… said he owed money.'

'What did this bloke look like?'

'I don't know; I was down the food bank. Barry must have been in the pub, for a change. Next door neighbour told me.'

'Did Barry know a man called Nathan Dukes, or a bloke named Grant Bolton, both in their late forties?'

'She thought for a few seconds. 'Not as I know of, but he wouldn't have told me anyway. Secretive bastard he was: never told me nowt.'

'Fair enough. Who's your next door neighbour?'

'Mrs Arlington. She said he was banging on the door, shouting.'

'We'll need to speak to her. Get a description?'

Audrey Cliff butted in. 'Good luck with that. Wini's got cataracts. Blind as a bat.'

'Well, it can't do any harm. Is it possible Barry might have had money stashed in a savings account or something like that to pay for the TV?'

'I just told you, he pissed it all up the wall, Inspector. Every penny! We can barely afford to put the heating on, let alone get three square meals a day. Mum's been helping out.'

'I'm assuming Barry borrowed the money for the TV then, and it wasn't from the bank?'

'Knowing him, it would be from someone dodgy down the pub.'

'So it's fair to say Barry never had any money because of his drink problem, which led him to bouts of violence?'

'Twatted her more than once!' Audrey butted in again, supporting her daughter. 'Glad to see the back of him. He's been nowt but trouble these last few years. He came home with black eyes, or something broken, every other week,' the old woman rasped in a familiar Potteries' dialect. 'Smacked her about plenty. Our Tracy's well out of it now.'

'Did Barry see his GP recently for any health issues?' Blake asked.

'What's that got to do with him being murdered? Never went. "Quacks", he called them. Always banging on about packing in smoking and drinking. Same bloody lecture every time you go. Only bloody pleasure we got left,' Tracey Gibson said, retrieving a disposable green lighter from her tracksuit bottoms' pocket. 'Chuck us a fag, Mum?'

'We thought you should know Barry's post-mortem revealed severe cirrhosis of the liver. According to the pathologist the prognosis wasn't good.'

'You mean he'd pickled his liver,' the old woman said sarcastically, taking the cellophane wrapper off a twenty Superkings pack.

'I'm afraid so. Life expectancy six months at the most. Sorry to break it to you like that but those are the sad facts.'

Tracey Gibson's eyes filled up, and she sobbed in between long draws on her fag.

'I hate to mention it Mrs Gibson, but Barry's toxicology report also revealed ecstasy was present in his blood. Did you have any knowledge of him taking drugs of any sort?'

She looked annoyed. 'E's! Bloody hell! I knew he did coke sometimes?'

'How could he afford it?'

'Exactly!' Audrey interrupted, 'You never said anything to me about sodding coke.'

'I didn't want the hassle of you going off at me. It was bad enough with the booze.' Tracy Gibson said to her mum.

'So, where do you think the money for coke came from?' Blake asked.

'I don't think he paid for it. Told me he was doing errands around the estate for a bloke.' Tracy said.

'Errands?' Blake asked her.

'Up to no good probably. I begged him not to get involved in anything dodgy, but he just ignored me. Wouldn't tell me what he was up to. Still never got any money off him though.'

'Was there anyone in particular he was involved with?'

She thought about it for a minute. 'Now you mention it there was this one guy called Stomper he hooked up with now and then, but I don't know his real name. All I know is Barry was out every night of the week, in the pubs with god knows who.'

'How often did he meet this Stomper bloke?'

'I don't know, maybe once every couple of weeks.'

'Really! So it's possible, Barry owed this bloke money, and in return he ran errands for him, taking drugs as payment?'

'I just don't know. Like I said he was very secretive. Will you get the bastard that killed him; he wasn't much of a husband, but he was mine for best part of twenty years?'

'I can assure you there will be a thorough investigation. We're looking at several lines of enquiry. If you can think of anything that might be relevant don't hesitate to give me a call.' Blake passed over his card. 'In the meantime, our family liaison officer, Sue Collins, will be your main point of contact. She'll be keeping you and the family informed of how the investigation is progressing.'

'Her who was round here yesterday?'

'Yes. Right, if there's nothing else, we'll see ourselves out,' added DS Murphy, desperate to hurry proceedings along, feeling like he'd choke if they stayed in the stinking living room any longer.

As they got to the front door Blake asked Audrey Cliff, who stood in the hallway, 'What number does Mrs Arlington live at?'

'The one on the left… sixty-one.'

'Thanks.'

Murphy tapped on number 61. After a few minutes standing around, he increased the intensity which did the trick. An elderly lady wearing tortoiseshell spectacles, with jam jar-bottomed lenses opened the door on a chain and peered through the gap like a frightened mouse.

'Who is it?'

'Mrs Arlington, it's DI Blake and DS Murphy from Hanley police. We won't keep you long. Is it possible we could come in for a minute?'

'Not while my son isn't here. I don't see too good any more. What do you want?'

'Not to worry. We can ask you through the door. Mrs Gibson next door told us you spoke to a visitor she had a couple of weeks ago. He was banging on the door shouting after Barry Gibson. Can you remember?'

'My eyes are failing, not my memory,' she said, sharp as a tack.

'What did he say to you?'

'I told him they were out. He said, Tell Barry I'll be coming back for the money he owes. Then he went. Barry's dead, isn't he? Is that what this is about?'

'I'm afraid so, and yes, it could be related. Did this man sound local to you?'

'Potteries, you mean?'

'Yeah.'

'I think so.'

'We know your sight is poor, but can you tell us anything else about him?'

'Not really, everything's blurred these days.'

'Did you hear him leaving in a vehicle?'

'I think so.'

'Did you make out the colour of that vehicle?'

'Oh, I'm not sure. White, or silver maybe. Nothing bright.'

'OK, sorry to have troubled you, Mrs Arlington. You've been a big help, take care?'

On the drive back down Bloodland Road, the detectives discussed the case whilst creeping through the speed cameras.

'So, some scumbag debt collectors were on Barry Gibson's case?' Blake said.

'Seems that way. Doesn't tie into the crime scene though. These people are savvy. Unlikely they'd kill him in a public place. In fact it's debatable they'd kill him at all. He only owed them for a TV. Not a massive debt?' Murphy said.

'Judging by what Gibson's missus said he'd made enemies all over the place. But one thing is for sure, we need to speak with this Stomper bloke as soon as, he could be our man. Someone knows who he is.' Blake said.

Back in the incident room, Nick Pemberton was bragging about his weekend conquest to a young constable. He'd pulled her at the Duke of Bridgewater pub in Burslem; according to him she was a fit 27-year-old redhead who rode him like a Grand National jockey.

'Don't believe a word he says,' Murphy interrupted, winding him up.

'Ignore him, he's just jealous. The last time his helmet got knocked off was in the nineties at the Stoke match when the Zulus run amok through the town,' Pemberton retaliated.

'Oh, your jibes cut like a knife. Actually, the missus blew the dust off my truncheon on Sunday while we watched *Antiques Roadshow*.'

'Wehay! I'd loved to have heard what value their rare artefacts expert put on that ancient piece of mahogany.'

The group burst into laughter.

'Gentlemen! Need I remind you this is a police station and we're in the middle of a murder enquiry? It's like a bloody episode of *On the Buses* in here. Can we stick to the job in hand?'

'Hand job!' Pemberton said with a cheeky grin.

'Seriously, is there anything new on the suspects?' Blake asked.

'Sorry, boss,' Pemberton said. 'Yeah, there's been dozens of calls about the CCTV still in the *Sentinel*.'

'Have any of the callers mentioned the nickname Stomper?' Blake asked.

'I can check for you, but not that I know of. Is he a suspect?'

'The victim's wife mentioned Barry had been socialising with him recently. We really need to find out who this guy is. Hardly an inconspicuous handle is it?'

'Kernel Mustard has sent out a posse of constables to follow up those lines of enquiry. We should know more later.'

Blake sounded doubtful. 'Let's hope that gives us more to work with. Have the local taxi firms been contacted yet, to see if anyone picked up a man fitting the suspect's description between nine-thirty and eleven p.m.?'

'PC Evans is working her way through the taxicab list,' Pemberton said. 'No hits yet, I'm afraid. Maybe he caught the bus, or walked?'

'Would you like me to see if Evans has any leads, chief?' DS Murphy asked.

Blake grinned. 'It's OK, John, I'll have a word with her. Good point about the bus; has anyone spoken to First Bus or Wardle Travel?'

'Not yet, boss, but I'll get somebody onto it as soon as,' Pemberton replied.

'Did you discover any irregularities in the witness statements, John?' Blake asked his DS.

'No, just the ramblings of beered-up wasters. The murderer legged it well before we arrived. None of them owned up to missing a drinking partner, although judging by the state of them, it's unlikely they'd dob a mate in.'

'Worth bringing any in for questioning?'

'Yeah. If we turn up the heat maybe someone will expose a drinking bud?'

'OK, draw up a shortlist of the most helpful and evasive witnesses? We'll bring them in for further questioning. Putting them under a microscope in the interview room might jog a few memories. At least they're likely to be sober this time.'

Pemberton rocked on his chair. 'Don't bank on it, judging by what PC Haynes told me. Says the majority looked like they'd converted their gyros into beer tokens.'

It was 11.30 a.m. and Blake was in desperate need of a pre-lunch coffee boost. The curvaceous figure bending down to retrieve a cup of the black shit the vending machine company passed off as coffee was unmistakably PC Casey Evans. He hated to admit it but John was right; she was an absolute stunner. God knows why she joined the force; that face and body wouldn't look out of place on the cover of a lad's mag, or some other trite fashion monthly.

He asked her, 'Any leads on the taxicab line of enquiry?'

'Not yet, sir. You wouldn't believe how many private hire companies there are in Stoke-on-Trent. Called twenty-five already. Just another thirty to go!'

'Tedious, I know, but it needs to be done. I'll see if I can get you help to lighten the load.'

She shot him a flirtatious smile. 'Thanks, sir; that would be great.'

His eyes averted her gesture. 'Don't thank me yet; I'm about to add to your workload. Can you call First Bus and Wardle Travel and get them to circulate the CCTV still of our suspect to their drivers?'

'Will do, sir.'

Coffee in hand she turned and strutted along the corridor towards the incident room. Did she just give him a signal or was he imagining it? It had been months since he'd cavorted with the opposite sex and the brief encounter left him feeling a little unhinged.

CHAPTER 35

DI Blake decided there might be mileage in re-questioning some of the drinkers from the White Horse crime scene, before any of the cheap pubs opened. Hopefully, they'd be sober.

Arthur Cumberbatch and his son Raymond were first on the list, although his previous encounter with the pair had established they were dumber than barstools. It would take a huge leap of faith to think this daft pair were involved in Barry Gibson's death. They'd struggle to knock the top of a pie, let alone poll axe a six-foot skinhead. But they still needed re-questioning.

'What we doing in here, duck, pubs open soon; me and Wazz haven't had breckie yet.'

'It's DI Blake to you, Mr Cumberbatch. We're reassessing the witness statements taken on Friday the 5th, in the White Horse. And since you and your son seem to be the only pair who knew the deceased, we want to make sure we haven't missed nothing.'

'I see. What do you reckon, Wazz?'

'Yeah, sound, Dad.'

Blake glanced at his highlighted notes. 'Mr Cumberbatch, in your original statement you said:

"'*We've known Big Gibbo for a few years. He normally drinks in the Burton Stores. Bit of a lad, if you know what I mean. Likes a bloody good row that one. He offered plenty of 'em to step outside. He could turn real nasty.*"

'Going back to what you said about *he offered plenty of people outside.* Can you remember anyone in particular, say a regular you know from any of the pubs you and Raymond use? Does the name Stomper mean anything to either of you?'

'Never heard of him; all I know is, most of the regulars knew better than to row with him. He got on with most of them; it was usually strangers,'

'I see. This brings us onto the altercation you witnessed between Barry Gibson and the "big youth" you referred to. I know you gave us a brief description on the night but it's possible you may have remembered a bit more about him since Friday?' Blake said addressing Raymond.

Cumberbatch's son didn't respond immediately. 'Can't remember.'

Blake jogged his memory. 'A broad youth about five ten, dark hair wearing a top and trousers. It's a bit vague to say the least?'

'How do you mean?' Raymond said dimly.

'I hate to state the obvious but that probably describes several punters in the White Horse on Friday. We need more specific details. Can you remember his hairstyle, facial and body marks; such as moles, scars tattoos or anything else distinguishing about him? What colour was his top? Did it have a logo? Was he wearing jeans, chinos or more formal trousers? Come on Raymond, this is a bloody murder inquiry!'

'Murder! I thought Gibbo was in a fight?

'He was, but the killer stabbed him with a knife in the head.'

'Oh shit! Sounds really bad?'

'It is, so can you remember anything?'

'His hair was longer on top, greased over to one side. Like footballers have it.'

'OK, that's a good start. Any marks or tattoos?'

'Now you mention it, I think there was a tat on the back of his neck poking just above his collar. Chinese writing or summet.'

'Now we're getting somewhere,' Blake said, taking notes. 'Facial hair or anything like that?'

'Just a bit of stubble.'

'And moving back to his clothes. Anything at all you can remember?'

'Na, pub was too packed, it was darkish.'

'You're sure?'

'Yeah.'

'OK. Your dad said the youth ordered loads of pints. How many would you say?'

Arthur Cumberbatch butted in. 'About ten, I reckon.'

Blake ignored him and carried on probing Raymond. 'So he'd have been with a big group of mates. Do you remember anything about them? Think hard.'

'Nah, it was too packed so I couldn't say for sure. Blokes were coming and going all night.'

'But you remember the incident fairly clearly?'

'Yeah, only because Big Gibbo was involved.'

'To recap. Your dad said the big youth stood up to Gibbo?'

'Yeah, then the landlord stepped in and fetched the bouncer.'

'That would be Mr Darryl Connor, and the bouncer was Nathan Dukes.

'Ar, that's them.

'So you're saying Nathan Dukes had a word with Barry Gibson?'

'Yeah, but we couldn't hear what he said.'

'And there's nothing else at all you want to add?'

'Like what?'

'Did you notice anything after things settled down?'

'No, we never saw Big Gibbo after that. Thought he must have gone another pub. Then you lot turned up later.'

'Unfortunately, the *big youth* who rowed with Barry Gibson has disappeared. His name's Grant Bolton, and there's a warrant out for his arrest. Do you know him?'

Cumberbatch gave his son a worried look.

'No.'

'Thanks for your cooperation. You've been very helpful.'

CHAPTER 36

Stoke-on-Trent's new state-of-the-art forensics lab was a five-minute spin around the ring road. Blake had phoned earlier that morning and arranged a meeting with Langford Gelder, the city's senior forensic specialist. He preferred the old city lab housed in a grand three-storey Edwardian building. Sadly, the powers that be declared it no longer fit for purpose and it had been boarded up since closing in 2001. Worst of all, the car park was smaller so, unless the forensics team were at a crime scene, there were no spaces.

A glance over the lab's low perimeter wall confirmed his parking theory. Unable to get a driving pool car, he'd been forced to take the Jag. Unimpressed, he parked it in the terraced street opposite, mindful any dozy twat could knock his pride and joy. The receptionist recognised him. After scribbling in the visitor's book, he strode along a clinical corridor towards Langford's office.

'Tom,' Gelder greeted him, opening his door, 'what can I do for you?'

'I'd like to go through the Barry Gibson murder case forensics again?'

'Did we miss something?' he said, puzzled.

'Not sure. It's more a case of double-checking everything. Still no arrest, although DS Murphy may have identified a potential suspect, but it's early days yet.'

'CCTV?'

'Yeah! Sadly we don't have a face shot though.'

'Nothing at all to go off?'

'Bastard's wearing a hood.'

'What about the timeline…? Can you place him?'

'Time stamp is within the hour mark.'

'No hits on the fingerprints?'

'Afraid not. He placed bin bags on his hands. Those weren't recovered at the crime scene, and there was far too much cross contamination from other drinkers to establish anything solid.'

'Nothing on the DNA side of things?'

Blake let out a heavy sigh. 'Another blank. The suspect is not in the database. Could be a first offence, but I very much doubt it, judging by the level of violence and the fact he tried to hide the body. Doesn't exactly look like a panic merchant. He may have been arrested pre-DNA. Compulsory testing wasn't rolled out until 1995.'

'Suppose it's possible. There are positives though. The forensic podiatrist unit have produced clear images of both the suspect's footprints. There are also contact samples of the perpetrator's clothes fibres, which transferred to the victim when attempting to hide the body.'

Blake's brow furrowed as he considered the limited forensic evidence. 'That's disappointing. We both know the first thing he's likely to do is to dispose of those.'

'Unfortunately true, Inspector, but that's all we've got to work with at this stage. These size tens have leather soles, which means unique marks,' Gelder imparted holding up an A4 image of the suspect's footprints.

'That's a good thing, because they would be easy to identify. And there'd be blood transferral from the floor.'

'Anything turned up regarding the knife?'

'Another blank I'm afraid. Pathologist thinks it could be something called a drop point blade; a survival knife.'

'Nasty?'

'Yeah, I'm sure you've read the report?'

'I have, Inspector. Killer forced it into his brain, no way he'd come back from that.'

'Thanks, Langford, it is what it is. Just means we've gotta work much harder to get him.'

Gelder shrugged. 'Sorry I couldn't be of more help.'

CHAPTER 37

DI Blake's team had yet to establish the whereabouts of Grant Bolton. The fact he'd argued with Barry Gibson in the White Horse on the night of his murder, clearly made him a prime suspect, although they couldn't rule out Darryl Connor, Nathan Dukes and Dave Millburn who'd also had the opportunity.

He was convinced they were lying about not really knowing the victim: a web of deceit he planned to get to the bottom of.

It seemed Bolton had gone completely off the grid. Judging by the inactivity of his phone records, he must've ditched his contracted mobile. A door-to-door in the Milton area drew a blank; even his landlord was after him because he owed a month's rent. A search of his property didn't bring any new evidence to light. The only thing they had to go on was his Facebook profile which provided clues as to the type of person he really was. Judging by the pictures of paint-balling events, survival courses, videos of camping trips on remote Staffs moorlands, and SAS guide books he'd listed as his favourite reads, he was some kind of survival fantasist, which fitted the pathologists original profile of the killer. Someone knew where he was and they intended to find out who.

Back at the station, Blake's frustration was showing. They'd had to release Nathan Dukes without charge. He'd been in custody for forty eight hours and apart from circumstantial footprints at the scene they had nothing concrete on him; he claimed not to know anyone called Stomper, and the search of his property drew a blank.

He crushed and slam-dunked his second disposable coffee cup into the incident room bin.

'Have you sent stills of the CCTV footage out to the *Sentinel*?' he asked Nick Pemberton who sat swivelling his chair.

'It went off straight after you spoke to John this morning. It will be in tonight's edition,' he said, glancing over at DS Murphy sitting two desks along.

'Great, at least that's sorted.'

Pemberton moaned. 'There's still a bloody multitude of tasks in the action book, which Kernel Mustard hasn't sanctioned. I'll have to run them by him first. You know how anal he is on protocol.'

'I know it's early days but we've got limited evidence to work with,' Blake said.

'Wait till Tuesday's press release; we'll be inundated with calls from the public identifying the suspect.'

'You wish.'

'Langford not turned up anything useful then, I take it?' Pemberton asked Blake.

'All we have to show for Friday night's graveyard shift is frigging shoe prints and fibres!'

He reflected on Barry Gibson's prostrate body lying in a sea of blood, like a freshly slaughtered abattoir carcass – a fact which focused his attention on the present arduous task of building a case, brick by brick.'

Earwigging, DS Murphy chipped in. 'Seriously! No clear suspect fingerprints or DNA?'

'As you know John, the crime scene was contaminated with hundreds of elimination prints. And of course Nathan Dukes and Darryl Connor trounced all over the bloody floor. Originally we thought it looked like a fight gone wrong. According to the post-mortem the victim received a nasty blow to the face, which busted his nose causing him to fall backwards onto the trough, cracking his skull like a nut.'

'Poor bastard probably never saw it coming.'

'Head-butt, you reckon?'

'That's what the pathologist said. However, he was adamant the knife wound to his brain killed him.'

'Ironic though. Poor bugger had cirrhosis of the liver. Smithson said Gibson would be dead within six months anyway.'

'Jesus, that's uncanny. Our man probably did him a favour in the end then?' Murphy said cynically.

'It looks that way, John.'

CHAPTER 38

Blake sat in between Chief Inspector Robert Coleman, and Alice Lowe, the station's press officer. For some reason unknown to him, the Barry Gibson murder case seemed to have generated interest further afield than the Staffordshire Borders. Apart from the usual suspects from the local rags, a group of seven unfamiliar faces sat three rows in, eagerly awaiting to speculate on the available evidence. Rightly or wrongly he put the press in the same category as the majority of scrotes he nicked. A bunch of parasitic losers living off the misfortune of others. However, in certain circumstances he knew they played a vital role. Especially when mass distribution of CCTV images were needed.

Alice Lowe opened proceedings. 'Ladies and gents. Thank you for attending the Barry Gibson case press release. Before we begin, just a few house rules to take note of. In the event of an emergency there are two fire exits, the entrance which you all came through and another on the sidewall.' She pointed to her left, like an air hostess. 'Usual rules apply. Please don't interrupt the police officers unless you are prompted to do so. There will be an opportunity at the end to ask all relevant questions. If you really can't resist the urge to interrupt, please raise a hand and wait patiently for a response.'

Blake smirked inwardly knowing this bunch of muck rakers wouldn't last until the end before picking holes in their case and questioning their integrity. Glaring across the room he adjusted the microphone, and addressed the eagerly awaiting ensemble of around fifteen journalists. 'As you know, on the fifth of June, at approximately ten-fifty p.m., the body of Barry Gibson, formally of the Heath Hayes Estate, was discovered in the gents by the doorman of the White Horse pub in Hanley city centre. Our SOCO team processed the crime scene but unfortunately due to there being too much cross contamination we were unable to identify a specific suspect. Forensic evidence leads us to believe Barry Gibson was involved in a fight, during which he slipped on a wet floor and in the process hit his head on the stainless steel urinal trough.

'Realising his victim was still breathing, his callous assailant forced a sharp object, possibly a knife through the skull into his brain, which the coroner informs us accelerated blood loss. The murderer then dragged him across the floor and hauled his body into one of the cubicles, where he bled to death. The good news is we have CCTV footage of a stocky man, approximately six-feet tall, wearing a black cagoule with the hood up, leaving the scene and heading up Stafford Street at ten-thirty p.m. On the left arm of the coat there was a distinctive badge. This relates to the Northern Soul music scene and shows a fist within a circle with the words "keep the faith" around the inner edge. We have issued a warrant for the arrest of another man. Grant Bolton was seen arguing with the victim in the pub, not long before he was killed. He is currently on the run, and we are very keen to speak with him. There are also three undisclosed witnesses helping us with our enquiries, and we're looking to identify a fifth man known to the victim by the nickname Stomper.' Blake concluded, surprised that there'd been none of the usual unhelpful interruptions.

Taking back the baton, Alice Lowe prompted the press for a show of hands. The *Evening Sentinel*'s crime reporter was first in line.

'Jim Roachford, *Evening Sentinel.* Judging by what you've just said it's possible any of these men could be the murderer, Inspector Blake? And, can you tell us how the perpetrator managed to escape the pub unnoticed?'

'Again, forensic evidence shows our man exited the gents' toilets through a small window leading onto Old Lane.'

'Surely someone must have seen him?' Roachford asked.

'As I just said, we have CCTV evidence of our primary suspect. Come on, Jim, keep your eye on the ball,' Blake said sarcastically.

Changing tack, Roachford asked. 'In your opinion was this a stranger killing or could the killer be known to the victim?'

Blake gave him a noncommittal glance. 'It's hard to say really. All family have been eliminated as suspects. However, because of the lack of forensic evidence we are continuing to look at Barry Gibson's associates, amongst other lines of enquiry, but the arrest of Grant Bolton, and CCTV angle are our primary objectives.

Like an MP on *Question Time*, Blake continued to begrudgingly engage with the hacks.

'Brian Welland, *Birmingham Mail.* Inspector, is it true the victim was an alcoholic and therefore could he have goaded his attacker, and got the upper hand before the knife came into play?' He threw Blake a curve ball.

'Naturally that's something we considered before the post-mortem, but the truth is we'll never know exactly what happened. All *you* need to know is the killer is still out there, and we're doing everything in our power to catch him,' Welland clamped up.

Like a lemming, Jim Roachford's familiar ginger beard popped up again. 'Is it true you questioned The White Horse landlord, Darryl Connor, in connection with the murder?'

'I'm afraid I can't comment on that at this time,' Blake said bewildered at how the bloody hell he'd got hold of the information, concluding he'd probably badgered Connor's wife. They'd soon know he'd been released without charge.

His reply caused a ripple of gossip until a pretty young woman in black-framed geek-chic glasses waved from the back. 'Lisa Faulkner, *Leek Post.* It's rumoured that the victim could be violent and made a lot of enemies due to his alcohol addiction. Can you confirm that?'

Being from a fairly rural paper he was expecting a more subtle approach from her, but should have known better. She was a journalist after all. No doubt she'd bunged cash-strapped Audrey Cliff a wad of notes in return for dishing the dirt on her pariah of a son-in-law. 'Please let's show some respect for the deceased. To clear this up, I can confirm Barry Gibson was an alcoholic; however we have yet to substantiate any links between his drinking and his untimely death. Wild speculation and alcoholic clichés won't help us find Barry Gibson's killer. Let's not vilify the victim just because of his drink problem?'

Seeing Blake wading through a mire of journalist antagonism, his chief inspector jumped in to bolster his detective. 'Ladies and gentlemen, let's keep the questions relevant and civilised; as DI Blake quite rightly pointed out we don't deal with speculation, but rather forensic evidence and facts. We're trying to enlist your help here.' He gave a nod to Alice.

'That concludes today's press conference. Thank you for taking the time to attend and respond. If you have any further questions you can contact me via the usual channels.

After Coleman had left the room. Blake sighed deeply, gathered up his notes and zipped them into his folio. 'That never gets any easier,' he said to Alice Lowe. Hacks really wind me up!'

'I've become immune to it. Dealing with them all the time nullifies their verbal drivel. It's either that or I've subconsciously developed a bullshit filter. Although I do think they can really help on this case?'

'Hate to admit it but I have to agree. Considering the woeful lack of forensics we've got.'

'How you getting on with the landlord and the bouncer?'

'Had to release them. The CPS won't charge either; too much circumstantial evidence. Either could have done it, but we just don't have anything concrete, even though both had strong motives and opportunity. Gibson was a real nasty bastard, and it looks like he was a sex pest as well as a violent drunk. Unfortunately both have a history of violence. Nathan Dukes actually broke Gibson's arm last year and the landlord's got form for GBH. He spent two years in Featherstone, but until we can eliminate the mystery CCTV man, we're no closer to a conviction.

'Any leads on the whereabouts of Grant Bolton? The fact he absconded looks extremely suspicious. Seems to me he could be a strong contender?'

'We're working on it, but as yet there have been no sightings, or intel on him.'

CHAPTER 39

The man sat slouched down in the seat of his car, and stealthily watched the security guard and his German Shepherd lock up and climb into his car just outside the front entrance to the Furlong Social Club in Baptist Road, a former seventies working men's club in the back streets of Burslem, not covered by cameras. It was ten p.m. and he'd use the cover of darkness, and the back alley to break into the property.

The heat was definitely on. The police were probing deeper into the Barry Gibson murder case. He couldn't risk them finding evidence linking him to the victim. The night before he sat contemplating how to get the pictures into his possession over a few cans of lager. He weighed up several options and but nothing seemed viable, except getting the photos back and destroying them. This would buy him valuable time. Getting in wouldn't be a problem, he'd broken into several of these types of properties over the years. All of them had dark alleyways leading to backyards with high gates. In this instance the adjacent business properties were unoccupied; up for sale, and the other side looked empty too: judging by the shuttering ply covering the windows.

He grabbed the top of the old rendered breeze block wall with both hands and shimmied up, before dropping down into the yard. A dog barking startled him. Bollocks! Had that security guard come back? He stood there frozen to the spot, hand on a PAVA spray in his jacket pocket, before realising the noise was coming from down the street. Breathing a sigh of relief he moved closer to the back door, fished in his jacket and pulled out a fifteen inch jemmy bar. Considering this was a community centre the security was crap; whoever ran the place was failing to protect the property. A cheap shitty aluminium lock seemed to be the only thing stopping him entering, although there could be shot bolts as well, but he doubted it. He jammed the chisel end of the bar between the frame and the door, forced it deeper, before yanking hard to the side. The softwood frame splintered and cracked easily. He worked the bar around until it freed the locking mechanism. Leaning on the door he gave it a gentle shove with his shoulder; it swung open with ease. As he stepped cautiously inside the large catering kitchen, light filtered through a gap in the door. He popped his head through the door to double check it was unoccupied

He moved forward and pushed the door with his gloved right hand, and entered the large meeting room; its decor still a throwback to the seventies. Thankfully the blinds were down so anyone passing in the street couldn't see in. He made his way past the PVC red padded bar, over to the back end of the room. Two wall lights, with low watt bulbs cast shadows across the empty lino dance floor. Looking around he spotted what he'd come for. Three locked display cabinets fixed to the artexed wall, containing photos and memorabilia from several decades of the now derelict William Adams & Sons factory. It was years since he'd last visited the place on an open day welcoming ex-employees from the pottery firm. He remembered sitting there drinking pints of lager with the others, reminiscing on the five years they worked at the factory: young men in the prime of their life with good wages, and an even better social life. Twenty-nine years later he occasionally thought about the place.

He couldn't remember exactly which cabinet the photos were in, so started with the first one on the left, but the light was too dull to see properly. He fished his mobile from his pocket, tapped the LED torch on, and scanned the six by four inch black and white, and colour pictures pinned to the blue felt back panel.

The first picture was a group shot of nearly all the employees, in their clay-stained white trousers and tops in the courtyard next to the factory entrance. He spotted a stone and half lighter version of himself, with a mullet hairstyle on the second row back. The others were scattered amongst the group.

Preceding pics followed various stages of a typical pottery factory production line. He quickly scanned through them. *Where the hell are those snaps of the kilns?*

He moved onto the second board, which seemed to be full of shots from Christmas 1988. He remembered being leathered at the works do here; dancing around with older women from the Sponging and Lithograph departments. Putting nostalgia to one side he moved on to the third board. There they were, a series of photographs of him with the old crew, albeit he had his back to the camera, pushing a trolley away, but the others could name him. God they were crazy times. Soon as they got paid on a Friday lunchtime, they'd hit the pubs until four p.m. Then head home for a bath and get straight back out around seven until the pubs and clubs closed at two the following morning. They were like wild Embassy-smoking dogs who'd shag anything that moved in a skirt.

A twenty year old Barry Gibson leaned on a cart full of ware waiting to be loaded into the kilns. The group of young men were all of similar height and build apart from one youth, who was broader across the shoulders. The only one he couldn't remember stood on the end of the group of five, with a red cap obscuring his face. There was only three years between the four of them, although the broad lad was considered the baby of the bunch, being almost five years younger than Gibson, who was twenty-two at the time.

The next few pictures were taken in a social environment. They showed the group drinking with three women, he couldn't remember their names, except one, he'd never forget her. *Karen Kennedy.* A very pretty but troubled redhead, who came down from Dundee with her abusive stepdad and mum in '86. She was his first love until things went badly wrong in her home life and she dumped him. The stepdad buggered off back to Scotland and twelve months later the mother died from a heroin overdose leaving her 18-year-old daughter homeless around the Potteries. At the time the devious Barry Gibson was dabbling with drugs; chasing the dragon, and dropping acid at the weekend at illegal warehouse raves in the Midlands. He copped off with Karen, and within a few months got her on the skag. When she was off her head, he pimped her out like a sex slave. Within six months, like her mother, she became totally dependent on heroin: then just seemed to disappear. Where did she go, he thought, glaring at that vile parasite Barry Gibson?

He glanced at his watch. Shit, his trip down memory lane had wasted twenty minutes, and he needed to get the pictures and get out of there. He was about to fish the jemmy bar from his jacket when a sudden noise startled him.

'Come on boy, I think I left it in here.'

Should he go now or wait? Adrenalin surged through his veins, his heart thrashed wildly. Taking deep breaths, he prayed the guard would leave after a quick look around. He stealthily dropped to the floor and hid behind a DJ booth cobbled together with shuttering ply, painted black. The last thing he needed was to tackle a bloke, especially one with a vicious dog in tow. He was a hard bastard, but definitely not a stupid one. Hand on his PAVA spray he crouched trying hard to lower his breathing. God forbid the dog would pick up on his scent.

'It's here,' the guard said to the dog, retrieving his mobile from a table near the bar, 'Bloody battery's low; I might not be able to ring your mum after all. We'll just have to chance it with the chips. Come on boy?' But the dog wouldn't budge. It started to growl and pull on its lead.

'What's up lad? There's only us here. We checked everything earlier.'

The dog stood rooted to the spot. The guard flashed his torch down the bottom end of the room. For a split second it passed over the DJ booth. The man watched the light arc back across the bar. He waited with gritted teeth; hand on his PAVA in preparation for a fast exit.

In those tense few minutes his heart thrashed wildly, as he listen to the guard step up to the edge of the bar. He lifted the latch on the top and paused behind it. Lowering his breathing he could hear the dog panting. He prepared for the worst.

The guard's footsteps came closer; he stopped again in the middle of the dance floor and scanned the torch around. He was just about to make a run for it back through the kitchen, when the guard's phone rang, its ring tone echoed in the darkness. 'Hello? It's your mum, old lad. Okay, okay. We'll be home in half an hour, going to fetch some chips, if you fancy them? Great, mushy peas as well? Ta-ra! Come on lad there's nowt here. I'm bloody starving.' He made his way back across the dance floor through the meeting room, towards the front entrance, closing the doors behind him.

He heard the distant sound of keys turning, and breathed a huge sigh of relief, as a car engine turned over. He crept from behind the booth, dashed silently across the room, and stood in the window peering cautiously through the slotted blinds into the darkness outside. He watched the guard's car headlights illuminate the front windows of the houses opposite and disappear out of the street.

Back at the opposite end of the room he began to work the jemmy bar into the centre of the first cabinet's doors. He yanked it hard and the tiny lock on the front bust open. He sneezed loudly, then again. Bloody allergies. He must have dislodged years of dust settled on the inside, top edge of the cabinet doors. One by one he removed the pins holding the pictures, and placed them on the floor. He moved on to the second cabinet. Only this time the glass cracked, and a large shard dropped out, almost slicing into his shin on its trajectory to the floor. It shattered into pieces across the floor, just missing the photos. Fuck!

Stepping over the glass he retrieved the pictures. He couldn't take the risk of leaving any behind, even if he wasn't in them. It would look royally suspicious only stealing the ones containing him and the others. Standing looking around the room doubts whether this was such a good idea after all entered his head. Maybe it was unrealistic to think the cops would find the twenty-nine year old photos, and connect them to the murder victim. Ultimately, he couldn't take the risk. A quick check of his watch revealed he'd been in the Furlong Social Club almost an hour; it was time to get out, whilst he still could.

CHAPTER 40

After their fruitless search of the Stoke-on-Trent area, Hanley police widened the net to encompass the Staffordshire moorlands. Because it was a murder enquiry Blake twisted the Chief Inspector's arm into commandeering a NPAS helicopter from the national operations centre in West Yorkshire. Their on-board search camera technology was brilliant at identifying suspects from the air. And because of the amount of ground it could cover, although expensive, it saved masses on manpower.

Blake sat in the incident room watching a live feed streamed from the helicopter. It was passing over the Ramshaw rocks area of the moorlands, close to the Derbyshire border: nothing but sheep, climbers, ramblers and farmers going about their daily duties. After a couple of hours of checking back he felt concerned that he may have got the location wrong; quite literally a needle in haystack.

After several hours the search proved fruitless, but as the NPAS officer informed Blake; detecting a suspect was always subject to being in the right area, at the right time; not every search led to an arrest. He'd just have to reassess the information they had on Bolton, and establish new search criteria.

CHAPTER 41

Ibrahim sat by the edge of the lake in Hanley Park reading a five day old copy of the *Evening Sentinel.* A murder, in a city centre pub he'd heard about, took up most of the front page, and he was concerned that Charlie Bullard's association with the landlord could attract unnecessary attention from the cops.

Police have started a murder investigation, after the body of 48-year-old Barry Gibson was discovered in the men's toilets of the White Horse pub in the city centre, on Friday the 5th of June. Forensic evidence at the scene revealed he'd been involved in a fight with another man. A post-mortem examination later showed that although the victim fell and sustained a head trauma; his assailant forced a sharp object, which the pathologist said was probably a knife, into the wound, leading the victim to bleed out where he lay. Police have interviewed the pub's landlord, doormen and customers who were drinking in the pub at the time, but have yet identify a clear suspect, and are appealing for other witnesses who were in the vicinity of the pub between ten and eleven p.m. to come forward.

He glanced at his watch, it was 2.30 p.m. He folded the paper and walked through the park's historic landscape, past a gaggle of noisy Canada geese, shading from the sun under one of the many willows which surrounded the lake. He climbed the grass embankment up onto the canal towpath. After striding a couple of hundred yards along the winding crushed stone, he found Charlie Bullard sat in an army green deckchair on Caldon Canal.

He was staring intensely at the luminous orange tip of his float, which bobbed in front of the reeds on the opposite canal bank. Suddenly the tip lifted and then dived below the murky water. Charlie reacted to the bite, striking his rod hard-right with both hands. It bent in a large arc, tip to butt as the fish plunged deeper to avoid capture. Skilfully, he played it with a smooth pumping action, winding his reel to bring the fish closer to the waiting landing net he'd slid into the water. A sudden flash of gold sparkled just under the surface as a large bream capitulated and floated into the waiting net.

'Calculated force conquers the will of nature,' Charlie proclaimed with a wide grin. 'If only the pigs were that easy to master we'd be laughing.'

'You've pulled plenty of jobs over the years,' Ibrahim said smugly, acting as if they were above the law and the rules didn't apply to them.

'Yeah, and been collared a few times as well. Lost the best part of my forties to prove it. It's not the eighties any more. There's CCTV, silent alarms wired straight to the cops, helicopters with heat-seeking cameras and all manner of surveillance technology. The odds are in the cops' favour.'

'Give me credit, Charl, this won't be a smash and grab raid in broad daylight. Those days are long gone. Like I mentioned to you on Friday at the casino, we'll swap the real Hoard for replicas.'

Both their mouths clamped as an elderly lady walking a black Labrador passed behind them on the towpath. When she was out of earshot, Charlie asked, 'How the bloody hell are you going to do that?'

'To be honest, switching the gold is the easy part. The hard bit is getting in and then getting out unnoticed. Obviously the swap needs doing after hours when the museum is closed to the public and the staff are off the premises. Given your experience, that's where you come in.'

With a bewildered look, Charlie rubbed the back of his neck. 'Eh?'

'Basically, we need someone on the inside of the building. I spoke to our financier yesterday. He told me the best line of attack is to hack into the security cameras and doctor the digital image feed when the museum is closed.'

'So what do you need me for?'

'To be the inside man, but you won't be alone. We've turned the caretaker. He retires at the end of the year and his state pension is crap. We've offered him more than enough to make his retirement cosy. He's told us he can get agency staff when needed. Also which agency it is. That's the one you'll get registered with. Once everything is in place, the caretaker will call them and ask for you.'

He frowned. 'What if they offer it to someone else?'

'They won't.'

'I think you're being overconfident.'

'Trust me, Charl, when the call comes, you'll join him for the day.'

With a worried look on his face, he said, 'But that means I'll be exposed to the cameras. If this goes tits up it's my neck on the chopping block. Another stretch would kill me, I'm fifty-four this year, you know.'

'Like I said we'll doctor the cameras. Leonard will hack into the system, so they don't capture the switch. Instead they'll only show the previous two hours, but with the timeline unaltered. You'll be a ghost. This might sound ridiculous, but you'll be in partial disguise. A full beard, dyed hair and a flat cap.'

He scoffed. 'Sounds like a bloody *Carry On* movie. Besides you know I've got previous form. The first thing the Old Bill do when this kind of shit goes down is scan their database for known suspects, local and national.'

'Speaking of suspects, have you seen this?' Ibrahim unfolded the *Sentinel* and passed it over to Charlie.'

Bullard skim read the front page. 'Yeah, I'd be lying if I said I hadn't.'

'That's your cousin Darryl's pub, isn't it?'

'Yeah.'

'How reliable is he?'

'Daz is old school, he knows to keep quite. He's done time, you know.'

'What for?'

'GBH. Stoved his wife's lover's head in with a bar stool, at his old pub. I was there at the time; he got sent down.'

'Fucking hell, why didn't you say before?'

'Didn't think it was relevant since he's not directly involved.'

'That's all we need, another sodding con with a record linked to this job. If the cops start digging about can we trust him to keep his mouth shut? Not that he knows the full details anyway.'

'Yeah, Darryl's safe as houses, mate.' He didn't dare tell Ibrahim Connor knew about the heist, he'd go mental.

'You see where I'm coming from? We both know the cops work by leaning on those with records and their known associates. Is this murder anything to do with him?'

'Why would you say that?'

'Because it happened on his premises, and according to the report he's been questioned. Doesn't look good, does it? Bloke with previous for GBH in a pub; ends up running another pub where a bloke was battered to death.'

Charlie didn't reply. He glanced at his float trying to dodge the question.

'What about your nephew Mickey?' Ibrahim continued.

'We'll be okay. For starters he's in Manchester. Unlikely they'd twig that.'

'I hope not, because we're doing this job.'

'Don't worry I've already told him what the consequences would be if he mentions anything to anyone.'

'Okay, let's leave it at that for now.'

'Going back to the job. Until everything has been checked and double checked we won't even consider making a move? OK, let's say I get in and the cameras are nobbled, what then?' Tension filled his expression.

'The gold pieces are so small you could fit most of them in a rucksack, making it easy to get them out of the building undetected. You'll do the switch and Leonard will take care of hacking the cameras.'

'So I'm the man on the inside, pure and simple?'

'Yeah, you're the best man for the job because I know you'll keep your nerve. Besides, I only work with people I can trust,' Ibrahim said pandering to his ego, while trying to reassure him. 'We'll do everything we can to make sure you're not detected. The Collector's providing us with the latest fingerprint cover-up technology. It's called liquid bandage. It works well in situations where you can't be seen to be wearing gloves, which is ideal because you can't wear them during your day working at the museum. Then, after hours, you can slip on the gloves. I've arranged a group meeting this evening; we OK using your flat?'

'How many people?'

'Just the guys from the casino on Friday.'

'Make it eight-thirty?'

CHAPTER 42

Since Dean Taylor's arrest four days ago, Yusuf Benzar had found it hard to calm down. He was seething. The pigs had intercepted their gear and lost his brother the six grand he'd paid to their Afghan connection. Because of his stupidity, the bigger shipment would have to be delayed indefinitely. To get a handle on the situation he'd called Dean's mate Carl Draycott, who'd received a message from his bent lawyer telling him the heat was on and to lay low. Knowing the police would be looking into his affairs made him feel very uneasy. Instinctively he felt someone was watching him but he couldn't be certain. With this in mind he'd stayed away from the flat in Shelton and slept at his neglected terraced house in Hanley.

Stealthily he exited from the back of the house and made his way over to Tindale Street where he'd covertly parked his other, untraceable motor.

Undetected, he drove his black BMW and turned a sharp left into Marchwood Street, Hanley, travelled fifty yards, and parked in the dotted resident zone outside number sixteen. Unlike his brother, Yusuf's aspirations towards building a property portfolio were stunted by his inability to control problem gambling. Over the years it had cost him significantly and emotionally. He used to own six properties but was forced to sell four to pay off casino debts of over three hundred thousand.

Number sixteen was now his last source of income from rent, aside from the two hundred quid a week his brother tossed him for helping out with The Dojo Martial Arts School, and the Slipware Tankard bar. The loan sharking he dabbled in had gone tits up recently. He was still owed thousands by those filthy scroungers on the Heath Hayes estate. Nathan Dukes brought in less than a grand on his last collecting mission. Next week, he'd go with Dukes and leave a trail of fucking casualties.

He hated being reliant on his brother for handouts; it wound him up how Ibrahim seemed to amass piles of cash, while he lived beyond his means, head bobbing just above water.

Ibrahim refused to give him lump sums as he knew the gambling demon within would blow it. He even let him live rent-free, but that was beside the point. These bastards in number sixteen were taking the piss and he wasn't having it. If they didn't cough up tonight he'd chuck them out.

He rapped the knocker on the traffic-stained plastic door and waited. The net curtain in the rotting front window twitched. He knocked again, then dropped to his knees and shouted through the letterbox. 'Your rent's well overdue. Open the fucking door!' Through the slot he saw one of the tenants, a greasy-haired rocker named Damien run through the house in a panic to lock the back door. Yusuf was steaming. He took a step back and kicked the front door hard. 'Open the door, or I'll kick it in, you pair of bastards.' Still no reply. 'I know you're in there!'

There was no way the shot bolts would give in through kicking; it needed more force. He jumped around to the back of his BMW, opened the boot and heaved out a Tactical Mini-ram.

Clasping the handles of the fifteen-pound ram he swung it hard into the lock edge of the door. It cracked, shattering white plastic shards onto the pavement. On the second swing police sirens could be heard in the distance. By now several neighbours looked on in horror from their doorsteps as Yusuf finally caved the door in and ran inside chasing his scared shitless tenant through into the kitchen like a possessed madman.

The rocker tried to escape through the back door. He frantically fumbled at the brass handle, only managing to creak it open a couple of inches before Yusuf lunged at him, grabbed his hair and slammed his face into the wood, crushing his fingers agonisingly in the gap. Yanking his bloated fingers free, he slid and cowered on the floor as a barrage of heavy blows rained down into his head.

'You fucking disrespect me, you dirty bastard,' Yusuf raged. 'Where's my money!'

'Ah, ah shit – I'll get it to you next week, definitely!' The rocker screamed in pain before passing out, his nose streaming blood onto the laminate floor.

The next voice Yusuf heard was that of the police who'd stormed the property. Before he could react he was wrestled to the floor, face pushed hard onto the laminate by a copper, whilst another huge officer sat on his back and handcuffed him with force.

'We're arresting you for breaking, entering and assault,' DS Murphy said, catching his breath.

The officers managed to get him up, but he resisted, wrestling with them violently. 'Fucking get off me, pig scum!' he shouted in defiance, continuing to thrash around as the sergeant read the rest of his rights.

It took the threat of being tasered to eventually calm him down. Two uniformed officers bundled him out of the property, shouting expletives into the cage of a police meat wagon waiting in the street.

Twenty minutes later Yusuf Benzar lay on a foam mattress staring around a stark cell at Hanley police station; belt-less, without shoelaces, awaiting interview. The first thing that crossed his mind was how pissed off his brother would be about his arrest.

The duty sergeant slid his door hatch and informed him he was entitled to a lawyer and a phone call.

Yusuf could tell by his brother's tone he was livid; despite this, Ibrahim knew his idiot brother would only get one call so within minutes of hanging up he called their lawyer, Bryant Preston, his accountant's brother.

The pokey interview room's spotlights glared off the walls. Bryant Preston sat poised next to Yusuf, pen and paper laid out on the table. DI Tom Blake and DS John Murphy sat opposite, staring at the arrogant scowl on Yusuf's face.

Blake knew DI Clive Moore from the drug squad would be furious with him for jeopardising his surveillance operation on Benzar. Having initiated the op himself this was serious egg on the face. Unwittingly DS Murphy arrested him, but how was he to know? It looked worse for them caught napping on the job. How the bloody hell did he slip under their noses undetected? Total incompetence. Besides, they couldn't ignore such a public display of breaking, entering and assault. Brushing off the consequences of shooting himself in the foot, he hit the record button on the tape machine and kicked off the interview.

'OK. Let's start off with what we know.'

'You've been arrested for breaking, entering and assaulting the resident of number sixteen Marchwood Street, Hanley. What do you have to say regarding this?'

Yusuf paused, then consulted Preston before answering. 'I didn't break in. It's my house.'

'We have half a dozen witnesses who saw you obliterate the door with a police battering ram.'

Again, he consulted his lawyer before answering with caution. 'I'm entitled to get in my property?'

'Why didn't you knock like any normal person?'

'I did; they wouldn't come to the door. Those bastards are squatting. They've not paid any rent for two months.'

'So you thought you'd smash the door in and beat the shit out of one of your tenants? If you read your tenancy agreement it clearly states you have to apply for an eviction order from the courts. They engage the services of bailiffs on your behalf when a tenant needs removing. Do you have a tenancy agreement, Mr Benzar?'

'No comment.'

'Mr Benzar, you know answering no comment to any of our questions can become part of the case against you?'

Blake glanced at DS Murphy, and shook his head in disbelief at how many landlords thought they could do as they pleased. It seemed whole streets of inner city areas were being bought up cheaply by unscrupulous crooks looking for somewhere to launder their dodgy cash. He recalled this was the fifth landlord he'd dealt with so far this year, concluding they'd rent properties to anyone with a deposit, no background checks or contracts, making it difficult to prove the facts, as everything was verbal. There was no way of establishing a paper trail of whether the tenant had paid rent or not.

Yusuf sat arms folded in defiant silence. Both officers knew from experience that statements of no comment were avoidance tactics.

'You can be prosecuted for renting a property without a tenancy agreement,' DS Murphy pitched in.

Blake interrupted. 'For the tape, Mr Benzar is shrugging his shoulders at DS Murphy's last question. Your tenant is in hospital receiving treatment for a broken nose, a fractured cheekbone, a dislocated jaw and three broken fingers. That's a serious assault charge you're looking at. If we hadn't arrived when we did, you could have killed him. There's no way you'll be leaving this station tonight. A search of your vehicle turned up a hunting knife and six wraps of cocaine in the glove box. So, on top of the assault we have possession of class A drug and a concealed weapon. It's not looking good for you at all, Mr Benzar.'

Blake stood up and sauntered over to the corner of the room to a blue plastic evidence box sat on the floor. He retrieved its contents. 'For the benefit of the tape I'm showing Mr Benzar two clear evidence bags containing the aforementioned knife and cocaine. Do you acknowledge these items retrieved from your BMW belong to you?'

'It's a fucking set-up. I've never seen those before!' Yusuf pleaded, desperately trying to detach himself from the implications of the evidence. But his irritability showed. Lately his coke usage had spiralled out of control. Most weeks there'd only be one wrap in the glove box, six made him look like a small-time dealer.

'Interview terminated at nine-thirty. Take him back to the cells, sergeant. We have more than enough evidence to charge your client with,' Blake said, addressing the lawyer who, judging by the solemn look on his face, knew there was little he could do to help Yusuf, apart from stopping him digging an even deeper hole.

CHAPTER 43

The drug squad looked like a bunch of muppets after they failed to detect Yusuf Benzar leaving his property on the fifth day of surveillance. Whilst he was in custody, DI Moore and his team raided his terraced house in Hanley, but didn't find anything apart from beer, condoms, a wrap of personal, and a credit card statement. All six officers returned to the station with faces like smacked arses, and questions to answer.

This, added to DS Murphy's premature arrest of Benzar, made them all look like a bunch of amateurs. The Chief Inspector would be furious. DI Blake unwittingly heaped further embarrassment on Moore's team when he pointed out the credit card statement was registered to an address in Cliffe Vale. Deflated, in fear of additional failure, Moore passed the search over to his colleagues in CID.

Yusuf Benzar's second property was a cedar-clad apartment overlooking Caldon Canal. Newhaven Court was part of a complex that included the restoration and conversion of the world-renowned 1887 Twyford Sanitary factory facing Etruria Road. Before cheap imports flooded the market in the eighties, thousands of the UK's sinks, troughs and toilets originated from the factory. Now it was the desired location for young professionals.

They parked opposite a couple of hundred-and-twenty year old bottle kiln ovens protected to preserve local heritage.

Blake and DS Murphy climbed out of the Astra pool car and made their way around the front of the building. 'Nice location, Tom,' Murphy said as they climbed the stairs to the third-floor apartment.

Blake retrieved Yusuf's confiscated car keys from his jacket. Aside from the BMW key-less fob there were only two other keys on the ring. 'I'm guessing it's this one,' he said, slipping the newish-looking key into the lock on the light oak-panelled door.

The open plan apartment took Blake by surprise; it had the stamp of an interior designer. The living room and kitchen merged seamless top end modern design with high-tech gadgets. A huge black corner sofa dominated the far corner of the room. A long, white, granite worktop floated over four backless high stools and ran parallel to dozens of high-gloss concealed kitchen cabinets. Floor-to-ceiling glass fronted windows leading out onto a decked balcony overlooking the Caldon Canal ran the opposite side. The whole place had had thousands thrown at it.

'Looks like Benzar's spent serious wedge on this gaff,' Blake said.

'Yeah,' Murphy jested. 'Whoever said crime doesn't pay.'

'There is one consolation.'

'What's that then?'

'Depending on whether we find anything, he might not be enjoying this for the next few years.'

'You reckon?' Murphy remarked.

'We've got him for possession and assault; as long as the victim presses charges, that is.'

'Always tricky that. We both know career criminals intimidate their victims. The guy he pummelled was just a kid; doubtful he'll stand his ground against that nasty bastard.'

'We'll see.'

Before the pair started searching the doorbell chimed.

'That'll be Evans,' Blake said, making his way to the door.

'Really?' Murphy said with a glint in his eye.

'John, you're old enough to be her father.'

Most of the coppers at the station thought PC Casey Evans was beautiful. They'd nicknamed the fearless five-foot-eight brunette Daisy Cutter after Daisy Rose Cutter, the famous American female wrestler, after she took down and arrested a six-foot-four shoplifter single-handed. She had a figure most women would kill for and, at just twenty-one, a promising career in front of her.

'Wow, this is plush,' she said entering the apartment.

'It's very nice, but we're not here for a viewing. Let's get to it. We're looking for anything incriminating. Drugs, cash, mobiles, stolen goods and information on Benzar.'

'OK, boss. Where should I start?' Evans said, removing her hat.

'You do the bedroom?' Murphy said, giving a crafty wink to Blake, who shook his head, disapproving of his suggestive innuendo.

'I'll take the living room and bathroom,' Blake said.

Murphy moaned. 'That's right, leave me to sift through all those bloody kitchen cupboards.'

Blake grinned. 'DI privileges. Got to pull rank on you sometimes, John.'

'Tell you what. You lie on the sofa and I'll let you know when we've finished,' Murphy said sarcastically. The banter between them helped to ease tension through long fourteen-hour shifts when tempers could fray through tiredness.

Murphy was on his second cupboard when PC Evans shouted from the bedroom.

'In here, sir. I think I've found something.'

'She's a quick worker, Tom.'

They both entered the bedroom to find her rummaging inside a sliding mirrored wardrobe.

'Look, sir, there's a safe.' She pointed to the heavy-looking box sat in the bottom.

It was an old cast-iron job; the kind you might see in the finance office of a pre-WW2 factory. On the front of the rusting grey chest was a circular brass plate with a coat-of-arms in the centre, and the words 'Milner's 212 Patent, Fire Withstanding' embossed around the plate.

Blake scratched his chin. 'Well, that's weird. What do you make of it, John?'

'Looks like something from the Museum uptown.'

'Yeah, Benzar must be hiding something valuable to use this antique fortress?'

'Must weigh a bloody ton!'

'Makes you wonder how the hell they got it up three flights of stairs? Anyway, I'll give the station a call and get them to lean on the suspect for the keys. We need to get moving on this. His solicitor will be pushing for bail. Have you found anything else, Casey?'

'Not yet, sir.'

'Carry on looking.'

Fifteen minutes after Blake had called the station his mobile rang. The desk sergeant informed him the prisoner was uncooperative about the keys. Blake suggested giving his car another search.

Murphy returned to the kitchen and carried on rummaging through the cupboards. He smiled inwardly after discovering the majority of them were empty, apart from one which contained three packets of dried pasta meals, an assortment of tinned soup, beans and spaghetti. Judging by how clean the oven was and the stack of microwave meals in the freezer, he concluded Benzar was an archetypal bachelor who didn't cook.

'Anything, John?'

'Nothing yet, boss.'

'How about you?'

'Bugger all. It's too clinical in here… there's no newspapers, coffee rings on the table. Dirty dishes in the sink. It's almost as if no one's lived here for a while. Mind you, he was moonlighting at the house in Hanley.'

'Might have a cleaner?'

'Might be OCD?'

'Doubt it, but you never know.'

'True.'

'My gut's telling me any incriminating evidence is locked in that humping great antique in the wardrobe.'

'Definitely. No point in having a safe if you're not going to use it. Any news on the keys yet?'

'Williams has one of his PC's giving Benzar's BMW the once over just to be sure.'

'Maybe, it'll turn up here?'

'It'd save a lot of hassle. I'll let you know once I've done the bathroom.'

Blake looked in amazement. Loads of space in the main living area, but the bathroom was tiny. So small in fact, they'd fitted a bi-fold door to save space. Compromised interior design he thought, emptying the linen basket next to the walk-in shower. Two pairs of socks, and a skimpy red thong spilled onto the floor. Looked like he'd had female company recently, although he avoided scrutinising the knickers closely. Whilst replacing the basket lid, he noticed something strange about the toilet roll holder. It'd been fixed on a raised tile, much smaller than the others, whereas the rest of the wall tiles were flush; an afterthought or just bad workmanship? Judging by the amount of cash spent on the rest of the place he doubted it. Removing the toilet roll revealed the tile was covering something. He pulled at it but it wouldn't budge, although there was minor movement there. A knock on the tile gave a hollow sound. He shouted through the hallway. 'John, I think I've found something.'

DS Murphy joined him in the bathroom. 'Cosy.'

'There's something not right with this tile. I've tried pulling, but it won't budge.'

'Try sliding it?'

They both gazed in anticipation. 'Bingo!' Blake said, animated, as the tile inched to reveal a recess containing an old brass key held in place with modelling clay. 'Let's see if we can unlock his secrets.'

They made their way back into the bedroom. PC Evans had emptied the entire wardrobe onto the bed and was diligently rummaging through the pockets of a pile of tailored jackets. 'Got expensive taste this one. Boss, Armani, Ralph Lauren.'

'Hold fire a minute, I think we've found the key to the safe.'

'That was quick.'

'Seek and ye shall find,' proclaimed Blake with a philosophical grin.

'Couldn't have done it without me though,' Murphy hinted, trying to bolster his male ego in front PC Evans.

'Yeah, thanks, John. Let's open Pandora's box?' He inserted the key, turning it anti-clockwise to an audible click. Grasping the handle on the edge of the door, Blake pulled, but it remained steadfast. Murphy leaned in and turned the handle in the centre to the six o'clock position.

'You'd have been shit on the Crystal Maze, Tom. Try now?'

'OK, here goes.' The door creaked open, revealing a compartmentalised interior. Stacked at the bottom on the left-hand side were three hardwood boxes. Sitting above those on a shelf were piles of twenty-pound notes, each one bonded with a red sleeve. A brown A5 notebook sat on top.

'Looks like he's been busy, John.'

'What's in the book?'

Blake retrieved it and removed the elastic strap. On the first page there was a list of postcodes, written in neat capitals, each one assigned a number. These numbers repeated down the right-hand side of the next few pages. Next to each one were a series of dates, and amounts in pounds, spanning twelve months.

Blake scanned the postcodes. 'Judging by this, he's a bloody loan shark. Jesus! There are initials BG in here, and there's a grand next to them.'

'No kidding. What's the postcode? I'll give DC Moore a call to see if they match.

'ST6 8DL.'

Murphy dialled the number. Minutes later DC Moore confirmed it was Barry Gibson's address.

'Looks like Benzar might have put a contract out on Barry Gibson. As I mentioned before though, unlikely they'd do it in such a public place.'

'That means the other poor buggers in this book are at risk. We'll need to contact them soon as,' Murphy said.

'You're not kidding. Unscrupulous bastards, loan sharks. Any known associates?'

'Several, according to his record. Two were sent down last year, but Benzar's always distanced himself from the shitty end of the stick until now.'

'He's shot himself in the foot this time.'

'We need to pull in some of his associates. See if any squeal. Keep an eye out for mobiles and SIM cards we can get names off. There's more than enough evidence to do him for ABH and unlicenced money lending, and that's excluding what we find in those boxes.'

'He's got enough capital here. I'll wager you a tenner there's more than twenty grand,' Murphy proposed to his boss.

'How about drinks at the Smiths Head instead?'

'You're on.'

PC Evans looked on in amazement as the pair of them jested.

'I'm going for thirty K.'

'Thirty-five. I tell you what, if we nail him before play's out, I'll buy everyone in CID a pint.'

'Done.'

'I think I have been,' Blake said, leaning in to retrieve the boxes, which appeared to be locked. 'This guy's paranoid. Any more keys in there? Have a look in that drawer,' he said, referring to a small metal panel inside the safe.

'We're in,' smirked Murphy, jangling three tiny skeleton keys in the palm of his hand.

'Casey, you stay here, count and bag the cash, whilst John and I scrutinise these in the kitchen.'

Blake laid the first box onto the granite worktop. 'Should be interesting. What do you reckon, Murph; smack, crack or coke? Deal or no Deal?'

'Could be any, but judging by the apartment and the motor I'll take a stab at coke.'

'Sure you don't want to phone a friend?'

'Just open it, man.'

'Deal!' Blake scoffed.

'Well, would you look at that?' Blake said, gawping inside. 'A box of sex toys, dildos and lubes.'

'Picture the scene. I'm charging you for possession of illegal vibrating cocks.' Murphy burst into laughter, slapping his palm on the granite.

Like teenage lads discovering their dads' porno mags, full of hairy chicks, under the bed, the pair of them cracked up.

PC Evans popped her head round the door. 'Have I missed the joke?'

Blake slammed the box lid shut and the two detectives gave each other a covert glance.

'Looks like it's your round, sir. Forty grand in total.

'OK, thanks, Casey. Anything left to sift through in the bedroom?'

'Just the bedside drawers.'

'If you could finish up in there, we won't be much longer.'

'You reckon he pushes poo uphill without a wheelbarrow?' Murphy said after she'd gone.

'Your guess is as good as mine. Let's get these other two boxes opened and head off back to base.'

In the second box the detectives found a digital video camera containing graphic photos of the suspect performing sexual acts with a pretty brunette. All of which were time-stamped Friday the 5th of June, the night of the murder.

'I think that confirms he's not gay, John.' Blake dropped the box back onto the worktop, but noticed the bottom lift a touch. 'Hang on, the bottom of this box is loose.'

'False one, maybe?'

Blake pushed one side of it. 'Voila!' he said, retrieving an old faded blue Nokia mobile. Not seen one of these for years.' He pressed and held the on-off button, but the battery was dead. Sliding it into an evidence bag, he said, 'We'll get this scanned with the Radio Tactics data acquisition. And finally!'

'Have we won a car?'

'Nope, it's a bag of brown powder. Looks remarkably like the one we found in Dean Taylor's man bag; it's even got the same bottle kiln logo. There's loads of empty bags in the box. I reckon this will have the same chemical compound as that heroin.'

'Shit, there's a few grams there. Bad habit, or dealer?' Murphy asked.

'Dealer, I reckon. Smack's too street-level for this guy. Whichever, we've more than enough to charge him.'

CHAPTER 44

Yusuf Benzar sat in interview room three with a look of desolation on his face. He'd been festering in a cell for five hours, pegging out for a fag and a decent cup of coffee. The two lines of coke he'd snorted before caving his tenant's front door in had worn off and his head was swimming in paranoia. The thought of the pigs rummaging through his apartment mortified him. Worst of all, if those bastards found his stash he was fucked. When they pressed him for the keys to the safe he'd stalled them by feeding the desk sergeant a bullshit story about losing them six months ago.

DS Murphy entered the room, followed by Blake who was carrying a pile of clear bags containing his gear. A sudden look of dread appeared on his face and he slumped in the chair.

Murphy hit the record button on the tape machine. 'Mr Benzar, do the contents of these seven evidence bags belong to you?'

'No.'

'For the benefit of the tape I'm showing Mr Benzar evidence recovered from the safe in his flat. A large bag of uncut heroin, forty grand in twenty-pound notes, a digital camera containing sexually explicit images of Mr Benzar and an unknown female, a notebook containing the initials and postcodes of people he appears to have loaned money to, implicating him as an illegal money lender, a three-inch hunting knife and six wraps of cocaine.'

'None of that is mine.'

'Funny that, because we found four of them locked in an antique safe inside the wardrobe at flat number twenty-eight New Haven Court, and the other two in the glove box of your BMW. If the items don't belong to you, then please divulge the name of the person you're looking after them for so we can contact them to corroborate? Do you know a bloke who goes by the nickname Stomper?'

'No comment.'

'Furthermore the initials and postcode of a recent murder victim Barry Gibson is listed as owing £1000 in the aforementioned notebook, giving you a motive to kill him. And guess what? Gibson was stabbed in the head with a knife like the one you carry around. The forensics lab is looking at it.' Blake glared at Yusuf's solicitor, who sat prostrate, fingers entwined, knowing there was bugger all he could do for his client apart from recommend him to plead guilty to the looming possession charges in return for a more lenient sentence.

Preston informed Yusuf he concurred with the detectives, but under no circumstances should he admit to being involved in the murder, considering the circumstantial evidence.

Benzar sat arms crossed, lips taut. Eventually, after a few minutes of silence, he snapped. Banging his handcuffed fists on the table he shouted, 'You set me up, pig bastards.'

'There's overwhelming evidence to convict you of drug dealing and illegal money lending, pure and simple.'

'I didn't kill this Gibson bloke!'

'Explain your connection to the victim then? Why is his name and postcode in your address book with the sum of thousand pounds next to it?'

'He borrowed it.'

'When was this?'

'A few weeks ago.'

'How much had Barry Gibson paid off his loan?'

'Nothing, that bastard tried to take me for a ride.'

'So you sent someone to kill him, or did it yourself. Send out a warning to everyone else who owed money. Isn't that what happened, Mr Benzar?'

He looked rattled. 'You think I'd have someone killed for a thousand pounds?'

'Frankly, yes. You're a known drug dealer with zero morals, and a history of violence. Your tenant is currently in hospital receiving treatment for a broken nose, a fractured cheekbone, a dislocated jaw and three broken fingers. That's GBH. Luckily the incident was only a mile from the station, any further and you'd have killed the poor bugger. Now, where were you between nine and ten-fifty on Friday evening the fifth of June?'

He turned to consult with his solicitor. After a moment's pause: 'I was in the Genting Casino until around twelve-thirty. You can call my brother Ibrahim, he'll tell you.'

'Don't worry, we will do,' Blake lied, knowing Ibrahim Benzar would furnish his brother with an alibi. He wouldn't waste his time.

Benzar continued to protest. 'I'm telling you I didn't kill him. I lent him money, that's all. Where's your evidence, pig?'

'We'll be speaking with a few of your associates, see what they have to say,' Blake said nodding to DS Murphy.

'Interview terminated.'

'Take him back to his cell, DS Murphy.'

After Benzar had left the room, Blake called the casino and arranged an immediate meeting with the head of surveillance.

Forty minutes later Blake returned to the station, annoyed and disappointed that Benzar's casino alibi checked out. There were several shots of him and his brother during the time the murder was committed. And the fast tracked forensics on the knife was negative. He'd just have to settle for charging him with the evidence they had. Bailing him in the hope of new evidence coming to light would be too risky.

DS Murphy fetched him before the duty sergeant.

'Yusuf Benzar, I'm charging you with assault, possession of an illegal weapon, two counts of possession of class A drugs with intent to supply and running an illegal money-lending operation. Do you have anything further to say?

'Seni lanet olasıca öldüreceğim.' I'll fucking kill you,.

'Don't worry; we'll get that rant translated. Any threats will be taken very seriously,' Blake said, handing him his charge sheet. 'Take him back to his cell, DS Murphy?'

CHAPTER 45

The ten-by-ten windowless room suited Leonard Vale's people-averse personality down to the ground. The tech geek was comfortable when left to his own devices, especially when they were electronic and hooked up to the Internet. Just as long as he could put several hours a day gaming and squeeze in a once-a day oil change with sex cams, he was happy as a pig in shit.

However his primary focus was to monitor the Potteries Museum cameras, which the gang had infiltrated, through an undocumented back door. During a planned CCTV maintenance the caretaker placed a tiny tracking device at the rear of each one, which routed a signal back to him. Once they were ready to move, he'd hack into the system and take over the feed.

This secret location was command HQ for Ibrahim's operation. Two Panasonic CF-20 Tough Books on the desk in front of Leonard were hooked up to a powerful satellite feed from a remote US server with a roving IP.

The room was only accessible through a secret entrance door behind the back of a shelving unit full of stock – there was even a caravan Portaloo, small bed, kettle and a fridge – which had its supplies restocked daily.

In the event of a raid by law enforcement, a warning light alerted the room's occupants if the stockroom had been breached. He'd practised his exit strategy several times. A small loft lid opened electronically at the pull of a cord, dropping a telescopic ladder, allowing him to escape into the loft spaces above, from where he could access any of one of several empty properties in the row of shops in Piccadilly.

The Collector's M.O. inspired Ibrahim. He insisted the reason he'd never been caught was because his pro outfit only used the best personnel and equipment available.

Glancing at the small CCTV monitor wired to the shop's front camera, he saw two official-looking men in suits approach the entrance. Who were they this early, he wondered nervously, glancing at his phone; it was only eight a.m.

CHAPTER 46

It would be hard to miss the place, thought Blake, looking at the garish green sign above a window display, which wouldn't look out of place in a performance of Aladdin. Several rows of multi-coloured Shisha pipes filled the front window. It was one of those small mini-markets, which had popped up in the city over the last few years, the majority of whose proprietors were immigrants with newly acquired bank loans.

Blake and his sergeant entered the shop. Open-fronted chill cabinets covered all three walls while a centre shelving unit dominated the rest of the available floor space. A crystal beaded drape in the left corner hung above the doorway leading to the back of the premises.

Blake addressed a short, painfully thin Asian guy who was on his knees topping up what appeared to be the spice shelf with large packs of pungent powders from a box on the floor.

'You the owner?'

'No.'

'Who is then?'

'Who asking?'

Blake flashed his warrant card. 'DI Tom Blake, Hanley CID and this is my colleague DS Murphy. We're looking for Ibrahim Benzar.'

The shifty-looking assistant paused nervously before answering. 'He's not here.'

'Can you give me your boss's number please?'

'I don't have.'

Blake's instincts told him this guy was either being deliberately unhelpful or was scared of his boss. Whichever, it was widely acknowledged employees such as these were often illegals with no work visa. He turned up the heat knowing a quick mention of customs would prise him open.

'Listen, I'll only ask you once more. After that customs will pay you a visit to check if your work visa and passport are valid. Give me your boss's number now.'

Without hesitation, the guy climbed to his feet, paced over to the counter and retrieved a business card from under it. Blake gave DS Murphy a knowing look and called the mobile number on the card.

After multiple rings there was an answer. 'Hello?'

'Is that Ibrahim Benzar?'

'Who's asking?' said a voice with a slight Eastern European accent.

'Detective Inspector Tom Blake. We have your brother in custody.'

'Our lawyer is dealing with it. Why are you calling me?'

Blake moved to the other side of the shop and lowered his voice. 'I'd like to make you aware of how serious your brother's situation is. Possession of a large quantity of class A drugs, forty thousand of untraceable cash, and, of course, there's the assault on his tenant.' Blake knew these kinds of criminals rarely acted alone and in most cases they were part of an organised syndicate, which often contained several members of the same family. Brothers, cousins, uncles and even mothers were not immune to being party to it.

'I don't speak to cops. Our lawyer deals with them. If that's all, I'm a busy man?'

Blake tried to evoke a response from him. 'Your brother's looking at least eight to ten years in prison.' His intention was to draw Benzar into a face-to-face in his shop. He took a couple of seconds to realise the line had gone dead. 'He's hung up on me,' he moaned to the shop assistant, who looked worried about retribution for giving his boss's number to the cops, which Blake inferred as a sign of the level of fear his paymaster instilled.

CHAPTER 47

PC Evans and DC Chris Longsdon arrived at the Social Club, Burslem. Dennis Miller greeted them, standing on the front steps puffing away at the last remnants of his fag. He ushered them through the doors into the main bar area.

'We've had reports of a break-in,' Evans said.

'Ah, that was forty-eight hours ago!

'Mr Miller. Each crime reported to us is prioritised, and fortunately because no one was hurt, and not much has been stolen, the break-in was down the list I'm afraid to say. Just the way it works, with all the cuts.'

'Fair enough. I'm buggered if I know why they've done it. Just bloody mindless vandalism,' he said.

'What exactly is missing?' DC Longsdon asked him.

'That's the funny thing. Whoever did this only stole old photographs of the William Adams Pottery.'

'And there's nothing else at all been taken? Often it takes a while for you to realise, because of the shock.'

'We've had a good look around, officer. Everything seems to be here.'

'Any idea what time the break-in took place?' Longsdon asked.

'Not exactly sure, but Jeff Greenhall, a local security guard who watches over several buildings in the area, called me around ten o'clock on the night it happened. Said the place was all safe and sound. So, I'm presuming it must have happened sometime after that.'

'Did the security guard enter the building?' Longsdon continued as Evans took notes.

'Yeah, he said the dog was acting funny, but everything looked fine, so he went home.'

'Dog?'

'Yeah, it's a German Shepherd. Goes everywhere with him, like his best mate: although it's getting on a bit now,' Miller said.

'I see. Going back to the stolen photos. Who, or what exactly were they of?'

'I've been into amateur photography, most of my life: and since this place has a lot of history linked to the old William Adams pottery site down the road. In '93 I decided to share some of my great memories with people who use this place. Quite a lot of them used to work there. It's only the strong sense of community that got everyone through the hard times. Bit like the miners, if you see what I mean.'

Both, Longsdon, and Evans had family who'd worked in the pottery industry during the '80s and '90s so knew exactly what he meant.

'Anyone specific in these photos?'

'Ah, loads of local blokes young and old. Of course some of them are dead now and others I've not seen for years.'

'Names would be helpful. It seems quite a personal sort of burglary, like they were only after the photographs. I mean how much beer and spirits do you keep on the premises?'

'Oh, I dunnow exactly, about three grands worth.'

'Which begs the question why didn't they take any of it?'

Miller rubbed his chin, 'That's exactly what I said to the cleaners this morning. Something's definitely suspicious about this break-in.' he said, pointing to the broken cabinets.

'Okay, we'll give forensics a call and see if there's a SOCO available to come and give the place a dusting for prints. Just out of interest do you have copies of these photos?'

Miller mused for a second. 'Well bugger me I never thought about that. You know, think I might have in my workshop. I used to keep folders with dates and everything. Although when I took over this place I stopped: takes up a lot of my time now.'

'What period where the photos from?' Longsdon asked him.

'At a guess I'd say between 1968 up until the factory closed in 1993.

'Okay, if you could have a good look later today. That might shed some light on the motive for the burglary. Give me a call on that number if you find them,' Longsdon said passing over his card.

CHAPTER 48

Ibrahim owned several properties across the city, although he was not interested in generating income from rent. All were poorly maintained terraced houses in rundown areas. He used these to house illegal immigrants who worked for him off the books. From a business point of view it was far more profitable to let tenants live rent-free, but on low pay.

The Africans lived in Shelton, an inner-city area made up of predominantly turn-of-the-century terraced houses with a diverse ethnic and student community. Frederick and Jozef Simbala were orphan brothers, forced by the death of their parents to survive any way they could on the tough Nairobi streets. Both were members of the Mungiki, a criminal organisation labelled as the most dangerous gang in Africa. Their involvement in multiple kidnaps, extortion rackets and a spate of violent murders in the country's largest slum, Mathare, caused them to flee Kenya twelve months earlier via illegal trafficking routes to Belgium.

First impressions of the pair were misleading: dark, lank and skinny, wearing faded charity shop T-shirts and jeans, but the evil pair were capable of anything. Ibrahim learned from his apprenticeship with the Black Wolves gang in Turkey back in the eighties: never have direct involvement with any form of crime. It was much smarter to orchestrate at a distance from the business end of things. He only used the Simbalas for unsavoury jobs that required brazen force.

He met the brothers in the Mediterranean Café on the A5006 Shelton. There were no CCTV cameras, making it an ideal place to conduct business. It was 9.30 a.m. and the place was empty.

He ordered a Turkish coffee and joined the shifty-looking pair who sat sipping green tea at a corner table. Retrieving a Manila envelope from inside his jacket he laid a sheet of A4 with a photograph of Isabel Blake attached to it onto the table.

'One of my men has been watching this detective's house for a few days. His daughter goes to college Monday, Tuesday, Wednesday and Thursday mornings.'

The Simbala brothers remained silent as Ibrahim went through clear orders of where the target could be found and where to take her, accompanied by his driver, once abducted.

'Keep this simple. We want her unharmed and detained for only twenty-four hours. She normally leaves the house at around ten a.m. and makes her way along the road mentioned here to an unobserved rural bus stop. When you leave this building, turn left past the pharmacist. One of my men is waiting in a silver BMW. He will take you to the bus stop and then drive you to the secret location. Do you have everything you need?'

Frederick Simbala nodded, glancing at a tatty-looking rucksack between his feet.

'OK, it's now nine thirty-five. Keep the information safe, but once you reach the secret location, burn it. Understood?'

'What about payment?'

Ibrahim glanced around the café. Lowering his voice, he said, 'When you have the girl, my man will pay you the amount we agreed. Here's two hundred each, just to whet your appetite?' He slid the folded twenty-pound notes across the table.

'How we speak with you?'

'I was just coming to that,' he said, sliding an old pay-as-you-go mobile across the table. 'It's charged, with just one number programmed in. If you need me for anything, call the number, but do not mention my name. I'll call you around half past twelve to check you have her. Under no circumstances call anybody else. If you do, I'll know, so don't even consider it.' He left the café and made his way back to his car.

CHAPTER 49

The man's leather gloved hands clenched the wheel of a stolen silver BMW three series. He drove steady past speed cameras on the city centre ring road, listening to a discussion about local football on Radio Stoke.

The two African brothers sat motionless in the back gazing out of the windows at the banners, advertising the city's world famous pottery firms, hanging from every lamp-post in the central reservation.

The BMW picked up pace as it sped down Botteslow Street and set off along Leek Road heading towards Milton Crossroads before turning right towards the remote bus stop just outside the rural idyll of Bagnall village.

'Get ready, we'll be there in two minutes.' The driver warned his passengers, turning off the stereo as the car climbed the steep incline of Bagnall bank. 'Ah! What's that frigging rancid smell?' Glancing in the rear-view mirror he saw the evil pair daubing a heavy cloth with liquid from a brown glass bottle.

'Chloroform. Stops dem resisting.'

The driver knew he was no angel, but this kind of shit was a touch disturbing. The sort of thing you'd see in one of those serial killer movies, he thought, trying to dismiss it from his mind.

The bus stop was two hundred yards ahead. He turned the corner easing off the gas. It was 10.15 a.m. and Isabel Blake was perched on the seat of a larch panelled bus shelter; the bus wasn't due for ten minutes. The BMW cruised past as Frederick Simbala eyeballed her taking a last glance at the photo just to be sure. The driver turned the car around and drew parallel with the bus stop.

The electric window on the rear of the vehicle descended and Frederick Simbala leaned through. ''Ello, we looking for da Stafford pub?'

Isabel unwittingly leaned in closer to the car door to give directions. It was over in seconds. The African grabbed her blouse, pulling her head down. Before she could scream he smothered the chloroform-soaked rag over her face. Her eyes rolled violently, her body went limp as she passed out, suspended by Frederick's clenched hand resting on the door sill.

Jozef jumped out the vehicle and scampered around the opposite side to catch her. The pair then bungled their unconscious victim into the car boot and locked it.

'Go, go!' They shouted and jumped back in slamming the doors behind them.

'Fuck! How long will she be out for?' the driver panicked, concerned about the implications of being involved with an abduction in broad daylight.

'No problem, she be OK. Just drive.'

He hit the pedal, took a sharp left down a lazy incline. After twenty minutes of navigating winding country lanes through the Staffordshire Moorlands, they reached the safe house. A derelict farmhouse stepped back three hundred yards from the road. It was in a desperate state of decay: broken guttering, crumbling brickwork and blackened windows. The driver pointed the car round the back of the property. He'd been there briefly the night before with a bag of tools and enough supplies for forty-eight hours. Breaking in had taken little effort; the rusting hasp and staple pried with ease from the rotten doorframe. The place looked much worse in daylight.

With the kitchen door propped wide open, the three of them returned to the sound of muffled screams and banging coming from the boot of the BMW. Isabel Blake had regained consciousness and was desperate to get out.

Frederick Simbala went to the back of the vehicle and retrieved a Glock 17 pistol from his rucksack. The driver nervously scanned the area before flipping the boot. An extremely frightened Isabel Blake jumped up and frantically cried for help. Frederick placed his finger on his lips, whilst jamming the Glock hard against the side of her head.

'Shh! Or I pop ya, bitch. Git outa da car,' he demanded.

She shook uncontrollably, gulping down breaths while attempting to stay quiet. Although the chloroform had worn off, she felt disorientated, struggling to comprehend finding herself in this nightmare situation.

They forced her into the dishevelled kitchen and made her sit on a dust-covered dining room chair sat ominously in the centre of the room. Cracks of light seared through several broken panes of the filthy windows. Large church candles littered the room in preparation for darkness. The whole place smelled of stagnant mildew and damp.

Face ashen white with fear, the 19-year-old brunette protested, 'Why are you doing this?' she sobbed; worried why the white guy had disappeared, leaving her at the mercy of the two crazed Africans.

'Give us na trouble an you'll be home tomorrow,' Jozef Simbala explained in a feeble attempt to reassure her. He was not in charge of the situation but rather assisting the other mad bastard holding the gun.

The driver stood around the back of the dilapidated farmhouse gazing across the rolling fields through an opening in a grove of Sycamores in bloom.

He fished his mobile from his jeans and called Ibrahim. 'It's done, make the call.'

'She OK?'

'Yeah, but these madmen are scaring her,' he said anxiously.

'Don't worry; they're under orders not to hurt her.'

'Try telling them that.'

'Tell Frederick to get the bike ready and keep the phone I gave him close.'

'Will do.' The driver ended the call.

The plan was to grab Yusuf outside police headquarters in Hanley fifteen minutes before the prison van was due to ship him off on remand. Once Frederick was in lower Bethesda Street on the bike, Inspector Blake would release his handcuffs. The speeding Honda would take him to a van waiting in a remote lane. That's how it was supposed to go; whether it would was a different story. He was just carrying out orders like a good foot soldier. But being party to abduction freaked him out. The sooner they released the girl the better.

Isabel Blake needed to urinate. Frederick Simbala untied her from the chair and passed her a filthy blue plastic bucket.

'I need privacy!' she pleaded.

But it was to no avail; the African just stared at her, shook the bucket and snapped, 'Just piss der.'

She hesitated, but the urge to pass water became too strong. She'd resisted for two hours and was now desperate. Composing herself she edged into the corner of the room like a frightened cat. Stooping, she slid her knickers to the ankles and hovered over the bucket holding her denim knee-length skirt down in a desperate attempt not to reveal anything. To her horror, Frederick stood watching rubbing his crotch in a provocative manner, as the other brother slouched on a dishevelled sofa opposite. Trapped in the corner her eyes darted around the darkness. Disturbing images of what might happen flashed through her mind as she teetered on the edge of this nightmare.

Suddenly the white guy entered the kitchen and defused the situation.'What are you doing? The boss gave strict orders not to touch the girl, back off!' he threatened, worried about her safety.

'Chill. Killing time, man. Remember, I's got da gun.'

CHAPTER 50

It was 9.30 a.m. when Kat's phone trilled, she looked at the call ID; it was Ibrahim. Not wanting to sound too desperate she let it ring another couple of times before answering.

'Hi.'

'Kat, just calling to see if you're available for lunch this afternoon?'

'This afternoon,' she paused, 'yeah OK! Where do you have in mind?'

'I know a great country pub, which does really nice steaks; if you fancy it?'

'That would be lovely. What time can you pick me up?'

'Shall we say eleven p.m.?'

'Yes, in the car park in Foxley Lane.'

'Okay, see you then.'

'Bye,' Kat said trying to contain her excitement.

She really didn't think he'd call again, after their one night stand. Besides, she was bored of hanging around the house. All the cleaning was done, and she'd fetched the pizzas from the shop for tea. This would inject a bit of excitement into her life.

Grinning she headed upstairs to take a shower, choose an outfit and put on some make-up.

After a twenty minute drive through glorious sunshine and pastel shaded farmland they arrived at The Lion; a refurbished 16th century coaching inn on the Staffordshire–Shropshire border.

Ibrahim parked his Audi at the side of the pub. The car park was less than half empty, just the way he liked it. At least they'd get some privacy. He'd booked a table in the conservatory which overlooked a small carp fishing lake at the rear. It was a real romantic place.

'Wow, this is nice,' Kat said as the waitress led them to their table.'

'Wait until you taste the steak and dauphinoise potatoes.'

'Sounds lovely,' she smiled nervously feeling a little apprehensive on only their second date. To be honest I was surprised when you called this morning.'

'Why, I really thought we connected last time.'

Kat's cheeks reddened. You can say that again she thought, after shagging him for hours.

'And I'm not just talking about the sex,' Ibrahim lowered his voice. 'I like you, Kat. You're beautiful and have a really easy-going personality.'

'Thanks, I like you too,' she said realising how cheesy that sounded.

'I wanted to call you before today, but I've been working on something big; there's lots of important stuff to sort out.'

This piqued Kat's interest, 'Sounds interesting, what's that then?

'Sorry I can't talk about it,' he said guardedly.

'OK. Don't worry about it, we're here now. It's probably for the best we're out of Stoke. If Carl finds out he'll go ballistic.'

'I wouldn't worry about him, he's a dick. This might sound a bit stupid, but I won't intervene in your relationship, unless you want me to, that is? But if he hurts you in any way, I may not be able to resist giving him a kicking. Anyway, don't worry about that now. Excuse me for a minute; I need to make an important business call,' he said leaving the table, strolling through the bi-fold doors leading to the empty outside patio area.

Kat sat watching him pace around on the phone, wondering what the hell she was getting into. Clearly Ibrahim was a man of means and probably dangerous, but she really fancied him. He treated her with respect. She decided to carry on behind Carl's back, see what happened. Maybe there could be a future in this, although she promised herself not to do anything foolish like leave Carl on a stupid impulse.

CHAPTER 51

At 11.30 a.m. Blake stepped outside for some fresh air. Police headquarters were built in the seventies and the four-storey modular box was boiling in summer and freezing in winter. Over the years the council had upgraded the interior, but from outside the building was still one of those 1970s architectural disasters.

His phone rang, but he didn't recognise the caller ID. 'Hello.'

'Listen carefully, what I'm going to tell you is important,' the man on the other end of the line informed him in a slight eastern European accent.

'Who is this?'

'Don't ask questions, just listen. You have Yusuf Benzar in custody, yes?'

'Who wants to know?' Blake demanded.

'I said no questions.'

'Yes, we do.'

'Tell me what time he's being transferred tomorrow.'

'Why would I do that?'

'Because your daughter's life depends on it.'

Suddenly, Blake's blood ran cold. 'Who the hell is this? How did you get this number?'

'That doesn't matter. If you want to see your daughter again, you'll shut up and listen. We have her and she'll be safe, just as long as you follow my orders. Don't tell anyone else about this call, especially other police. Her life depends on it.'

Was this a sick joke, a hoax? A disgruntled criminal with an axe to grind, or was this happening. For the first time in his life, he was speechless. The information wouldn't compute. He'd had personal experience assuring relatives during a kidnap case back in '98. The hopelessness he'd seen in their eyes flooded his mind. But nothing could prepare him for this agony.

'How do I know you're not lying?'

'We'll call you back and put her on the phone. Stay where you are.'

A painful few seconds passed before his mobile rang, another male voice spoke, only this time the accent was much stronger. He couldn't place it. 'Listen, Mr Police!'

'Where's my daughter, you bastard?'

The African held the phone to Isabel's mouth. 'Dad, I'm scared, they've got guns,' Isabel pleaded, trembling, holding back the urge to cry.

He was distraught upon hearing her. Taking a deep breath, he said, 'Darling, try to stay calm and do as they say, and I'll come and get you soon as I can. I love you so much.'

The African came back on the line. 'Ya get it, Mr Policeman?

Livid, Blake responded. 'You harm her and I'll kill you!'

'Ya tink.'

The line went dead. Blake stabbed the call end button to close the line. 'Think, think man.' He paced up and down the pavement in disbelief.

Moments later, the return call came through; it was the other sick bastard who was pulling the strings.

'Hello?'

'Is anyone else there?'

'No.'

'You sure?'

'Yes.'

'OK, is that proof enough for you?'

'You hurt her in any way and I'll find you and cut your bollocks off, you twisted bastard.'

'I understand you're upset, she's your baby, but give me the time and place of Yusuf's transfer?'

'I'll lose my job.'

'Which would you prefer, job or child?'

'OK, OK, nine-thirty tomorrow morning outside the station in Hanley.'

'For definite?'

'Yeah.'

'Bring him out at nine-ten.'

'I can't. We have strict protocols on prisoner transfers.'

'It's not up for negotiation, just do it. I'll call you again tomorrow morning at eight, make sure you answer, and remember, no other police. Don't try to be a hero. Do as you're told and your daughter will be back with you unharmed, understand?'

Blake's mind imploded. It's one thing to investigate crime against strangers but no amount of training could prepare him for the abduction of his own daughter. He felt a sudden dizziness as the physiological changes adrenaline imposed on the body took hold, gripping him in emotional torment. All kinds of irrational fears ran through his mind. He needed to speak to someone fast, someone he trusted. He put his phone away and stumbled nervously back into the station to find John Murphy.

His DS sat huddled over the keyboard on his desk in the CID's open-plan office.

'You OK, Tom? You look like you've seen a ghost?'

'John, I need a word in private, urgently?'

'I'm all ears.'

'Not here. Across the Smiths now, mate.'

'Seriously, it's only early.'

'It's Isabel; she's in real danger.'

'OK, you head on over there, I'll join you in five minutes,' Murphy replied with a puzzled look.

CID liked a drink more than most, and the Smiths Head, situated a hundred and fifty yards across the ring road from the station had been ingrained in the local police culture for more years than anybody cared to remember. The pub stood long before the station existed, but had gone through several reincarnations over the years, the latest being a modern bar and restaurant with heated terrace. It was unrecognisable from its traditional roots.

Blake entered the bar, knowing it was unlikely any other officers would be in there before lunchtime. Drinking on duty could lead to disciplinary action and was never justified. The body blow he'd just received was enough to drive the Pope to a stiff one.

Ten minutes later Murphy entered the tacky bar, which was redder than the average brothel. He spotted his DI in the corner, staring at an empty pint, ready to neck a whisky chaser.

'A bit early, Tom?'

'Nerves are in tatters, I needed something to calm me.' He lowered his voice. 'Sit down, mate, you won't believe what's happened. Somebody's taken Isabel and they're blackmailing me.'

Murphy hesitated. 'Shit, is she OK?'

'Spoke to her on my mobile earlier. She's really scared and I'm seriously worried what they might do to her if I don't follow their orders.' He stared nervously at Murphy.

'Doesn't make sense. Why would anybody abduct your daughter? I know we've put loads of scrotes inside over the years, but most of them are dimwit burglars or drug dealers. None of them have the nous to pull a stunt like this.'

'You reckon?'

'Absolutely. What's going on, Tom?'

'You know that Turkish wide-boy we charged yesterday? It's something to do with him. Seems he's part of an organised firm and they want him released tomorrow.'

'How do they expect you to do that; just let him walk? The prison van's coming for him in the morning. He'll be banged up on remand by dinner time.'

'I know, and that's the problem... these bastards want me to walk him out in front of the station twenty minutes before the van arrives. Handcuffs unlocked.'

'Seriously?'

'Deadly.'

'And there's no other way?'

'That's what I wanted to discuss with you. I've only just found out. One thing they're adamant about is if any other police get involved they'll harm her. Can't take the risk, John, not after what happened to Dylan and Jenny. It would finish me if I lost another child.'

'I understand, Tom, rock and a hard place. And you're sure they're not bluffing?'

'They've got guns. Izzy told me on the phone.'

'Shit, that's worrying. And no one else in the station knows?'

'No. I've weighed up the options, and I can't see a way out apart from giving these bastards what they want.'

'It goes against my better judgement, but I think you're right. The fact they know you have a daughter and could get to her tells me these people should be taken seriously. By the time we could get any kind of angle on them, they'd be long gone. It's too risky. Just let them have the scum.'

'Thanks for your input and support, John,' he said with a heavy heart. 'It's on my head. Now you need to distance yourself. Just make sure you look shocked when that bastard escapes.'

CHAPTER 52

Blake barely slept a wink all night. How could he, knowing his only child was at the mercy of those animals? The hopelessness he felt was unbearable. Downing four tumblers of single malt knocked him out for about two hours, and after that he spent the small hours watching TV and reading Mel Sherratt's *Taunting the Dead*, but the harder he tried to rationalise the situation with his copper's brain, the more it hurt. It was the longest night of his life. The bottom line was he didn't give a shit about freeing the Turkish wide boy. Nasty bastards like him had a habit of shooting themselves in the foot; it was just a matter of time. His sole focus was Isabel's safe return; just the thought of her name brought tears to his eyes.

He was one of the few officers who'd maintained a reasonably normal family life. The death of his wife and son ten years ago had cemented their father and daughter bond. He'd raised Isabel with the help of his wife's parents who'd been massively supportive in getting him through an extremely painful chapter in all their lives.

He glanced in the gilded mirror over the fireplace in the living room. The dark shadows under his eyes made him look like death warmed up. It took a hot shower, two strong coffees and a double bacon and cheese oatcake to awaken his senses. Suited and ready for action, he glanced at his watch; it was 6.30 a.m. There was no way he could hang around the house waiting for those bastards to call at eight, the tension was killing him. DS Murphy called twice already to offer support and enquire if there was any news, but, apart from the deeply distressing conversation with Isabel yesterday, he'd heard nothing, which only increased his anxiety.

The skies were clear and the air warm. The roads were quiet with few cars around apart from shift workers and delivery vans. Blake reached the station at 6.45 a.m. having devised the next course of action, spending fifteen minutes at his desk so as not to arouse suspicion from fellow officers; not that any would be there until at least eight. He then went down to the cells to discreetly tell Benzar of his pending escape: a moral dilemma he didn't want to dwell on for fear of doubts.

He headed downstairs to the cell block on the ground floor facing the compound. There were twelve cells and Benzar was in number eight. The thought of telling the bastard that in around an hour he'd be a free man made his flesh creep. To his dismay there was nothing he could do under the circumstances, except facilitate the career criminal's escape. Even so, it tested his moral fibre to the limit.

Blake informed the duty sergeant that he needed to speak with the prisoner before he went out on remand. The sergeant opened cell eight and told Blake he would be along the passage if needed. Yusuf Benzar sat on the edge of his mattress in a standard-issue prisoner tracksuit, looking worse than Blake felt. Hair a scraggy mess, blood-red eyes and the demeanour of a con determined not to let slip he was eliminated from the game.

'What do you want, pig?'

Blake ignored the derisory comment and lowered his voice to a whisper. 'You're being shipped out on remand in an hour. I'll take you to the pick-up point out front of the station. But you're not going to prison. Those bastards you work for have made arrangements for your escape. When we leave the cell, your cuffs will be on but unlocked. Just play along, then when I nod at you do what you have to do, understand?'

Benzar's face lit up as he gave a smug grin. 'They've got to you, detective; every man has a price.'

Blake was too wrung out to respond and certainly didn't want to alert this scumbag about his daughter's abduction, so he turned, conceding defeat. There was only one thing he was interested in now and that was Isabel's safe return; police morality could take a backseat. He popped his head around the door. 'Sergeant, officer leaving cell!'

CHAPTER 53

Blake looked nervously around waiting for the inevitable to happen. It was nine a.m. and he stood on the pavement outside the station, Yusuf Benzar standing to the left of him. His handcuffs were unlocked, and he had a self-satisfied look on his face. Like an abstract movie in slow motion, those fateful few minutes seemed to take an age to pass.

Suddenly, a black Honda road bike roared as it accelerated down Lower Bethesda Street screeching to a halt, smoke streaming from its twin chrome exhausts. The rider dressed in jet-black leathers signalled to Benzar with a hooked thumb over his shoulder, his tinted visor hid his identity, like a ninja.

He cast the cuffs into the road, jumped on and gripped the handrail on the back seat. The rider throttled up and the bike's induction turbo propelled it blindly across the busy ring road at soaring speed through oncoming traffic, escaping collision by milliseconds.

The traffic ground to a halt as a white Transit van slammed on its brakes and spun sideways across the ring road, causing a four-car collision. Two other cars swerved in a desperate attempt to avoid the pile up with the van, and rammed into the crossroad's traffic lights.

The steady flow of the morning commute was shattered by the splintering sounds of car alarms and screaming injured motorists. Like a ghost, the bike disappeared along Lower Bethesda St.

Blake stood numb, his shoulders curled heavy over his chest. The station entrance doors flung open and several officers dashed towards him. A sudden feeling of nakedness crept over him and for the first time in his career he felt exposed and out of control of the situation.

'My office, now!' screamed Chief Inspector Coleman.

Like a scolded child, Blake slouched ten yards behind him back into the station.

'What the hell happened, DI Blake?' barked Coleman from behind his huge antique mahogany desk, his face bright red, as if he was about to explode.

Numb with shock, Blake stood staring around the chief's inner sanctum. On the wall behind him hung framed certificates portraying his rise up the greasy pole. Turn of the century sepia-tone photographs in embossed frames hung nostalgically on the opposite wall: a horse-drawn prison van, a group shot of PCs with walrus moustaches, outside the old station house. and, dominating the row, an imposing image of Coleman's great-grandfather, Sir George Mathews Coleman, mounted on a large stallion in full police dress, his sword resting across highly polished boots.

'How the hell did a prisoner escape right from under your nose? More worryingly, how did his cohorts know the transit time? We never divulge or publish that information to anyone apart from the prison service. Nobody outside the station would know, which makes me think someone inside is looking at a serious misconduct charge as this incident reeks of leaked information. Who knew this prisoner's transit time besides you and the duty sergeant?'

Blake acted dumb. He considered telling Coleman everything but knew he couldn't until Isabel was safe.

'Well, DI Blake, are you going to answer?' Coleman continued.

He couldn't give a credible reply. He felt as if a huge rock had dropped in the pit of his stomach. His blood pressure was dropping. Hesitating, he blurted, 'I really don't know what to say, sir; it happened so fast there was no time to react.' The room blurred and before he could say any more his knees buckled and he lost consciousness.

Coleman jumped around the desk, dropping to the floor. He could see Blake's chest cavity rise and fall; his DI had fainted.

For sixty seconds, the detective lay motionless on the carpet in front of Coleman's desk, his complexion porcelain white.

Blake's eyes opened a crack and the room slowly came back into focus. For a few minutes it felt like peering through the lenses of unfocused binoculars. Within a few seconds, his brain caught up with the light signals streaming through his eyes and the haze lifted to the sound of Coleman's voice as he peered over him.

'Tom, Tom, can you hear me? You fainted, man.'

'Er, d… did I?' Blake slurred, half-conscious.

'Are you OK?'

'I think so.'

'I suggest you get checked out at A&E and then head off home, and that's not a request; it's an order. You've been putting in long shifts recently, and this incident shows you need a break.'

He sat up slowly. 'I'll be fine after a strong coffee.'

'It's not going to happen. Refer your tasks to DS Murphy for today. I'll get one of the constables to drive you home.'

'What about my Jag?'

'A squad car can follow and bring the constable back. It's not negotiable, Tom. Get some rest, and as long as you're OK, I want you back in my office first thing in the morning. You can explain then; clearly you're not up to it now.'

Blake knew it would be pointless arguing with him; orders were orders, and they'd been delivered with Coleman's usual finality.

Thinking about it, the enforced break from work couldn't have come at a better time, given the current situation with Isabel.

CHAPTER 54

Blake stood in his kitchen staring at his phone, which lay on the granite worktop, willing it to ring. It was 10.30 a.m. and Yusuf Benzar had escaped. He'd stuck to his side of the bargain, so why wasn't it ringing? What were those scumbags playing at?

His nerves were shot to bits, and he was seriously concerned for Isabel's safety. One thing was for sure, he didn't give a shit about the consequences of being found aiding a prisoner's escape. Coleman might even involve professional standards to look into it; those bastards did more probing than an endoscope. What could they find? It wouldn't be the first time a prisoner had absconded from police custody. No one else knew the truth apart from DS Murphy, who he trusted implicitly. All that mattered now was Isabel's safe return.

Abduction of a child was every parent's worst nightmare, and he stood to lose more than most considering Isabel was his only living child.

Glancing round the kitchen his subconscious focused on a picture taken of Isabel and Dylan in their school uniforms when she was ten, and he was eight. It evoked happy memories of play-fighting with both of them on the lawn. Closing his eyes, he could almost feel the warmth of the sun on his face, hear the sound of their laughter and the panting from Daisy their old chocolate spaniel who'd romped around with them. The kids loved that rescue dog dearly. Sadly, now in heaven with his son and wife; at least he liked to think of it that way.

The abrupt ringing of his phone jerked his mind back into the present, but the caller ID revealed it was only DS Murphy.

'Hello?'

'You OK, Tom? I heard you fainted on the carpet in Coleman's office earlier.'

'It's embarrassing. I bet it's all around the station by now?'

'Not really, people are just concerned for you. Any news on Isabel?'

'I'm waiting for the call now. To be honest, John, I'm getting worried. That bastard is free now, so where's my daughter?'

'I'm coming round. There's no way you can deal with this on your own.'

'It's OK, I can manage,' he said, playing the martyr.

'No chance, those animals are armed. Much safer if we collect her together.'

'If you insist. Much been said about the prisoner escaping?'

'You know what it's like – just wild speculation. Don't worry, let's concentrate on getting Izzy back.'

'Shit, another call's coming in. Gotta go, this could be them.'

'OK, call me straight after?'

Blake nearly dropped the phone, his hand noticeably shaking as he ended the call abruptly and switched to the incoming call, praying it would be good news. 'Hello?'

'You know the bus stop at the end of your road? Your daughter will be there in forty minutes. Make sure you're alone, no other police, or the girl gets hurt.'

'You bastards followed me home. How do I know I can trust you?'

'You don't, but if you want your daughter back just be there.'

The line went dead. He felt elated before realising getting emotional wouldn't help; he needed to don his police head fast. Forget revenge; just get Izzy home. These bastards would get what's due eventually.

Moments later he heard the familiar crunch of rubber on gravel. Peering out of the kitchen window, DS John Murphy climbed out of the Astra pool car and approached his front door with a carrier bag in his left hand.

CHAPTER 55

Isabel Blake's mouth was dry. Every muscle in her body ached. Exhausted from the mental torment of not knowing her fate, she'd dosed off for less than an hour on a bloodstained mattress in the corner of the dishevelled kitchen, refusing to eat anything they'd offered, scared it might be drugged. Eventually she begrudgingly took small bites from a bread roll they'd buttered in front of he, concluding it would be a safe bet after seeing her abductors open the packet and eat some.

Now untied, she glimpsed at his blurred face through tears. Wiping them away with grimy hands, she focused on the pistol he held tightly.

'Please, let me go,' she pleaded. 'I promise I won't tell anyone.'

Jozef Simbala didn't answer but paced around the derelict kitchen anxiously. His orders were to drive and then release her three hundred yards from the bus stop where they'd snatched her. Rarely did he have to operate alone. Frederick, being much stronger and the more aggressive of the two, always took charge of the jobs they carried out. Without the intervention of his brother's insane gun-slinging antics back in Africa, he'd have been dead years ago. A lot was riding on this; he needed to step up to the plate. If the cops found them, deportation and life in prison, once back on Belgian soil, was certain. '*Na fuck ups, bro.*' His brother's words echoed in his head.

Her mind raced through several preservation options. Was there just one black guy watching over her? Where were the other two? Was this her chance to make a run for it?

The African glared at her. 'I is takin ya back.' His uptight posture hinted at his flagging confidence on flying solo. 'Ya can gettin da car?'

Forming a steeple with her hands, she pressed them to her lips. Tearful, she glanced towards her remaining captor to express thanks. 'Oh god!'

The African motioned to her waving the Glock towards the door. She cautiously exited the dark prison, squinting at the blinding morning sun. The sweet summer air livened her senses, but she needed her dad's reassuring embrace more than anything.

The silver BMW was tucked out of sight in a large decaying barn opposite the house. She felt the tip of the Glock pressing hard in between her shoulder blades, letting her know he was still there.

'Git in da back?'

As she sat on the cream leather seats, a horrible thought entered her head: What if this maniac is taking me to a remote place to shoot me? Can I trust him?

Trembling, she edged closer to the door as the BMW eased along the gravel driveway towards the road. The African stopped at the end of the pathway, looked left to right surveying the empty road. Before he could pull out, Isabel flung the door open, and made a frantic run for it up the road. He slammed on the gas; the back wheels spun in the gravel sending the BMW sideways into a skid.

She managed twenty blistering painful yards barefoot before the car's front bumper clipped her heels, tossing her violently onto the road with a thud. Her head crashed hard against the tarmac, split open, leaching blood onto the pocked surface. Her eyes flickered at the silver BMW, disappearing into the distance, and then darkness.

Isabel Blake's twisted body lay unconscious like road kill in the gutter. Blood trickled from a gash above her temple, pooling underneath her shoulder on the warm tarmac.

An elderly orange Austin Marina eased around the corner and came to an abrupt stop. Its occupants squeezed themselves out stiffly and stared in shock at the young female victim lying bleeding before them. A grey-haired lady in her seventies fished an old mobile from her bag and called an ambulance.

CHAPTER 56

'God, you look like shit, Tom,' Murphy remarked, gawping around the kitchen, which appeared unusually untidy with dishes piled high in the sink. Understandable, given the circumstances.

'Thanks for the compliment.'

'Any news yet?' Murphy asked.

'They followed me home. Must've been watching our movements for a while. Just had a call informing me to pick Izzy up from the bus stop at the end of the road. They must've taken her somewhere near to here. Less chance of being seen in a rural setting.'

'Bastards! Definitely organised crime this lot. What's Isabel's routine like?'

'Doesn't really have one apart from college. She catches the ten o'clock bus from the stop I mentioned: every morning, Monday to Thursday.'

'I hate to say, but it sounds like you're right. Who did Yusuf Benzar make his call to?'

'His brother to arrange a lawyer.'

'You reckon he's involved?'

'Definitely, but there's no proof. I've had the kidnappers' calls traced. Drawn a blank.'

'I'm not surprised. We both know crims use operational phones. Let's get the brother in for an informal chat, see if he lets anything slip.'

'Tomorrow after my meeting with Coleman. I've got to tread really carefully. Remember, apart from you, no one knows.'

'Point taken. If they get wind of this you'd be looking at a suspension while they investigated.'

'Thanks for reminding me, John.'

'Sorry, mate. The last thing you need is those anal probers from Professional Standards sniffing about,' he jibed, trying to ease the tension.

'Anyway, got to go,' Blake said nervously.

'No way I'm letting you do this alone. You need backup.'

'Appreciate the concern, John, but they clearly stated if anyone else turns up, Izzy gets hurt. I can't take the risk.'

'I understand, mate, it's your daughter. Take this with you then?' He fished in the bottom of the carrier bag he'd been holding since arriving. 'It's for protection.' He passed over an odd-shaped heavy object wrapped in a stained rag.

Blake gave him a troubled look. 'Is that what I think it is?'

'My granddad's Webley Mk six pistol,' Murphy said, unwrapping the rag to reveal the weapon. 'This baby's seen a ton of action. Wasted a few Krauts in the Battle for Berlin in forty-five.'

'You can't be serious, John? This isn't some game. Isabel's life's at risk. If I start waving that thing around someone could get shot. Put that bloody antique away before you get us both arrested.'

'Just trying to help, Tom. Normally in a situation like this there'd be a firearms team standing by. You're completely exposed.'

'Tough shit. I'm not scared of these bastards. Once Izzy is safe, I'm going after them.'

'Is that wise? They know where you live. If this was a normal case I'd say go for it but don't forget you're flying solo. Just get Isabel home and we can talk about it.'

'Promise me you'll wait here until I get back?'

Begrudgingly Murphy agreed to stay put.

CHAPTER 57

Blake travelled four hundred yards in his Jaguar before stopping opposite the bus shelter. He was running on pure adrenaline. The tension had being building for almost twenty-four hours and had reached the point of no return.

Staring out of the open passenger window at the empty bus shelter, he reflected on his life. At forty-five his police career included three promotions, and hundreds of convictions. In contrast, his personal life, excluding events of the last day, had settled down. Although no matter how positive his outlook he'd spent the last ten years raising his daughter whilst trying to bury the pain of losing his wife and son in a fatal hit and run. Grief counselling helped but no amount of talking could ever bring his family back. It was the sheer finality of death that made him feel so overwhelmed and helpless at times.

Taking a deep breath to compose himself, he glanced at his watch. What the bloody hell was going on? He'd been at the agreed rendezvous point for almost thirty minutes and apart from the odd passing car it was a complete no show. A sudden feeling of impending doom crept over him. He picked up his mobile and speed dialled DS Murphy for support.

'Tom, what's happening?'

'Complete no-show, what should I do now?'

'Call them?'

'Tried that, there's no answer. They make all the running.'

'Just sit tight for another ten minutes. Then we can refocus.'

'I'm going out of my head waiting. Izzy is the only thing I have left. If they harm her, I'll blow their bastard heads off with that pistol of yours.'

'Tom, try and remain calm.'

'Gotta go. There's an incoming call; it could be them.'

The voice of the East European delivered heart-wrenching news. 'Listen, there's been an accident, your daughter got hurt. It wasn't meant to happen. The people responsible will be dealt with,' Ibrahim said, almost apologising.

Wiping back tears, Blake screamed at him. 'You'd better pray my daughter's OK or I'll personally hunt you down and make sure every last one of you gets banged up for the next twenty years, you evil bastards.' His rant was in vain: the line was dead.

Blake frantically scanned through his contacts before speed dialling Royal Stoke A&E admissions desk. All he got was the engaged tone.

His mouth became dry. Shaking, he took another deep breath and stayed on the line.

After an anxious minute the receptionist put him on hold while she checked if his daughter had been admitted.

The deadly silence only increased his fear.

She confirmed Isabel was involved in a hit-and-run and was on her way via ambulance. Distraught, he ended the call, hit the gas and sped off to the Royal Stoke University Hospital.

CHAPTER 58

Yusuf Benzar stood on the deck of the fifty-two foot 1968 refurbished Danish trawler, gazing out over the stern at the disappearing Liverpool dockland skyline as the boat ploughed a steady seven knots through the choppy Mersey Estuary, heading into the sunset towards the Irish Sea.

His brother paid the captain a hefty five grand for the charter of his impromptu escape from the UK. Yusuf being a wanted man had meant legal exit routes were off limits.

Charlie Bullard had arranged it. He'd struck up a friendship with a Bristol fisherman who'd spent time in the same prison wing as him in 1980.

The retired captain's boat was registered in a false name with the Liverpool dock authorities. He topped up his pension with day fishing charters acquiring casual crew members when needed. On this covert trip to Port De Pêche Lorient, a six-foot three, dark-haired second mate Simon Platt assisted him. The experienced deckhand could be relied on implicitly to keep his mouth shut. Besides, fourteen hundred quid for a seven-day trip couldn't be sneered at.

It'd been a covert operation from bike to van all the way up the M6 motorway to Liverpool where he'd checked into The Steam Liner Hotel on the Albert docks under an alias.

Below deck Yusuf glanced around his new home for the next few days. The mid-ship living area was lined with unvarnished marine ply, making it look like the inside of a cheap builders' hut. The log burner, tatty three-piece sofa in brown velvet and small flat screen TV huddled under a porthole in the centre, did little for its ambiance.

In the privacy of his room, he unzipped the leather holdall Ibrahim supplied for the journey and laid its contents out on his bunk mattress. Apart from a toiletries bag, and some essential clothes, there were two important-looking bubble-wrap envelopes. 'Personal use' was typed in bold text on one and the other had 'Payment' on it.

Opening the first revealed two wads of cash separated by pale-blue sheaths. In the second envelope were two folded sheets of A4 stapled together, an untraceable mobile phone, a slimline digital camera loaded with hundreds of images of the Staffordshire Hoard, flight tickets from Rennes–Saint Jacques Airport in France to India and a fake passport.

Yusuf knew this was the last chance to redeem himself with his brother. Although the circumstances weren't ideal, even he could see it was a good opportunity to get clean and start a new life somewhere else. Sibling jealousy aside, deep down he knew his brother would not cut him adrift altogether.

He unfolded the paper and read the list of chronologically typed instructions.

1. The boat will arrive in Port De Pêche Lorient, France on the 15th. Take the train to - Rennes Saint Jacques Airport, then Air France Flight no: AF 8125 to India.

2. Once in India (Chhatrapati Shivaji International Airport Mumbai) call this number +918436408888. Our contact will pick you up, take you to your accommodation and arrange an evening meeting with the Jeweller.

3. We have already negotiated a price. Do not try haggling; stick to the thirty-grand deal agreed: fifteen upfront and fifteen on completion. Do not give them all of it up front!

4. The Indian will contact you and bring everything to your hotel.

5. Call this number 0789 5532210 to contact me when everything is ready for export to the UK.

Keep the phone fully charged and by your side at all times. I'll call you later. Any problems, call on the number above. During any phone conversation do not mention details. Keep a low profile, and stay off drugs and alcohol.

I know you can do this.
Yours,
Ibrahim.

CHAPTER 59

Mickey Connor was in over his head to the tune of thirteen thousand on his credit cards. Most of the debt, and even more disturbing crippling interest rates, were down to his brain-dead ex-missus. Over a twenty-four-month period, the jobless, lazy slapper had waded into his plastic big time. The spree began when she purchased a fifty inch state-of-the-art TV, gallivanted on a hen week to Benidorm, which ended up being more like ten days and fifteen hundred quid on account of her buying endless rounds for a minibus of fatties from Lancashire she barely knew. The only thing he'd knowingly been party to was a first-class trip to Disneyland Florida with her and his little girl.

The baggage handler sat in the Silk Wheel pub on Selkirk Road, staring at his pint as if it were a magic lantern. He etched a pound sign in the condensation on the side of the glass whilst contemplating the bizarre phone conversation he'd had with his dad last week, offering him a lifeline.

He'd not seen him for around two years, and it had been even longer since they'd spoke on the phone. Considering his current financial predicament the call couldn't have come at a better time. Micky had gone off the rails when Connor Senior was sent down for beating up a bloke who was having an affair with his mother. With his dad inside he headed off to Manchester to live with a mate and start a new life, after five years of struggling with crap jobs around the city he landed a position at the airport.

He glanced at his watch. It was nearly 7.30 p.m. and his dad was about to introduce him to a dodgy bloke who was offering to pay off his debt for a favour. Reading between the lines the whole thing sounded highly illegal; not something he'd normally touch with a barge pole. But he was desperate and, as the saying goes, 'beggars can't be choosers'. So, there'd be no harm in listening to the proposal, he thought.

At 7.45 p.m. he considered going home to sink his sorrows with a few bottles of Suede Head when his old man entered, accompanied by a well-dressed foreign-looking bloke, putting paid to that idea.

'Pint, son?' Darryl asked him, cupping an imaginary glass.

'Suede Head, please.'

Five minutes later the three of them sat in a private corner away from the bar. Darryl Connor introduced his companion as a businessman from Stoke named Kareem. Knowing full well his real name was Ibrahim, and he was a serious player.

'What's this all about then, dad?'

'Since it's Kareem's gig, I'll let him explain it.'

Ibrahim Benzar took a shifty glance around the pub before asking, 'You're a baggage handler at the airport?'

'Yeah!'

He laid the bait. 'Your dad tells me you're having money problems?'

Mickey blushed. 'What's that got to do with the job?' he asked, unimpressed his own father had betrayed his confidence.

'We can help you with that in return for a favour.'

'What do you want me to do?'

'In a few days' time we have a suitcase coming through Manchester Airport and need it picking up before it goes through customs. If you know what I mean.' Ibrahim gave him a cocky wink.

'If it's drugs, or arms, you can count me out! No way I'm getting involved in that shit. Big-time prison sentence.'

'Chill, it's not drugs or guns,' Ibrahim reassured him.

'Don't mean to be rude but what are you smuggling?' Mickey asked.

Ibrahim paused, knowing Mickey wouldn't get involved if he didn't reveal the cargo, 'Replica jewellery.'

'Seriously?'

'Yeah.'

'Why do you need me then? Surely you could just declare that through customs no bother. Just pay the tax, job done.'

'Look, I can't go into details,' Ibrahim said 'but we can't do it that way. That's all you need to know.'

'How much we talking?' Mickey asked.

'If you pull it off without problems, seven up front, seven on delivery.'

'Seven hundred quid?'

'Thousand.'

Mickey's eyes widened. 'Fucking hell! Fourteen grand just to bring a suitcase full of fake jewellery through the back door!'

'That's the job. I'm going to the gents. You can talk it over with your dad? When I get back I need to know if you're in or out.'

Ibrahim stood up and made his way over to the men's, leaving Mickey limited time to objectively ponder his dodgy proposition.

'Is this guy for real?' Mickey asked, his voice changing pitch.

'Yep, deadly serious. You've got about five minutes to make your mind up. He doesn't mess about. He'll just find somebody else. Thought you wanted the banks off your back?'

'I do. The weekly interest is bastard killing me.'

'It's what they call a no-brainer then, innit?' His dad said like an annoying second-hand car dealer.

'What's in it for you?'

'Finder's fee.'

He shot him a disapproving stare. 'Sodding fiddler's fee!'

'Unfortunately, I've got some money troubles of my own son.'

Ibrahim returned from the gents and pressed for an answer. 'Do we have a deal?'

Squirming in his chair, ill at ease Mickey, agreed, lured by the prospect of squaring up with the bank in one payment.

'Great, now we celebrate.' Ibrahim ordered three single-malt whiskys from the passing barmaid. With a warm whisky glow inside, Mickey sat there listening to the details of what his role was, which in principle sounded easy enough, although the rational part of his brain was telling him if caught he'd be sacked with the possibility of a custodial sentence. He knew full well those anal twats at customs operated a stringent no mercy policy.

'OK, here's how we're playing this. You keep this mobile charged and with you all the time. It's untraceable,' Ibrahim said, passing it over.

'OK.'

'I'll text you forty-eight hours before the plane lands with the flight numbers and information about which case it is. Don't use the phone to call anybody else.'

CHAPTER 60

It was ten hours since the Danish trawler left Liverpool docks Yusuf slowly opened his eyes and looked around the unfamiliar surroundings of the tiny cabin, which would serve as his makeshift bedroom for the next few days. Having been in a prison cell most of the day before and then travelling for a further twelve hours, without regular meals, fatigue and tiredness were starting to drain him of mental clarity. Climbing off the bunk he felt the boat rise and fall under his feet. Steadying himself with an outstretched arm on the handrail, he flung open the cabin door and went in search of food.

Up in the control room, the captain was perched on a high seat carefully rolling himself a smoke. The balding 58-year-old's face had more lines than an ordnance survey map. A real lived-in sailor's complexion, which had probably weathered more storms than a lighthouse.

'Looking rough, boy,' he said in a distinctly Bristol dialect.

Too tired to respond, Yusuf asked, 'Where's the food?'

'You'll be wanting to see Simon for that.'

'Who?'

'My man over aft there.'

Not fully comprehending the captain's strange accent, Yusuf nodded in agreement, then ambled out of his domain, clinging onto the side of the boat. Cool sea water sprayed his hands and face lightly as the boat ploughed through the choppy summer waves. The second mate's pale-blue gill trousers mirrored the sky as he rocked back and forth on the deck in the morning sun. Yusuf cautiously approached him, still trying to get used to the boat's movement.

'Captain says you'll show me where the food is?'

Nodding in acknowledgement, the seaman stopped what he was doing and made his way over to the hungry Turk. 'This way,' he said, passing him without so much as a wobble before disappearing through the door below deck. Almost losing his footing on the near-vertical stairs Yusuf eventually made it to the tiny kitchen, which consisted of a Formica worktop displaying several pan burn rings, an ancient cream microwave, a kettle, two electric rings and a lopsided cupboard stacked full of tinned and dried food goods.

Pointing inside the cupboard the second mate guided Yusuf through the supplies. Best bet, if you're looking for quick meal, is one of these packet pasta meals. Slap it in a pan of boiling water, job done! Tea and coffee are in the jars. Milk's in here,' he said, knocking on the rust-spattered fridge door located under the worktop.

Being useless in the kitchen, Yusuf took his advice and opted for the packet pasta. Within ten minutes he sat at the tatty breakfast counter on a high stool, scoffing like a starving street urchin.

The captain informed him that his passage to the France would take almost four days, barring freak weather. Being only ten hours into the arduous trip, the thought of swaying constantly with bugger all to do except listen to the radio or read, made him feel nauseous. Moving over into the mid-ship lounge, he dropped onto the sofa, picked up a dog-eared two-day-old copy of a UK national newspaper and skimmed the headlines.

Not been a regular newspaper reader, he couldn't believe how much bad news there was. Everything from child abduction to major terrorist plots being foiled. He'd soon seen enough of this so-called news to last a lifetime, so ambled back to his bunk for a long overdue rest.

CHAPTER 61

Upon arrival at Stoke Royal University Hospital, Blake discovered the car park was chock-full, so he abandoned his car on a grass embankment, disinterested in the consequences. He dashed over to the reception desk and barged his way to the front, to the displeasure of the other queuing visitors.

The receptionist directed him towards the Critical Care Unit. On the second floor he buzzed himself through and was greeted by a young male doctor wearing large-framed eighties-style specs, who looked fresh out of med school.

Blake followed him to Isabel's bedside. Seeing his only child lying prostrate on a ventilator with tubes in her mouth and arms flooded his mind with distressing images of his deceased wife and son. Fighting back tears he bit his lip in anguish.

'I… is she going to live, doctor?' he murmured painfully.

'She's taken a nasty blow to the head from ground impact. Apart from that her other injuries are superficial: cuts and scratches. There's no broken bones or spinal injury, which is unusual. Normally there's multiple fractures when a vehicle hits a pedestrian. Your daughter's on a ventilator because the head trauma has made her breathing erratic. The next forty-eight hours are critical. If she pulls through that, then hopefully she'll improve. But there's no guarantee; the brain is very complex. Fortunately, the CT scan revealed nothing to be concerned about. I'm afraid all we can do is wait.'

Like a sniper shot taking him down, Blake dropped into a high-back visitors' chair next to the bed. Bringing a shaky hand to his forehead, he sighed deeply, wondering if he'd been singled out to receive triple his share of devastation by some divine power.

'I want to stay with her.'

'Of course, I'd expect nothing less. This ward is designed for twenty-four-hour visitors. I know it's a very distressing time, but I can assure you Isabel will receive the best possible care we can provide. We'll be checking on her around the clock. If you have any further questions, or need to speak to me any time regarding your daughter, here's my number.' The young doctor passed over his card.

Blake nodded a polite gesture of thanks but the shock rendered him mute of any meaningful reply. He just sat there looking at the myriad of medical devices hooked up to his precious girl. Two that he recognised instantly were the heart monitor and the ventilator. The other hi-tech screens and devices, although obviously designed to assist bodily functions, scared the hell out of him. It all looked so serious.

He was no stranger to an ICU unit, but questioning a victim's family, although sad, didn't engage the kind of emotions he was experiencing; it didn't even come close. Empathy was endearing but lacked the heart-wrenching intensity of blood ties.

Blake spent a few hours pacing around Isabel's bed before the tension became just too much, so he decided to go into the station to see if there were any developments in the Barry Gibson murder case. He desperately needed a distraction.

CHAPTER 62

Taking over temporary operational duties from his DI, DS Murphy stood in front of three white boards in the major incident room. The first one had gruesome pictures of the murder victim Barry Gibson, bloody and slumped in the toilet cubicle of the White Horse. Posted below it were sequential crime scene images. The second board contained pictures of Nathan Dukes, Darryl Connor, Dave Millburn and Yusuf Benzar.

He cleared his throat and the assembled team quietened. He was just about to read from his notes when DI Blake entered the room and shuffled to the back and sat down. DS Murphy gave him a sympathetic smile.

'This is the second briefing of the Barry Gibson murder case. Having gathered more intelligence about him from family, friends and known associates over the last few days, we now have a clearer picture of the type of man he was. It seems Mr Gibson made a lot of enemies especially in an area of the town we affectionately refer to as the Bermuda Triangle: e.g. Tontine Street, Parliament Row and Percy Street.

Because his drinking habits often escalated into abusive behaviour, he was prone to the odd fight in and around that area. In fact, Barry Gibson was involved in two altercations in the White Horse on the night he was murdered, the second one led to his death. Unfortunately one of the key suspects Grant Bolton; the first man he argued with, escaped arrest from a derelict factory in Tunstall. His DNA has been taken from the scene, and we know he's got form for football violence. So at this point he can't be ruled out.

Because Gibson was a known troublemaker, by several landlords and door staff, we questioned Nathan Dukes, one of M8's bouncers, whilst he was in custody. We discovered that in the line of his work he was involved in a fight with Barry Gibson. Medical records show that Dukes stamped on his arm after ejecting him from the Burton Stores a couple of years ago, due to an alleged sexual assault on Dukes' girlfriend. Barry Gibson had to have pins and reconstructive surgery to his arm. Murphy pointed to the next mugshot. 'We also questioned the landlord of the White Horse Darryl Connor who's done time for GBH. Again there is a link between Connor and the victim. When he and his Polish wife first took over the pub, Gibson made sexual and anti-Polish remarks to her. She subsequently made a complaint to the police. However, Connor claims Gibson later apologised to him and his wife, and they both forgave him. Which was probably a shrewd business, not personal decision, based around Gibson putting money behind the bar regularly. Both Darryl Connor and Nathan Dukes had means, motive, and opportunity to murder Gibson. Dave Millburn, a second bouncer at the crime scene was also questioned, but we couldn't establish any link between him and the victim, and his DNA has been ruled out by SOCO as circumstantial. To recap, the pathologist confirmed that a small, very sharp knife was forced into the wound Barry Gibson sustained to the back of his skull, and then left to bleed out, but there's still no clear suspect.

DI Blake stood up and interjected. 'John if I may clarify this point, I think it will help?'

'Go ahead, boss.'

'Drop point blades are popular survival knives, because they are extremely tough. But, although they're easy to conceal, this isn't the weapon of choice for the average nut-job on the street. It's the kind of blade used by survival specialists, but could equally be used by someone into camping. Unfortunately they're relatively cheap, and can be bought online. These kind of knifes are mainly owned by males who either collect weapons, or are survivalists. DC Longsdon, get on to Connor's, Dukes', and Millburn's banks. Pay specific attention to any online purchases from survival or weapons websites. Even if we don't find the murder weapon, lets at least trace it to a suspect?

'Another point of interest is our victim's toxicology report. This shows not only a high level of alcohol in his blood stream, but also a potent compound of MDMA ecstasy. If he was a regular user then there'll be a dealer involved. Meaning it's quite possible he owed money to him for drugs. We know Yusuf Benzar is a dealer. It's possible he could be the source supplier through a smaller distributer, who we think might be a bloke known to Barry Gibson as Stomper… which is another motive to consider. As yet we've been unable to identify who Stomper is, and he remains a suspect.' Blake said before giving Murphy the nod.

'Thank you, boss. To further muddy the waters both the bouncers and the landlord used the toilets that night. Connor and Dukes also kicked in the door, traipsed through the blood and contaminated the scene, making it even more difficult to prove or disprove either of them carried out the killing. Interestingly Connor went missing around ten, for a whole fifty minutes. We have him on CCTV for some of that time, but it appears he went off the radar just after ten, and wasn't seen again until he returned to the pub when the incident was called in. Unfortunately, apart from trace elements of the victim's blood on his shoe soles, obtained when he entered the gents, we don't have anything else on him *yet.* The shoe prints in the window where the murder exited are the same size as Dukes' and the landlord's, but the tread pattern doesn't match those worn by either on the night. However, because both left the pub during the murder time-line, and they were wearing very similar black polo shirts and black trousers… M8's uniform, it's quite possible they could have changed into a spare uniform, and shoes at some point, before calling it in. We later learnt that both men had cars parked close by; sadly this was overlooked at the time, but later searches of those vehicles were negative. Its possible plastic bags were used to dispose of the incriminating clothes. Ultimately, nobody would have noticed if they had changed. Bearing this in mind, Dukes and Connor still remain suspects until proven otherwise.

'What about Barry Gibson's outstanding debt to the escaped prisoner Yusuf Benzar? Surely he must be a key suspect?' the office manager, Nick Pemberton, asked.

'I was just coming to that. Because Benzar has absconded we have very little to link them apart from the fact that our victim owed him a grand. There's also no evidence to place him at the scene of the crime. In fact his alibi is rock solid. He was at the Genting Casino when the murder took place. Although we can't rule out that Benzar didn't put out a contract on Barry Gibson. Interpol have issued a Code Red for his arrest and extradition. But it's unlikely he'll surface anytime soon considering the serious drug charges brought against him,' Murphy paused and took a slurp of his tea.

DC Moore held his hand up like a patient school kid. 'Is it possible all of the suspects could be linked to both Benzar brothers in some way?'

'It's a line of inquiry we'll be pursuing. I'm giving you an action… get onto Nathan Dukes' and Darryl Connor's mobile service providers and access their records. See if we can find any call history to Yusuf Benzar, or his brother Ibrahim. And finally we still need to consider the CCTV evidence of a man captured leaving the alley at the back of the White Horse. He could be our man, but as yet the public appeal has yielded nothing.'

CHAPTER 63

Ibrahim was absolutely livid at the balls-up the African brothers made of the kidnapping and subsequent escape of Isabel Blake. He knew it was only a matter of time before this pair of animals were arrested, and he couldn't guarantee their silence. Ultimately, there was too much at risk, and he decided they were expendable. He picked up his phone and dialled the heist benefactor.

Vivaldi's 'Four Seasons' ring tone drew the Collector's gaze from his precious gallery of stolen paintings.

'Session key?'

'Six-four-three-seven-X.'

'Code confirmed.'

In the fast-evolving world of corporate espionage and military strongholds, crypto phone technology was standard across the board. It was a case of: if you can't beat them, join them.

'We have a problem.'

'And that is?' the Collector asked, gazing at the ambient lighting casting shadows over the vaulted brick ceilings of his secret underground gallery.

'Yusuf was arrested; we needed to leverage his release. So we kidnapped the arresting detective's daughter and bargained a switch for Yusuf. Unfortunately, the people I used fucked up. The girl escaped and they put her in hospital trying to recapture her, leaving us with some loose ends to tie up.'

'Your brother is a serious liability.'

'I know, but he's family,' Ibrahim said, trying to justify his actions.

'Kindred loyalty is endearing, but it's a weakness,' he said in the direct manner Ibrahim was accustomed to. 'You should choose your people more carefully.'

'They've done OK in the past.'

'Past results don't always guarantee future success: first principle of good economics. No matter, we need to see beyond this trite interruption to our plans. Do these people need a vacation?'

'Definitely. One-way tickets.'

'OK, send me the details through our usual secure channel and I will arrange for one of my operatives to organise their tickets.'

Although the Collector hated corporate business, he'd taken some powerful strategies from America's best business minds and implemented them into his crooked arsenal. Like a chess-master he was always one step ahead of the game and his network of highly renumerated operatives could be dropped anywhere in the world within twenty-four hours.

'Anything else?'

'No. We have a final meeting soon to ensure everyone knows their role.'

'Excellent, make sure there's no more fuck ups. Your people need briefing properly to make them aware of their commitments to this project. Once you are ready let me know and a courier will drop the operational cash off. The rest will be delivered on completion,' he said, gazing at the priceless 'Storm on the Sea of Galilee' taken from the fourth chapter of the Gospel of Mark in the New Testament.

The picture was one of thirteen grandmasters stolen from the Isabella Stewart Gardner Museum in Boston in 1990. This heist was considered the largest art theft in world history, with a collective value in excess of $500 million.

The Collector's appetite for the world's greatest art and antiquities knew no bounds and was parallel with a serious addiction. His gallery spanned three floors and contained a secret passageway down to the beach. Over a thirty-year period he'd filled it with priceless stolen artefacts, valued at around nine-hundred million.

On the premature death of his father as an only child, he'd inherited his Texas oil fortune at just nineteen. But after only two years at the helm, he sold the oil empire for the tune of one billion to a large conglomerate.

He visited the gallery at least twice a day and sat on one of the carefully placed Chesterfield sofas, basking in delusions of grandeur, whilst listening to soothing classical music, and savouring the smoke of his beloved Dunhill Red cigarettes.

Sometimes the euphoric feelings he got from the experience would be so overwhelming he'd masturbate. But right now his number one priority was the procurement of the Staffordshire Hoard. The largest haul of Anglo-Saxon gold ever found in the world.

He first became aware of the Hoard's discovery via CNN World News. However, due to the covert nature of his lifestyle and his criminal record, he didn't venture from US soil. When the Hoard tour brought the ancient treasure to the National Geographic Museum in Washington DC, he was ecstatic at getting within touching distance of the exquisite collection.

CHAPTER 64

Blake could tell by the look on Coleman's face it wasn't good news.

'Take a seat, Tom?'

He sunk down into the leather like a knight about to fall on his sword.

'I'm afraid it's bad news. After yesterday's debacle featured in last night's *Sentinel*, you've left me with no choice but to assign you to duties away from the public. What I'm struggling to comprehend is how the bloody hell the prisoner arranged escape from the confines of his cell, and then pulled a Houdini act on the handcuffs. It beggars belief, to be honest. Shit rolls downhill, Tom. Yesterday I had an interesting conversation with the Regional Commander, or, should I say, took it with both barrels. Let's just say the noises coming from HQ aren't good at all. There's talk of an internal investigation.'

Blake hesitated for a moment deliberating how to tell his CI what really happened. What was the worst they could do? He'd already been assigned to desk duties. There'd be an inquiry so best to come clean he thought; surely the powers that be would realise the immense pressure he was under. After all his daughter's life was at stake. Nobody would really blame him, would they?

Coleman's brows knitted in a frown. 'Well, Inspector, what do you have to say?'

Blake jumped straight in. 'Sir, the day before yesterday I received an anonymous call from some criminals asking probing questions about Yusuf Benzar's transit time to remand prison the following morning. At first I thought it was some kind of wind-up, until they dropped the bombshell that they'd abducted my daughter Isabel. Eventually she came on the phone extremely frightened saying they had guns.'

Coleman looked shocked. 'Seriously, Tom?'

'Yes, sir.'

'I wasn't expecting that, it's terrible news. Why didn't you come to me straight away? I would have put a team on it immediately.'

'I'm afraid it wasn't an option, sir. They threatened to harm Isabel if any other police were involved. I just couldn't take the risk. I hope you understand?'

The muscles in Coleman's face tightened, concealing his emotions. 'Tom, I'm really distressed to hear this. Is she OK?'

'No, sir.' His eyes welled with tears. 'I negotiated her release but Isabel tried to escape and was involved in a hit-and-run. She's in intensive care.'

'Oh my god! I really don't know what to say.'

'There's nothing you can say, sir; she's on life support at present with a serious head trauma.'

His tone of voice changed. 'Jesus, that's bloody awful! What have the hospital said?'

'She's on a ventilator because the head trauma has affected her breathing. The next forty-eight hours are critical. If she pulls through that they're hopeful she'll improve,'

For once Coleman was speechless.

'I'd really appreciate it if we kept this quiet for now, just until Isabel starts to pull through. I realise that will be difficult with regards to professional standards, but I don't want anyone else in the station knowing yet.'

'I can't make any promises, Tom, but I'll do my best to keep the vultures at bay for now. I take it DS Murphy knows about Isabel?'

'He knows about the hit-and-run and her admittance to the ICU. But not about the abduction,' Blake lied, to protect his DS.

'Tom, I strongly advise you to take immediate compassionate leave. We can discuss how long you'll need once Isabel's on the mend. And, before you say anything, I insist.'

Blake knew better than to argue, besides there was no way he could continue working at present. His mind was shot and he needed to visit the hospital regularly.

Coleman stood, came round to the front of his desk and placed a sympathetic hand on his shoulder. 'You take care, Tom. Look after your daughter. I'll explain the situation to the Regional Commander. I'm sure he'll understand; he's got children of his own. Regarding getting the bastards that did this I'll discuss our options with DS Murphy this morning and keep you in the loop.'

Blake stood and shook his hand. 'Thank you, sir. It eases some of the burden knowing you're on side.'

The hospital chair was designed to be comfy, but Blake simply couldn't relax whilst his daughter lay opposite, hooked up to a myriad of Intensive Care equipment. The duty nurse informed him that during his absence there'd been positive changes to Isabel's condition, and the consultant would be on the ward in a few minutes to give him a more detailed prognosis.

Alert, he became acutely aware of movement. Suddenly he heard voices in the corridor. The consultant stood in discussion with the duty nurse before entering the room.

'Mr Blake? I'm Doctor Rani, head consultant of the Intensive Care Unit,' he said, offering a reassuring handshake. 'You'll be pleased to know that Isabel's making good progress. Her heartbeat has returned to normal, and she could breathe unaided by the ventilator for two hours early this morning. We will try again later. Hopefully she'll be able to come off most of this equipment within the next forty-eight hours. She's young and her immune system is strong.'

'Thank God!' He sighed with relief. 'Will she be OK? I mean her brain?'

'It's early days yet but fortunately her scan showed no underlying brain damage. The signs look good at this stage, but we can never be one hundred per cent until a patient regains full consciousness.'

Blake felt a sudden floating sensation as the heavy burden he'd been carrying around for the last two days lifted. Wiping back tears of joy, he found the strength to believe everything would be all right. 'Thank you, Doctor, I can't tell you how much that means. Is there anything I can do to help Isabel?'

'Most definitely. I was just coming to that. Relatives can play a key role in a patient's recovery by helping to stimulate their senses. If you could bring some of Isabel's favourite things in. Talk to her, show family pictures. Read her favourite book and play music she likes. The most important thing is to stay positive whilst in your daughter's company. I know it's difficult, but best to leave your worries at the door. Research shows just as positive things are felt and sensed, so are the negatives.'

CHAPTER 65

The African brothers fuck-up of the Isabel Blake kidnapping highlighted their limitations. The fact there was such a personal police connection to the kidnapping meant their arrest was imminent. Ibrahim couldn't take the risk of being connected to this. Hence the swift call to the Collector to arrange their disappearance.

At ten a.m. the next day a taxi pulled up in Coals End Street, Shelton. A broad man about six feet, wearing a camel trench coat, retrieved a small black overnight case, from the cab's boot. His slick hair was gelled back, and his clean-shaven face gave no clues to his business. To the groups of students heading toward the university, he was just another non-descript businessman. This was exactly the type of professional the Collector used: someone who could blend in with their surroundings undetected, working under the radar, leaving no trace like a ghost in the shadows.

Veda Brimnull, AKA the Executioner, was only known by a handful of shady gangsters, as one of the UK's most dangerous assassins who'd never been caught. People who acquired his services did not know his name. They simply wired fifty per cent of his thirty thousand fee and the details of the contract.

Within two hours of an encrypted conversation with the Collector, Brimnull knew where the African brothers lived and, using Google maps, had identified a vantage point behind their house from where he could take the shots undetected. But first he needed coffee and a sandwich. He hated takeaway food; it was unhealthy garbage. A Parma ham and cheese salad baguette nestled in his case alongside the tools of his trade.

It was far too risky to break and enter during broad daylight, so he checked into the Grand County, a Victorian hotel situated close to Stoke train station, to freshen up before changing into street clothing. After showering he lay on the bed reading Bram Stoker's *Dracula*, fascinated by the atmosphere of the period and the vampire's ability to seduce women. A recent series of BBC Two programmes on Gothic horror and their authors had rekindled his interest in the classics. He'd polished off Mary Shelley's *Frankenstein* just the week before. He loved books, because, unlike films, they lasted much longer, immersing the mind in another world for days; providing pure escapism from any troubling thoughts.

An hour later he strolled up College Road, using his mobile satnav to guide the way. Once in Coals End Street, he glanced at the African's house, before briefly checking out the alleyway and derelict row of properties opposite.

Later that evening, under the cover of darkness, he returned to the alleyway and stealthily moved towards the house directly opposite the Simbalas. He pushed the rotten black tongue-and-groove gate; it swung open, and he entered the heavily littered terraced yard, sliding the bolt across behind him. Surprisingly, it was still intact.

The usual galvanised security panels were screwed to all the downstairs windows and doors.

He clicked on his mini LED torch and shone its powerful beam into his rucksack, retrieved a battery screwdriver and set to work removing the eight screws securing the panel over the back door. Within minutes it was leaning up against the window.

He entered through the rain-sodden door into a galley kitchen, with empty cupboard carcasses attached to the walls. He flashed the torch around the foul-smelling back room to ensure it was empty. A rat's eyes glinted back at him before scurrying off under the stairs. Pistol in hand, he crept up the stairs carefully making sure each tread was safe.

Once in position in the bedroom overlooking number 32, he saw the entire row was derelict so the chances of being disturbed were minimal. The upstairs window wasn't boarded, which made things a lot easier. He retrieved his headlight from the bag, switched it on and assembled the twenty-grand purpose-built sniper rifle, which fitted with ease into his rucksack and could be dismantled in less than one minute. He made all his own bullets. Each untraceable batch was different, and he always destroyed the jig after the job.

He attached the night vision sites, then propped the rifle against the far wall and moved over to the window to assess opening it. It was pointless using a silencer if you were going to shoot through glass, pure stupidity. Disappointingly, sliding a jemmy bar under the sash window revealed it was jammed. He sprayed the sides with liquid oil and waited a few moments for it to work free. Moments later the rifle poked through a four-inch gap and rested on the windowsill pointing directly at the darkened rear windows of number 32 opposite.

Would they be on time, was the key question in his mind? Ibrahim had informed the Collector he'd made arrangements for the pair to be in the property for 10.30 p.m. They were unwittingly expecting a payoff for the kidnapping. It was now ten p.m. He waited, listening to soothing classical piped through headphones plugged into his mobile.

Suddenly, the lights came on and one of the African brothers stood in the bedroom window smoking a cigarette. Could he take the first shot now, or would that alert his brother? Where was he, he thought, angling the rifle's sights onto the downstairs window overlooking the backyard? 'Gotcha!' He was sitting in an armchair in semi darkness, swinging a chain of rosary beads.

Veda knew the window of opportunity was slight and the guy downstairs was likely to be there longer than his brother, who, after finishing the cigarette, might leave the room. Decision made, he adjusted the sights a fraction until Frederick Simbala's forehead was dead centre in the cross hairs. Without hesitation he eased the trigger. No kickback, no tracer fire, just a silent thud as the rifle discharged its deadly shot through its silencer. Motionless he watched the victim drop to the floor like a deer being felled. Seconds later Jozef Simbala lay slumped in his chair, head pegged back, blood flowing from a hole the size of a penny like a lazy stream into his left eye and down his face.

He stayed put for a further twenty minutes of observation, just to make sure, before stealthily drifting away like winter clouds passing under cover of darkness. A 7.30 a.m. the taxi ferried Brimnull away, just as a dark-blue unmarked delivery van pulled curbside of number 32 Coals End Street, Shelton.

CHAPTER 66

Two men in black overalls climbed out of the dark-blue unmarked transit van. The first and broader man walked around to the back of the vehicle, opened the doors and latched them. The second retrieved a key to number 32 from a disposable bin liner and glanced around the street to make sure nobody was watching.

He opened the front door wide and dropped the bag on the carpet. They both returned to the van and slid out a fully assembled wardrobe covered with protective bubble-wrap. Jostling it into the front room, they closed the door behind them without uttering a word. Before stepping any further, both donned silicone gloves, forensic body suits and booties over their shoes. Padding through into the sparse middle room, they scanned around. It was dominated by a dated-looking 80s-style cream leather sofa and armchair.

Jozef Simbala lay motionless in the armchair, head leaning towards his left shoulder. A handful of blowflies danced around a small gunshot wound an inch above his bulging eyes, staring towards the bullet entry hole in the back window as if they'd almost seen it coming. Which they both knew was impossible; bullets exceeded three thousand feet per second.

In sync the two men made the sign of the cross. The unofficial undertakers adopted catholic protocols and felt it was important to ask for God's blessing.

'Murder victims they may be, but everyone's entitled to a blessing,' said the broader man in a rough Scottish accent, through his paper mask.'

'Wi'out doubt,' said his brother in agreement.

Rituals over with, they peeled the corpse precariously from the chair and carefully heaved it into an open body bag laid out on the dank floral carpet. The only sound in the room was the bag's long zip being drawn. Moving the body to one side they climbed the stairs.

The sinister cleaners had devised a devilishly simple but effective way of removing cadavers undetected. Their MO involved delivering a brand-new wardrobe and removing an old one, if indeed there was one. The older vessel acted as a coffin. In the absence of an old wardrobe they simply unwrapped the new one and used that instead. They took advantage of the fact that, unlike the old days, people living in ethnically diverse areas such as this often didn't know their neighbours. Half the properties were landlord-owned with a high turnover of tenants, which meant vans moving furniture were a common sight and rarely raised an eyebrow.

They located a sturdy plywood wardrobe in the front bedroom, but on opening it were shocked to find an evil-looking shrine daubed in black paint built inside its interior. An old wooden fruit box covered in occult paraphernalia sat vertical upon a shelf spanning the middle. On top of it a devil's head sat in the centre of two animal skulls, staring at them with its tongue hanging out. A crucifix hung from the end. Two six inch skeletons swung on chains below the ominously smirking figure of Lucifer.

Startled, the broad man said nervously, 'What the fuck is that?'

'Looks like a shrine.'

'You dunni say,' the other said sarcastically. 'I know it's a bloody shrine! Seen a film with stuff like this in it. It's Voodoo. That's what that is. Bad medicine, doll's curses and all that shite!'

'Makes sense since the deceased are African?'

'Whatever it is, it's giving me the bloody creeps. Let's get him bagged and away outa of here quick, sharp,' he said, glancing at the slumped corpse of Frederick Simbala lying in a heap on blood-stained carpet under the window.

'You dunni think we'll be cursed for this?'

'That's all bollocks,' the other said, scattering the sinister objects from the shrine onto the bed. With that they levered the wardrobe through the door and inched it down the stairs manning the top and bottom.

Moments later the Simbala brothers lay side by side in the middle room, bagged like cargo waiting to board a ship. It was a squeeze but both corpses just about fitted inside the wardrobe leaving the door about an inch from closing. They tightened two ratchet straps around the top and bottom clamping the doors firmly shut.

With the makeshift coffin loaded onto the aluminium trolley in the front room, the men removed all forensic attire, apart from their gloves, glanced around the street again, before wheeling the wardrobe to the back of the van.

Within twenty minutes the vehicle and its cadaver cargo hurtled northbound up the A500 towards the M6 motorway. With no passports, visas, national insurance numbers or birth certificates, like a passing storm in the night, the African brothers never existed.

By the time they reached the North Link Ferry crossing at Scrabster, Scotland, the light was fading. A flame-orange and salmon glow painted the sky as the setting sun on the horizon signalled another warm summer day would follow. The Hamnavoe Ferry crossing to Stromness on the Isle of Orkney took one and a half hours. The sea rolled calmly as the ferry cut through the deep waters.

The two men relaxed in the Hawksfall lounge sipping tea, gazing in wonder at Britain's highest vertical cliffs and Orkney's famous Old Man of Hoy, a 449 foot high sandstone Sea stack jutting out from the cliffs of the island of Hoy like a castle turret guarding the island.

They disembarked the ferry and headed along the winding B9047, which curled like a snake through the violet heathers that carpeted the island. After thirty minutes they turned into the gravel path leading up to their remote stone cottage and its outbuildings overlooking Pegal Bay. Forty thousand pounds richer.

This was their fiftieth clean-up job in the last ten years. Soon they would have enough to retire, but for now their huge fifteen by thirteen feet outdoor log furnace needed stoking to a temperature of a hundred and seventy degrees.

Climbing out of the transit Bryce Kennan gave his brother Fraser a sheepish grin. 'A wee dram?'

'Oh aye, definitely. It's been a nightmare of a dee. The furnace can wait, there's nae rush.' Bryce retrieved the keys to the stone cottage from his jeans and opened the back door to the kitchen.

'Glen Grant or Old Pulteney?' Fraser asked opening a pine corner cupboard, which they stored their expensive whisky collection in.

'Fancy a touch of vintage Glen Grant.'

'Coming up, son.' He laid out two cut-crystal tumblers on to the worktop and poured out a generous two-finger slug in each.

They chinked glasses and took a ritualistic sip in unison.

'Superb!' Bryce said, savouring the dry cheek pulling, spicy cinnamon and raisin ten-year-old single malt.

'Aye, better than a shag that.'

'No' quite, son. I'd prefer banging the back out of a filthy trollop, but I kin where you coming from.'

'Same again?'

'All day pal, all day.'

Twenty minutes and four glasses later they drew the transit closer to the furnace ready to load the cadavers once it was hot enough. The Tennessee Furnace's door was thirty-five inches wide, which enabled them to load and incinerate large objects with little fuss. Irrespective of what they shoved in, it kept their cottage warm during the severe Highland winters.

Fraser stumbled whilst lighting the pilot light. His brother almost spilt the logs from the wheelbarrow. The pair were half cut, acting, like a couple of amateurs.

'I'm pissed, bro!'

'I know; it's our last job. Let's take another drink and come back later. This pair ain't going anywhere.'

Wobbling back to the house they decided to finish the job under the cover of darkness. By three a.m. the bottle of Glen Grant was empty and they could hardly stand.

'Let's call it a night, I'm creamed,' Bryce said.

'Why did we sink all the Granty. Not good, we've got business to take care of.'

'Fancy a tea to lubricate your throat?'

'Just the one mind?'

Fraser staggered into the kitchen, but slipped on the tiles and upended a chair. 'Shite, man!' he groaned, lying in heap rubbing his leg. Dragging himself up he regained his balance by holding onto their ancient gas stove, a relic they couldn't bear to part with because their dearly departed mother spent fifty years cooking the best lamb dishes on the island on it.

He turned the ring nearest the front on and tried to light the gas with matches. After three attempts and a burnt finger, the blue flame danced under the kettle. Fraser staggered back towards the living room using the walls and doorframes to keep him vertical. Bryce lay across the sofa snoring loudly.

'Tea for one it is!' he slurred, slumping into the armchair opposite his brother.

Outside heady summer winds gathered, sweeping across the cotton grasses and dense scrub of Pegal Bay, towards the cottage. In the kitchen a small transient window was propped open about an inch, its arm lightly jammed, but unlatched. A sudden gust of wind blew the gas ring out. The kettle stopped boiling as a second blast blew the window shut. Deadly butane gas from the large outside storage bottle hissed slowly into the kitchen, replacing oxygen with its silent death.

CHAPTER 67

Airbus 4580 from India landed on time at terminal one of Manchester airport. Mickey Connor intercepted the small black trolley case with the luminous green address tag, displaying the code word Midas. He placed it on a trolley of damaged cases and wheeled it away from the CCTV monitored conveyor belt of inbound luggage, to a storage facility where lost and damaged cases were placed temporarily before being dispatched. Once the door shut behind him, there was a small window of opportunity to transfer the boxes of Hoard replica pieces into his rucksack unobserved.

He fumbled nervously with the suitcase zip. A quick glance at his watch revealed he'd been in the storeroom for one minute already; any longer than five minutes would appear suspicious. Flattening the rucksack he slotted it into a gap in the trolley's wooden pallet base and exited the room. The cameras would pick it up as an empty trolley. It had taken a week of sleepless nights mulling over several permutations to devise this simple but ingenious method.

To his annoyance he'd have to give up a grand of his fourteen thousand smuggler's fee to a minor customs officer named Jeff McIntyre. This was the amount they'd agreed for him to turn a blind eye when checking staff bags at the end of the shift. Greedy Scottish twat stated he wouldn't do it if drugs were involved. The bastard practically blackmailed him, though Connor never divulged what the goods were, instead fed him a line about fake designer watches from India.

Later that evening he met Ibrahim in the Silk Wheel pub and staggered home pissed as a newt, fourteen thousand richer, but after weighing in McIntyre, and paying off the credit cards his ex-Mrs had run up he'd be left with nothing.

CHAPTER 68

DI Blake took compassionate leave to look after Isabel, during which he subtly asked about her abductors. Unfortunately, because of the head trauma, her memory hadn't fully returned. The only thing she could remember was two black men in a silver BMW; everything else was a blur. He passed this information onto DS Murphy.

Ever since her discharge from hospital he'd been fussing around her like she was an invalid, although there was no denying the horrendous migraines the doctor said would pass were debilitating.

Since regaining consciousness she developed a bizarre craving for warm, Staffordshire oatcakes smeared in peanut butter; nothing else seemed to appeal. And because Blake had no work to occupy him, he'd taken the opportunity to blitz the house, acutely aware that the vacuum cleaner was off limits.

During the time she'd spent camped on the sofa, they'd watched *White Chapel* series two, at least one episode of *Waking the Dead*, and laughed at Tony Hill's plastic carrier bags and eccentricities in the award-winning BBC drama *Wire in the Blood*. It was ages since they'd spent any quality time together. Just a pity it wasn't under better circumstances, Blake thought with a worried look at the scar on his daughter's partially shaved head.

The sight of it brought horrible memories of the fatal hit-and-run that killed his wife and son flooding back. He took a deep breath to calm roller coaster emotions that could drag him into a downward spiral of dwelling on the past. Clinging to Isabel, he swore to make the bastards who did this to her pay severely. But first he needed to focus on her convalescence.

After lunch, whilst Isabel took a nap, he wandered barefoot around the back garden nursing a large glass of Shiraz. It was a lovely summer afternoon, and the cool grass felt like deep velvet underfoot; the long garden seemed to come alive. A swarm of gnats spun frantically around the lid of his composter next to the summerhouse, a couple of song thrushes chirped merrily hopping from branch to branch of the elder in full bloom, its soft white flowers like tiny snowflakes. The soothing effects of wine and nature mellowed his anxiety.

Thirty minutes passed before he decided to wake Isabel. If she slept too long, she wouldn't sleep later. He sauntered back down the path towards the French doors when his heart suddenly hammered hard in his chest.

'Isabel!' he shouted, frantically running across the lawn. He jumped over the patio wall to find her lying unconscious on the decking. She must have tried to get his attention before collapsing. Blake whipped his phone off the garden table and called an ambulance. The operator asked if she was still breathing and prompted him to place her in the recovery position. By some miracle her breath was slow but steady.

Ten minutes later the paramedics gave her oxygen before whisking them off to Royal Stoke in a blaze of blue flashing lights.

Upon arrival at the hospital the paramedics handed Isabel over to the Intensive Care team who performed extensive tests to determine why she'd blacked out. After a few hours they'd stabilised her and the doctor informed Blake a further MRI scan revealed a small tumour the size of a pea. He was upset and angry there'd been no mention of this after the first scan a week ago.

'Mr Blake, I'm afraid the first scan didn't pick this up because it was so close to the edge of the cranial injury. 'I'm really sorry, now we've spotted it we can act quickly depending on the type of tumour it is.'

'Has the accident caused this?'

'No. The tumour appears to be a few months in growth, which means if your daughter hadn't been knocked down, it may not have been discovered until she started getting severe symptoms later down the line. It's a horrible twist of fate.'

Hearing this felt like a huge wrecking ball crashing into his head. He stood there paralysed, unable to speak. A sudden coldness spread through his body.

Lowering his voice to a whisper, almost not wanting to hear the words, he asked, 'Will she survive?'

'The tumour is tiny, and because we've discovered it early your daughter's chances of recovery should be very good. However, until the biopsy results are back, we can't be a hundred per cent. It all depends on what type it is; this will determine treatment.

'When will you know?'

'The biopsy will be done within the next few hours and we can fast track the results. I can appreciate this is very traumatic for you. As soon as the results come back I'll let you know straight away.'

Like a badly produced reel-to-reel movie, disturbing images of his wife and son's funeral in 2005 flashed through his mind. Sat shaking uncontrollably in a church full of mourners he'd felt desolate.

The consultant placed a hand on his arm. 'Mr Blake, are you all right? Would you like me to call someone for you?'

Barely hearing the question he wandered without sense of direction like a zombie down the corridor and headed out of the hospital car park, a broken man with no destination in mind.

Later that day Blake received a call from the consultant, requesting his presence to discuss Isabel's' test results. Back on the ward the young consultant told him it was a grade-two metastatic tumour and chemotherapy wasn't an effective treatment. In cases such as Isabel's a specialised form of treatment known as 'Proton Therapy' had proved effective in destroying these types of tumours. Sadly, the NHS had limited funding for this kind of treatment, which was extremely expensive, and it was unlikely his daughter would receive this in the UK. If he could raise the funds, or get a grant from a cancer charity, then they could refer Isabel to the US where they specialised in this ground-breaking treatment.

Later that evening, with his daughter still in hospital, Blake sat in disillusionment in his kitchen nursing a double whisky. Eventually he called DS Murphy who helped him drown his sorrows with half a bottle of Glenfiddich. Around 3.30 a.m. they'd finalised a four-pronged plan to raise the money for Isabel's treatment, which included applying for an urgent grant from the cancer trust, a JustGiving page in Isabel's name, a major whip-round of all the officers at the station, and a loan against the house. First thing in the morning Murphy promised him he would hop over to the *Evening Sentinel*'s main office, directly across the road from the station, and call in some favours – God knows they owed him plenty - and hopefully get the story published with a link to Isabel's JustGiving page within forty-eight hours.

CHAPTER 69

Murphy was woken by the lovely aroma of filter coffee, wafting into the open-plan kitchen and living room of Blake's house. He'd crashed out on the sofa around four, managing three hours kip. Blake, on the other hand, understandably tossed and turned until around five before dropping through sheer exhaustion. He rang the hospital at 6.30 a.m. after dragging his bones out of the shower, which did little to refresh him.

The ambulance crew had reported the hit-and-run incident to the police, but as yet the driver and vehicle had not been identified. Murphy vowed he would put some resources into getting the bastards who did this.

'Can't understand it, Tom. How the bloody hell can no one have seen anything. Weren't there any witnesses?'

'Just an old couple who found Izzy. The scumbags who ran her down had already left the scene. It's a really remote moorlands road, where she was found. There's no cameras.'

'Once I've been to the *Sentinel*, I'll have a look at the case report.'

'Get me a photocopy would you?'

'I'll drop it round after work. What time you back from hospital?'

'I'll be there most of the day. I'll call you later.'

Pumped up with Italian coffee, Murphy left Blake's house and joined the commuter traffic on Leek Road, heading towards the city centre. Blake had an early-morning appointment with his bank manager.

CHAPTER 70

Katrina Osborne shut the door of number 32 Cooper Street behind her, picked up her striped beach bag containing a change of clothes and make-up and headed towards the narrow passageway leading towards Foxley Lane. Ibrahim was picking her up at nine a.m. Thankfully Carl had already left for work forty minutes before.

The private-number-plated Audi Tropic was the only vehicle parked on the tarmac at the end of the alleyway. Ibrahim Benzar sat in the driver's seat skimming through messages on his phone. It had only been a few days since their lunch date. She never imagined there'd be a third date so soon, and she was a little nervous at seeing him again. This time they were off to Buxton, a beautiful spa town in the Derbyshire Peak District. Ibrahim had booked them into the Manor Hotel opposite the park, which she thought was pretty presumptuous.

She climbed in and kissed him on the cheek. He placed his phone into the doorwell pocket, and responded by kissing her on the lips.

Twenty minutes into the journey they'd reached the steep hill leading towards Ramshaw Rocks. Ibrahim stuck his foot down, and as the road levelled off, miles of barren Staffordshire moorlands came into view.

Huge five-storey sandstone houses lined St John's Road leading towards the town. Most of them were converted into hotels or nursing homes. Ibrahim turned left into Manchester Road. A minute later they'd parked outside the beautiful Victorian Manor Hotel. Their room wouldn't be ready until twelve-thirty, so they sat on a tan studded sofa and ordered a pot of coffee. Katrina gazed out of the large Victorian bay window at two huge trees in full bloom, gently swaying in the summer breeze. The sun was just starting to break through the dense cloud cover which had lasted most of the morning, but was now thankfully beginning to roll away eastwards leaving patchy, but promising clear, skies ahead.

Classical music piped subtly in the background of the empty lounge. A beautiful Red Admiral butterfly flew through the open window and danced around them, almost as if Mother Nature had choreographed it to perform. It was one of life's sublime moments. Katrina thought.

They finished the coffee and decided to wander into town. Although small, Buxton's architecture was very impressive; the magnificent Devonshire Dome being second in size only to St Paul's in London.

Ibrahim took her hand in his as they crossed the road and strolled towards the Crescent; a grade one listed building currently undergoing a fifty million pound restoration to transform it back to its former glory of an eighty bedroom spa hotel. Derbyshire council were aiming to put the town back on the national and international map as one of England's leading spa towns.

Turning round Kat pointed towards Saint Anne's fountain; a steady stream of the famous Buxton mineral water poured from an aged bronze lion head into the stone trough below it.

'Last time I came here was with my parents when I was a kid. You can drink the water from that fountain,' she said walking towards it.

Ibrahim followed her. They stood waiting for a rambler to fill his small bottle before each taking a sip with cupped hands. It was warm, but refreshing.

'Let's take a walk around the park?' Ibrahim suggested.

They entered through a gate in the cast-iron railings holding hands. It was such a beautiful Victorian park. The river meandered lazily through the middle, cascading over man-made waterfalls of rocks. A miniature steam train towing carriages full of excited kids, holding onto their parents tooted its horn and continued circling the track in the centre of the park.

'Can't believe the train's still running; my dad used to take me on it,' she reminisced.

Ibrahim leaned in and kissed her. 'What's happening with Carl? Does he suspect anything?' he said changing the subject.

'I don't think so.'

'Where did you tell him you were going tonight?'

'Said we'd been invited to a friend's hen night, out of town.'

'We?'

'Me and Luna.'

'And he believed you?'

'He got suspicious about who was paying for me. I told him Lune had a six hundred quid tax rebate and was treating us.'

'Okay, just as long as he doesn't harm you. I'll kill him if he touches you.'

'That's a bit extreme isn't it? She gave him a worried look.

'I suppose so, but I really like you Kat; I'd love us to spend more time together?'

She felt flattered, 'Let's just see how things work out. We might hate each other by tomorrow.'

'I don't think so,' Ibrahim said placing his hand on her lower back, ushering her.

They followed the path over the bridge and doubled back, past the bandstand heading towards the town.

Later that evening Ibrahim had booked a meal for 7.30 p.m. at a petite Italian restaurant in the town. After, a lovely romantic meal they strolled back towards the hotel for a nightcap. Unfortunately because there weren't many guests the bar had closed early, but Ibrahim managed to wangle a bottle of Prosecco and two glasses, to take up to their room.

Standing outside room fourteen, they kissed. Her lips felt soft and warm. Breaking off, he slipped the key into the door and ushered Kat through. Placing the glasses down on the dressing table he opened the wine and poured two generous measures. He removed his jacket and a hung it on the hook on the back of the door. Kat sat in the chair in the corner and removed her heels.

Ibrahim passed over the wine; she took a sip and looked at him.

'I could get used to being treated like a lady,' she laughed.

Ibrahim placed his wine down and padded towards her on the deep pale grey carpet.

'Put some music on your phone. The Wi-Fi is pretty good I tried it this afternoon,' Kat asked.

'What do you want to listen to?'

'Something slow and smoochy,' she smiled.

'Really?' Ibrahim took her hand and pulled her from the chair into his arms.

'What about the music?'

'Okay,' he fished his phone from his pocket and logged into his Youtube account. 'I've got just the thing here,' he said scrolling through his playlist, before tapping the auto-play button to start on Luther Ingram – *If Lovin You is Wrong I Don't Wanna be Right.*

He leaned it on the mirror and turned up the volume, then held her in his arms and embraced her.

Overcome with emotion Kat's eyes welled, a tear ran down her cheek. Ibrahim wiped it away gently and kissed her again.

'Don't cry, everything will be OK, trust me.'

'You're an old romantic,' she said holding his gaze.

They dropped onto the bed. He slowly unbuttoned her shirt dress and tossed it to the floor. She lay in her best lace underwear gazing at him, as he hurriedly undressed.

Unlike last time she wanted him to make love to her. Instinctively he knew, and responded by gently parting her legs and entered inside her whilst breathing on her neck. Slowly, his lips moved to hers and he kissed her, whilst softly stroking her hair. She climaxed as Bill Withers hit the last chorus of *Ain't No Sunshine When She's Gone.*

CHAPTER 71

The following day Isabel's story appeared on page two of the *Evening Sentinel.* Taking up half a page, including a photograph of her and Tom in happier times, it told of the compelling but tragic events that had led to the detective losing his wife and son in 2005, before tactfully moving on to Isabel's illness and pointing sympathetic readers to her JustGiving page; summarising with a *Crimestoppers'* number for anyone with information relating to her abduction and hit-and-run incident.

The newspaper started the ball rolling with a donation of four hundred quid from all the staff. This added to the two grand from the whip-round at the station, but left eighty-seven thousand to raise. Blake pleaded with his bank manager, but because he still owed forty thousand on his twenty-five-year mortgage, the slimy bastard offered him a loan against that of just fifteen-thousand, leaving a massive seventy-two thousand short fall.

The cancer charity said they were stretched to the limit with hundreds of grant applications for treatments in the current tax year. The hospital told him that, without treatment, Isabel might live another twelve months, a devastating thought he refused to consider. There was absolutely no way he'd let this happen, even if it meant selling everything he owned. Whilst it hurt like hell, it was a time for action, not wallowing hopelessly in self-pity. With a sense of renewed determination he called DS Murphy.

'John! Just wanted to thank you and everyone at the station for all the money they've pledged, the support is overwhelming. I'll try to call in on my way back from the hospital later.'

'Mate, I know you'd do the same for me or any other officer. How's Isabel?'

'The hospital are keeping her under observation for the next few days. I'm worried about her coming home. She could have another blackout. I've asked the mother-in-law to come over and look after her.

'Shit, that could be difficult. If you need extra help I could sit with her?' he offered.

'Thanks, appreciate it, just need to take it one day at a time.

'How'd you get on at the bank?'

'Bastards will only lend me fifteen grand.'

'Seriously? Soulless parasites!'

'I know, I'm gutted, but that's the situation. I pleaded with him, but you know what they're like. I'm going to sell my car and cash in some bonds. Still leaves around sixty-five grand to find.'

'I've got three grand in savings you can have.'

'No, John, you've done enough. I can't accept that,' Blake said, choked at Murphy's compassion.

'It's only money; I want you to have it. If you don't, I'll donate via JustGiving.'

'I'm not going to talk you out of it, am I?'

'No.'

Holding back tears, Blake paused for a moment at his friend's unbelievably kind gesture. 'I don't know what to say, John. Honestly, I'm touched.'

'No need.'

Blake could hear Nick Pemberton's familiar voice in the background.

'Sorry, Tom, I've got to go; new info's come through on the Gibson murder case. Have you looked at the hit-and-run incident report?'

'Yeah, nothing to go on, apart from the old couple's statement. They didn't see anything, thank God they called an ambulance'

'I'll call you in the morning if anything else comes in. Apparently a witness has come forward in the Gibson murder case, says she recognises our man on the CCTV picture.'

'Maybe some progress at last.'

'Take care, mate.'

CHAPTER 72

Blake thrashed around the sofa like a man drowning in the deepest ocean. Beads of sweat ran down his face as his temperature soared. The same lucid dream tormented him regularly. His wife's beautiful smiling face turned to the back of the car checking on little 8-year-old Dylan Blake.

Then without warning her head slams violently into the dashboard throwing her body round like a rag doll. The car spins before the huge force of impact with a dry stone wall leaves him unconscious.

Clouds rapidly pass through his flickering eyelids as blurred consciousness returns. Slowly his hand reaches out, but is touched by a silicone glove. He cries out for his wife and son. The paramedic shakes his head; his solemn voice delivers the heart-wrenching blow: 'They're gone.'

Early morning sun streamed through a chink in the curtains and glared off the glass coffee table. Blake shielded his eyes with a cupped hand, dragged his aching carcass off the sofa and reached for his mobile vibrating across the glass like an air hockey puck. He'd had another terrible night's sleep.

'Hello?'

'Tom, you OK?'

'Bit knackered mate, rough night.'

'I can't imagine. How's Isabel?'

'Still under observation'

'Shit mate, I'm really sorry to hear that. If there's anything you need just ask?

'Appreciate it, John. You've already done enough mate,' he said gratefully.

'I've got news. Patrol were called out to an abandoned BMW on the fields behind the Heath Hayes estate. Apparently kids have been playing in it for a few days. Someone tried to torch it but botched the job. The perp stuck a rag in the petrol tank, but a bloke training his greyhounds disturbed him. One of the dogs attacked him. Turns out he legged it before he could light the rag. The dog walker's identified him as a black male in his thirties. God only knows why he didn't report it sooner.'

Tired and impatient, Blake said, 'Don't want to sound rude, mate, but where's this leading?'

'Trust me, it's relevant. You said Isabel vaguely recalls a BMW and two black guys. We did a routine trace, which revealed the car is stolen. After scouring footage within a fifteen-mile radius, this vehicle's been picked up by a camera on Leek Road at the Milton crossroads leading up to Bagnall, on the day Isabel was taken.. Maybe I'm clutching at straws, but this has to be worth checking out. SOCO have recovered prints from the vehicle. I ran a PNC, drew a blank, but got a match for both sets on Interpol's UK feed; two brothers from Kenya wanted for murder and kidnapping in Belgium. Both are illegals. That's too many relevant facts to be coincidence?'

'Shit! I think you're right.'

'Brussels police are still after them for the murder of a kidnap victim. A rich diamond merchant's wife, who they shot after discovering the majority of their ransom money was fake. If we can identify them as known associates of the Benzar brothers, we may be onto something.'

'You reckon they could have used them for Isabel's abduction?'

'Afraid so.'

'I'll bring Ibrahim Benzar in for questioning. See if we can rattle his cage. I've asked Coleman to clear a search warrant for his home and businesses; it's being processed now. I know you're on leave, but I think we can swing it for you to be present at the house search. This will sound callous but is there any chance you can get Isabel's DNA, so we can test it against DNA found in the car?'

'If it helps nail these bastards, I'll get it over to you later today.

CHAPTER 73

Ibrahim Benzar sat behind his desk in the office at the back of the Slipware Tankard bar, scanning high-end villas in Ibiza. All the meticulous heist planning and his brother's latest fuck-up had drained him, he desperately needed a break.

A knuckle wrap on the door disturbed him. 'Not now, I'm busy.'

'Sorry to interrupt, Mr Benzar, but the police want to speak with you,' his bearded barman said nervously through a gap in the door.

'I told you if the police call I'm not here, you idiot.'

'I know, but they threatened to arrest me and storm the office if I didn't cooperate.'

'Keep them at the bar. I'll be out in a minute.' He panicked, before frantically speed dialling Bryant Preston, his solicitor.

'Bryant, it's Ibrahim Benzar. I think I'm about to be arrested. Be at Hanley police station in twenty minutes,' he said forcefully.

Ibrahim shut the laptop down and picked up his phone. But before he could even slip his jacket on DS Murphy, DS Jamieson and PC Haynes barged his office.

'Mr Benzar, can you accompany us to the station? We want to question you in connection with your brother's escape from custody.'

'Am I under arrest?'

'Let's just say you're helping us with our enquiries at this point,' DS Murphy said, not letting on about the kidnapping.

'Cuff him, PC Haynes,' Jamieson said.

'What's with the handcuffs?'

'Just a precaution, Mr Benzar,' PC Haynes replied.

Within twenty minutes Ibrahim Benzar sat next to his lawyer opposite DS Murphy and DS Jamieson in interview room two of Hanley police station. With an air of defiance he shot the detectives an arrogant look. DI Blake sat in the observation room down the hall staring angrily at Benzar on a twenty-inch monitor. He was finding it hard to resist the urge to barge in and rip his head off. Fortunately for the suspect Chief Inspector Coleman was sitting by his side.

'Right, Mr Benzar, here's what we know. On the eleventh of this month at 9.20 a.m., your brother Yusuf, aided by a high-powered motorcycle, escaped police custody from outside this station, causing a serious road accident. We suspect his escape was facilitated by the organised gang he associates with. This group used Detective Inspector Blake's daughter as leverage in a vile abduction plot. These people threatened to harm her if he didn't cooperate without informing his colleagues, compromising his ability as a policeman to act accordingly. The outcome of this kidnapping was near fatal. One of the kidnappers brutally knocked her down in a vehicle as she tried to escape. As a result Isabel Blake is now on life support in Royal Stoke.'

Jamieson cut in. 'However, before she was readmitted to hospital, Isabel told us two black men driving a silver BMW abducted her. Do you have any association with Frederick and Jozef Simbala?'

'Never heard of them!' he dismissed.

'We've run a PNC check on you. Unfortunately you don't have a record in the UK, but like the Simbalas you're also on Interpol's database with a criminal record for money-laundering and racketeering in Turkey. You served a four-year prison sentence in Diyarbakir Prison.

Benzar glanced at his solicitor, who nodded.

'That was a long time ago. I run legitimate businesses now.'

'I'm afraid we only have your word for that and, until we can confirm this, you're a key suspect in facilitating your brother's escape and Isabel Blake's abduction,' DS Murphy stressed, glancing at his lawyer.

Again, he turned to Bryant Preston before answering. 'I had nothing to do with Yusuf's escape,' he said defiantly.

DS Jamieson cut in. 'DI Blake received several calls from his daughter's abductors. Having spoken to you over the phone before in your mini-market, he's convinced you were the man blackmailing him?'

Rattled he said, 'That's a serious accusation. Where's your evidence?'

'Our tech team have examined DI Blake's phone records. The GPS mobile triangulation of the blackmailer's calls was suspiciously close to your home address – 56 Wade Road, Etruria.'

'Are you serious? That could have been anyone.' Benzar's solicitor continued taking notes before consulting his client.

'I think you'll find it's a valid line of enquiry. We've spoken to DI Blake's mobile provider. They've informed us that the phone used was a pay-as-you-go, with several numbers, which shows the caller tried to avoid being traced. Can you confirm your whereabouts on the tenth of this month, between ten and eleven in the morning?'

'I was at my martial arts gym, the Dojo.'

DS Murphy could tell by his quick fire response and twitchy body language he was back-peddling.

'Where's your gym?'

'Just off Marsh Street, Hanley.'

'Can anyone confirm this?'

'No, I was on my own; my instructor doesn't start work till twelve-thirty.'

'Did you drive to the gym that day?'

'Yes.'

'What's your vehicle registration?'

Benzar leaned towards his solicitor for acknowledgement; he had to answer.

'ABL I3.'

'We'll check CCTV footage.'

A worried expression appeared on Benzar's face.

DS Murphy's phone rang. 'OK, thanks for letting me know, will do, thanks Casey... That was PC Evans confirming we have a search warrant for your businesses and home address. Is there anything you want to tell us before we proceed?'

'Bastards!' His nostrils flared. He glanced at his solicitor for intervention, but Preston just nodded in agreement with the officers.

'Take it that'sa no, then?' DS Jamieson said sarcastically.

CHAPTER 74

Over the next couple of hours, three teams of four officers led by DS Murphy simultaneously searched Ibrahim Benzar's properties. At his home – flat 56 on Wade Road, Etruria – DI Tom Blake joined Murphy, and, since the property was empty, Coleman couldn't complain he was in breach of his current leave status. The flat was almost a carbon copy of his brother's a few streets away. Judging by the colour scheme and furniture layout of the contemporary interior, it looked like the same designer. Only this time it was a two-bed with a bigger bathroom, complete with a Jacuzzi bath.

'Tom, you start in here, while I take the bedroom,' DS Murphy said, switching roles with his DI.

'OK, boss!' Blake saluted, mockingly standing in the centre of the open-plan living room kitchen.

'You really should be at the hospital, Tom.'

'Going this afternoon. Can't sit around doing nothing while Izzy lies there, covered in tubes. It's driving me insane!' Blake said, just about to rummage through a high-gloss black cabinet next to the huge white leather sofa, but before he could open it his phone rang. He tapped the green answer button.

'Hello?'

'Mr Blake, it's Sister Owen from the Intensive Care Unit at Royal Stoke. Great news, Isabel is awake!'

'I'm on my way now!'

Elated he dashed towards the front door and shouted, 'John! Isabel's awake, I'm going. Let me know how you get on here.'

'That's fantastic, give her my best wishes.'

Disappointingly, the combined search of Ibrahim Benzar's flat and businesses yielded nothing incriminating. The CCTV footage in and around the city centre roads leading to the Dojo hadn't picked up his car on the day of his brother's escape. The crafty bastard claimed he'd dropped it off at Waxed handwash a couple of streets away, for a full valet. PC Evans called them to confirm this, and predictably they said it was there all day. The blackmailer's call couldn't be linked to him either and therefore had to be dismissed.

They'd failed to find a connection between him and the Africans. Instinctively both DI Blake and DS Murphy knew he was the organ grinder but didn't have enough evidence to charge him with anything. They released him from custody later that day with a warning not to travel outside Stoke-on-Trent for the next forty-eight hours, knowing criminals such as Ibrahim Benzar rarely got their hands dirty. Often there was a hierarchy to organised gangs, comprising multiple levels; the boss, senior advisers, bent accountants, techs and foot soldiers. Therefore, stealth, surveillance and informants all played a major role in bringing them to justice. But since they'd questioned two of the main players, one of which had escaped, the next course of action would be to pay Benzar's accountant a visit.

CHAPTER 75

'Mr Preston, we know you're in there? Open the door or we'll be forced to ram it through,' DS Murphy shouted through the wide-panelled Victorian door of the accountant's third floor Chambers situated in Albion House on Chambers Street, Hanley

A paranoid Malcolm Preston heard the screech of tyres outside and knew it would only be a matter of minutes before the cops ransacked his filing cabinets looking for links to Ibrahim Benzar, who'd warned him not to hang around if they came calling.

Without hesitation he yanked down the loft hatch and swiftly retrieved the telescopic maintenance ladder, clambered up, dragged the ladder back and shut the hatch. Then he frantically crawled through the loft space into the empty office opposite, which exited on to the fire escape running down the rear of the building onto the car park. As wood splintered, and the door banged open, he fled from the car park in the caretaker's battered Fiat Panda. Since the rusting chariot was worth less than executive relief at the knocking shop, he always left the keys in the glove box. Ironically he'd boasted for years that no one would nick the heap of shit. If he could get to Tesco he'd dump it, then jump into one of the shopper's taxis waiting outside. He'd be on platform one of Stoke station, ready to board the hourly London Euston train.

'Looks like he's already scarpered, Sarge,' PC Haynes exclaimed.

'Question is, how did he know we were coming. Something's not right. It's the second time a suspect in this case has escaped.' It's almost like someone is tipping them off.'

'I'm not so sure, Sarge.'

'PC Evans only called about five minutes ago pretending to be a potential client. Preston claimed he was quiet and could see her straight away so where is he?' Murphy responded scanning the room.

'Get your point. No one passed us on the stairs,' Haynes said.

'We're three floors up! There's only one way he could've escaped. Through the roof,' Murphy said pointing to the loft hatch.

'Grab one of those chairs, Roger, see if you can get it open? Crafty bastard might still be up there.'

DS Jamieson lifted the top moulded plastic chair off a pile of three stacked in the corner, then positioned it under the hatch and stood on it. 'Can't reach. How tall is this accountant?'

'I don't know, but one thing is for sure he's not Peter Crouch,' Murphy said glancing up at his outstretched arm, which was a good five feet short of reaching the hole in the hatch.

'Look for a pole with a hook on the end?'

After a few minutes of foraging Preston's office the four officers drew a blank.

'Must have taken it with him. Evans, get down to reception; see if they have anything that will do the job?'

Minutes later she returned with a red-faced, portly bloke in his early sixties who stood puffing like a steam train in a paint stained overall.

'This is Roy Cooper. He's the caretaker for the Chambers.'

'I'm getting too old for those bloody stairs. This young lady tells me you want to access the loft? Where's Malcolm? He's usually here until four.'

'That's what we're trying to establish, Mr Cooper.'

'You wunna find him up there. Is he in trouble?'

'All depends on what we find.'

Regaining his breath the caretaker tugged out a thin telescopic rod with a hook on the end, from his pocket. He extended it, opened the hatch and clawed the ladder down. Murphy found the torch on his phone and climbed up.

Leonard Vale left the secret surveillance HQ above the Euro Mini-Market in Piccadilly discreetly by the back entrance. He'd only moved a few feet along the passageway leading onto the car park when a broad figure wearing a balaclava frightened the life out of him. Leonard froze to the spot as the sinister figure approached.

'What you up to, Ginger, sneaking around in back alleyways? Having a crafty wank?'

'Who are you, what do you want?' Vale said, shitting himself.

'Tell me who you're working for, geek?'

'What do you mean?'

'Let's put it this way, I know you don't work in the shop. I'll give you five seconds to tell me what you're doing up there, before I start cutting off fingers.' the man said wielding a small, razor sharp blade in his right hand.

The blood drained from Vale's face.

'Please, I can't tell you; my boss will kill me, literally.'

'Have it your way.' the man said grabbing his left wrist tightly, before hovering the blade millimetres above his index finger. The man grabbed him around the throat and pinned him to the wall. 'Stop pissing me around,' he retorted.

'Ger… off, your st… rangl?' Vale spluttered through choked breath.

The man eased his grip.

'OK, OK. Don't hurt me, I'll tell you.'

'What you doing then?'

'Surveillance,' Vale blurted, fearful for his life.

'On what?'

'Can't say.'

The man tightened his grip again.

'The Potteries Museum.'

'Why?'

Vale raised his right hand, unable to speak, face white through lack of oxygen.

The man released his grip.

Vale gulped air, 'Sworn to secrecy.'

'Come on, I won't tell anybody.'

'I can't. No chance.'

The man turned then rammed his fist into Vale's stomach. Winded, he keeled over, breathlessly writhing around in agony on the ground.

'Tell me or I'll cut your fucking throat?'

Holding his stomach, Vale rose gingerly to his feet. 'OK, OK,' he capitulated.

'He's pulling a job.'

'Where?'

'Potteries Museum.'

'You taking the piss?'

'No, he's robbing the Staffordshire Hoard.'

'No way? If I find out you're telling porkies, I'll come to 28 Lawton Road and cut you up while your asleep.'

Vale was shocked, and scared this stranger knew where he lived. 'Just leave me alone!'

'Dunna worry? I don't associate with fucking orange losers,' the man said, holding the blade to Vales throat.

'How's he getting the gold out unnoticed?'

'We have a man working on the inside, he's smuggling it out,' Vale blurted, before revealing the plan, and dates of the robbery in more detail.

Balaclava man took it all in. 'Tell anyone about this and I'll cut you up and feed you to the pigs, understand geek?' he said walking away.

Tormented by the thought this psycho knew his address he turned around, but the passageway was empty.

CHAPTER 76

'DS Murphy, we've just received a call from a member of the public. A woman says she recognises our CCTV suspect in the Gibson murder case. She reckons his name is Carl Bentley,' PC Evans said.

'Any hits on the system for him?' Murphy asked.

'I've only done a quick PNC. He's a convicted football hooligan, with numerous arrests in the mid-nineties.'

'Did this woman leave a name?'

'Yes, a Miss Luna Ellis, sir.'

'We'd better get her in for an informal chat. Better still, I'll arrange a home visit for later today if possible?'

PC Evans nodded. 'OK.'

'Oh, Casey, while you're at it, can you access me Bentley's file?'

Katrina Osborne sat nursing a coffee and a fag, facing the sun in her shabby terraced yard when her mobile trilled.

'Kat, it's me, Luna.'

'Hi babe, what's up?'

'You still want to leave Carl?'

Kat frowned, wondering where this was leading. 'Yeah, but like I told you before, I can't; he owns the house. Anyway, why are you asking, bit weird?'

'Promise you won't be pissed off with me?'

'Spit it out?'

'I was sifting through a pile of *Sentinels* from the last ten days looking for the number of a cheap electrician when I came across a story that freaked me out.'

Kat clutched her elbow. 'What you on about? I'm not in the mood for guessing games, my arm's killing me.'

'What's up with it?'

'That bastard pushed me over last night. I banged it on the hearth. He was pissed again. I hate him,' she said, eyes welling up.

'Do you want me to come over?'

'I need to get out. Can we meet uptown?'

'Have you got any copies of the paper from the last couple of weeks? Tuesday the ninth is the one you need?'

'Hang on?' She entered the house and padded over to the front room in her slippers to retrieve the dog-eared *Sentinels* piled on a shelf ready for recycling.

She sifted through them. There were several days missing. 'No, haven't got it.'

'Get online and click on the link I've just emailed you,'

'Seriously, babe, this is getting on my nerves. Just tell me what the bloody hell you're rambling about?'

'Remember that murder in the White Horse pub in town recently?'

'Heard something about it on Radio Stoke, why?'

'There's a picture of a suspect in the paper. Police are asking the public if anyone recognises him.'

'And?'

'I think it's your Carl!'

'Don't be stupid!'

'Just have a look now?'

Kat opened her email on their laptop. She clicked the link and skimmed through the article. Her arm throbbed.

'What am I supposed to be looking at?'

'The CCTV picture… it's Carl.'

Kat felt betrayed. 'Don't be stupid.'

'It is, I'm telling you I recognise his build and the Northern Soul badge on his coat.'

Kat stared at the grainy image. A cold sensation crept over her. She realised the man's build and clothing did look like Carl's. Her hands trembled as they hovered over the keyboard. He'd paid a seamstress to sow the badge on his black cagoule.

'You still there?' Luna asked.

Kat's eyes darted around like a cornered fox; her stomach lurched. She got up and paced around the room numb with shock knowing only too well Carl was aggressive, especially after a drink.

'Are you OK?'

'I can't believe it.'

Luna could hear the tremor in her voice. 'I don't know how to say this: I've called the police and shopped him. Sorry, Kat, but he's gone too far. I'm worried for your safety. He needs locking up.'

Kat sighed deeply, attempting to release the tension. 'I… I'm glad you did!'

Taken back by her friend's admission, Luna paused before slipping back into support mode.

'It's my day off. Get a taxi to mine; I'll pay. We can talk this through, over a bottle of Pinot?'

Still reeling from the shock, Kat's body went into autopilot.

'Give me half an hour.'

'You know they'll interview him. It's difficult, but they'll want to speak to you as well. They always do,' Luna said.

Kat nodded nervously, brushing imaginary creases from her denim skirt.

They were in Luna's living room. Kat had already downed a large glass of Pinot Grigio and was contemplating a top-up when Luna's phone rang.

'Hello?'

'Can I speak to Luna Ellis, please?'

'Speaking.'

'This is DS John Murphy from Hanley CID following up your call to us, regarding the Barry Gibson murder investigation. Are you available for an informal chat today?'

She moved over to the window. Head dropped, hugging the receiver, she shot Kat a guilty backwards glance. 'Yes, but it would have to be later. I'm just going out,' she lied.

'We're on shift until six this evening. Shall we say four-thirty?'

Luna hesitated, realising there was no going back, then agreed.

'What's your address?'

'Flat 52 Braithwell Court, Park View Road, Hanley.' Feeling uncomfortable and pressured, she glanced at her sixties retro wall clock; it was only eleven a.m., so she agreed. Returning to the sofa, she placed a reassuring hand on Kat's arm. 'That was the police.'

'What did they want?'

'An informal chat.'

'About Carl?'

'Yeah, they're coming here at half four.'

It was all moving too fast now, and Luna was having second thoughts about the whole thing. Why had she given them her name and number? What an *idiot*! The thought of having the cops round gave her the jitters. To make things more complicated, she felt obliged to support Kat. After grassing on her partner, it was the least she could do. What a mess.

'This is a nightmare, Lune. What the bloody hell am I supposed to do? If he finds out it was you, he'll go ballistic. I'm scared.'

Luna tried to reassure her with a hug, but the damage was done. Kat didn't reciprocate; she felt stiff and lifeless.

'He'll never know, the police definitely won't tell him. We've just got to keep our nerve and see what happens,' she said, voicing support in a tone that lacked confidence.

'It's all right for you, you don't have to live with him.'

'I'm sorry, but you need protecting from that psycho. It could have been you killed.'

'What if he's innocent and it's someone else with a similar badge on their coat?'

'Come on, Kat, is that likely?'

'It's possible.'

'Don't even go there.'

'I know it's a mess, but it's your chance to get away, start a new life. You deserve better.'

'With what? I've got no job, and could end up homeless.'

'There's no way I'll let that happen. You could live with me until you get back on your feet.'

Kat sat dejected staring at the carpet.

'I'm here for you a hundred per cent, whatever you decide.'

'If I move in with you, he'd kick off. He might be a nasty bastard but he's not stupid. He knows you don't approve of our relationship. You'd be the first person he'd suspect of shopping him.'

'I just feel so guilty. If I hadn't made that bloody call none of this would be happening.'

'Too late now, the police are involved. I need to get some air.'

CHAPTER 77

It was 7.30 p.m. when DS Murphy and DS Roger Jamieson entered Cooper Street, Milton, followed by two uniformed officers in a patrol car. Their shift should have finished over an hour ago but the arrest of Carl Bentley was far too important to wait until morning. It was the first real lead in the Barry Gibson murder case and they were keen to question the suspect before someone let slip he'd been grassed on, giving him time to abscond.

Murphy sent the uniformed officers around the back of the house, blocking off the alleyway escape route, while he rapped on the tatty front door, which looked like it belonged in a skip. They waited a few moments before knocking again. Murphy glanced up at the second floor window. The netting twitched, someone was definitely in the house.

Suddenly Murphy's airwave set crackled and jumped into life. 'Suspect leaving property rear entrance. Will detain. Over.'

'Joining you now, over. Bastard's legging it, Roger!'

The two detectives dashed down the street and dived left into a passageway, leading to the back of the properties three doors along. Bentley was cornered in his yard, protesting his innocence to the uniformed officers.

'This is police harassment! I've done nowt,' he said, cowering behind a vintage scooter.

'Going somewhere?' DS Murphy asked, looking at the clothes poking out of a partially zipped shoulder bag, Bentley had tossed to the ground. 'Carl Bentley, I'm arresting you in connection with the murder of Barry Gibson. You do not have to say anything…' Murphy continued to read him his rights.

The uniformed officers cuffed and led him through the house towards the patrol car. The two detectives joined them as they shoved Bentley in the back.

CHAPTER 78

Interview room two was only marginally better than room one, but thankfully in this magnolia box, the air conditioning worked. The suspect wore a retro Stoke City top, and sat cross-legged, resting his cuffed hands on his lap. The Formica interview table was bolted to the floor just in front of him. Both detectives wore short-sleeved shirts, whilst the chubby legal aid lawyer looked as if he was melting in his pinstripe suit. Fifteen minutes into the interview it became clear to Murphy that Bentley was definitely trying to hide something. His fidgeting paranoid behaviour led them to believe he was stoned, and his evasive manner was starting to irritate them.

Bentley claimed that on the night of the murder he went round the pubs in Milton with two mates for a few pints before going back home to his missus. At this stage they couldn't disprove anything so were determined to carefully probe, whilst his lawyer seemed content to let him get on with it, uninterrupted, which was a rarity.

'I'm telling you I was at home with me missus watching TV. Call her, she'll tell you.'

'Don't worry, once we can locate her whereabouts, we will. The number you gave us goes straight to voicemail.

'You've been identified from the CCTV still in the *Evening Sentinel*.' Murphy slid the aforementioned picture across the table.

Bentley scrutinised it. 'Are you taking the piss? That could be anybody?'

'Maybe.' Murphy sounded doubtful. 'But we have a witness who swears it's you. Now why would they do that?'

Bentley's eyes shot nervously around the room. 'Someone is trying to frame me with this shit.'

'Look, Mr Bentley, you're a suspect in a murder case, and in order for us to eliminate you, your alibi needs to check out, and we'll need DNA samples and fingerprints from you. It's in your best interests to cooperate. Is that clear?' Murphy insisted.

'Crystal,' Bentley said arrogantly. 'Any chance of a smoke?'

'What do you think?' Jamieson said, sarcastically. 'It's not the eighties anymore.'

'Did you know of, or have any connection with, Barry Gibson, or a man with the nickname Stomper?'

'No!' Bentley said abruptly.

'Are you absolutely sure?'

'Yeah.'

'Well, Mr Bentley, that's a lie.'

'We have information that you do,' Murphy said, knowing the mobile data retrieved from Yusuf Benzar's old Nokia was tenuous.

'What info? I don't know him,' he countered.

'I'm afraid I don't believe you. We retrieved your mobile number from a drug dealer's phone, a dealer who Barry Gibson owed a thousand pounds to. There were only five numbers on it and the call history shows dozens of calls to your number.'

Bentley tried to act dumb. 'I haven't got a clue what you're talking about.'

'You must think we're stupid. We know toe-rags like you have loads of SIM cards.'

Bentley paused and glanced at his lawyer, who shook his head subtly. 'No comment.'

'Yusuf Benzar! Is that who you get ganja from?' Murphy said.

'No comment.'

'Yusuf Benzar is a known heroin dealer with a history of violence and intimidation, and he's an illegal money lender. Do you normally have multiple conversations with people you don't know? I think not. Wouldn't you agree, DS Jamieson?' Jamieson nodded.

'Did you pay Barry Gibson an unannounced visit at his house on the Heath Hayes Estate, on the seventh of May?'

'I just told you I don't know him.'

'Strange that, because someone fitting your description was seen hurling abuse outside his house on that date,' Murphy lied, knowing Mrs Arlington couldn't identify him due to her failing eyesight. There was definitely a connection between Bentley and Yusuf Benzar and he'd keep probing until it came to light.

'This is total bollocks! I don't know either of these blokes you keep banging on about. Where's your proof?'

'Apparently Barry Gibson owed a thousand quid to Yusuf Benzar,' Murphy said, continuing to speculate. 'I think you were collecting that money for him, which gives you a motive to murder. Only Barry wasn't in that day. In fact each time you went round to collect the money, he avoided you. When you saw him in the White Horse gents, you seized the opportunity to confront him, but he kicked off, so you head-butted him, leaving him unconscious on the floor. But Gibson knew who you were. You couldn't take the risk of him regaining consciousness, so you finished him off… stabbed him in the brain with a knife.' Murphy tried to force Bentley into confession.

Bentley looked at his lawyer. 'Why are they trying to put this on me? I was in Milton drinking that night.'

'I think you were in Hanley drinking at the White Horse.' Murphy said.

Bentley stared vacantly at the wall behind the two detectives.

'Aren't you going to say anything, Mr Bentley?' DS Murphy asked.

'I've already told you, I don't know this Barry Gibson.'

'This is going nowhere. Take him back down to the cells while I sort out a search warrant. We'll see what turns up at Mr Bentley's house,' Murphy said to DS Jamieson.

Bentley's face turned ashen, as he looked at his lawyer for confirmation.

'I'm afraid so. Whilst you remain a suspect, it's within the law for the police to search your property.'

'Hopefully we'll bring you back a few souvenirs,' DS Jamieson added.

DS Murphy spent the next half an hour trying to locate the suspect's partner. Eventually he found her. Turned out she was a close friend of the witness who shopped Bentley, which seemed rather suspicious. He sent a patrol car to pick her up. Whilst awaiting her arrival at the station forensics took a DNA swab and fingerprinted the reluctant prisoner, but to the team's annoyance the results wouldn't be back until mid-morning the next day.

CHAPTER 79

Within minutes of the police forensic van drawing up outside Carl Bentley's house, curtains twitched and several Cooper Street residents stood brazenly rubbernecking at the four-man SOC team as they entered through the front door of the two-up, two-down run-of-the-mill terrace.

Jeff Foxhall, head of the team, swept the kitchen whilst his colleagues spread out into the other rooms. He checked the microwave first. If alerted to a police raid suspects tried to dispose evidence quickly. Drugs were flushed down toilets and incriminating SIM cards were blasted in a microwave. Sure enough, in the centre of the microwaves glass rotation plate, there was a blob of molten plastic.

He dusted the microwave for prints and then swabbed the worktop next to it. The tape picked up heroin residues from where someone had recently been weighing and bagging.

An hour into scouring the property they'd found two large transparent bags of brown powder, which tested positive as heroin, and nine ounces of cannabis resin in a bedside cabinet draw.

Foxhall called Murphy. 'Detective, it looks like our man's a pretty serious dealer. More importantly, looks like he's been burning stuff in a fire basket, in the backyard. It might be coincidence but we found the remains of a shoe sole. Unfortunately it's far too incinerated to get any forensics from. Everything else has been burned with an accelerant so it's mainly ash. As a precaution I'll bag it up, but I'd say it won't produce anything from an evidential point of view.'

'What'd you think?'

'Crime scene footprints.'

'Exactly! Bring it in. They can go off to the lab tonight with the suspect's DNA samples,' Murphy said.

'Also, there's a Lambretta in the yard. One of those vintage jobs. Do you want us to give it the once-over?' Foxhall asked.

'Definitely. Judging by what you found so far he's probably hid stuff all over the place

'OK, speak to you when you get back.' Murphy ended the call.

The SOCO officer lay his toolkit on the ground and knelt beside Carl Bentley's vintage TV 200 1965 Lambretta, looking for a way to remove the side panel. The two-tone blue-and-white paint was immaculate, and the scooter had been lovingly restored by a serious enthusiast. A quick turn of the chrome lever on the ocean-blue side panel exposed the rear-wheel shock absorber, engine and petrol can. There was a small mahogany box wedged in the space between the petrol, and water cans. He cautiously laid it on the seat. After a minute of prizing with a flat head screwdriver, the lid popped open, revealing four clear bags, containing dozens of pills, each one embossed with a tiny bottle kiln. He opened one and performed a colorimetric chemical test to detect the presence of methamphetamine or MDMA ecstasy. Still wearing his silicone gloves, he speed-dialled DS Murphy.

'John?'

'Added to the other drugs, I've found a couple of hundred high-strength ecstasy pills stashed in the scooter. This is turning out to be a significant haul.'

'Great work, Jeff, if we don't get him for murder we'll nail him for possession with conspiracy to supply.'

'We're coming back in now.'

'OK, cheers.'

'Almost forgot Kyle found two bags of SIM cards, one gaffer-taped to the underside of his wardrobe, and another in the toilet cistern.'

'Great, more ammunition!'

Murphy decided to celebrate the small victory with a coffee.

CHAPTER 80

'After performing a forensics sweep of your property, SOCO discovered a large quantity of class A and B drugs stashed in various locations. Ecstasy pills, heroin and nine ounces of cannabis resin to be precise.

'The SIM card you blasted in your microwave turns out to be one of many. Thankfully, our team are very thorough. The bag you taped to the underside of your wardrobe, and another you hid in your toilet cistern, contained a selection, so stop pissing me around and start telling the truth; else we'll add wasting police time to the list of charges.'

The colour suddenly drained from Carl Bentley's face, and his lawyer seemed devoid of a response.

'So, what do you have to say?' Murphy continued.

'I prefer pay-as-you-go phones.'

Murphy glanced at DS Jamieson. 'Seriously! Like I mentioned earlier, stalling won't help your cause. Our tech analysis team are retrieving the call data from those as we speak.'

'So what?'

'It's only a matter of time before we link them to the heroin supplier, Yusuf Benzar. We know you work for his brother Ibrahim. The quantity of class A found at your property is enough to send you down for years and that's excluding the small matter of Barry Gibson's murder.'

His body tensed. 'Why are you still trying to pin that on me? I didn't kill anyone.'

'I'll ask you again. Where were you on Friday the fifth of July, in the evening?'

'I've already told you, I went Milton for a few pints and then watched TV with the Mrs later. Are you deaf or summet. It's on that tape if you play it back?' Bentley said sarcastically, pointing to the tape player.

'I'll tell you where you were; in the city centre drinking, selling ecstasy and coke.'

'Yeah right, course I was. Look into your crystal ball, did you?'

Humouring him, Murphy replied, 'Haven't you heard they're standard issue now? Window to the world, it's called CCTV and we have a witness who's identified you pacing suspiciously up Stafford Street on the night in question, with your hood up.'

'Bullshit! I went for a few beers in Milton, then home to the Mrs, she'll tell you,' Bentley protested.

Murphy held back from probing Bentley about his dubious alibi, and reverted to questioning him about the Ee's, 'Barry Gibson's toxicology report shows he took ecstasy as well as consuming tons of alcohol. That ecstasy has exactly the same chemical compound as the two hundred Kiln embossed tablets, discovered hidden inside your scooter. Bit of a damning coincidence that wouldn't you say? Furthermore, I checked the drug lab reports on the police national computer.'

'What's that got to do with me?'

'Sixteen year old Katy Hayder died in January this year; from taking the very same Kiln Ee's you've been knocking out. Which is another damning coincidence we can't ignore, since its likely they came from the same supply batch,' Murphy knew it was a tenuous link he couldn't prove, but he wanted to rattle Bentley.

'You can't pin that on me. Anyone could have sold her pills. Those Ee's weren't mine anyway; someone planted them in my scooter. Bastard set me up!' Bentley protested.

'You can't seriously expect us to believe that?'

'It's the truth!'

'Well, they were found in your possession and unless you can give us a name of your supplier, it doesn't look good for you.'

'That Turkish wanker Yusuf Benzar's behind all this, I'm telling you.'

'Really? The thing is, he's on the run at present. Escaped from police custody, so unless we capture him soon, and he admits all this gear found at your house is his, you're pretty screwed. Highly unlikely that's going to happen is it, Carl?'

Devoid of a response Bentley sighed deeply, and slumped back in his chair.

Knowing he had nothing concrete linking Yusuf Benzar with Bentley, until the phone analysis was done, Murphy moved onto the murder weapon, 'Where have you chucked the knife? These things have a habit of turning up when you least expect them.'

'What knife?'

'The one you stabbed Barry Gibson with. Does the ganja cut itself up?'

'You're talking bollocks.'

'All this time wasting will add at least six months to his sentence,' Murphy said addressing Bentley's lawyer.

Katrina Osborne sat in Hanley's police station reception, anxiously waiting to be interviewed. All kinds of disturbing thoughts coursed through her mind. Could Carl really be a murderer? He certainly had an uncontrollable temper. Maybe Luna just wanted to rattle his cage in the hope the police would find sufficient evidence to do him for drug dealing? Whatever happened to him, this was her chance to break free from the bastard. As Luna rightly pointed out she'd done nothing wrong and could do so much better than that loser.

Suddenly the door leading to the back offices of the police station opened and a beer-bellied detective in his early forties with mousy receding hair called her through.

'Ms Osborne, I'm Detective Sergeant John Murphy. We're ready for you now, if you'd like to follow me, please?'

She edged across the reception, nerves getting the better of her. Once seated in interview room two, he introduced DS Jamieson and offered her a cup of tea.

'Don't worry, Miss Osborne, you're not under arrest. This is just an informal chat to establish a few facts about your partner Carl Bentley. I can appreciate you must be concerned given this is a murder enquiry. We've brought you in to corroborate his alibi. You're entitled to a duty solicitor. Would you like one to be present?'

Flicking her fringe, she declined the offer.

'But first, DS Jamieson and I want to ask you about Carl. It will help us build up a picture of his personality and social activities. Can he be violent?'

Unconsciously clenching the bruised arm he'd inflicted on her recently; she couldn't resist the urge to tell them about his physical abuse. 'He loses it sometimes, after too much beer.' Her eyes welled up as she held back tears.

'Has he ever hit you?'

'Not really.' She said curling her lip nervously.

'I don't want to upset you Miss Osborne, but could you be more specific? Has he ever abused you in any way at all?'

'Yes,' she murmured, ashamed to admit it.

'I'm sorry we have to ask these sensitive questions. When was the last time he was violent towards you?'

'The other night. He pushed me and I fell onto the fireplace and smacked my elbow.' She slid her sleeve up revealing a large greenish bruise, swollen blue around the edges.

DS Jamieson gave Murphy a judgemental glance. 'Phew! Looks painful?' Murphy said. 'Does this kind of thing happen often?'

'No. He's just normally a mouthy bastard when he's pissed.'

'Has he ever threatened you with a knife? Something small, easily concealed in a coat or trouser pocket?'

'No, never! Why do you ask that?' She said shocked.

'Because the murder victim was stabbed with a small knife.'

'I see,' she gave him a worried look.

'Going back to my previous question. What led him to push you?'

'We were arguing over money and stuff.'

'Anything in specific?'

'Not really. I lost my job a while back and he doesn't give me enough to live on.'

'I'm sorry to hear that. And he's been violent before this?

'A long time ago when we were on holiday in Corfu. He slapped and punched me, but nothing since the elbow.'

'I see,' Murphy said, trying to empathise. 'How often does he drink?'

'Mainly at the weekend.'

'Which pubs?'

'Local. He uses all the Milton pubs, The Foxley, The Millrace, Traveller's Rest, Miners Arms and Bar 41.'

'Has Carl mentioned being involved in any fights, or disagreements recently? Has he come home with any cuts or black eyes?'

'No, nothing.'

'Does he venture into Hanley much?'

'Not often.'

'Is it possible he was in Hanley last Friday evening?'

'Suppose, but I didn't see him.'

'You were in town last Friday?' Murphy knew Bentley was lying all along.

'Yes, Luna and me.'

'Miss Luna Ellis?'

'Yes.'

'That's interesting, because on the fifth of July, Carl told us he was with you at home watching TV around ten-fifty p.m. when the murder was reported. Judging by what you've just told us, that's not true?'

'He said we were at home last Friday night?' Taken by surprise she welled up again.

'Afraid so. It helps to remember your movements that evening. It's OK, take your time?' DS Jamieson said, offering her a clean tissue.

Kat sighed before recalling one of the most unforgettable nights she'd had in years, until emotions got the better of her. Tears rolled down her cheeks. They'd been together for twelve years, and deep down she still had feelings for him. She felt so lost and alone, mindful that the truth could send Carl to prison, but there would be serious consequences for lying.

'Sorry, Ms Osborne, but I have to press you about Carl's alibi last Friday. Were you with him at home at between ten and eleven p.m.?'

Her eyes dropped to the table, and the detectives saw she was wrestling with her conscience.

In the end her gut instinct prevailed. After a moment's pause, she uttered, 'No!', before realising there was no going back.

'What time did you hit the town, and which pubs did you use?' Murphy asked.

Nervously she recalled the evening's events.

'Er… started off in the Auctioneers, then sat on the terrace outside the Slipware Tankard.'

'What time did you stay in the pubs till?'

'Around half eleven.'

'And after that?'

'We ended up in the Genting Casino.'

'Just Luna and yourself?'

She paused again before reluctantly divulging. 'And another person.'

'Was it another man?'

After more silence, she nodded.

'Can you tell us his name?'

'It was a one-night stand.'

'And you didn't ask his name?'

'Not really.'

'I know these questions are very personal, but it's important we check who you were with. Especially since Carl lied about being with you.'

Again, she nodded nervously.

'Is there any reason you don't want to tell us his name? Do you think he's given you a false name?'

'No.'

'You sound certain, how do you know?'

'I don't want to get him into trouble.'

'Is he married?'

'Divorced, I think, but I doubt he'd admit he was with me.'

'Why?'

'Would you?'

'Depends on the circumstances. I'm sure you appreciate how serious this is. We're dealing with a murder inquiry, in which your partner is a key suspect. My forensics team swept your property around an hour ago; they discovered significant quantities of class A and B drugs, amongst other evidence. Those have been fast tracked to the lab. Carl's DNA and fingerprints will be tested against those found on the victim at the crime scene. If they match it's likely he'll be charged with murder. We don't want to charge you for perverting the course of justice, but we need a name.'

Kat looked racked with worry.

'You said it was a one-night stand. Where did you go after the casino?' Murphy continued.

'I left Luna with the man's brother. He booked a room at the Willow Hotel.'

'His brother?'

'I'm sure his names Yusuf.'

Murphy's eyes lit up as she revealed their escaped prisoner was with her friend on the night of the murder.

'What time was that?'

'Not sure. Around half past twelve, I think.'

'And you stayed there until what time in the morning?'

'Got back home about half six.'

'Did Carl kick-off when you got in?'

'He wasn't there, so I got into bed and made out like I'd come home. He came in around eight, said he'd crashed on his mate's sofa.'

'Which mate?'

'Johno.'

'What's his real name?'

'John McKnight.'

'Does McKnight live in Milton?'

'Yeah, he lives in one of the council flats just off Bagnall Road. Don't know the street name.'

DS Jamieson noted the name in his pad. Playing good cop he chipped in. 'We'll be speaking to Mr McKnight to verify this. We understand this is upsetting you, so DS Murphy and I will give you a few minutes to think it over, but we need a name? Would you like a top up?' He pointed towards her empty plastic cup.

With that they left her to mull it over, knowing full well a break from questioning would intensify the pressure.

They returned to the interview room ten minutes later. Kat had composed herself. The tears had dried up, and she'd touched up her eye blusher and ruby lipstick.

DS Murphy placed the tea on the table in front of her and asked, 'Do you have a name for us, Ms Osborne?'

Without further hesitation she said, 'Ibrahim something. I don't know his second name. He's originally from Turkey.'

Alarm bells went off in Murphy's head. 'Where would we find him?'

'I don't know where he lives, but he owns one or two businesses in Hanley.'

'What businesses?' Murphy asked already knowing the answer, but wanted her to confirm it.

'A bar called the Slipware Tankard and a gym called the Dojo.'

Those two added to the Black Sea Mini-Market made it quite a property portfolio. Murphy thought.

She stalled. 'What will happen to him?'

'We just need a brief chat with him to prove he was with you all night. If that checks out OK, you're both in the clear.'

'What do you mean, if it checks out? I've done nothing, and neither has he.'

'It's standard procedure, that's all. I'm sure everything will be fine.' The Benzar brothers were involved in two key investigations at present. The fact Yusuf Benzar was on the run and they'd arrested and searched Ibrahim's properties recently, supported his theory that they were dangerous and organised. Was it just drugs, or were they planning something much bigger? Whatever they were into, he and DI Blake were determined to take them down.

'Benzar, that's your mystery man's surname. Ibrahim Benzar. I'd steer well clear of him, love; he's a right nasty bastard that one. We've issued a warrant for the arrest of his brother Yusuf, who escaped police custody a few days ago.'

'What's he done?' Kat said with a worried look.

'I can't go into detail as the investigation is ongoing, but let's just say there's large quantities of drugs involved,' Murphy informed her.

By the tired look on her face Murphy could tell the interview was feeling more like an interrogation and decided they had enough information for now.

'OK, thank you for your cooperation. We'll speak to Ibrahim Benzar in due course. You're free to go, but if you think of anything else, you can call me on this number?' He placed his card on the table.

CHAPTER 81

It was 9.30 p.m. and Carl Bentley had been in custody for over two hours. Both detectives were determined to push on with a murder case that had so far yielded zero clues in a week, before opening up in the space of twenty-four hours. Bentley's false alibi opened up new lines of inquiry, and they needed to question two persons of interest before they had time to concoct different versions of events.

'Best if we split up on this one, Roger. You take PC Evans with you and head on over to Milton to have a chat with John McKnight and Terry Clarke. They might let something slip. I'll have a wander across to the Slipware Tankard with PC Haynes to check out Katrina Osborne's story. Something's not right here. Ibrahim Benzar was only released from custody twenty-four hours ago, and we need to question him again, only this time about an alibi for the missus of a suspected murderer.'

'You think they're linked in some way?' Jamieson said.

'I really don't know, but she's been shagging his boss behind his back; there's definitely some association here, but the clock's ticking. If there's not enough evidence, he'll swerve the murder charge.'

'OK John, Evans can ride shotgun.'

'Naughty!'

'It's been a long day and I'm too knackered to flirt.'

'I'll call you around ten-thirty,' Murphy said, looking at his watch.

'Synchronised.' Jamieson smirked.

The Slipware Tankard was only a few hundred yards away from the station. Murphy made a quick call to DI Blake.

'Tom, we've arrested a suspect in the Barry Gibson case.'

'Who?'

'A bloke named Carl Bentley; he's got previous for football violence. A woman recognised him from the CCTV still in the *Sentinel*, and called it in. Roger and I are about to question Yusuf Benzar's brother, Ibrahim, regarding Carl Bentley's alibi Meet us outside the Slipware Tankard in twenty minutes; I think you should speak to him again.'

Leaving Bethesda Street, Murphy and PC Haynes crossed over the tarmac island and joined Lower Marsh Street on foot. Outside the Slipware Tankard they waited for Blake to arrive.

Ten minutes later the three of them stood at the bar. A bearded bartender, with a sleeve tattoo covering his right arm and two pierced ear plugs they could see through, stood behind it.

Murphy flashed his warrant card. 'DS Murphy, Hanley police. Can we speak to the owner Ibrahim Benzar? Is he on the premises?'

'Er, not sure, I'll have to check. Just hang on there a minute and I'll find out?' he said, before disappearing through an opening at the end of the bar. Returning a few minutes later he asked. 'What's it about?'

'Never mind that, son. If he's on the premises we want to speak to him, or would you prefer PC Haynes here arrests you for obstructing our enquiries?' He'd been on duty over fourteen hours and didn't have the patience to take any stalling bullshit from some frigging Edwardian Pirate with an art degree.

Moments later the scolded barman returned red-faced with the well-dressed Ibrahim Benzar.

'Mr Benzar? Our paths cross again.'

'This is police harassment. I told you everything I know when you locked me up the other day. I'm busy. You've got ten minutes. Come into my office.'

Blake and Murphy followed him through the bar into a compact but well decked-out office. Ibrahim sat behind a glass desk; in the right-hand corner sat a vintage safe, suspiciously similar to the one they'd found in his brother's flat.

This was the third time in a week he'd spoken to this smarmy bastard, and Blake was convinced Benzar was the orchestrator of his brother's escape and his daughter's kidnapping, but had nothing concrete to prove it.

'John, could you give us a moment? I want to speak with Mr Benzar off the record. I don't want to compromise you.'

'If you're sure, sir, but I don't like it.'

'I'll be fine,' he reassured him.

Murphy closed the door behind him.

'What do you want, officer?'

Blake launched into Benzar. 'It's DI Blake to you, and you know full well what you've done.' He leaned over the desk and angrily faced him, just about resisting the urge to land a punch in his face. 'You blackmailed me into facilitating your brother's escape, and now my daughter is in intensive care because those animals you paid to abduct her nearly killed her.'

Benzar sat there with a smug look on his face before calmly responding. 'I'm sorry to hear about your daughter, but as you know my brother is mixed up in drugs, and he keeps terrible company. I run legitimate businesses. Why would I get involved in his shit?'

'Because,' Blake continued ranting, 'he's your brother and you're both criminal scum. You seriously think I believe that bullshit? I'll dig deep until I find what's really going on here and when I do, you'll be locked up for so long you'll need a pension book when you get out.'

'That's a strong accusation. Unless you have any proof I suggest you calm down or you'll be hearing from my lawyer. If you've finished threatening me, you can leave before I call him.'

Blake took a deep breath before opening the office door and calling DS Murphy and PC Haynes back in.

'Don't worry, we'll be leaving soon, but not until you tell us where you were on Friday fifth of June in the evening. We're investigating a murder that took place that night.'

'I haven't killed anybody.'

'A key witness in our investigation has told us she was with you on the night in question. Is that correct?'

'Depends?'

'On what?'

'What she said.'

'That you spent time at the Genting Casino in Hanley, followed by a one-night stand at the Willow Hotel. Is that correct?'

'Yes.'

'What time were you there until?'

'Nine in the morning.'

PC Haynes retrieved a notepad from his top pocket and took down the details as DS Murphy continued.

'Do you employ a Carl Bentley?'

'What's this got to do with him?'

'It's a simple question.'

'He drives for me.'

'What kind of driver?' Murphy asked.

'Supplies, stock and suchlike.'

'Don't the brewery deliver your beer?'

'Yeah.'

'So what's Carl Bentley's role in your businesses?'

'He helps out.'

'In what capacity? Be more specific.'

'He takes money to the bank, picks up supplies… anything I need him to do.'

'Was he drinking in this bar last Friday?'

'How would I know? I was only here for around an hour. What's with all the questions about Bentley? What's he done?'

'I'm afraid I can't divulge information regarding Carl Bentley.'

'I've had enough of this shit; if you want to ask me any more questions I'll call my lawyer.'

DS Roger Jamieson glanced at PC Evans as she sat next to him in the Vectra pool car heading from Terry Clarke's in Fairfield Street, Milton towards John McKnight's flat on Bagnall Road. It made a nice change to have a female officer accompanying him. Lardy-arsed DS Murphy often stank the car out with farts, especially after a night on the ale.

He refocused and indicated to pull into Bagnall Road. He parked outside a seventies maisonette near the top of the road, which was hemmed off by cast-iron railings through which acres of unkempt fields leading to Bagnall Woods, were visible. According to the address they'd been given. John McKnight lived in flat thirteen on the upper floor. Hopefully, they'd catch him unaware.

Evans pressed the intercom. After a moment's silence, a timid voice crackled through a damaged speaker. 'Who is it?'

'Am I speaking to John McKnight?'

'Yeah.'

'It's DS Roger Jamieson and PC Evans from Staffordshire Police. We'd need to speak with you in connection with Carl Bentley's arrest, can we come in?'

'I was just going out,' McKnight said trying to avoid them.

Jamieson looked at Evans and shook his head before thumbing the button hard. 'I'm afraid you'll have to delay, this won't take long.'

After a moment's silence McKnight permitted them entrance. The door clicked and Jamieson held it open, ushering Evans through.

John McKnight's flat looked like it needed a serious mothering. A knackered coffee table sat in the centre of the unvacuumed living-room carpet, covered in mug rings. Piles of lads' mags were scattered on the shelf below. A film of dust covered his TV screen. A strong smell of freshly sprayed deodorant lingered in the air. Judging by his food-stained T-shirt, grubby jeans and sweaty appearance, he'd tried to mask the unpleasant BO exuding from him.

'What's this all about?' he said, sweeping his greasy fringe to the side.

Keeping him on his toes, Jamieson said, 'Hardly dressed for going out, are you, Mr McKnight? Why did you lie to us?'

'I… err… am later, after a bath.'

'Well, the sooner we do this, the sooner you can bathe.' Jamieson smirked at Evans. 'Mind if we sit?'

'No,' he said, leaning against the cheap MDF fireplace surround.

'OK, we'll cut to the chase. We're here to corroborate Carl Bentley's alibi for Friday the fifth of July. During his interview he told us he spent the evening drinking around the pubs in Milton, accompanied by yourself and Terry Clarke. Is that correct?'

'Er… last Friday. Yeah,' McKnight replied, his complexion flushed.

'Take us through the evening. From the time you met, to which pubs you drank in. We want to build up a picture of your movements.'

McKnight gave Jamieson an uneasy look, his brow moist with sweat. The detective could tell he was frantically trying to cobble together a version of events that might fit Carl Bentley's statement, but since he couldn't know what his mate had said he became extremely tense at the prospect of bullshitting his way out of this.

'Err… we met in the Millrace pub at eightish, I think.'

'Is that the pub just over the bridge on Maunders Road?'

'Yeah.'

'How long did you stay in there?' Jamieson asked him as PC Evans squirmed, whilst taking notes in an armchair under the window that was littered with cigarette burns.

'Not sure… for a couple of pints.'

'An hour or more?'

'Yeah, about an hour.'

'OK. And after that?'

He paused to wipe his brow nervously. 'Can I get a glass of water?'

'Of course, it's your flat.'

McKnight got up and disappeared into the kitchen. Jamieson lip-synced to Evans, 'He's lying!'

McKnight returned looking even more jittery, a glass of water shaking in his hand.

'You OK, Mr McKnight. You seem very edgy?'

'I'm fine.'

'OK, as I was saying where did the three of you go after the Millrace?'

'The Foxley.'

'Where's that?'

His eyes flicked to Evans. 'On Foxley Lane.'

'How long did you stay in there?'

'Can't remember exactly, a while.'

'So when we speak to the landlord and bar staff they'll confirm this?'

A sudden look of dread came over McKnight. 'Suppose so.'

'Look, Mr McKnight, I don't want to appear cynical, but we both know you're feeding us porkies. Do yourself a favour. Whatever misguided loyalty you feel compelled to uphold, don't bother. It's as transparent as that glass of water. Make no mistake, Carl Bentley is in deep shit. If you don't want to be arrested for perverting the course of justice, I suggest you start telling the truth?'

'I am,' he said unconvincingly.

'Funny that, because your version of the evening's events is different from Terry Clarke's.'

The colour drained from his face. 'Is it?'

'OK, have it your way. PC Evans pass me your handcuffs. John McKnight, I'm arresting you for perverting the course of justice…' But before Jamieson could finish, McKnight capitulated.

'OK, OK, hold on! Just give me a minute, please?' he protested.

'You've got exactly one minute to come clean. Understand? No more pissing about. Were you, Carl Bentley and Terry Clarke drinking in Hanley on the evening of the fifth of June?'

'Yeah.'

'Now we're getting somewhere?' Jamieson said to PC Evans, who'd resumed taking notes.

'So, why is your mate telling us he spent the evening in Milton, when Terry Clarke's saying you went into town? He's hiding something?'

McKnight shrugged. 'I dunno.'

'What time did you get into the city?'

'About half eight.'

'Bus or taxi?'

'Taxi.'

'First pub was?'

'Wetherspoons.'

'Until what time?'

'I can't really remember.'

'Bloody try. This is a murder case.' Jamieson was getting annoyed at McKnight's monosyllable answers.

'A pint and a shot, then we went to the Black Bull. What's Carl supposed to have done?'

'Let's just say Carl Bentley is helping us with our enquiries into a murder, which took place last Friday in a city centre pub.'

McKnight twigged. 'I read about that in the *Sentinel.* Bloke found dead in the White Horse.'

'We need to wrap this up now, Mr McKnight. Tell us where you went after the Black Bull, and what time you headed home?'

He paused and took another sip of water before answering. 'We stayed in the Bull until last orders.'

'We'll be checking CCTV from the pub and speaking to the landlord and his staff.

McKnight looked deeply worried.

'How did you get home?'

'Walked, about half eleven.'

'All three of you?'

'Yeah, we wanted some air, it was hot.'

'You can't seriously expect me to believe that?'

'We did.'

'OK, that's it for now. But we'll be checking everything. If you're lying, you'll be arrested.'

CHAPTER 82

On the day before the heist, Charlie Bullard stood in the grotty kitchen in his council flat overlooking the city, spooning filter coffee into a percolator, when the call from the Agency came through at ten a.m.

'Hello?'

'Can I speak to Brian Calcot? It's Louise here from Work Supply.'

He hesitated for a moment. Taking a deep breath, realising he'd almost blown it, he replied, 'Speaking.'

'We have a couple days work for you at the Potteries Museum. The caretaker there asked for you personally.'

'Oh yeah, Arthur Mitchell?'

'Yes, that's him. Can you start tomorrow at 7.30 a.m?'

'Yes, I'll be there on the dot.'

'Great. Any problems call me. You have my number?' OK, thanks, Brian. Bye.' The kettle shook in his hand as he poured boiling water into the glass coffee pot. Pushing the plunger, he realised there was no going back. It'd been years since he'd felt that rush of adrenaline that could only come from ripping off the establishment. It was the ultimate natural high, although the flip side of the coin was less euphoric: contemplating another ten-year stretch in prison was enough to bring on a panic attack.

Bollocks to it, he thought! The chance of a million, or slowly decaying in a substandard council dwelling surrounded by junkies. Looking round at the garish orange walls of his shit flat shored up any nagging doubts. In the worst-case scenario what would he really be giving up; ninety quid a week unemployment benefit, just enough food to live on, loneliness and the limited prospects of an ageing con.

He drained his mug and fished his mobile from the cluttered wicker basket on the worktop. 'Come on,' he uttered impatiently under his breath as Ibrahim's phone went to voicemail.

Hesitating, he stammered. 'It's me… Charl… important… you call me ASAP?'

He needed something stronger than coffee to calm his nerves so decided to head into town for a well-earned beer.

The White Horse pub was deserted, except for two blokes huddled in the corner nearest the window. It wasn't company he needed; a decent pint of Titanic and a nod from his cousin Darryl behind the bar would suffice. More importantly, why wasn't his phone ringing? It was less than twenty-four hours until the job and the organ grinder had gone AWOL. He was on a second pint when his mobile vibrated on the bar.

'Hello?'

'Charl, is that you?'

'Left a message on your voicemail, we need to meet, it's important. Where are you?'

'White Horse pub in town.'

'I'm at the Dojo, just give me ten minutes then come down to the office?'

'OK, see you in ten.'

If there was one thing he'd learnt it was never to discuss anything dodgy on a mobile; he was strictly old school face-to-face. That's how business should be done. Besides, any dumb shit with half a brain knows the cops can access phone records.

Bullard drained the rest of his pint, but just as he was leaving, Darryl Connor collared him. He'd just cleaned the gents. His regular cleaner had left him in the lurch after the Barry Gibson murder, and because of the negative publicity he'd failed to replace her. That vile sex case even managed to do damage from the grave. Good riddance to bad blood, he thought to himself.

'Everything okay Charl? Had a call from Mickey, he's done his bit.'

He looked nervously around. 'We can't talk about it, Daz.'

'Yeah I know. Just saying like, so you know.'

Charlie wasn't supposed to tell him about the heist, but after a recent lock-in he accidentally spilt the beans, when he'd had far too much to drink. Just like his son, Connor had money worries of his own, so Charlie persuaded Ibrahim to loan him 15k, with minimal interest to help pay off what he owed his beer supplier, who'd threatened to stop his barrel orders, and take him to court. Because of his criminal record legit loans weren't a viable option. Problem was, any default on the debt and half the pub he ploughed all his savings into, would be Benzar's.

Bullard left the pub and strode off, down Albion Street past the magnificent, renovated Bethesda Chapel. At the bottom he crossed the busy T-junction that linked up with Piccadilly and ducked through Birdcage Walk, before reaching The Dojo.

Being a black belt in karate from the age of seventeen, Ibrahim understood the needs of its client base.

Charlie entered the building and made his way across the blue crash mats laid out on the wooden gym floor to Benzar's back office.

Ibrahim was sitting behind the desk in his karategi uniform, glaring at the computer screen when he arrived.

'Charl, sit down, mate.' He pointed to the red plastic chair in front of the desk. 'So, tomorrow is the big day?'

'Yeah,' the ageing bank robber said nervously.

'Relax, we've planned this carefully. As long as you stick to what we practised, everything will be OK,' he said with scary optimism.

'I know, but I can't help feeling nervous. It's the first job I've done in years, I'm shitting bricks.'

'I understand this is a big deal, but you won't be on your own. We'll be in constant contact with you all night. Leonard will handle the cameras and alarms.'

'That's the whole problem; I'll be flying solo if this goes tits up. I'll be the one going down for it. With a rucksack full of bloody Hoard replicas, and a bunch of keys. It's not like I'd be able to plead breaking and entering. They'd know instantly what I was up to.'

'OK. I'd scheduled for us to go through everything again this afternoon, but since you're here, we can do it now. I think it will help you to focus and calm down. I'm nervous as well. That's why I'm here letting off steam. Just give me five minutes to change, and we'll head on over to the bar and run through it again using the replicas.'

'OK,' Charlie agreed, but still felt indecisive. He knew throwing the towel in this late in the day was not an option. Benzar had invested serious time and a decent wad of the Collector's cash into the planning stages of the job. Ultimately, a U-turn was out of the question unless he fancied being sized up for a six-by-two mahogany box with brass fittings.

CHAPTER 83

Ten minutes later, Charlie perched on a Chesterfield sofa, in one of the private rooms above the Slipware Tankard bar. He knew what was coming next. Ibrahim fixed them a couple of whiskys before locking the door and wheeling the dustsheet-covered replica display cabinet from the corner of the room. Arthur Mitchell, the museum caretaker they'd turned, provided details of the company who manufactured the cabinets, and they'd downloaded the design PDF. It had cost two grand to get this made by a local joinery firm.

'Sink that, and we'll run through it again.'

With two pints and a triple measure of single malt inside him, Charlie's nerves finally subsided. 'Okay,' he said, entwining his fingers, stretching his arms in front of his chest in preparation.

At this stage, things couldn't be going better for Ibrahim. The complete sets of gold replicas had arrived at the airport a few days ago, without detection. Mickey Connor played a blinder. He'd spent hours, wearing silicone gloves, scrutinising and comparing them to those in the official Hoard book. He'd even visited the find spot at Ogley Hay near Lichfield and excavated soil, with which the gold was to be dusted to add authentication. To the untrained eye, they would be hard to detect. Although he knew a Hoard specialist would eventually spot the fakes, by that time the lot would be safe with the Collector in the USA.

Ibrahim removed an old, large, framed picture of the town, tapped in a code, and retrieved eight clear plastic boxes from another of his built-in safes. He laid them down on top of the cabinet, put a pair of silicone gloves on, then tossed Charlie another pair.

'I'll load it up. Then you have another crack at it.'

'Our Mickey did the business then; any problems?' he asked Benzar.

'Like clockwork. But that doesn't excuse your cousin from paying what he owes me. Mickey got plenty for his part.'

'I know that.'

'But does Darryl? His tills will take a hit after that murder. Punters will be scared to go in there, especially the women. Bad publicity like that can ruin a business.'

'Of course, you'll get it all back.' Charley said waiting patiently. In truth he didn't know if he would. Maybe he'd have to bail Darryl out from his share of the heist?

'Bastard cops were nosing around here yesterday, asking questions about it?'

'Why, what's this murder got to do with you?'

'Remember Katrina from the casino the other week?'

'The fit blond?'

'Yeah. Her partner's that arse-hole Carl Bentley who drives for me. Seems he's a suspect.'

'How do you know?'

'I have my sources. Those dumb cops think I don't know what their game is. We need to be real careful now, that's all I'm saying.'

'You don't think they know about the job do you?' Charlie sounded worried.

'No, definitely not, but just to be sure I've cut Bentley lose; now he's been arrested. Not that he knows shit all anyway.'

Charlie waited patiently until the pieces were in place, and the cover was locked down. Ibrahim passed him a black rucksack. 'Your toolkit is in there.'

Then he dragged a side table the same height as the cabinet next to it, rolled out a paper template onto it and fixed it down with blu-tack.

'You ready?' Ibrahim asked, setting up the stopwatch on his mobile. 'Just pretend I'm not here?'

'Yeah, right.'

Charlie unzipped the bag and rummaged its depths before locating a set of keys, a powerful LED headlamp, a black twelve-inch torch and a small work belt loaded with tools needed to do the job. By this time Ibrahim began to draw the blackout blinds adorning the sash windows.

'Shit, it's dark in here.'

'Good practice. It could be darker in the Museum. No use doing it with the lights on! This will be the last time before the real thing,' Ibrahim warned him.

Charlie shrugged half-heartedly. 'Suppose you're right.'

'Anyway, like I said, I'm not here.'

Charlie laid the rucksack on the floorboards, switched on the LED headlamp, tilting it downward to his line of vision, clipped on the tool belt, then opened the first lock. Within seven minutes the locks were open and the cover lifted to a forty-five degree angle like a car bonnet. He clicked the torch on and rummaged around in the bag again until he located the ten-inch tablet loaded with images showing the exact position of the pieces. Placing it inside the cabinet, at the top, he switched the tiny bits of gold piece by piece, until the template contained all them.

With a small bottle of glass cleaner, he sprayed the cabinet cover and wiped it down, before locking it. He stood back for a moment mentally checking he'd not forgotten anything. To ensure each step was completed efficiently, leaving no trace evidence, they decided he should refer to a simple numbered checklist, printed on a laminated presentation card. As Ibrahim watched, the Collector's mantra echoed in his head '*The world's richest forgers and art thieves weren't often apprehended, because they planned meticulously for every outcome, including fencing the goods*'

'Finished!' Charlie said gratifyingly.

'Forty minutes flat,' Ibrahim said, tapping his phone, rising from the Chesterfield. 'You're forgetting something?'

'What's that?'

'The checklist! You gotta run through it.' He raised his voice to emphasise the point.

'Oh, bollocks!'

'At least it happened now, not on the job. Best to do it before you start and after you finish that way you're covered.'

Charlie scanned the torch in a large arc around the work area, checking he'd left nothing. 'All sorted.'

'What about that spray bottle on the table?'

'Oh, fucking hell!'

'Listen, take a break. I'll fetch you a coffee from the bar before you do it one last time.

'You're joking! Do it again?'

CHAPTER 84

Nine days after the break-in at the Furlong Social Club. DC Longsdon received a package delivered by Dennis Miller, the club's caretaker. On the front of the envelope a sticky note, handwritten in Biro, explained the reason for the delay was that, having not seen the duplicate copies for over twenty years he'd struggled to locate them amongst thousands in his collection. Longsdon tore open the flap of the A4 envelope and emptied its contents onto his desk. A pile of six by four inch photographs documenting five decades of the William Adams & Sons Pottery, spilled out. He separated the black and white from the grainy colour pics, and began to skim through them. Each picture showed employees posing in the department they worked in at the pottery firm.

That was when it hit him. Quickly he isolated five photos and studied them closely. A young Barry Gibson was in each of them… less tattoos, but it was definitely him. The big question was, who were the other young men with him? Whoever they were, the body language implied they were mates, as well as work colleagues. Could one of these men have stolen the photos in an attempt to hide his identity; maybe it was the killer?

He picked up the phone and called DI Blake, who was back in the station, as his mother in-law was now looking after his daughter.

Ten minutes later Blake stood behind Longsdon staring intently at the five photos laid out on his desk. 'Brilliant work, Longsdon. This is a very significant development in the Barry Gibson murderer case. It shows that whoever stole the copies from the Furlong club is desperately trying to disassociate their links to the victim. As you pointed out over the phone, it means our murderer is one of these men,' he said staring at the faces of Nathan Dukes, Darryl Connor, Grant Bolton, Dave Millburn and a fella with a red cap, pulled over his face, 'We need to identify him, which complicates things. I think it's time we had a serious chat with Connor and Millburn, but first we need to double our efforts in locating Grant Bolton.'

CHAPTER 85

Six hours locked in an artefact's storeroom, with a dog-eared crime paperback, a bottle of water and a pack of sandwiches for company wasn't his idea of a riveting evening. He was piss bored. Luckily there was a large stainless steel sink with running water. At fifty-four, Charlie Bullard increasingly needed to urinate at regular intervals, far more often than a few years ago. He'd pissed like a race horse since ten o'clock; probably nerves more than water intake being the culprit. The all-important text arrived at midnight on his crypto phone.

Cameras and alarms doctored. You have a four-hour window. I will call later to check progress. If you have any problems, contact me ASAP. Turn phone to silent vibrate mode. Don't forget session key number.

Charlie donned the forensic suit, boots and silicone gloves, and meticulously doubled-checked the contents of his rucksack, before unlocking the large exhibits storeroom, situated close to the entrance of the Natural History Zone.

Easing open the fire exit doors leading to the room, he stealthily moved forward into the darkness of the cavernous space. Like Aladdin exploring the genie's cave, he swept his torch in an arc. It was a taxidermist's paradise, full of stuffed animals, fossils and birds from in and around the Stoke-on-Trent area, each one behind glass screens or in Perspex display boxes.

His torch beam shone upon a large raven, its eyes reflected back at him, creepily suggestive, as if watching him. Moving on, past the section laid out to represent the Staffordshire Moorlands, complete with dry stone wall and winter skyline, a large stag surrounded by pheasants took centre place; its haunting glass eyes glared as an even bigger raven straddled a dead rabbit, entrails hanging from its beak.

Eerily the whole room seemed to come alive. Walking through the Woodland Trail, and into the Bronze Age displays, he kept his head down. On entering the 'Death and Burial throughout the ages' section, he illuminated the classic Benjamin Franklin quote:

"In this world nothing can be said to be certain, except death and taxes."

How bloody true, he thought. Stepping backwards something sharp nudged him in the lower back and startled him. Nervously turning around, half expecting a security guard, he shone the torch across a late nineteenth-century, two-wheeled coffin bearer, surrounded by display cabinets full of Victorian death and mourning artefacts. This place was giving him the creeps. Every display took on a new sinister meaning in torchlight.

Turning the corner he bumped into a large Perspex cabinet; a flash of the torch revealed the Arnold Bennett Zone. The cabinet contained several items which belonged to the famous local writer, including his Gladstone bag, a pair of shabby leather slippers and his book on watercolours.

Regaining his composure, he entered his favourite part of the museum: the local history zone, an L-shaped corridor divided into a series of rooms from the early nineteen hundreds, all containing original fixtures and fittings. First up on the left was the bar of a local pub, complete with Edwardian drinkers accompanied by *Harry Hewitt's Billy;* a legendary local greyhound that won dozens of races before the First World War. Next to that was a complete pharmacy from around the same period; its carved mahogany shop front and counter had been beautifully preserved. He almost dropped the torch as it illuminated a female mannequin clad in a black ankle-length Edwardian dress. Her ghostly white face glared at him as she sat rocking a lifeless baby in the chair next to a cast-iron range.

Taking a deep breath, he paused before finally reaching his destination, slightly disturbed at his night at the museum. All the artefacts seemed to be alive.

On entering the Anglo-Saxon kingdom of Mercia the ominous sight of eight large display cabinets confronted him, strategically laid out at the entrance to exhibit the Hoard to the visiting public. Each cabinet had two alarmed locks securing the glass frontage.

Removing the rucksack, he retrieved a large folded plastic sheet, draped it over the cabinet on the far left, before laying his sterilised tool kit, including the cabinet keys onto it. Hopefully this would stop any trace evidence being transferred onto the glass. The Collector stressed the importance of using unopened high-grade forensic equipment for a delicate job such as this. It was much harder to trace.

Lastly, he placed the ten-inch tablet containing a series of numbered HD photographs Ibrahim's cousin had taken. Recreating the original positioning was vital. Pointless replacing everything with the replica pieces, only for them to be discovered as fakes because the positioning was wrong. The Dad's Army security guards were on a rota, watching over the gold, and everyone would notice if the pieces were in the wrong order.

Turning on his headlight to illuminate the work area, he dropped to his knees, inserted the barrel key into the first lock and turned it anticlockwise. Repeating the same for the next lock, they opened like a dream. Early days yet but, so far so good, he thought, trying to keep a lid on his nerves. He carefully leaned the tablet showing picture number two against the hinged glass of the open cabinet, double-checking it was the right one before removing the first piece of delicate gold with a pair of sterile blue tweezers. This extremely delicate operation needed executing with maximum efficiency and finesse. The replicas sat inside tiny compartmentalised boxes, each box, and each piece of gold, meticulously numbered to avoid error. Thankfully each cabinet only contained about a hundred pieces. The other two thousand two hundred were kept in a safe in the artefacts storeroom. Lucky for them, the caretaker had told them these were only checked every couple of weeks.

Switching the first seven cabinets went better than he could have imagined. With those locked down and cleaned, he moved on to the final treasure chest, repeating in his head, I am calm and relaxed, I am calm and relaxed, an Emotional Freedom technique mantra he'd discovered via YouTube. He found this simple, self-hypnosis very calming.

A glance at his watch revealed it was four a.m. Still plenty of time left, he reassured himself. As before, he lifted the cabinet lid with caution, but there was a horrible creaking noise. The kind old rusty door hinges made when they needed lubricating. 'Bollocks!' he uttered under his breath. His heart skipped a beat, and, nervous, he spun around, instinctively looking to see if anyone else had overheard, before remembering he was alone in the deathly silence of the Kingdom of Mercia.

It was 4.10 a.m. and there was no time to dwell. He'd got this far, without hiccups. There was no way he'd let himself falter at the last hurdle. Tapping his temples he repeated the mantra. Nerves composed, he continued. Within the next half an hour the switch would be complete. All that remained was to lock down, clean-sweep the work area and get back to the storeroom to empty the safe containing the rest of the Hoard. He'd then get his head down until the caretaker let him out at 6.30 a.m.

Pulling the cabinet cover revealed it was stuck. He took a deep breath and pulled harder. Still it wouldn't budge so he pushed it from the side, but still no joy.

'Oh fuck!' he groaned anxiously. It was jammed solid. Taking another deep breath, he stepped back and wiped beads of sweat from his brow. The bloody forensic suit was making him sweatier than a dervish's jockstrap. With the hum of air conditioning in the background he pondered what to do next. A horrible thought entered his head. 'What if this bastard cover won't go down? I'll be well and truly fucked.'

Without hesitation, he fished the crypto phone from the rucksack and called Ibrahim.

'Session code?' Ibrahim asked bluntly.

Charlie could barely see the screen. Wiping the sweat from his eyes, he said, 'Four, three, seven, eight.'

'What's up?'

'There's a problem,' he whispered, looking around the room, paranoid.

'What fucking problem?'

'The last cabinet won't shut.'

'Have you sprayed the hinges?'

'Not yet.'

Ibrahim demanded immediate action. 'Do it now!'

'OK.'

'Stay on the line.'

After a minutes silence Charlie spoke again. 'Given 'em a good blast, just waiting for it to soak in.'

'Careful you don't break anything,' Ibrahim said, trying to remain calm, realising Charlie could lose the plot if he abused him at this crucial stage.

'It's no good, still won't budge.'

'Hold on a minute while Leonard looks for a solution online.'

Charlie felt nauseous like a heavy rock had dropped in the pit of his stomach. A sudden noise overhead startled him. The silence from the other end of the phone only increased his irrational fears. He yanked the water bottle from the bag and nervously gulped down the last few drops.

'Charl, you there? It's Leonard.'

'Yeah.'

'Listen, according to this quick fix, you need to lift the lid gently, then rock it up and down carefully before trying to close it. Spray again as well?'

'OK, giving it a go now,' he said with the slightest glimmer of hope in his voice.

CHAPTER 86

The rider sat on a stolen scooter, opposite the side exit of the Museum, in a black crash helmet, visor up, with a thin breathable scarf hiding the lower half of his face. According to that ginger geek Leonard Vale, Charlie Bullard was due to leave the building around 6.30 a.m. Because of CCTV he hadn't arrived too early, and planned to follow Bullard until he could take the rucksack where there were no cameras.

Like clockwork Bullard slowly exited the building, giving a cautious look around. He noticed the man on a bike but didn't appear wary of him. To be sure the rider waited until Bullard had turned left and headed towards the traffic lights crossing over the ring road. Slowly the rider exited the street and eased down the road keeping his target in full view. They must be doing the switch in Shelton.

Bullard continued down the A5006, before crossing over and turning right down a side street. This was his window, it was now or never. The rider throttled up and took a sharp right down the same street. Where was he? He lifted his visor and scanned the area in a panic. He noticed a cobbled alleyway leading down the back of the rows of terraced houses. Without hesitation he mounted the pavement and gunned the scooter down it. Bullard was halfway along when he noticed the scooter racing towards him with intent. Attempting to dodge it he dived through a half open gate into one of the terrace backyards. The rider screeched the scooter to a halt, leaving the engine running; lowering his visor he chased after him. Bullard was cornered, his back against old outbuildings.

'You don't know who you're stealing from. He'll have you taken out, you stupid fucker!'

The rider ignored him and lunged at the rucksack slung over Bullard's shoulder, but as it slid down his arm he frantically managed to cling onto the other strap. A moment of tug-of-war ensued, before the assailant pulled a small razor-sharp blade from his pocket, and slashed through the taut strap. Bullard fell back onto the ground as the rider dashed out of the yard, jumped on the scooter and spun away in a blaze of trailing smoke out of the alleyway.

Bullard lay there numb with shock, trying to contemplate what had just happened. Months of planning, thousands of pounds of investment, and the famous Staffordshire Hoard, gone! How the hell was he going to explain this to Ibrahim? Since there were only a handful of people who knew about the robbery this was definitely an inside job; got to be. Still shaking he patted his pockets for his phone. A feeling of dread crept over him as it dawned on him; he'd left it in the front pouch of the rucksack. 'Oh fuck!' He dragged his sorry ass up and headed for the Slipware Tankard bar, absolutely shitting it.

CHAPTER 87

In a rage, Ibrahim Benzar hurled his mug of coffee at the painted brick wall so hard, it smashed into dozens of pieces, exposing a chunk of bare brick. Charlie looked in horror at the exploded coffee stain splashed all over the wall like a modern art installation.

Benzar sat down after hearing the news of the mugging. His face ashen white as a sudden coldness hit his core.

'Who would have the balls to do this? Make no mistake, he's a fucking dead man walking, I'll whack him myself if I have to. Ahhh!' He slammed his fist on the desk, 'It's got to be an inside job. No one else knew about it. So, you're saying there was a moped outside the museum when you came out?' Ibrahim asked him again.

Charlie almost dared not to answer, 'Yeah, but I was so focused on getting out of there, and to the drop-off point I barely noticed him.'

'Are you serious, man?' his facial muscles tightened.

'I'm afraid so.'

'This is some kind of double-cross! What am I supposed to tell our buyer, he's already invested shit loads in this venture? We need to get that gold back soon as. The longer it's out of our hands the worse it gets. There's no way this arsehole can shift it. No one knows it's been nicked except us. Why didn't you call me straight away?'

Charlie stuttered 'My… mobile… it's in… the rucksack.'

Without another word Ibrahim grabbed his phone from the desk, and speed dialled Charlie's burner. It rang and rang, but no one answered. He stabbed the end call button in disgust.

'If he's dumped the phone we are totally fucked. Have you told anyone about this job, anyone; even family?'

'Of course not, what do you take me for?'

'I want everyone together right now,' he said tightening his grip on the arms of the chair.

Forty minutes later all the gang sat wide-eyed in amazement facing Ibrahim Benzar. No one dared speak.

'I've been racking my brains about who could have done this and drawn a blank, which leads me to think one of you fucking idiots has told someone about the robbery, and I'm pretty convinced it's not Charlie', Ibrahim accused them. 'Well come on, someone speak?'

'You can't seriously believe it's any of us?' Why would we take all those risks and lose the chance of a million quid,' Malcolm Preston said, bravely acting as unappointed spokesman.

Ibrahim glared at him, 'Well someone has, and when I find out who it is they'll be hanging from their bollocks on a meat hook, and that's just for starters. Do you understand?'

Arthur Mitchell plucked up the courage to respond, 'None of us would *ever* consider double-crossing you,'

'What have you got to say for yourself, Leonard?' Ibrahim stared at him noticing his face begin to redden. 'Well, come on let's hear it?'

Vale bowed his head. He didn't speak. Ibrahim slid open his desk drawer and retrieved a hand gun. In a panic Vale darted towards the door, but before he could open it Ibrahim tightly gripped his greasy ginger mop, and forced the weapon into his mouth. Vale shook uncontrollably as the other three men gawped in horror at what was unfolding.

'Give me one good reason not to blow the back of your skull open? Have you told anyone about the job?' Ibrahim said pushing the gun further in, choking him.

Vales eyes bulged, tiny optical veins stopping them from bursting out of their sockets. He nodded rapidly. Ibrahim withdrew the gun, but kept it aimed at his face.

'A bloke in a balaclava, with a knife threatened to kill me if I didn't tell him about the job. Said if I told anyone he'd come round my house and carve me up; he knows where I live. I was petrified,' he said staring everywhere but at the gun.

CHAPTER 88

'What the bloody hell do you lot want now? I've told you everything I know,' Dave Millburn retorted.

DI Blake and DS Murphy sat opposite him in an interview room one. Having already been questioned twice this latest interview felt like police harassment.

'New evidence has come to light which means we need to ask you some more questions, Mr Millburn. This is an ongoing murder investigation.' Blake said.

Millburn shot him a look. 'What new evidence?'

'A member of the public has come forward and provided us with incriminating photographs.'

'What photos?'

'Pictures linking the crime scene witnesses to Barry Gibson.'

'Is this some kind of joke?'

'How long did you work with Barry and the others on the kilns at William Adams & Sons?'

Millburn's face reddened; he looked shocked, 'A few years, but I really don't see how this is relevant?'

'When we initially interviewed you at the White Horse crime scene, you denied knowing the victim. In fact, you went out of your way to distance yourself.' Blake glanced down at the original interview notes. You said, "*Seen him around town from a distance, but that's all,*" but judging by these photos. You, Nathan Dukes, Darryl Connor, Grant Bolton and some fella in a red cap we've yet to identify all worked and socialised with Barry Gibson.'

The revelation made Millburn more anxious.

Blake continued, 'So, my concern is why did you lie to us? Wasting police time is an offence Mr Millburn, and you've been doing it from day one of this investigation. Clearly you have something to hide, and we intend to find out what it is?'

'This is bollocks. So, I knew Barry back in the day, doesn't mean I killed him does it?' Millburn scoffed.

'The fact he ended up murdered whilst you were working the doors of the White Horse, and denied knowing him, is too much of a coincidence for us to ignore. Furthermore, someone broke into Furlong Social Club in Burslem recently. There was over three-thousand pounds worth of booze in the place, but not so much as a bottle of wine was taken? The raider smashed open three display cabinets, and stole photographs of workers from the William Adams Pottery, dating from 1968 to 1993.'

Millburn stared at him arrogantly. 'And you're telling me this because?'

'We're pretty certain that Barry Gibson's killer is in these photographs.' Blake said laying the five pictures out onto the table.

Millburn glanced at them nervously, but kept his mouth shut.

'Who's the lad in the cap?'

'Can't remember his name, it was years ago.' Millburn said evasively.

'You worked with a bloke for five years and can't remember his name, I'm afraid your bullshitting again. Can you smell something in here, DS Murphy?'

'Yeah I'm getting a whiff, it's definitely getting stronger by the minute.'

Millburn sneered. 'We weren't really mates; he worked in a different shop to us: just jumped into that photo.'

'We'll find out who he is. You clearly know the others? You work the doors with Nathan Dukes for Darryl Connor, at his pub.'

'I already told you, that was a one-off, because one of the lads let me down.'

Blake continued. 'This break-in was targeted. The raider knew exactly what he was looking for, which tells us one thing.'

Millburn seemed shifty, but remained silent.

Blake glared at him, 'This raider is the murderer, and he's desperately trying to cover his tracks. He'll slip up and we'll be there when he does. Do you hear me Mr Millburn?'

'Hard not to, but I still don't see what this has to do with me?'

'Where were you between ten p.m. and eight a.m. on the ninth of this month?'

Millburn thought for a while. 'I'm a busy man Inspector. That was over a week ago. Although I do remember because that was one of the only nights I was at home with the Mrs; takeaway and TV I seem to recall, but to be sure I'd have to check my diary and get back to you.'

'How convenient, you just do that, but I want your whereabouts confirming within the hour, or I'll be charging you with wasting police time.' Blake knew they couldn't place Millburn at the scene of the break-in.

CHAPTER 89

Disappointed with the outcome of Dave Millburn's interview, Blake needed a caffeine boost. As he pressed the coffee with extra sugar button on the vending machine, DS Murphy shouted down the corridor.

'We've got Darryl Connor in interview room one when you're ready, boss. Oh, by the way I've spoken to Dave Millburn's Mrs, she works across town.'

'His alibi for the night of the break-in at the Furlong Social Club checks out?'

'Fraid so.'

'How frigging predictable.'

Blake sighed deeply. He was sick of the sight of those idiots associated with the White Horse pub. Darryl Connor was another slippery tosser with form for violence.

'Sorry to have hauled you in for another chat Mr Connor, but we have some new evidence in the Barry Gibson murder case, and thought you may be able to help us with it?' Blake said attempting to put Connor at ease, before dropping the bomb.

'Not sure I follow Inspector.'

'Well it was a long time ago.'

Connor looked puzzled. 'What was?'

Blake laid the photographs side-by-side in the middle of the table. He wanted to assess his suspect's reaction. 'Do you recognise these?'

The colour drained from Connor's face as he nervously picked up the first picture with a shaky hand, and stared at it. 'Bloody hell! Where did you get these from?'

'I have my sources. So, why didn't you mention you'd worked with Barry Gibson, Dave Millburn, Grant Bolton, and this guy with the cap pulled over his face, between 1988 and 1993. Who is he by the way?'

Connor stared at the picture. Honestly, I can't remember. He didn't work with us on the Kilns.'

'So this anonymous youth just jumped into the shot?'

'Must have done.'

'You don't seriously expect us to believe that?'

'Hang on a min, he paused, 'Now I remember! It's Stomper; that was his nickname anyway. I really don't know his real name?'

This took Blake by complete surprise. Surely it couldn't be a coincidence, that the bloke Barry Gibson's Mrs mentioned, and a lad who worked at William Adams Pottery, were in fact the same person? Even though Connor might have seen the police appeal in the *Sentinel*, Blake didn't reveal the connection. The landlord might warn him. It was best to let it run. See if things developed.

'I'll ask you again, why didn't you mention about your history with the other witnesses, when we first questioned you at the pub? It's very suspicious.'

'I don't know. It didn't seem relevant.' he said, cheeks flushing, like a teenager lying to his teacher.

'Please don't insult my intelligence, Mr Connor. I've heard so much bullshit from the witnesses in this case, it's starting to make me retch. You conveniently failed to mention it because you're scared of the consequences of being linked to Barry Gibson's murder. You can't hack another prison sentence at your age, especially now you've got the Mrs and the pub to think of.'

'What I am supposed to have done?' Connor asked.

'I was hoping you would tell me. But it looks like I'll have to spell it out to you. We're convinced Barry Gibson's murderer is in these photographs, but I'm now of the opinion he didn't act alone. He may have had accomplices. Witnesses who pretended to unwittingly contaminate the crime scene. After all, you guys have known each other for years. And realising the severity of the situation, you all created an elaborate smokescreen to send us on a wild goose chase after an anonymous murderer.'

Connor continued the charade. 'We reported it to the police as soon as Barry's body was discovered.'

'It all seems a little too convenient to me. Three old workmates just happened to be in the vicinity of a fourth, who'd been killed. Your deception is slowly starting to unravel, and when the final curtain drops, one of you goes down for life!

'Where were you between ten p.m. on the ninth of this month and eight a.m. the next morning?'

'What's this got to do with Barry's death?'

'Trust me, it's relevant. Those photos were stolen during a break-in, and they were the only thing taken.'

Connor thought for a moment. 'Er… I seem to recall I was in the pub all night with Dominika. We tided the stock room, and then had a few beers. It sticks in my mind because I filled in order forms, dated the ninth.'

'Was anyone else there?'

'No.'

'You seem pretty sure? Let's hope you're telling the truth, because we'll be checking. In fact, what's her mobile number? DS Murphy will call her now.' Blake decided to play hardball, allowing Connor no time to coerce his Mrs into providing an alibi.

CHAPTER 90

'A hundred grand in cash! Are you fucking joking?' Ibrahim was absolutely steaming with rage at the ransom demand.

'If you want to get the gold back that's the price; it's non-negotiable,' said the man on the other end of the line.

Ibrahim thought carefully for a few seconds knowing what was at stake. If he lost it with this double-crossing bastard it would all be over. 'You'll have to give me twenty-four hours to get my hands on that kind of cash.'

'Twenty-four hours, no more. I'll call back on this number with instructions. Don't even consider double-crossing us.'

Ibrahim clenched his fist and agreed reluctantly. A hundred grand was a shit load, but in the scheme of things a mere fraction of the 5 million they were due. He'd just have to take the loss. One thing was sure, once everything was finalised he'd put some resources into finding these bastards. They were dead men walking.

He dismissed the group, slipped the gun into his jacket pocket and walked over to the other side of the room to access the safe sunken beneath the floorboards in the far corner. On his knees he lifted the white floorboard revealing an impenetrable firecracker box securely bolted to the joists on both sides. On the last count he knew there was eighty grand cash in there, but he really didn't know where the next twenty grand was coming from, leaving him with a big problem. Yusuf's arrest had already lost them forty thousand.

CHAPTER 91

Twenty-four hours later, Ibrahim was only a couple of miles away from Knutsford service station, between junctions 18 and 19, on the M6 in Cheshire. The switch was due to take place in the café, situated in the gantry over the busy northbound M6. A very public place, he thought glancing at the pistol handle poking out from under the brown envelope, containing the cash on the passenger seat.

He parked and purposefully headed across the car park contemplating who would have the balls to pull this stunt?

Just a few spaces down from Ibrahim's Audi, a man sat behind the driver's wheel of his rental car, watching him. In the passenger seat a woman in her early twenties sat nervously with Charlie Bullard's rucksack on her lap. On the journey down she'd been instructed to get a coffee and join Ibrahim at his table. The man had sent a photo of him to her mobile phone. He retrieved Bullard's stolen burner from his door pocket and made the call.

Ibrahim sat sipping cappuccino whilst thumbing through the Daily Star. A constant stream of lorries and cars flew underneath the gantry. All kinds of irrational thoughts ran through his mind. He wasn't confident that he'd be able to control his anger, but had to admit it was a smart move to send a woman to do the switch.

'Is this seat taken?' a young woman wearing Charlie's rucksack asked.

Ibrahim gestured for her to sit, 'You do realise you're putting yourself at risk by getting involved in this?' he said, noticing her fear.

'All I know is I'm swapping this rucksack for an envelope,' she said nervously clenching the right shoulder strap.

'Enjoy the money they're paying you because you don't have long to spend it.' Ibrahim unintentionally raised his voice, which attracted stares from a family of four sitting at the table behind them.

'Are you threatening me?' she asked fearfully, before glancing around the room.

'Let's just say you've been warned, now let's get this over with before I lose my temper!'

'Put the envelope on the table, I've been instructed to count it in the ladies', before giving you this,' she rolled her shoulder and glanced at the rucksack.

'Yeah right, and I'm an idiot. I'll tell you now, that's not happening, so call your boss to re-negotiate.' Ibrahim shot her an angry stare.

A muffled message coming from a police airwave set startled them both. The woman froze. Nervously, Ibrahim glanced at a motorway cop in a Hi-Viz jacket ordering coffees at the counter; then another cop joined him. Shit! There were two of them, he thought.

A moment of deadly silence followed as they both sat there waiting for the cops to leave. God forbid they'd take a seat.

Carrying two lidded cups in a cardboard tray they walked towards their table. The woman's complexion turned white; she looked as if she'd faint any second. Avoiding eye contact, Ibrahim pulled out his mobile and began nonchalantly flicking through his messages. As the cops levelled with their table, one of them noticed the woman's demeanour.

He paused and glanced at her. 'You OK love, you don't look well?'

'I'm… fi… ne,' she said almost alerting him that something was wrong.

Ibrahim interrupted, 'She gets car sickness on the motorway, Officer.'

'Fair enough,' he said.

The airwave set blasted again, this time Ibrahim listened carefully.

'Safe to talk shire 591 over?'

'Roger, go ahead?'

'RTA just before junction 24, what's your estimated response time, over?'

'About ten minutes, on our way.'

Ibrahim breathed a huge sigh of relief as he watched the coppers make their way out of the café door. With a worried look the woman got up, fished her mobile from her back pocket, paced towards the window and dialled.

Ibrahim never took his eyes off her. She was totally out of her depth.

She returned to the table and renegotiated, 'Says he wants proof all the money is there; wants it counting.'

'And how am I going to do that in here; you'll get us both arrested, don't be dumb. The best I can do is take a picture on my phone in the men's. But let's get one thing clear I'm not leaving without that rucksack, even if I have to rip it off your back you stupid bitch. I'm done fucking around.'

Realising there was no other option she sat at the table waiting for Ibrahim to come back from the gents.

'He says it's okay to do the deal, after you've sent the picture to him.'

Ibrahim took a deep breath, 'That's it then, no more of this shit. And I want to see some samples of the gold first. She glanced around the room nervously, then fished in her pocket and pulled out a clear bag containing sword fittings; pommel caps, hilt plates and garnet set pyramids.

Ibrahim scrutinised them. A minute later he received a text…

DO THE SWITCH. If you follow her after I'll call the cops!

With gritted teeth he slid the folded Daily Star across the table, hiding the brown envelope inside. The woman grabbed it and left the rucksack where she'd been sitting. Ibrahim was desperate to follow her but didn't call the man's bluff; since he didn't know who he was dealing with it was too risky. He grabbed the rucksack, unzipped it and rummaged through; all the boxes loaded with the gold where there. He breathed a sigh of relief. At least there was still some honour left in the criminal world.

CHAPTER 92

The Sepang blue RS5 Audi Tronic eased into the lower bay of Liverpool One car park. This stolen-to-order beauty had cost the Turkish gangster less than half the manufacturer's on-the-road price of sixty-thousand. A London syndicate had nicked it to order: affording Ibrahim uninhibited motoring in this exquisite coupé for the past six months.

The journey from Stoke to Liverpool took longer than Charlie had expected, due to traffic. Before setting off from the Potteries, Ibrahim informed him that, with a cargo of £3.3 millions' worth of ancient gold stowed on-board, he should stick to the speed limit religiously.

The switch was due to take place later that evening in a room at the four-star Hilton overlooking Albert Docks, on John Sears' Way. The Collector's man in Europe was overseeing the deal. Ibrahim and Bullard were scheduled to meet his specialist artefacts' authenticator in the hotel bar at 6.30 p.m. After the nerve-wrenching experience of the heist, Charlie was enjoying all the mystique.

'It's like being in *Ocean's Eleven*,' he said to Ibrahim, as they wheeled their trolley cases across the highly polished marble floor of the hotel reception. 'I need a drink.'

'Let's check in first. Take a seat there,' Ibrahim said, pointing towards the modular leather sofas opposite the reception desk.'

Because businessmen from all over the world frequented the hotel they'd blend in relatively unnoticed; although Ibrahim made an obvious point of mentioning to the receptionist, that they were attending a business conference at the Echo Arena. With the formalities over, they took the lift to the third floor.

The adjoining rooms had spectacular views overlooking the Albert Docks UNESCO heritage site. Charlie dumped his case in the spacious double wardrobe, opened the mini-bar, and flipped the top off a cold beer. It'd been years since he'd stayed in a posh hotel and this place would do nicely, he thought. With its super king-size bed, modern en suite, panoramic view and, most importantly, fridge stocked full of beer.

In the next room, Ibrahim secured the Hoard in his safe and made a coffee from one of the complementary sachets. Whilst he languished in a large swivel chair, gazing through the floor-to-ceiling glass, he thought about the five million. A light tap on the door brought him back to the present. Padding across the carpet he peaked through the spy hole at Bullard's silvery moustache.

'Charlie, come in?'

'Quality room that.'

'Glad you like it. Fancy lunch?'

'Yeah, I'm starving, man.'

'OK, I'll book us a table at Jamie Oliver's; it's only five minutes from the hotel. Italian OK with you?'

'The TV chef?' he animated.

'Yeah, just a franchise; he won't be cooking.'

'Sounds good.'

'Give me twenty minutes to freshen up and I'll give you a knock.'

'OK.'

CHAPTER 93

Over prawn linguine and pizza, they covertly discussed the last couple of weeks' intense heist preparation, and the audacious bastard that stole the gold from them. Above them, the glass walkways of the busy Liverpool One shopping centre filled up. After they'd finished Charlie lifted his glass in the hope of a top-up, but Ibrahim shook his head at the waiter, putting paid to his desire for more Chianti.

'Can we have the bill please? No more alcohol, Charl; you need to keep a straight head for the meeting. Once that's done, we can party.'

'Party!' His face lit up anticipating going on a bender with Benzar.

'Another meal, a couple of bars, then onto Eros Divine.'

'What's that place then?'

'Lap dancing club.'

'Seriously?' Charlie grinned.

'Yeah, thought I'd blow some cash. I've booked a VIP. booth for eleven. We get champagne and a couple of girls to ourselves for an hour.'

Demonstrating the desperation of single bloke who rarely got his rocks off, the ageing bank robber rubbed his hands together.

'Anyway, it's three o'clock; we need to get back. You take a nap, watch TV, while I prepare for the switch.'

Back in his room, Ibrahim set up the money counter and then lay on the bed. The heavy lunch had made him feel drowsy. Lying there he mulled over the arrangements of exchanging half the gold for two million cash, and the second half on completion of an online bank transfer into a Cayman Island company account, set up by his accountant Malcolm Preston.

Ibrahim woke after a nap; it was 5.10 p.m. He showered, wrapped himself in a towel and opened a beer from the mini-bar. Finally, after weeks of planning, payday had arrived. Sitting upright on the bed, he felt apprehensive. Could he trust the Collector? Apart from weekly phone calls during the months leading up to the heist, he'd not seen the eccentric millionaire for over eight years. Even with the two hundred thousand upfront, payment for personnel and equipment, he still had nagging doubts whether the cash would be kosher. Five million seemed an absurdly large sum to part with for a collection worth just three point three million, although he was aware mega-rich collectors were more interested in the status of owning some of the world's rarest artefacts, as opposed to their monetary value. Equally worrying was how long it would take the museum to discover their Anglo-Saxon kingdom of Mercia was full of gold-plated Indian tat.

He drained his bottle, slipped on some boxers and pulled on a navy polo shirt. Padding across the soft carpet to the window, he gazed out across the Albert Docks. Sun rays sparkled, flickering like tiny stars on the dark waters of the Mersey Estuary as a steady stream of tourists sporting backpacks ventured across the busy six lane ring road towards the city's dockland bars and restaurants.

Turning back from the window, he slipped on his jeans and loafers and ran a comb through his hair. He grabbed his wallet and left the room, heading towards the lift.

It was 6.25, and the fashionable hotel bar with its glass chandeliers and zoned high-back Chesterfields was filling up with an eclectic mix of businessman, couples and groups of young woman, probably hen parties judging by the chinking of champagne flutes and their rowdy excitement. Ibrahim arranged for the Collector's authenticator to call him at 6.30 p.m. Jefferson Newbridge was a rare artefacts specialist with a specific knowledge of ancient gold. And the Collector told him he could trust the 65-year-old implicitly.

Suddenly his mobile rang. 'Hello.'

'Jefferson Newbridge, we have a scheduled meeting at six-thirty.'

'Where are you?' Ibrahim asked, scanning around the bar until he noticed a grey-haired gent in a two-piece Harris Tweed suit, and green pinstripe tie, sat in the far right-hand corner, offering up a pint in acknowledgement. He slipped Charlie forty quid to get the drinks in and joined the eccentric-looking professor.

'Hi, you must be Jefferson?' he said offering a firm handshake.

'Yes, please sit.'

Ibrahim dropped into the high back Chesterfield, facing the professors, affording them a degree of privacy. 'Can I get you a drink?'

'I'm OK, thank you, got one here,' he said in near-perfect Queen's English.

Charlie came trundling over, dodging four-luscious looking girls in skinny jeans with outrageously big hair. He tried hard not to spill the drinks, but the two pints of lager were a quarter of an inch lower by the time he'd stopped gawping at them and sloshed them onto the table.

'Charl, this is Professor Newbridge.'

Charlie nodded in acknowledgement as he stood wringing his hands free of surplus beer. 'Back in a minute, I'm going to wash my hands.'

Give his cock a good rub, more likely! Ibrahim thought, after that blatant perving. After taking a long slurp, he asked the professor. 'How do you want to do this?'

'I suggest we finish the drinks and reconvene at your room to look at the goods. Once we've established everything's genuine, I'll fetch my luggage. What room are you fellows in?'

'Three-four-five, on the third floor.'

They made unrelated small talk for a further fifteen minutes before leaving the bar.

Back in the room Ibrahim poured two whiskys, one to calm his nerves and another for Charlie, who sat in the swivel chair reading a complimentary copy of the *Mail.* He'd already retrieved four of the eight boxes, containing the Hoard pieces, from the safe and was pacing up and down the narrow space between the bed and the door in nervous anticipation of the professor's arrival.

A sudden tap on the door focused his attention. Peering through the spy hole he saw the distorted outline of the professor's tweed suit. The eccentric entered towing a sturdy-looking black trolley case, with a smaller tan briefcase perched on top of it. He laid the briefcase on the bed, retracted the other case's telescopic handle and let it rest by his side.

'Please sit down, Professor.' Ibrahim gestured towards the leather chair under the writing desk.

'Can I offer you a drink?'

'A glass of water would be fine, thanks.'

Ibrahim eased past him to fetch a bottle from the mini bar. Upon returning he noticed the professor had removed his jacket and linked a microscope to a small laptop he'd laid out with several other tools onto the desk, presumably equipment needed to authenticate the gold.

Rising from the chair the Professor heaved the trolley case onto the mattress, clicked the combination lock and slid it towards the opposite side of the bed, where Ibrahim sat eagerly awaiting to scrutinise its contents.

'I think you'll find it's all there, one million in used twenties and seven hundred in fifties. The other three hundred is in the briefcase, but feel free to count it?'

Ibrahim carefully unzipped the case cover and folded it back to reveal deep piles of neatly packed notes. He gasped, his head spinning. Never in his entire life had he seen so much money in one place. Charlie stood speechless at his side gawping at the fortune laid out before them, and that was only bloody half of it, he thought! Switching on the note counter they set about the tedious job of counting and checking the cash was kosher.

The Safescan 2210 electronic banknote counter was a small portable device with built-in UV counterfeit warning detection and the ability to count a thousand notes per minute.

He fed the machine with the first pile of twenties. This crazy gadget even printed an itemised receipt at the end, providing a complete breakdown of the number of notes, batches and total value.

The professor looked on sceptically before asking to see the gold. Ibrahim passed him the first box while Charlie continued to feed the counter. He carefully opened it and sat in awe of its contents. The gold glistened under the powerful LED desk lamp.

'So this is the world-famous Staffordshire Hoard? I must say it's an absolute treat to see the pieces of this rare collection up close. Thirteen hundred years of history right in front of me. It's like opening Pandora's box to sixth- and seventh-century England,' he said, squinting through the viewing tube of the microscope, whilst gently caressing the first piece with a pair of tweezers. 'I'm presuming these pieces have already been gold-tested by the British Museum. However, since we can't obtain those results legally, my employer requested this second test.' He lightly scratched the surface of several pieces and performed analysis on them to identify what type of alloys the gold comprised of. 'Beautiful filigree work, amazing skill. It's so delicate and intricate… no two pieces are the same, an absolute joy to behold. The garnet inlays of this sword pyramid originated from India, the level of craftsmanship is astonishing. Look at this magnificent folded cross… you can see from the core it was crafted in two parts; there's still plenty of soil trapped in the carving. Ruddy shame the settings used to decorate it aren't here. They'd have probably been rubies.'

Spouting numerous superlatives, the professor methodically worked his way through both boxes, spending a few seconds analysing each piece. After an hour he declared emphatically that the exquisite collection was genuine.

Tell us something we don't already know, egg-head! thought Charlie, visualising how he intended to splash his first hundred thousand, whilst reloading the last pile into the counter.

With a wry smile, the professor said, 'I think that concludes our cash transaction.' He retrieved a seven-inch tablet PC from his jacket. We can settle the bank transfer if you login to your account here.' He pointed to a portal on the screen below a Dominion bank logo.

Ibrahim tapped his phone to display the account details and nervously entered the password. Fifteen minutes later the screen returned a balance sheet showing a 3 million sterling deposit. He loaded the professor's cases with the boxes containing the remaining pieces of the Hoard.

'Shall we part over breakfast? Eight-thirty OK with you, chaps?'

Ibrahim agreed, carefully pondering how to best secure the cash whilst they were out on the lash that evening. 'Make sure to stuff your safe with as many boxes it will hold.'

'They'll be collected later via secure currier in the guise of a taxi,' the professor informed him.

Ibrahim should have guessed the Collector would have all bases covered. 'What you up to this evening, Professor?'

'Nothing much, couple of glasses of Shiraz in the bar, then I'll retire with *Gold From The Dark Ages*.'

'Couldn't tempt you into a few beers with me and Charlie?' Ibrahim asked him with a cheeky grin.'

'Will there be girls?'

'Might be.' He winked at Charlie.

Professor Newbridge looked excited. 'Bang on. The Dark Ages can go on a back burner; it's been months since old Harry's had a rub.'

The pair of them looked at each other, with a conspiratorial grin, trying hard not to laugh at the Professor's overtly public schoolboy mannerisms.

After he'd left, they split the cash in half and intended to spread it around both rooms. In the unlikely event of being robbed at least they'd only lose a few grand. Five hundred thousand went into each of their safes, whilst the other million was split into ten bundles, and stuffed in different hiding places around their rooms.

CHAPTER 94

Later that evening the three unlikely drinking companions sat sipping a forty-quid bottle of Venica Ronco Delle Cime, in Gusto, a top-class Italian restaurant on the Albert docks. Ibrahim raised his glass and announced a toast.

'Health, wealth and women.'

'Quite right, old boy,' added the professor as their glasses chinked together.

'Not a bad tipple, this cheap plonk,' he teased.

Ibrahim shot him a glance, but didn't rise to the bait.

'Can't believe we pulled it off,' Charlie marvelled.

'I know. It's crazy how after tomorrow you can start a new life. No going mad buying things that will draw attention to you. Flash cars and big houses are off-limits. How about you, Professor? I take it the Collector's sorted you out?'

'I have a standard fee for this kind of work, which is more than generous, although any extra donations would be received with gratitude.'

Ibrahim wished he hadn't asked, knowing full well the evening's debauchery would leave little change from two grand. The meal combined with VIP tickets to the lap dancing club had already cost three hundred and fifty quid, and he hadn't even paid for the Professor's ticket yet. Sod it, I've got shit loads, he thought.

'How about a tasty bird in hot pants sitting on your lap, rubbing her tits in your face?' he teased the Professor.

'Bang on. That'll do for dessert. Most grateful if you could extend to a shag.'

'You dirty old bugger!' Charlie said.

'Well, us old guys rarely get a sniff. I have needs same as the next man,' he declared like a sex-starved slave.

After the meal they downed brandies and headed over the cobbles to the Smugglers Cove pub, passing the huge Wheel of Liverpool on the way. It turned slowly, LED lights flickering and casting a shimmer of blue across the inlet waters as the light faded across the cloudless sky above the Mersey Estuary.

The dockland warehouse Smugglers Cove occupied retained original stone slabs on the floor, and vaulted ceilings, from which an anchor rope spanned the length of the bar, with crystal brandy decanters, converted into lanterns hanging from it. The bar front displayed a row of eight down-lit glass cabinets, each containing a plethora of nautical memorabilia; glass floats, fishing reels and small barrels of rum..

'Ahoy, shipmates,' Charlie jested with a warm brandy glow. 'I'll get these,' he insisted, eager to spend some of his newly acquired wealth. He'd almost forgot what it felt like to buy a round of drinks without worrying about being skint until the next benefit payment.

They polished off another couple of pints, by which time Charlie and the professor were merry as a couple of cabaret drag queens.

A taxi ferried them to Eros Divine. Ibrahim casually paid another seventy quid for the extra VIP ticket. At that moment he felt like a VIP, having just taken receipt of 5 million quid.

They entered the main room past two huge doormen clad in black. The scarlet studied interior, disco balls and low-level lighting didn't surprise Ibrahim. Whilst Charlie and Prof Newbridge looked as if they were about to self-combust as they gawped at the troop of beauties strutting about the boudoir, virtually naked wearing outrageous platforms. The disco balls sparkling reflections cast tiny diamonds across their pert breasts, which seemed to point seductively at the punters. A group of Japanese businessman were involved in a heady drinking game, whilst two skinny dancers took turns gyrating sleazily around a pole in the centre of their purpose-built booth.

A brunette in a tight basque, which showed her curvaceous figure, asked Ibrahim for his invitation before ushering them to their own booth. Five minutes later the champagne arrived accompanied by three hot dancers: a blonde in a tiny leather micro bikini, who the Prof said looked like Bardot; a mixed-race dancer with massive bangers in a fishnet body stocking; and Ibrahim's personal favourite, the brunette in the basque.

Charlie sipped champagne, mesmerised as the blonde performed, tantalisingly, inches away from his groin.

Within minutes the professor was warned about his roving hands and sat sitting on them, staring at the mixed-race dancer's cleavage like a starving dog gawping at meat in a butcher's window.

Ibrahim on the other hand wasn't feeling it; even though he found the brunette provocative, his thoughts focused on Katrina. Over the years he'd screwed plenty of lap dancers, but another emotionless conquest just didn't interest him any more. Not wanting to spoil the old guys' fun, he discreetly asked the brunette about extending their pleasure. She told him propositioning the dancers could get them unceremoniously thrown out, but for the right price the club's private suite upstairs was available.

She led Ibrahim to the reception where he negotiated a private session for the old boys with the manager.

After parting with another grand he returned to the booth, and whispered in Charlie's ear, 'I've treated you and Newbridge to a private showing upstairs. I'm heading back to the hotel now. Get your rocks off and I'll see you in the morning. Just don't stay all night? We've got business tomorrow.'

The dancers took Charlie and Newbridge along a corridor. The blonde tapped a code into the fire door at the end and led them upstairs like a couple of dogs on leashes. At the top of the landing there was a series of doors each one with its own lock. Within minutes the professor was lying prostrate stripped to his Bell & Smithson Y-fronts and argyle socks on a single bed.

Like a pole propping up a tent, his knob pointed to the ceiling. The beautiful mixed-race dancer tried her best to appear seductive, but was repulsed by the 64-year-old's perverted company. She grimaced while sliding his pants down, but was shocked at the size of his huge bald member as it cranked back into position.

Drunk and determined to get his money's worth, the saucy old bugger said, 'I'm as hard as a diamond cutter. Jump aboard for a ride on my ancient staff!'

She slid a condom on him and climbed on top facing towards the door so she didn't have to look at his depraved facial contortions while screwing him. The copious amounts of alcohol he'd consumed helped him hold back for at least ten minutes, at which point he let out a groan that sounded like a kicked nanny goat, before erupting like an inactive volcano. The poor woman would be haunted by visions of her encounter with the musty old bastard.

Charlie heard Newbridge's groans two doors along the corridor, whilst the blonde wantonly flogged his ass with a leather whip.

CHAPTER 95

Despite Blake's considerable efforts to prove otherwise, the lack of forensic evidence meant he couldn't charge Carl Bentley with Barry Gibson's murder. The burnt shoe and ash recovered from a fire basket at his property was so damaged, its evidential value was zero. And even though two of the witnesses eventually confessed they accompanied him for a drink in the White Horse pub on the night of the murder, and his missus proved his alibi was a complete fabrication, they still had nothing concrete, so the whole case against him would never stand up to trial. What they did have was overwhelming evidence he was a drug dealer.

DS Murphy returned from the cells ushering a reluctant Carl Bentley before the custody officer to be formally charged. He looked like shit. The dark moons under his swollen red eyes showed a distinct lack of sleep in the last twenty-four hours.

Blake addressed him. 'After performing a forensics sweep of your property in Milton our SOCO team discovered over two hundred ecstasy tablets, fifty grams of high-grade heroin and nine ounces of cannabis resin stashed in various locations. Pretty damning evidence, wouldn't you say? Carl Bentley, I'm charging you on two counts of possession of class A drugs with intent to supply, and one count of possession of a class B drug with intent to supply. Do you have anything to say in response?'

Bentley didn't reply, but judging by the devastated look on his face he didn't need to.

CHAPTER 96

Charlie and Newbridge reassembled over breakfast. It was 8.30 a.m. and the old guys looked like death warmed up after a depraved evening at Eros Devine club. The professor gave them a wry smile before announcing he'd banged like a barn door in the wind, until the early hours. They took this with a much larger pinch of salt than Charlie was sprinkling over his monster full English of two eggs, three sausages, three rashers of bacon, beans and hash browns.

'Just a small breakfast this morning, Charlie?' Ibrahim smirked, looking at the lone croissant and two slices of ham and cheese on his plate, which paled in comparison; judging by Charlie's ghostly complexion the horny old goat needed to refuel depleted energy stores.

They checked out of the Hilton by twelve-thirty. The professor headed south on the 2 p.m. train to Bristol, whilst Charlie dozed off in the passenger seat as Ibrahim cruised down the M6 with two million packed into the boot of his Audi.

When they arrived back in Stoke, Ibrahim made two calls, one to the Collector informing him the crazy prof was on his way to Bristol with the Hoard, and the other to Malcolm Preston for an urgent meeting. He'd not spoke to his accountant for a few days and the fact he wasn't answering his phone, worried him. Where the bloody hell was he? Maybe he'd taken that break to Kefalonia he'd told Ibrahim he was planning?

Thankfully the bespectacled number cruncher had already set up a private offshore investment company to launder the bank transfer. He'd also distributed the credit cards to each of the board members. He'd structured it to be simultaneously a British public company, tax-resident in Amsterdam, but whose businesses were Swiss-owned. This also included complex tax avoidance schemes for each of the gang. Essentially, each member of the team would be given four hundred thousand in used notes and the rest placed into the company's Cayman Island bank account, which was partitioned. Each of them had a credit card that could be loaded with a maximum of eight grand a month. As Preston pointed out, this would act as a brake to stop suspicion falling on any large individual purchases.

CHAPTER 97

Boskava was a small fishing village in the shadow of the mountains in the Trabzon province of the Black Sea coast in north-eastern Turkey. Relatively untouched by progress, it was hard to believe many of Europe's key Turkish Mafia bosses grew up in this idyllic region. But, behind the facade of the beautiful pastel-coloured houses and apartments of the village, lay poverty. Whilst the Black Sea yielded endless shoals of bass, over-fishing and the devastating effects of a large cannery, built three miles along the coast in the seventies, meant local fishermen were left picking up the scraps, or working long hours for low pay at the cannery. Neither option was conducive towards a prosperous life.

Since the mid-seventies a steady stream of young men from the village had been inspired by the success and wealth of the Calkan brothers, who started out with nothing, at the tender age of nineteen, but now owned Casinos, tobacco shops, restaurants and bars in Trabzon and the UK generating millions in tax-free revenue. The unscrupulous pair employed half the village's young men in one form or another, from tobacco smugglers, to drug mules.

Their rise to wealth had been both swift and defiant. Ibrahim and Yusuf were unwittingly drawn into their web with the lure of easy money running illegal cigarettes to the cannery, whilst skipping school. Watching his father struggle in the field of his smallholding each day galvanised Ibrahim into emulating the Calkan brothers. The rest, as they say, is history.

He'd spoken to his mother and father over the phone, but not seen them for five years. He drove the hire car from the airport through winding roads of lush vegetation and bountiful crops growing on the lower elevations and valleys, below dense pine forests stepping up the hills of the Eastern Black Sea Coast.

Ibrahim sighed, inhaling the hot midday air, immersing all his senses in the nostalgia of home.

The stone cottage where he'd grown up hadn't changed in years. Its decaying window frames, tired blue door, and red tiled roof sat on the hillside in the blistering sun, like an unkempt relic. He creaked the gate open, and strolled down the gravel path.

Turning the corner he instinctively knew his father would be out back working his crops. His spinach, beans and corn were regarded amongst the best in the region, though life was hard as profit margins were barely enough to see them through the barren winters. His mother sat on a stool, peeling potatoes into a large enamel bowl set on the ground. She dropped the knife and flung her arms around him.

'Baba! *Benim oğlum eve döner.* Father! My boy's returned home!' she exclaimed, joyously wiping tears from her eyes with a tea towel from the pocket of her faded black dress.

'Ibrahim! Welcome home, son.' His father rose from the ground dusting himself off.

His mother fetched two chairs from the kitchen and made tea. The three of them sat on the crazy paving reminiscing whilst sipping tea from small gold-rimmed glasses, loaded with beet sugar. He'd almost forgotten how good Rize Province Tea tasted, the bitter flavour complemented by the *kesme şeker* sugar.

His father removed his hat and wiped the sweat from his brow with a handkerchief. His denim smock and boots bore all the marks of hard labour. He looked tired.

Ibrahim reached into his camouflage shorts pocket and passed over a wad of Lira to him.

The proud man shook his head. 'Thank you, son, but we cannot accept. We have food,' he said, guessing the money would have probably come by illegal means. A strict religious upbringing ingrained stubborn values in the old man.

Not wanting to insult him, Ibrahim said, 'It's a gift to help, you must take it.'

Knowing her husband's conviction all too well, his mother quickly changed the subject. 'How's your brother, we've not heard from him for a while?'

'He's in India working on a business project,' Ibrahim said.

'India, why there?' she asked.

'We have suppliers there.'

Judging by their sons' colourful past, they knew it would be pointless digging any deeper so dropped the subject.

'Is he OK?'

'Yes, he's fine, don't worry.'

'It's about time you boys married and made me a grandma. There's plenty of nice Turkish girls in Boskava.'

'I live in England, Mama.'

'You could come home?' she said longingly.

'And do what? All my business is in England.'

She made sad eyes at him. 'You could sell up?'

His father shot her a stern look. 'Azra, the boy has a life in England. We don't see him often, stop pestering?'

'It's OK, Baba.'

That evening Ibrahim ate a traditional meal of fresh water trout, vegetables and laz bread for the first time in five years with his parents.

His mother was clearly elated by the presence of her beloved son.

After the meal they took more tea outside, and Ibrahim suggested taking his father into Boskava for plum brandies.

Apart from the cannery along the coast, the beautiful village remained true to its fishing roots. Whitewashed houses cascaded down the winding mountain road, leading the way to an idyllic beach and harbour. The cobbled streets were lined with traditional properties with wooden shutters, and small balconies of flower baskets in full bloom of pink bougainvillea.

Bar Yomra was an old stone winery squeezed between pastel-coloured waterfront houses and shops on the small harbour.

Proudly introducing his son in Turkish, his dad shook hands with several locals sat playing dominoes at tables perched on the cobbles, in front of the bar. Some of the old guys Ibrahim recognised from childhood.

Taking a seat overlooking the coloured fishing boats, lilting on the ocean, his father waved at the owner and ordered his favourite plum brandy and a pint of lager for his son.

Only minutes after the drinks arrived, Ibrahim had almost drained his glass in one gulp. His dad shot him a look. 'Slow down, son, you drink too much.'

'It's hot, I've been travelling most the day.'

'Your mother worries about you and your brother. We both want to see you more.'

'We're doing OK, Papa. It's great to be back home, but apart from you and Mama there's nothing here for us any more. You should come to England sometime.'

'Son, you know your mama won't go on a plane. I don't like flying myself. My trip to Istanbul in seventy-one to see uncle Memet was enough for me.'

'Aeroplanes are much more modern than that rust bucket you flew on, Papa.'

'Still, I don't like them and, besides, your mother gets exhausted these days. She'll be sixty-eight soon you know?'

'OK Pa, forget planes for now, let's enjoy our drink.'

After another round they took a stroll along the harbour. The breeze coming off the ocean felt wonderfully refreshing. A courting teenage couple sat holding hands on an old stone seat, which Ibrahim remembered having his first ever kiss on. How things had changed since then, he thought.

They returned to the stone cottage around ten by which time Ibrahim was shattered. He said goodnight to his parents, kissing his mama before retiring to his childhood bedroom. It felt surreal to be back where he grew up. He'd contemplated booking into a hotel, but knew it would offend his proud parents. Unbelievably, the old hardwood wardrobe he and Yusuf shared stood like a monument to the past in the corner. Glancing in the mirrored door he recalled arguing like fishwives for space on the rail, and in the drawers below. Thankfully they'd replaced the mattress on his old bed frame, which matched the wardrobe. Closing his eyes he drifted off with a warm glow of nostalgia inside.

After washing down a hearty breakfast of Trabzon Pidesi; home-baked bread topped with egg with two glasses of sugar-beet-sweetened tea. Ibrahim set out for a stroll down memory lane of the local area. Apart from a lick of paint and a few new roof tiles, the scattering of traditional houses, which made up the old village, hadn't altered much since his childhood.

Stopping on the ancient sandstone bridge, which spanned the river, he glanced down at the crystal clear water flowing endlessly over rocks. His eyes followed its winding journey through the lush meadow up towards the snow-capped mountain tops, before spotting the familiar bell dome and Byzantine architecture of the village's four hundred-year-old church in the distance.

A rusting nineteen-sixties tractor passed him as he paced towards the Christian shrine. It was almost 9.30 a.m. and his flight to Ibiza was due in a couple of hours, leaving just enough time to do what he had to.

The high stone walls of the crucifix-shaped chapel of Saint Albassor rose at least twenty-five feet before being capped with the region's familiar terracotta roof tiles, which sloped further skywards to the base of its bell dome, surrounded by eight portico windows. Locals worshipped there for centuries and it was hugely important to the community, influencing moral guidance and strength.

Ibrahim entered through the pillars supporting the tiered arches over the narthex. His footsteps echoed on the stone mosaic floor. A sudden drop in air temperature made him shudder as he crossed over into the nave.

Looking upwards, he marvelled at the faded frescoes of Christ adorning the bell dome. Sat on the front bench he reflected on recent events, facing the altar with its large statue of Christ carved from marble.

It was the first time he'd visited the church since childhood, and although not religious, he found the experience humbling. He was startled by a hand laid on his shoulder. As he turned, the priest greeted him. 'Ibrahim Benzar.'

'Father Degarmo!'

Having not seen him for over twenty years, he was amazed that the priest recognised him. Being devout, his parents insisted he and his brother accompanied them to church at least twice a week during their childhood. In the summer of 1980, Degarmo took over the reins from his predecessor Father Vincenzo, who'd died from a sudden heart attack.

That was the official line regarding his death, but both Ibrahim and Yusuf knew the truth. Vincenzo was a sick pervert who abused his position to prey on impressionable boys from the village. For years, none of them dared to speak out, paralysed by shame and fear, until Vincenzo performed a lude sexual act on Yusuf, leaving him distraught for months.

Ibrahim remembered being woken many times by his brother's disturbing nightmares. In the end they plotted to finish the vile child molester for good. Sneaking out in the middle of the night, the brothers broke into the vicarage and suffocated the evil priest with a pillow whilst he slept. His thrashing around and bulging eyes haunted their childhood, but over time they'd buried the events of that awful night deeply.

'What brings you here, my son?'

'I was visiting Mama and Papa, thought I'd come in for old times' sake,' he said, now regretting going near the place after the disturbing memory it'd evoked.

Degarmo sensed something was troubling him. He ambled over to a winged cherub statue holding a large shell. Uncovering the stoup's lid, he returned and blessed Ibrahim. Having shunned religion years ago, Ibrahim felt unexpectedly moved by the gesture, and thanked the clergyman, who acknowledged him with a bowed head, before silently exiting through a door in the south transept.

Before leaving, Ibrahim folded a wad of Lira and deposited it into the wooden collection box.

CHAPTER 98

Upon first glance, the morning post appeared to be the usual depressing crap, demands and bills. That was before Katrina Osborne discovered a brown envelope without a stamp and her name written on the front in biro, followed by three kisses.

Intrigued, she tore it open and emptied the contents onto the dining room table. Crisp, hundred Euro notes, a plane ticket and a folded note dropped onto the cherry wood top. Closer scrutiny revealed a ten-day return flight from Manchester to Ibiza. After the shocking events of the last week, this put a smile back on her face. The accompanying note wasn't exactly a love letter, more a set of instructions. What did she care? The prospect of a free holiday with Ibrahim on the sun-drenched island didn't change the fact her partner had been arrested on a murder charge, but it would offer a necessary distraction. Her spirits lifted considerably as she read the note again.

Flight leaves tomorrow at 7.30 a.m. Hope you can join me. Taxi will pick you up from your house at five a.m. Another taxi will meet you in Ibiza and take you to the accommodation. I'll join you tomorrow afternoon.

Love Ibrahim xxx

PS treat yourself to something nice

Gathering up the notes she couldn't contain herself. Throwing them up in the air like a lottery winner, she screamed with excitement as they scattered around the living room carpet. Jobseeker's Allowance didn't allow any luxuries, and over the last few months, apart from the odd dress from the reduced section, she'd lived a meagre existence.

She didn't have expensive taste and made a mental separation of the money, allocating five hundred or less for clothes and the rest for spending whilst away.

She glanced at the mantelpiece clock; it was 8.30 a.m. Closing her eyes for a few seconds she visualised several rails of New Look's summer collection, and some hot bikinis. Maybe she could even squeeze an appointment with Angelo at Siena Falcone, her split ends desperately needed attention. With a quick shower and a slap of make-up, she could be in the city centre for half-nine taking breakfast.

Climbing the stairs, a horrible thought stopped her dead. Where is my bloody passport? She'd not seen it for months, and, even worse, was it in date?

She ran to the landing and dived into the bedroom. Dropping to her knees she yanked the top drawer of her bedside cabinet and dumped its contents onto the bed: nothing but dozens of bras. The middle drawer was full of knickers, and the bottom one just socks.

'Bollocks!'

She slammed the bedroom door, before racing down the stairs intending to ransack the writing desk in the living room.

She turned the rusty key and lowered the lid of the vintage painted desk. One by one she rummaged through the small internal draws. Nothing but old bank statements and bits of broken stationary. By now panic started to set in. Where is it? No passport, no sodding holiday! It wasn't as if she could get another in twenty-four hours, no chance! The kitchen was her last hope.

Starting with the first wall cupboard she opened each door and scanned the contents. Disappointingly half of them were bare and the rest just contained odd cups and plates, mostly from charity shops. The cupboards under the worktop were filled with broken gadgets.

In a rage she swiped her empty morning tea mug off the worktop, sending it smashing into pieces across the tiled floor. Leaning both elbows on the worktop she buried her face into her hands and burst into tears. 'Fucking hell!' She needed a fag.

Out in the backyard, she leaned against the flaking rendered wall separating the house from next door and lit up. Taking a deep draw she wracked her brain to remember where that bloody passport was. Glancing across at the shed, which Carl kept Lambretta spares in, she saw a Dublin Scooter Club sticker in the corner of the window. In a sudden flash she recalled a weekend trip to Dublin a couple of years ago. That was the last time she'd used her passport.

Dousing her fag in the brimming ashtray on the kitchen windowsill, she entered the house to fetch the keys for the shed padlock. Moments later she was rummaging through a large archive box of receipts. Judging by how many there were, that bastard had spent a small fortune on Scooter parts. After losing her job they stopped going out together. Carl always claimed he couldn't afford to pay for both of them, which was bullshit; the lying twat went out every weekend.

Kat piled them on top of the bench next to his vice. Two sealed plain white envelopes stared at her from the bottom of the box. She ripped the first one open and retrieved the contents. Bingo! Two ten-year passports held with a rubber band. She placed them on the side and opened the second envelope; it contained several Polaroid photographs of some dark haired slapper, blowing a bloke off sitting on a scooter. Thumbing through the photos she realised it was Carl . In one he was taking the same *girl*, who looked barely legal, from behind. Not only had he neglected her, he'd been shagging a teenager. Even more reason not to feel guilty about going away with another man.

CHAPTER 99

Flight 2596B from Manchester touched down on the sun-bleached tarmac of Ibiza airport at 7.30 a.m. Katrina Osborne had dozed off for forty minutes, until she was woken by little feet kicking the back of her seat. The family behind had two girls under six and their mum found it difficult to contain the excitement on their first flight. She had been dreaming of Ibrahim, imagining how her first holiday abroad in over seven years might pan out. She recalled Carl being pissed and stoned for most of their fourteen nights in Kavos, in 2008. The crafty bastard didn't tell her his mates were there at the same time. While she topped up her tan, he went on the lash with those losers, culminating in a massive argument and him slapping her so hard it loosened a tooth, and the pair not speaking for the last five days of the holiday.

After going through arduous EU customs checks, she towed her Zebra-print case through the Arrivals Lounge, and scanned through the crowd before spotting a small, plump Spanish taxi driver with a comb-over, holding a card up with her name on it. He introduced himself as Carlos, then ushered her through the sliding doors into the glorious morning sun to an immaculate white Mercedes parked on the busy concourse outside.

She climbed in the back, kicked off her white pumps, and stretched out. 'How long will it take to get there?'

'Villa Hermoso Lugar; it's in Cala Llonga so about twenty-five minutes.'

'OK, thanks, Carlos.'

'Good flight?'

'Fine, thanks.'

As the Mercedes sped at a steady sixty along the E-20 carriageway, she rolled down the window, letting the warm summer breeze blow on her face. God, it felt good to be away from Stoke! She gazed at the barren landscape of dry grassy fields scattered with palms and cacti, amongst the traditional Finca farmhouses.

Every few miles, huge roadside billboards displayed pictures of models in bikinis and big name DJs, each one advertising the island's world-famous dance clubs. No matter what happened to Carl, she promised to enjoy herself.

Fifteen minutes into the journey, the taxi left the E-20 and followed the meandering back roads to an isolated group of three villas overlooking the ocean. The Mercedes came to a halt on the block-paved driveway of an expensive-looking villa.

'Villa Hermoso Lugar,' the driver announced, as Kat sat gazing at the beautiful properties.

'Is this the right place?' she said in amazement.

'Sí Señora.'

'How much is the fare?' she asked, rummaging through the wad of euros in her purse.

'No charge, el taxi paid, para. Señor Ibrahim paid franco. He's joining you later.'

Before she climbed out, the driver passed her a sealed Jiffy bag envelope, and a set of keys to the property. He retrieved her case from the boot, lay it down on the paving and handed her his card.

'Señora, you need taxi, call this el número?'

'Thank you, Carlos.'

He waited until she'd opened the front door before slowly backing out the driveway. Shutting the door behind her, she abandoned the case in the hallway and ripped open the Jiffy bag. It contained a wad of Euros – she calculated about six hundred quid's worth – and a note.

Katrina,

Champagne and food in the fridge. Explore the villa, relax and enjoy. My plane lands at 3 p.m.

See you later

Ibrahim x

Call me if you need anything: 07654228829

She moved across the marble floor into the minimalistic open-plan living space. Light poured in through the large patio windows from outside. For a moment she stood gazing at the stunning sea view before jumping onto one of the three modular sofas facing each other. Lying there, she contemplated spending ten days in paradise with a man she fancied the pants off.

Rising, she sauntered over to the doors looking for a way onto the patio. Sliding the handle on the door, she slipped through the gap and scanned around the huge multi-level, marbled area, split up into different seating zones to chill out, sunbathe or dine on. The sheer glass balcony gave unobstructed panoramic views for miles across the ocean.

Kat spent the next twenty minutes nosing around every room of the luxury six-bedroomed villa. The master bedroom opened onto a private balcony, with an amazing outside roll-top bath and sea views.

Hurriedly unzipping her case, she grabbed a white micro bikini, Mp3 player and sun cream from the zipped webbing compartment on the reverse side of its lid. She stripped, and slipped the bikini on, then made her way to the kitchen.

Opening the fridge she grabbed the bottle of Moët Chandon, popped it and poured a glass. She lay the flute down next to an expensive-looking lounger, inches away from the pool's edge.

Listening to relaxing chill-out sounds through headphones, she lay in a state of bliss for forty minutes, before scanning around the dry stone walls surrounding the villa, to make sure it wasn't overlooked. Dropping her bikini top on the ground, she drifted back off. The intense midday sun drenched her breasts, and she felt a million dollars lying in wait for her secret lover.

After a further thirty minutes of frying, she slipped into the pool, and basked like a mermaid.

She swam over to the infinity edge, and rested her elbows on the side. The cloudless sky and ocean view was stunning. Embracing the blissful surroundings gave her inner peace and for the first time in months she felt truly relaxed.

She climbed out and dried off with a large beach towel, padded over to the lower deck, toward a rattan love seat, and lay down like Cleopatra under its calico sunroof. Drifting off her senses were suddenly livened by a familiar hint of citrus and lemon carried on the breeze. Warm lips touched her cheek. She opened her eyes, and he was there.

'You look beautiful,' Ibrahim said softly, kicking off his boating shoes, and climbing beside her.

'When did you get here?'

'Not long ago. Sorry for sneaking up on you. More champagne?' he asked, lifting two ice cold flutes from off the decking.

'This place is amazing, must have cost you a fortune.'

'Seven hundred a day. We've got it for ten days.'

'Seven thousand! God, that's a lot of money.'

He gave her a cheesy grin. 'You're worth it.'

They drained the glasses, and he kissed and caressed her. Drifting down to her belly, he gently pulled the ties of her bikini bottoms and tossed them aside, revealing her neatly shaven flower. He gently parted her petals with his tongue. Aroused she groaned and raised her thighs. Not wanting to tease her any more, he ripped off his clothes and entered her. Sex under the shade of the love-seat canopy in the boiling afternoon sun was amazing.

Later that evening they drove along the coastal road in a vintage silver Maserati with the top down, heading for a beautiful restaurant on the Ibiza Harbour.

Kat stepped into Porcelain Tropic in a stunning, low-cut, backless dress, which he'd brought along as a gift, as well as six-inch heels and a droplet necklace lariat with crystals. He looked handsome in his navy blazer, polo shirt and chinos. They dined in stylish elegance in the converted church to the romantic sound of Spanish guitar. She gazed blissfully at a few thin strips of clouds on the horizon turning shimmering gold as the sun set.

CHAPTER 100

DI Blake checked the time on his phone: it was seven a.m. Slipping it into his jogging bottoms pocket, he went downstairs to check if there'd been any mail. Sifting through the usual marketing leaflets and crap he noticed a peculiar brown envelope with no stamp on it. On the front in black marker it read:

FAO DI TOM BLAKE. URGENT!

He placed the junk mail on the second step of the stairs and hastily ripped open the envelope. Inside there was a folded sheet of A4 with a message printed on it.

'What happened to your daughter was a tragic accident. Visit Shelton Cemetery and find George Edward Royston's gravestone by the canal (Died in 1857) – husband of Beatrice, father of Edward Royston. Dig a shallow hole in the gravel directly below his stone, until you find a tobacco tin.'

He opened the front door and stood on the gravel in his moccasins, trying to spot who'd delivered the cryptic message. Legitimate post would have only just arrived, and since the brown envelope was at the bottom of the pile, he deduced it must have been pushed through late at night or early morning.

More to the point, was this a sick joke, or was someone genuinely trying to help? Could this have come from the kidnappers? Unlikely. Maybe this was payback? Whatever it was, it needed investigating further.

After breakfast Blake drove along Cemetery Road, Shelton and took a sharp left, swinging in through the open wrought iron gates of Hanley Cemetery. Its small but impressive chapel was set back a few yards from the entrance. He parked his Jaguar next to an elderly Sierra, which looked in surprisingly good condition considering its age.

Climbing out of the car, he made his way towards the disused chapel, then stopped under the main archway, which was connected to five other smaller arches. He felt a strange sensation of being watched. Glancing upwards, the eerie face of a stone-carved gorgon, with pupil-less eyes and a sinister smirk, glared at him. On either side, two oak doors were barricaded with wooden straps. An acrid mire of pigeon shit stained the slabs below each doorway.

Across the graveyard, huge eighteenth- and nineteenth-century memorial stones scattered like a city of the dead amongst the grass. Tombs, elevated crosses, shrouded caskets and angels all perched on top of bottle kiln-blackened cenotaphs climbing to the heavens. The larger graves were surrounded by decorative ironwork displaying the decaying ravages of time. The first few he passed hid under the protective shade of a large oak tree, its outstretched branches touching the headstones like mother nature's fingers reaching out to the souls interned below.

He continued along the pathway leading to the lower end of the cemetery until, after a hundred yards, he reached a fork at the bottom. The question was, which path led to George Royston's tombstone? Being right-handed he instinctively veered that way, hoping to get lucky.

A small sign staked in the soil at the lower end of the cemetery informed visitors it was a conservation area. Meadow grass scattered with buttercups, daisies and dandelions carpeted the ground like a Claude Monet pointillist painting.

Thankfully, there were few memorials in this part, Blake thought. Royston's tombstone was an imposing cenotaph around seven foot high, topped with a marble angel praying over his remains. Like so many other graves, the ironwork surrounding his was in a state of decay. According to his faded memorial, he was an esteemed local council member who crossed to the other side in 1886, at just forty-six years old.

The stone chippings laid on top of the grave were relatively new, judging by how pearly white they were. He guessed they'd be something to do with a council preservation program. Nervously he scanned to ensure no one was watching, before clumsily climbing over the rusting ironwork onto the grave. The chippings were warm from the cast of the morning sun. He scratched at them like a cat burying its mess.

The vintage tobacco tin lay a few inches below the surface. Blake slipped it into his pocket, and hurriedly neatened up the stones before climbing off the grave. 'Bastard!' A sharp stab of pain shot through his leg.

He'd caught his knee on a razor edge of the ironwork, tearing his jeans in the process. Blood seeped from a small cut on his kneecap.

Ignoring the minor discomfort, he waded through meadow grass under a line of willow trees separating the cemetery from the towpath and perched on a metal bench facing Caldon Canal.

Glancing around again, he checked no one was watching before retrieving the tin. After a few seconds of fumbling it prized open unexpectedly, flirting two small gold objects dangerously close to the water's edge.

He scrambled to his knees to retrieve them from amongst the grass just as a fifty foot barge ploughed through the water. A retired couple in matching orange crocs, sporting grins, stood on the tiller end waving. Blake ignored them, anxiously trying to stop the objects falling into the murky depths of the canal.

With the help of a few shortcuts, it only took Blake fifteen minutes to get home from the cemetery. Leaping from the car he dashed across the gravel, opened the front door and entered the house, intent on calling the number on the cryptic note.

Well aware his police mobile call data could be examined any time, he opted for one of the pay-as-you-go phones he kept in the kitchen drawer, specifically for conversations like the one he was about to have. Not something he liked doing but even detectives were entitled_to a private life, he thought in justification.

Nervously he tapped the keys of an old slide top mobile, but, after the fourth digit, stopped, cancelled the call and laid the phone onto the worktop, contemplating the magnitude of the situation.

He fumbled the tobacco tin from his jacket pocket, prised it open once more and emptied the two gold pieces into the palm of his right hand. They gleamed in the sunlight streaming through the window. The ruby garnet inlay reflected the light. Turning them over like worry beads, the patterns looked familiar but he couldn't quite place where he'd seen them before, possibly some kind of tribal jewels? One thing was for sure, they looked old judging by the faded colour, tiny scratches and chips on the edges.

Whatever their provenance they were still only objects, and his daughter's life hung in the balance. Irrespective of the consequences, it was vitally important she received the proton therapy in America. Focused, he grabbed the phone and dialled without further hesitation. Within thirty seconds a voice with a Texas drawl answered.

CHAPTER 101

Coleman was uncharacteristically sympathetic towards Blake's plight, which might not have been the case if he'd not confessed the full facts of the prisoner's escape from custody. Even though Blake had delayed telling the Chief Inspector about his terrible ordeal, he still signed the compassionate leave forms laid out on his huge mahogany desk.

'I take it the fundraising went well then, Tom?'

'It's a little overwhelming how many strangers have supported Isabel's cause, sir. Very humbling.'

'I asked everybody at the station to contribute.'

Bullied them more like, Blake thought, extremely grateful for his intervention. The extra donations were significant.

'Take as long as you need. DS Murphy will handle your caseload in your absence; he's more than capable. Besides, from what you've told me, there seems to be a real sense of urgency with Isabel's treatment.'

'Thank you, sir, your support means a lot.'

'Don't mention it. I'd be there in a heartbeat for any of my boys. You never stop caring, even when they've grown up,' he said trying to empathise. 'When do you leave for the US?'

'Tomorrow.'

'When do they start treatment?'

Just the thought of it made Blake anxious. 'Immediately after a few health checks. Thankfully proton therapy has a good success rate. Apparently, it doesn't damage other healthy cells in the body like chemo does. It's very targeted.'

'That's excellent news, we'll all be praying for her at the station.'

'Thank you, sir,' Blake said, gratefully shaking his hand, before exiting his office.

He headed along the top floor corridor past the meeting room where Stoke-on-Trent's high command discussed new directives. The powder room, as CID referred to it, on account of most of what they sanctioned in there was purely cosmetic touching-up and tinkering unnecessarily with police procedure. The lift was still in maintenance mode so he tackled five flights of stairs to the lower echelons of the station where real police work took place.

Despite several email reminders from the policing Gods about efficiency and tidiness, DS Murphy's desk had the appearance of a 1970's schoolteacher's, stacked high with randomly distributed files and paperwork.

'PC give up the ghost, John?' Blake said sarcastically.

'Good to see you've got your sense of humour back. Top filing system that is; I know where everything is.'

'Pity no one else does.'

'How's Isabel?'

'Good and bad days. I hope to God now we've secured the funding for treatment it cures her.'

'What's the success rate?'

'About seventy per cent'

'That should comfort you. When you flying out?'

'Tomorrow. You OK with everything? Bentley's likely to go on trial while I'm away. Do we need to do anything before I leave?'

'Listen, Tom, we've covered all bases on that one. The forensics on the drugs are rock solid, but we don't have enough to put him at the murder scene. No DNA, fingerprints or footprints. There's not a jury in the land who'd convict him; the evidence is too circumstantial.'

'We've still got a lot to do. Keep a close watch on the other key suspects, while I'm away? One of them is bound to slip up, sooner or later.'

'Don't worry about it. You focus on Izzy's treatment and recovery.'

'Can't thank you enough for everything you've done, mate. It's a weight off my mind knowing the ship's in capable hands.'

'Remind me to keep PC Haynes off the rudder then,' Murphy jested.

Blake cracked a smile, 'Keep me posted on any developments John?'

'Don't worry I'll call you.'

CHAPTER 102

Out of the JustGiving funds Blake had booked two first-class places on a British Airways flight 2345A to Miami, costing three grand each. The doctor gave them the all clear, but cautiously provided flight socks, and a pouch of medications for Isabel. Even though she was still weak, she'd had no more blackouts and was feeling more like her old self; probably the placebo effect of her pending treatment.

After an ardours ten hour flight, which Isabel slept most of; the plane shuddered to a stop outside the South Terminal of Miami International airport. As their fellow first class passengers stood and stretched in the aisle, Blake called the Wellness Institute on his mobile to confirm Isabel's admittance time.

They disembarked the plane and headed down the tunnel into the concourse. Customs checks were slow and tedious, because of the new rules the US government had introduced for foreign visitors. After an hour and a half they were travelling down the carriageway, under the direction of their rental car's on-board Sat-Nav.

The Wellness Institute Hospital was in an idyllic coastal location, just off SR 112 road, half a mile along a private access road, six miles outside Miami.

Blake entered the plush reception, which looked more of a five-star hotel, than a hospital: expansive marble floors, high planters with palms, sensory music and glass coffee tables laden with magazines, were positioned in the centre of several expensive looking sofas.

After fifteen minutes of form filling he accompanied the orderly, pushing his extremely tired looking daughter to her room.

Once the nurses had settled Isabel into bed, Blake kissed her forehead and headed for a coffee. The in-house café looked like one of those high street chains; aged wood panels, and rustic steel fittings.

He ordered a Latte and sunk down into a leather wingback in a quiet corner near the window, overlooking the car park. Fishing out his phone he called DS Murphy.

'John, how's it going?'

'Tom, good to hear from you, how's Isabel? You at the hospital yet?'

'We arrived about an hour ago, she's dog tired after the flight.'

'I bet. She's resilient though, a real fighter.'

'Where she gets it from amazes me. Changing the subject, what's happening with the Gibson murder case? Any updates I need to be aware of?'

'We've been keeping tabs on the suspects, but there's nothing new I'm afraid to say.'

CHAPTER 103

Blake swung the Chevy SUV rental into the car lot at the side of the Ninth Street Diner on Washington Avenue. Compared to its competitors, who appeared to have spent thousands of dollars on architectural renovation and signage, it seemed like an unsavoury dive locked in a eighties time warp. The crumbling pale-blue exterior needed serious TLC.

The lights were on but Blake couldn't make out the interior through the maze of menu items plastered over the windows in white paint pen. It looked to be Miami's version of a greasy spoon.

Pushing the door open Blake entered and cautiously scanned the narrow room. A long stainless steel counter top, fronted by eight fixed chrome swivel stools sat on the back wall. The five tables in the window were empty apart from one, where a well-dressed portly man in his mid-fifties wearing a panama sat in the corner sipping coffee.

He'd arrived fifteen minutes early to assess the situation. A middle-aged Hispanic looking guy in a grease-stained apron – probably the owner, he thought – greeted him.

'What can I get ya?'

'Latte, extra hot, please.'

'Take a seat, I'll bring it over.'

The proprietor didn't comment on his accent, which piqued the interest of the man in the corner who glanced up and nodded in Blake's direction. He approached his table with caution.

He removed his panama and placed it on the seat beside him.

'Good evening, Mr Blake. Please take a seat. I believe you have a package for me?' he said in the familiar Texas drawl Blake recognised as the man he'd spoken to on the phone.

Not wanting to antagonise him with probing police questions, Blake politely sat opposite, intending to keep it focused and to the point. But before he could answer, the proprietor laid his coffee on the table.

'Thanks very much.'

'The English and their manners, so quaint,' the Collector remarked. 'I suppose you're wondering what this is about?'

'I'd prefer not to know, as that would implicate me in whatever is going on here.'

'Well, the people who hurt your daughter appear to have a conscience. Now I'm not an uncaring man, but since we're here to do business, can you show me the pieces?'

'How do I know you won't rip me off?' Blake said sceptically.

'You don't. But one thing I've learnt over the years is nobody likes being double-crossed. It leaves a nasty stain on one's reputation and generally ends up in some kind of revenge. As my dearly departed daddy used to say, "Thieves and hustlers burn in hell. It's an unspoken law of the universe. I give you my word that the money's good. Now I don't wish to be rude,' the Collector said, lowering his voice, 'but can you show me the gold?'

The whole situation was surreal. Blake felt like a player from a scene of some blockbuster scam movie: a midnight liaison with some oddball dealer, exchanging antique gold for a wad of cash.

Whilst retrieving the jewellery box from his inside jacket pocket, a sudden blast from an MPD police siren startled them both. The vehicles intense red light lit up the street like a fireball. Blake's heart banged hard in his chest. The white Ford Crown Victoria Police Interceptor cruised past the window before speeding off up the road, probably towards a shout.

'You seem nervous, Mr Blake? Don't worry about the boys from Intra Coastal; there's plenty of gang bangers to keep them busy of an evening.'

Before he could reply, a huge scruffy-looking man about forty entered the diner. Judging by his ponytail, oily jeans and Cuban-heeled boots with spurs, Blake concluded he was some kind of biker. In the minute's silence that followed, they heard him order coffee and bagels before sitting behind them in the last seat of the row in the window.

The whole thing was making Blake more nervous by the minute. A dodgy deal in a public place wasn't exactly his idea of discretion, but that was the situation. Besides, he needed the money desperately to pay for Isabel's treatment.

'What about him?' He asked lowering his voice.

'Slide me the package under the table. I'll take a look in the john.'

'How do I know you'll come back?'

'Mr Blake, you clearly didn't listen to what I was saying about honourable business earlier. We can't do business in front of that frigging

Ape Hanger. Besides, the john is only there,' he said, pointing to a set of louvre swing doors at the opposite end of the diner. 'We can't both go together; he'll think we're a couple of steers.'

After the week he'd had Blake could almost see the funny side of this. 'OK! But your only getting one of the pieces and if you're not out in five minutes I'll be coming in, deal?'

'OK, you gotta deal.'

As the Collector left the table and moved towards the gents, he noticed the biker stare longer than necessary at him. Or was he being paranoid?

Behind the relative safety of a locked cubicle door, the Collector held the Saxon pommel cap up towards the spotlights and peered wondrously through his loupe at the ancient gold. 'Amazing!' Satisfied the goods were genuine, he flushed, exited the gents and returned to the table.

'Everything in order?' Blake asked, concerned at how long the switch was taking. He'd expected some kind of checks but hadn't anticipated it taking more than half an hour tops. Glancing at his watch revealed it was coming up to the hour mark.

'Are you on the parking lot at the side?'

'Yeah, why?'

'I suggest we conclude business out there. I'm not real comfortable with the Ape in the corner. Mine's the black '61 convertible Corvette.'

Blake was losing patience, but this was America and if the hype he'd seen on CNN was anything to go by, it couldn't do any harm to be extra cautious.

'OK.'

'I'll leave now. You follow in, say, one minute, Mr Blake.'

CHAPTER 104

Blake glimpsed around the car lot checking for floodlights and cameras before opening the Corvette's passenger door, just about remembering it was on the opposite side. Thankfully, there was only one other car apart from his rental and the Corvette. An old rust bucket with two-toned doors sat empty in the darkness like a prop from a seventies movie.

True to his word the Collector sat behind the wheel, languishing in the off-white leather interior and polished Rosewood door trims, hands on his lap resting on a bulging manila envelope.

He tossed the package over to Blake. 'It's all there, hundreds and fifties. Feel free to count it,' he said, flicking a switch on the dashboard, which illuminated Blake's footwell.

Nervously he fumbled through each of the forty-five piles divided into thousand dollar bundles by red card. After ten minutes he was satisfied.

'OK, we got a deal?'

'Yes,' Blake said, taking a long photographic stare at him, as he passed over the other pieces.

'That concludes our business then. You'll not hear from me again. Don't call the cell number you were provided with; it's deader than Elvis,' he jibbed.

'OK,' Blake said, unimpressed, trying to stuff the inside pocket of his jacket with the envelope. It was far too thick, so he discreetly tucked it under his shirt and shielded it with a cupped hand stuffed in his side pocket.

He climbed out and slammed the door behind him, but before he reached his rental, the roar of a finely tuned V-Eight engine cut through the muted sounds of the city. In a blaze of headlights, he watched the Corvette swiftly exit the lot; within seconds its red brake lights disappeared down Washington Avenue like tiny snake eyes.

He retrieved the key fob from his jeans, pointed it at the car and plipped. The SUV's orange sidelights flashed, but before he could open the door he heard another type of click, followed by the cold pressure of a gun barrel digging into the base of his skull.

'I'll take that off your hands, you dumb fucking Brit.'

Blake froze, his muscles rigid. Was this a double-cross?

'Turn around real slow and chuck the money on the ground. Keep your hands where I can see 'em?' The scruffy ponytailed biker eased back to a car width away, aiming the gun at the centre of his chest.

'I need that money for my daughter's treatment. She'll die without it.'

'Tell someone who gives a shit. Just toss it over or I'll pop you right here.'

Realising he had little choice, Blake reluctantly bowled the package under arm across the ground towards the mugger. Kneeling down with the gun still trained at him, the biker scooped up the package.

'Turn around and put your hands on the hood. If you move an inch, I'll do ya!'

Blake's fear turned to anger, and with clenched fists he did what was asked.

He watched the man climb into the rust bucket, fire it up and swerve out of the lot like a madman, its solo tail-light bounced as it dropped off the kerb and screeched away. By now, pure adrenaline surged through him. Without hesitation he jumped into the rental, turned over the engine and spun out of the lot in pursuit with absolutely no regard for the consequences.

Blake knew his SUV was a much newer and faster vehicle, giving him a serious edge. If he could keep close to the biker, then ram him off the road when no other cars were around, there'd be a fighting chance of getting the cash back. He could hardly report it to the cops.

Glancing in the rear-view mirror an endless stream of suburban lights reeled away behind him. He narrowed the gap to three car lengths when a crossroads loomed about a hundred yards in front. Easing on the gas, he covered the brake. Surprisingly the three-lane road heading out of the city was quiet.

Suddenly the lights changed to red, but, instead of slowing down, the mad bastard slammed his foot down and swung the rust bucket left straight across the path of an oncoming truck from the right. Luckily it was only cruising and braked to avoid impact. The truck's horn howled, echoing like a ship in the fog, as it skidded and altered course. Tensely gripping the wheel of his stationary rental, Blake watched the biker's rear lights shoot a few hundred yards into the distance.

The lights changed, and he accelerated swinging a sharp left. The suburban sprawl thinned out as he continued in pursuit heading down a two-lane road. He burned through the gears glancing at the orange speed dial hovering over the seventy mark. What the hell was under that bonnet, he thought sweating profusely in the humid night air? Surely it couldn't match a car forty years newer, could it?

The winding road ahead twisted amongst the trees. Approaching vehicles were few and far between and, judging by its random swaying, the rust bucket didn't look to handle the combination of bends at high speed too well. Conversely Blake's rental tracked the surface with relative ease. Problem was, the loser in front was a native, meaning he'd know every turn-off and shortcut.

He estimated they'd gone about ten miles and there was no sign of him stopping. Holding his resolve, he ploughed on drawing upon the skills he learned on the police high-speed pursuit course.

Suddenly the road swung violently to the right, straightened for a few yards, before swinging back to the left out of an S-bend. His bonnet was now within touching distance of the rust bucket's back-end.

It bounced as if driving over a large rock; its brake lights flashed. Spotting his chance Blake tensed preparing for impact. Gripping the wheel he slammed his foot to the floor and rammed into the back, shunting his assailant's nearside wheels off the blacktop onto the grass lining the sides of the road. Blake swerved just missing a large boulder, and jammed on the brake bringing him to a screeching halt at the deserted roadside.

Darkness cloaked the surrounding area; a full moon silhouetted the trees like ghouls. He sat motionless, watching the car career over the edge of the road through a gap in the barriers, crash through a line of trees and rumble down a minor slope through dry grass. He traced its headlights until they halted and extinguished.

Jumping out, he zipped up his jacket and turned the collar up to shield his aching neck from the Pacific breeze. Stealthily he paced through the trees wielding a heavy fifteen-inch torch he'd found in the glove box. The distant sound of waves crashing against the shoreline put him in a heightened state of alert. Hundreds of chirping crickets echoed amongst the grass.

Emerging from the trees he could just about make out the hazy figure of the huge biker who'd abandoned his vehicle in the scrub and was stumbling across the moonlit beach heading towards a cluster of massive rocks for cover.

Warily Blake approached him from behind. Did he still have the gun? Gripping the flashlight like a police baton, he sprinted across the sand, closed in and shoulder barged him side on, sending him crashing onto the sand. Blake dived on top of him and launched the flashlight into the side of his head. The biker wailed in pain as it thudded hard into his temple, his legs thrashed around, violently attempting to fend off Blake who'd dropped the flashlight in the struggle.

Regaining balance he hammered his fist into the biker's nose. With bloodied hands the biker suddenly found a burst of strength. Shielding his face with an elbow, his free hand pushed hard under Blake's chin. His muscular arm forced Blake's head back, his other fist pummelled him hard in the kidneys. Winded, Blake swayed off balance to the side and the biker heaved him over. In one swift movement he whipped the gun from his jacket and shoved the barrel into Blake's forehead.

Pinned to the sand, hands held out in surrender, Blake clamped his eyes. Devastated, knowing his life was about to end, leaving his sick daughter stranded in America to fend for herself, he heard the click of the trigger, followed by a deafening blast.

CHAPTER 105

The gunshot echoed across the pitch-black sky, followed by an agonising cry. Blake's ears pounded, and his forehead burned with pain. Opening his eyes he lay motionless, gazing at the moon, its ghostly white refection pale as linen.

Something heavy lay on his chest. Fearful he glanced down; a tiny star glinted in the moonlight. A chrome spur on the end of a Cuban heeled boot came into focus. It took all his strength to heave the biker off. A stabbing pain shot through his arm.

Rising slowly he stood over the man lying sprawled out on the sand. He bent to pick up the heavily bloodied flashlight, turned it on and scanned the huge corpse. His head was splattered in blood. Closer inspection revealed a mutilated, partially burned-off face missing the left eye, blood leached from its empty socket. The cheek flesh flapped, like a charred piece of liver. His mouth was twice as wide as it should be, exposing upper jawbone and a skeletal set of molars. Blood trailed down his neck leaving an indelible stain on the sand as it filtered through the grains.

Blake shone the torch on the man's hand; it was clasped tightly around a piece of mangled metal. The back end of the gun had exploded, burning a hole into his wrist. The bullet obliterated his face on its deadly trajectory into his brain. He'd seen something similar in a cop drama, where a re-bored gun backfired.

Blake entwined his fingers and looked skyward. A bizarre twist of fate had dragged him from the clutches of death.

Dropping to his knees, he leaned in and checked the biker's jugular vein for a pulse, but struggled to find it through the river of blood trailing down his neck. No beat. He was dead as the driftwood that lay by his side.

What a nightmare; he'd only been in US for twenty-four hours and was embroiled in an illegal artefact's deal. Now, even worse, he was the victim of a robbery, which ended up in the death of the assailant. Calling the police would lead to detainment and probing questions. Ultimately he needed to get back to Isabel as quick as possible.

Frantically he rummaged through the biker's jacket. Patting him down, he realised the money wasn't there. Shitting hell! He must have left it in the car in a panic. Blake stood silent, listening for a sign that someone might have heard the gunshot. Nothing audible except the constant sound of waves crashing against the shoreline.

Left with no option, he dragged his aching body through the dark, across the deserted beach, back towards the rust bucket. The vehicle was embedded into a tree, bonnet poking up like a half opened can. Its windscreen was shattered, leaving shards of glass over the seats.

Blake's eyes adjusted to the dark; he could see the passenger door was still intact. Placing the torch on the ground, he pulled his sleeve over his hand and yanked it open. Retrieving the torch, he climbed in and scanned the dated coffee-coloured interior of the vehicle. It reeked of putrid cigarette smoke.

Where the bloody hell was the money, he wondered, trying the glove box but the impact must have jammed the lock.

He climbed back out, grabbed the top of the doorsill and launched the sole of his shoe into the glove box lid. It dropped open like a drawbridge, revealing the brown package sat beside some photo ID and what looked like a bag of weed. He grabbed the envelope in his left-hand and took a peek at the ID. James Darryl Carney, aged forty-three, Miami Florida. Judging by the date on the driving licence, it had expired two years earlier… hardly surprising. He tossed it back in the glove box and carefully closed the door.

Wading through the grass, amongst partially moonlit trees, back towards his rental, he glanced down at his jacket and hands; they were smeared in Carney's blood. If the cops pulled him, they'd throw the book at him. Besides, returning a rental car with a bloodied steering wheel would arouse suspicion.

With the cash tucked in his pocket, Blake anxiously made his way back across the beach to the ocean. The salty Pacific air flooded his senses, but somehow felt different, becoming eerily peaceful and calm. From seemingly nowhere the heavens opened unleashing a torrent of rain. He guarded the money under his shirt, but the envelope was getting damp. Through blurred vision he ran, stumbling in the heavy sand; rain sodden hair dripped into his eyes.

At the water's edge he scanned the beach before tearing off his clothes and stuffing the envelope under them to keep it dry. A deafening thunder boom echoed across the sky, exploding his head. Bolts of lightning splintered through the inky blackness. Highly charged forks of white heat ripped through the previously calm horizon illuminating the desolate beach for a split-second through the rain.

Apart from Carney's corpse, the vast Pacific and judgement from above, he was alone in this horrific predicament.

Kneeling in just his boxers, in a few inches of freezing sea water he spread his fingers wide and thrashed them around. Then with cupped hands he threw copious amounts over his face and chest, baptising away the blood. The lashing rain gave his body a second cleansing.

After an extremely paranoid thirty-five-minute journey back to his motel in damp clothes, Blake parked the rental in front of his ground floor room around three a.m. He'd offloaded the bloodstained jacket into a large dumpster at the back of a restaurant in downtown Miami. Unbelievably his shirt and trousers came out of the near-death experience wet but relatively unscathed, apart from back spatter drops of blood.

Momentarily sheltering from the rain under the small veranda spanning the ground floor, Blake slipped the key into the door of room fifteen and entered. Immediately he reached for the bottle of duty free Jack Daniels he bought on the plane.

He poured a three-finger slug into a tumbler on the dresser, then slammed it straight down without hesitation and refilled. The dark-amber liquid warmed his throat and the larger repeat dose took the edge off his shattered nerves.

Gazing around the room he contemplated calling John Murphy for advice, but, however much he needed support, his first call would be to the hospital to check on his daughter.

The night nurses' reassurance Isabel had eaten a hearty meal of chicken and potatoes and was soundly sleeping comforted him. However desperate he wanted to visit, it was out of the question at three-thirty a.m., battered and already half pissed.

CHAPTER 106

Blake woke the following day sprawled out on top of the floral-patterned duvet of the king-size bed, his head pounding. The searing Florida sun streamed through a gap in the curtains. He flung an arm over to the bedside cabinet to check the time. Bollocks! His mobile battery had died in the night. Thankfully, his trusty Rotary never missed a second.

Ambling over to the bathroom like a pensioner pushing a Zimmer frame, he grabbed the titanium timepiece off the Formica sink top. Shit, it was 8.30 a.m. already. A quick glance in the mirror over the sink showed a reddish swelling under his left eye, which, combined with his ghoulish white complexion, gave him the appearance of a phantom.

Leaving the bathroom, he stubbed his toe on something hard. 'Bastard!' Rubbing it in agony, he saw the half-empty bottle of JD he'd kicked across the carpet. The bourbon must've knocked his lights out.

Plugging his mobile into the charger, he called the hospital and arranged a 9.30 a.m. meeting to discuss Isabel's treatment program.

With under an hour to spare, he downed two Ibuprofen with half a bottle of mineral water then jumped into the shower. Its flow was weak, and the cheap curtain, with 'Welcome to Miami Dolphins' logos, did little to prevent overspray. He didn't care; the hot water eased his aching neck and back; besides there were far more important things to worry about.

He lifted clean clothes from his case, slipped on a polo shirt, jeans and brogues and headed across to reception in search of breakfast.

Blake entered the reception and found a man in his mid-fifties arched over a large wooden display stand, fastidiously tidying a plethora of tourist-attraction leaflets. His garish Hawaiian shirt was even more vibrant than his ginger comb-over. Sensing Blake's presence, he greeted him in accented Floridian. 'Mornin'.'

'Morning. Just wondering where I can order breakfast?'

'If you follow me, Mr…?'

'Blake.'

'Mr Blake, I'll take you through to our dining facilities. I'm Jeffrey Osgood, the hotel manager,' he said, leading the way out of the reception.

After ambling ten yards, he fished keys out of his pocket and opened a door to the self-serve dining room overlooking the empty lot.

With the worrying events of the previous evening heavy on his mind Blake scoffed a bacon bagel he'd warmed in the microwave, and made his way out to the parking lot towards the rental, thinking things couldn't get any worse, when a large dent in the front bumper glared right at him in the morning sun. Letting out a deep sigh, he rubbed his temples recalling ramming the rust bucket off the road, although that could be easily explained to Auto Rental. He'd feed them bullshit about some jerk banging into him; after all bumpers were there to protect the bodywork. But that was before he noticed a deep scratch running full length of the driver's side sill.

CHAPTER 107

Blake eased the rental into a bay by the reception, trying his level best not to cause any more damage to the already battered midnight-blue Chevrolet.

On the drive down he'd been mulling over the delicate payment situation. He'd already sent the initial £50,000 deposit via BACS. But there was no way he could bowl in and slap forty-five grand down on the counter. With this in mind, the second instalment was paid on three credit cards, taken out specifically. He'd drip-feed those with the cash over the next month.

Thankfully, unlike the NHS, there was no queuing and a twenty-four-hour dedicated care nurse was assigned to Isabel. Sophie McCarthy stood chatting to the receptionist as Blake entered the plush reception.

The petite south-east Asian receptionist he'd spoke to yesterday addressed him. 'Good morning, sir, how may I help you?'

'My daughter is a patient here – Isabel Blake, she was admitted yesterday for proton therapy?'

'Nurse McCarthy will take care of you,' she said, gesturing toward her colleague.

The attractive brunette smiled, revealing a glimpse of her immaculate pearl-white teeth. 'Mr Blake, I'm Sophie McCarthy, your daughter's dedicated nurse. If you'd like to come this way, I'll take you through to see her.'

He accompanied her down a series of clinical corridors lined with framed photographs of America's finest scenery until they entered into another small reception area facing a series of glass panelled doors, leading to the patients' rooms.

Isabel was in C6, a luxury suite with matching high-end mahogany furniture, and floor-to-ceiling sliding glass doors overlooking the Pacific.

Overcome with emotion, Isabel's eyes filled with tears. 'Dad!'

'I'll give you a few minutes alone,' McCarthy said, before closing the door behind her.

Blake sat on the bed and flung his arms around his daughter, fighting back tears, which eventually got the better of him. Dragging his sleeve across his face, he looked vulnerable. 'I really missed you yesterday, princess; how are they treating you?'

'This place is like a hotel. I've got my own bathroom and a fridge full of fruit, drinks and healthy snacks. What's happened to your eye?'

'Oh, that. I slipped on the motel bathroom floor and banged it on the sink.'

'There's ice in the fridge dad, get some on it?'

'I'll be ok.'

'Where were you? I was so worried?'

'I had to organise your funding, Izzy. It took longer than I thought. I called the hospital last night, but you were asleep. Anyway, I'm here now and we can spend all day together. When does your first treatment start?'

'The doctors want to speak to you about that?'

'Is everything OK? How did the scan go?'

'I had a panic attack; they had to give me something to calm my nerves. That's the second MRI in two weeks. Bloody horrible things.'

'I'm really sorry, I should have been here,' he said, feeling guilty.

She pointed to a two-seater perched in the corner. 'That sofa pulls out into a bed, Dad; you can stay tonight. We could have tea together and watch DVDs later?'

'At almost a hundred grand for ten days, I should bloody think so,' he joked. 'Your laptop and DVDs are in the car. I'll bring them in later, but let's get you sorted out first. I'm just going to have a word with the nurse. Back in a min.'

Although she'd perked up since the arduous flight, his fatherly instincts were telling him her enthusiasm for the high-end facilities was just a coping mechanism. Deep down, he sensed she was worried about the proton treatment.

Letting the door slip to, he walked the short distance across to the nurse station. Sophie McCarthy sat behind the counter focusing intently on a flat-screen monitor.

'Mr Blake?'

'Tom, please.'

'Tom, take a seat. Can I get you a drink before we begin?' She got up and gestured towards two leather wingback chairs opposite the reception.

'I'm OK for the minute, thanks.'

She followed him over and sat down cross-legged, glancing at a clipboard. 'I understand you've come a long way, and it's a very worrying time. But I can assure you your daughter is in the best place. I also understand you'll have questions about the treatment, but first if I explain how the Proton Program works, and what you can expect from our specialist team; it should help to relieve some of that worry.'

Blake listened intently. 'OK, thank you.'

'Proton therapy is very safe and has an excellent success rate with this type of tumour. Unlike other more aggressive chemotherapies, it minimises damage to healthy cells. Overall there's increased tumour control, or eradication. Another big advantage is the patient feels nothing during treatment. And, there are hardly any side effects after treatment.'

Her reassurances helped ease some of his anxiety. He was silent for a few seconds before asking, 'How many treatments will she receive?'

'One today, and then further treatments each day until there's significant regression in the tumour. I can't exactly say for sure. Dr Aston Jones will be along in a few minutes to discuss Isabel's MRI images with you.'

'Will she be poorly after?'

'It's worth bearing in mind that, apart from the tumour, Isabel is a healthy young woman with a strong immune system. I think the fact she's flown ten thousand miles proves that. You must be very proud of her?'

'I'm extremely proud.' Blake felt a wave of emotion rise in his chest, but suppressed the urge to cry with a couple of deep breaths. Seeing Isabel again for the first time in twenty-four hours stirred up all kinds of irrational fears.

'She's all I've got left. I lost my wife and son in a car accident some years ago. Isabel's been my rock ever since. I can't imagine life without her.' Unintentionally he heard himself appealing for sympathy.

'I'm sorry for your loss. I'm sure this must be very painful. If there's anything I can do to make your stay here with us more comfortable, please don't hesitate to ask? You can be with your daughter day and night at the institute if that helps. We have an in-house Relative Support Unit. I'll give you the number; you can talk to them any time.'

'Thank you. Isabel has already shown me the sofa bed. When will we know if she's in remission?'

'During the whole treatment we'll be monitoring progress, closely keeping Isabel under twenty-four hour observation. If everything goes well, which I'm sure it will, she'll be moved to one of our convalescence suites right on the beach. Our post-op after-care therapists are some of the best in the world. Is there anything else you'd like to know?'

'I think that's it for now,' Blake said, trying to process the info. She handed him a leaflet from the clipboard.

'Everything we've discussed is in our brochure. If you do think of anything, you can reach me here?' She pointed to the mobile number printed on the inside fold.

'OK, thanks, will do.'

CHAPTER 108

Blake placed a reassuring arm around his daughter as they descended towards the beach in the clinic's glass lift. 'I've spoken to Doctor Aston Jones, and he showed me your scan pictures. He reckons, because the tumour is small and was spotted early, you have an excellent chance of full recovery.'

With renewed optimism, she smiled coyly, 'I've already spoken to him, Dad; first treatment's this afternoon.'

'Try not to worry, love, I'll be by your side all the way through.'

She hugged him tightly. 'I know, Dad.'

'Just look at this place,' he said as they exited the lift, stepping out onto the neatly swept winding concrete pathway leading towards a stunning group of single-storey buildings made from a mix of redwood and white-washed blocks. Apart from a few minor cloud clusters, the sky was crystal clear.

Isabel stared ahead. 'I can see this place from my window. Sophie told me it's the Convalescence Centre. There's a coffee shop and a spa… it's unbelievable!'

'Bloody different from the NHS, Izzy. Let's get a drink, I fancy iced tea.'

'Make that two, Dad?'

The whole situation was surreal; Blake only wished it could have been under much better circumstances. Whilst the idyllic surroundings provided a distraction, there was no getting away from the fact that his only child was being treated for cancer. He promised himself one way or another they'd get through this.

The open-plan coffee shop had the appearance of a classy restaurant, without alcohol. Several families sat at tables, under huge sails suspended by wires. The impressive redwood decking spanned a large area, edged by a glass balustrade, providing an excellent view of the Pacific. Waves rolled and crashed hypnotically on the shoreline.

Blake ordered two iced teas and a club sandwich. The assistant said she'd bring them over to their table. Weaving through the chairs, they dropped into two rattan-cushioned seats perched on the edge of the decking close to the bar.

'Are you sure you don't mind me eating? Feels cruel.'

'I'm fine, Dad, stop worrying. I had a bacon toasty this morning. It's not really nil by mouth; just a break from food before the treatment.'

'Only had a small breakfast at the motel.'

'What's it like?'

'Basic, but clean.'

He leaned over the table and placed a reassuring hand on her arm. 'You'll beat this, princess.'

'Can we talk about something else? I'm fed up of all this hospital crap. Just want to feel normal for a few hours.'

'OK, what do you want to talk about?'

'Anything, not bothered. What's Miami like?'

'Not seen much of it, but what I've seen looks pretty amazing. Pastel-coloured buildings and wide palm-lined boulevards, just like in *Miami Vice.*'

She gave him a puzzled look. 'What's *Miami Vice*?'

'It's a cult eighties TV show set in Miami about two cops Sunny and Crockett, running around in white suits catching drug dealers.'

'Sounds cheesy.' She smiled. 'You're so ancient, Dad.'

'Cheeky, I'm only forty-five. Not ready for the care home yet!'

They both laughed. It was great to see her smile again after all she'd been through, he thought.

The iced teas arrived, and they both took a sip. A slight breeze coming off the ocean invigorated Blake.

Suddenly his moment of calm was shattered by an alarming announcement on Network News. He spun his chair around and stared at the large wall-mounted TV behind the coffee shop counter. The anchorwoman Robin De Haven delivered the report in her sixties-style wide-rimmed specs:

'A dog walker discovered the body of a forty-five-year-old Florida man on a remote part of Daytona beach off the coastal plain this morning. In a statement to Network News, Crime Scene detectives said the victim's vehicle was rammed off the coastal road and crashed amongst the trees. But the man died from fatal injuries not related to the crash, rather a single gunshot wound to the head, which appears to have come from his own gun, which backfired. Police also found a large bag of Marijuana in the victim's vehicle, and suspect this is a drug deal, which went badly. They are treating the death as suspicious and appealing for witnesses.'

Blake felt cold creep over him as the news switched to live camera footage of a young male reporter standing on the beach. The colour drained from his face. Swallowing hard, he turned his chair back around.

'What's up, Dad? You look like you've seen a ghost.'

'Just tired with all the travelling and stress,' he lied nervously, as all kinds of irrational thoughts cursed through his mind.

'Maybe we should go back now?'

'Just ten minutes more. Please, Dad… it's so lovely here.'

'OK, Izzy.'

CHAPTER 109

Blake stirred around seven a.m. the following day. Sitting on the edge of the sofa bed, he entwined his fingers and stretched his arms towards the ceiling. His morning ritual. He stood and slipped jeans and a shirt on.

Isabel was still sleeping peacefully; he watched her chest rise and fall, feeling reassured as she breathed. Considering he'd been shouldering the burden of the biker's death, and fear of being arrested in connection with it, he'd slept OK, after a relaxing evening spent chatting and watching DVDs with his daughter – though it was probably more to do with not feeling helpless any more; knowing Isabel was receiving the best possible treatment money could buy.

Removing the sheets and pillows, he folded and placed them neatly on the dresser before quietly collapsing the sofa bed.

Sliding the balcony door open, he slipped through and closed it behind him. The promise of another beautiful day loomed on the Pacific horizon. With the soothing sound of the ocean in the background, he retrieved his mobile from his jeans' pocket and called John Murphy, mindful the UK was five hours in front.

'Tom! How the bloody hell are you? More importantly, how's Isabel?'

'Not too bad considering she had the first treatment yesterday. I'm really hopeful it will cure her, John. This hospital is state of the art. Slept here last night to be with her.'

'That's great news, mate; we're all rooting for her at the station. How long's she in for?'

'Can't really say. Each patient is different… all depends on the size of the tumour. Thank god Isabel's is small, and, because they caught it early, she may not need too many treatments, but we'll know more over the course of the week.' For the first time Blake found himself able to discuss 'it' – the tumour – openly.

'How's Miami?'

'Like I mentioned to Isabel yesterday, I haven't had a chance to see much. To be honest, John, we want to get the treatment over with, and fly back home.'

'I can't imagine how difficult it must be,' Murphy sympathised.

'It's not easy. Listen, where are you?'

'Just nipped out the station to grab a pie.'

'You alone?'

'Why?'

'Can't discuss it over the phone, mate. How about I call you from a phone box later?' Blake said covertly.

'All sounds a bit cloak and dagger. You in trouble?'

'Sort of.'

OK, which mobile?'

'Your other one.'

'The burner?'

'Yeah.'

'I must nip home and get it.'

'Appreciate that, John.'

'What time?'

'What time is it there now?'

Murphy glanced at his watch. 'Twelve noon.'

'Izzy's having another treatment around ten a.m. Shall we say seven p.m. UK time?'

'OK.'

'Everything good with you? How's the Bentley case going? Has he been sentenced yet?'

'Yeah, Judge gave him four years for possession with conspiracy to supply.'

'That's good news at least.'

'I'm still not convinced he hasn't anything to do with the Barry Gibson murder case.'

'I know, John, but there wasn't enough evidence to convict him.'

'OK, speak later.'

'Take care, mate?'

'And you.'

CHAPTER 110

The forty-foot Vitress 420 Fly private yacht left Ibiza harbour heading for Morocco, its two guests relishing the thought of spending an uninterrupted few days in the exotic North African coastal capital of Rabat with its fascinating blend of architecture and cultures.

Clouds of white sea spray churned from the bow, leaving a hundred feet stream of wash behind, as the Bavarian craft carved through the deep Balearic at twenty-seven knots.

Katrina Osborne, feeling like a Bond girl, stood in a revealing salmon bikini, next to Ibrahim Benzar on the fly bridge. She watched in awe as the vast Balearic sprawled out in front, her bob blustered in the headwind. Ibrahim sat at the helm in his gold-rimmed shades, gripping the steering wheel like a rich boy cruising around town in a convertible.

She kissed his warm temple. 'This is a dream,' she said, watery-eyed from the wind. 'It's a gorgeous boat. Must have cost a fortune?'

'About a million.'

'How many days have we got it?'

'A few.'

Her face lit up like a small child's at Christmas. 'How long until we get to Rabat?'

'It's six hundred nautical miles. If we keep a steady twenty-five knots, a day and a half.'

'Why don't you get some sun on the bathing platform?' he said, easing down the throttle, slowing the yacht to a steadier ten knots.

She padded barefoot down the fly deck steps and edged over to the bow, sliding a cautious hand down the chrome side rail, like an acrobat on a tightrope. The ocean breeze washed over her, cooling the intense rays. Feeling the yacht rise and fall underneath her, she lay blissfully on the leather covered memory foam bathing bed.

Since landing in Ibiza, hardly a single thought about Carl's plight and Stoke had entered her head. Did that make her a callous bitch, or just someone who desperately needed to escape and gain new perspective on life?

She'd called Luna several times for updates, but Ibrahim warned her not to reveal their location, which she found suspicious, if not a little worrying.

After much interrogation Kat told her somewhere in the Balearics. Luna voiced concerns, said he was using her for sex. Instinctively Kat knew there was more to it than great sex. Ibrahim knew how to treat a woman. Expensive gifts, exotic locations and millionaire's toys aside, she felt the connection you only get when there is mutual respect and feelings developing between two people. As good a friend as Luna was, her opinion reeked of jealousy.

Around lunchtime they'd reached the Alboran Sea off the coast of Almeria and Malaga. Whilst Ibrahim sat motionless at the helm, sipping coffee, Kat spent the rest of the morning familiarising herself with the yacht, with a glass of iced Pinot Grigio in tow.

The sense of space below deck – with its stylish rose-wood interior, white leather seats and saloon master cabin with en-suite bathroom – blew her away.

By lunchtime Ibrahim had detoured towards land and anchored just off the coast of Malaga in a secluded bay. He made his way down the fly bridge steps, over to the rear bathing platform, which was submerged into the sea, stripped naked and dived off. Swimming in the crystal cool waters, he shouted at Kat to join him.

'I'm not a good swimmer.'

'You'll be OK, I'll look after you, we'll stay close to the yacht.'

Reluctant, she stood nervously on the platform. 'I can't.'

He swam closer and held out a hand. 'Just sit on the edge and lower yourself in, I'll steady you?'

Plucking up courage, she grabbed the edge.

'Take off your bikini first.' He grinned.

She glanced around. 'Seriously? You cheeky bugger!'

'There's no one here, don't worry?'

She paused, then untied her top and tossed it behind. With raised knees, she slid the skimpy bottoms off. Slipping into the sea, she screeched, 'Shit, it's cold!'

Ibrahim laughed. 'You English girls are so uptight.'

She swam frantically into his arms. Treading water, he pulled her close and they kissed. She felt liberated.

'It's OK once your body temperature gets over the shock. Don't let go of me though; it looks really deep.'

Sensing her fear, he guided her to the platform edge. 'Hold on here while I swim.'

Clutching the edge, she watched him for a few minutes, and, as he flipped and began to swim back towards her, she shouted. 'Don't be too long, I'm getting out.'

She heaved herself up.

He stopped and floated on his back. Salt water ran off her naked curvaceous hips and bum, and he felt himself getting semi-hard. He swam fifty feet, then rejoined her on the yacht.

Drying off, he slipped a robe on and climbed the steps back up to the fly bridge.

Kat was laying out a cold fish salad. They dined, sipping Prosecco he'd fetched from the wet bar.

Kat took another sip. 'Where are we now?'

'About four miles from Malaga.'

'How do you know?' she asked curiously.

'The instruments and chart plotter on the helm tell me where we are, how many miles we've done, weather forecasts and all kinds of other info. It's a computer you program before starting any journey.'

'Sounds clever.'

'It is. Without it we'd be lost at sea!'

'I like the idea of being lost.' she smirked whilst slipping her hand under his gown.

'Where did you learn to sail?'

'In Turkey. My old boss used to let me drive his yacht while he entertained clients,' he said, raising his groin in response.

'Must've been rich?'

'He was, but the yacht was a lot older than this; it was years ago.'

'Man of many talents, eh?' she said, leaning lower, her arm now up to the elbow under his robe.'

Fully aroused, he joked, 'I'll show you what I'm fantastic at.' Then, grabbing her hand, he towed her seductively to the side and turned her around to face the ocean. With both hands on the edge, she gazed at the waves gently lapping the boat.

He removed her robe.

Naked, she arched, the searing sun kissing her tanned back, white lines visible just below her waistline, where the skimpy bottoms had been.

His tongue traced her neckline, then he slipped his robe onto the deck and entered her from behind.

CHAPTER 111

Seventy-two hours later, Isabel Blake had been discharged from hospital mid-morning, and they were almost home. Her dad was elated by her response to the treatment.

Blake eased his nervous grip on the armrests as the plane finally passed through rough turbulence on its descent towards Manchester airport. Take-off had been fairly smooth, but landing was a whole different ball game; thankfully they'd be on the ground soon. Reflecting on recent events, he accepted that, although he'd been assigned to desk duties, he had been party to some kind of illegal artefacts trade, and almost died at the hands of a murdering thief. None of it truly mattered; just knowing Isabel was tumour free gave him immense inner peace. They could start making plans for the future.

Taking another slurp of Shiraz, he glanced across the aisle at his brave girl. She turned her head and gave him a tired smile.

'You OK, Izzy?'

'Yeah, Dad, I'm just shattered.'

'We'll be landing in a few minutes.'

The Boeing 787 Dreamliner from Miami touched down at Manchester Airport around midnight UK time. After the tedium of an eight-hour flight, DI Tom Blake didn't relish the thought of waiting for their cases; he simply wanted to get his daughter home safely.

As the plane eased to a standstill opposite the terminal, an incoming call from DS Murphy startled him. He peered through tired eyes at his mobile on the table in front of his seat, the green answer icon flashed. John probably wanted to know if they'd arrived in the UK.

'H… ello?' he said, a little disorientated.

'It's John, can you hear me?'

'Yeah.'

'You don't sound with it?'

He yawned. 'Just dozed off.'

'Everything OK with Isabel?'

'Great news, the tumour's in regression.'

'That's fantastic, mate.'

'I know, it's unbelievable. I can't tell you how happy we both are.'

'What time should I pick you up?'

'Around 12.40.'

'No problem. Listen, Tom, I don't want to put a damper on things but have you seen the news recently?'

'Just American stuff. Why?'

'You won't believe this. Someone has only gone and nicked the Staffordshire Hoard from the Potteries Museum. All three point three million quid's worth! Apparently they were displaying the whole collection, with most of it coming from Birmingham Museum on a two-week loan.'

'Shit! You're kidding?' he said, trying to sound surprised.

'Straight up. They discovered yesterday when the pieces were taken off display for cleaning. Haven't got the full details yet, but it appears they've nicked the originals and swapped them for replicas. It'll be all over the front pages of the nationals tomorrow.'

'Shit! Anyone in the frame?'

'We're looking at known suspects, but nothing yet. Anyway, don't worry about that now, I'll see you at arrivals. Call me before you go through customs, it will save waiting around.'

'Will do. Thanks, mate.'

After thirty minutes of queuing, Tom and Isabel passed through customs into the arrivals lounge.

John Murphy gave his boss a welcoming handshake and hugged Isabel, before taking their trolley. Once outside, he slung their cases into the car boot, which thankfully he'd parked right outside the exit doors of terminal three.

Blake eased Isabel into the back, making sure she was comfy and had everything she needed for the short journey, before jumping in the front next to his sergeant.

'How you feeling?' Murphy asked Isabel, indicating to pull out of a line of taxis.

'Tired, but I'm glad to be back.'

'Your dad tells me the treatment went well.'

'Yeah, really well.'

'That's fantastic news!'

Blake craned his neck to the back. Isabel's eyes were barely open.

'Try to get some rest, darling. We'll soon be home.'

'OK.'

'How was your flight?'

'Great, we managed an upgrade to first class. The doctors advised it, considering Izzy's condition. Turned out to be a real smart move, bloody expensive though.'

'I can imagine. Did you have one of those reclining seats with loads of space?' Murphy asked curiously.

'Yeah, plus tons of other perks,' Blake said, glancing in the rear-view mirror at Isabel, who'd dozed off, her head cranked awkwardly to the side.

'What's Miami like then?'

'I didn't end up seeing that much of it, but what I did see was spectacular.'

Murphy glanced in the rear-view mirror to make sure Isabel was sound asleep. He lowered his voice. 'What you told me on the phone sounds like a movie script. You're lucky to be alive, mate. Horrendous!'

'Don't I know it. John, you really can't tell anyone about it. I had no choice, absolute nightmare.'

'Goes without saying. I totally understand, I'd have done the same in your situation.'

'I don't think anyone else will see it like that, especially back at the station.' Blake sounded concerned.

'Maybe not, but what's done is done. Can't change it now. Let's just hope people don't find out about your illicit trade.' He knew they were probably from the Staffordshire Hoard, and judging by the guilty look on his boss's face, he knew as well, but wasn't letting anything slip.

After an awkward moment of silence, Blake asked what the weather had been like in the UK, as they cruised down M56 towards the M6 south at a steady sixty.

Murphy just had to ask, he couldn't resist any longer. 'The pieces of gold?'

Blake looked at him mournfully.

'They were from the Staffordshire Hoard weren't they?'

'The Hoard consists of over 3000 pieces; no one will miss a couple?'

'Bloody hell Tom, if this comes out you could be looking at a custodial!'

Blake looked remorseful. 'Will it come out, John?'

'Not from me. You did it to save Isabel's life. I understand, mate. There wasn't enough time to look at other options.'

'Exactly. I'm not proud of what I've done, but it was out of necessity.'

'You do realise this all leads back to those scum Benzar brothers? The kidnapping and the robbery.'

'I know. I can assure you those animals will pay for what they did to Isabel, but at present we have no concrete proof.'

'Could be risky, Tom! Once the team start probing, you never know what they'll find?'

'The thing is, John, we had a legitimate reason to be in America. It's unlikely Ibrahim Benzar would shoot himself in the foot. If he mentions those two pieces, he'd be admitting to the theft.'

'Agreed, but if he gets nicked he may try to use it as leverage. Are you prepared to take that risk?'

'No choice. If you don't mind, I'd rather not talk about it, John?'

CHAPTER 112

Stafford Prison's twenty-foot high perimeter wall and tiny barred windows sent out a clear message to its inmates. Built during the Regency period in 1793, this sinister-looking fortress was where the infamous Staffordshire poisoner William Palmer was hanged.

The huge oak gates opened slowly, and DS Murphy eased the Astra pool car into the secure visitors' entrance.

Blake hated prison visits. Over the years, he and Murphy had endured plenty. The fact that neither he nor his sergeant had their mobiles left them feeling vulnerable. Hardly surprising really; inside prison the police were a pariah.

Convicted prisoners often shared key intelligence on known associates, providing there was something in it for them. A mutually beneficial carrot and stick scenario, which led to arrests. Carl Bentley put a request in to see the detectives on the premise that he had new information regarding the theft of the Staffordshire Hoard.

The governor allocated them an interview room away from the main prison block. Michael Lawrence Porter, a tall thin bloke in his mid-fifties, wore a slightly eccentric autumnal-coloured tweed suit, accompanied by an emerald dickie bow, giving him the appearance of a winter tree. Fusty attire aside, he was well thought of by both prisoners and his superiors. DI Blake first met him at HM Brixton five years ago. Having done a wonderful job dragging that prison into the twenty-first century, he'd been headhunted for a repeat dose at Stafford.

'Chaps, wait here while we fetch prisoner Bentley,' Porter said, before disappearing along the corridor with one of his pristinely turned-out guards.

'Let's hope Bentley's not clutching at straws,' Murphy said sceptically.

'We won't know until we speak to him. He'll be pissed off, stuck in this dungeon, while the rest of the gang are on their jollies.'

'I bet. You reckon he was involved?'

'Probably, but from what you've told me he's no mastermind; we'll soon see.'

Moments later, Carl Bentley sauntered along the corridor handcuffed to the prison guard, behind Lawrence Porter.

'Go easy on him, he's only just settling in. Would you like tea or coffee?' Porter asked.

'Two coffees, white with sugar please.' Blake thanked him.

'Someone will bring those to the interview room soon.' With that, he left.

The guard led Bentley into the interview room. Removing the chain that joined them, he told the detectives he'd be in the next room if needed.

Judging by his ashen-white complexion and sleep-deprived eyes, Carl Bentley's short time in prison had emotionally drained him.

'Let's cut to the chase, Mr Bentley. What exactly do you have to tell us?' Blake asked bluntly.

He shuffled around nervously on his chair, avoiding eye contact, before replying, 'I know who knocked off the Staffordshire Hoard.'

'And who would that be then?' DS Murphy asked.

'What's in it for me?

'Depends on how good your information is.'

Although Bentley had little to lose, he was still mindful that other prisoners would be suspicious. He'd been taken from his cell by the governor, after only a short incarceration. A grass got nasties slipped in his food and the shit kicked out of him.

'It's spot on.'

'We only have your word for that,' Murphy said.

Blake made it clear to Bentley. 'I can't make any promises, but the CPS allows some discretion within the law. If the information you provide leads to the arrest of the perpetrators and recovery of the stolen Hoard, we may negotiate you some privileges and a reduced sentence, but there's no guarantees.'

'What sort of privileges?'

'Fags, extra phone cards, that type of thing.'

'You having a laugh?' Bentley scoffed. 'Phone cards! What about my bastard safety?'

'If the information you provide places you in danger, we can request you're moved to a different prison.'

'How long off the sentence?'

'That's not up to the police. We have to talk with the CPS. Again it all depends on the quality of your information.'

'Ballpark figure.'

'Up to twelve months, maybe.'

Bentley grimaced. 'Is that it?'

'The clock's ticking, Carl,' Murphy chipped in playing bad cop. 'We need to nail this today. Trust me, we won't be returning, so stop messing about and tell us what you know.'

Bentley sighed, knowing there was no going back. He lowered his voice. 'The Benzar brothers pulled off the Hoard job.'

'Your boss is Ibrahim Benzar. Is that correct?' Murphy asked.

'Yeah.'

'How long you worked for him?'

'About four years.'

'Doing what?'

'Driving.'

'In what capacity?'

'Picking stuff up.'

Bentley's evasive manner was winding Murphy up. 'It's like pulling teeth,' he moaned to Blake. 'He was like this when we charged him with dealing. A right irritating shit.'

'I told you before. It's on my record.'

'Oh yeah, delivery boy,' Murphy said sarcastically.

Blake interrupted. 'Tell us about Benzar?'

'He's a dodgy bastard.'

'Something we don't know?'

'Makes out he's an honest businessman. All that's a front.'

'For what?'

'Drugs, money laundering scams.'

'No doubt his brother Yusuf Benzar is involved in that side of things. He recently escaped police custody,' Blake said, fishing for links.

'I don't know much about him. I do know they've been planning this job for months.'

'I'm afraid that's bullshit. Yusuf Benzar's a known heroin and coke dealer, and since you worked for his brother, and have been convicted for dealing class A, it beggars belief.

'Anyway, we're not here to discuss your supplier. Were you in on the Staffordshire Hoard job?'

'No.'

'I find that hard to believe. You worked for Ibrahim Benzar for four years and didn't have a clue about the robbery. Not even a hint of it?'

'I only do the deliveries and run him about sometimes. He never told me bugger all.'

'So you've been turning a blind eye all that time?'

'Yeah.'

Blake's patience was running out. 'If you weren't involved, how the bloody hell do you know Benzar orchestrated this job? Because at the minute you're giving us nothing concrete.'

Murphy put the boot in. 'We know you're pissed off with Ibrahim Benzar for having a fling with your missus. I reckon they're having an affair.'

Bentley looked confused, 'What are you talking about?'

'The bogus alibi you gave us, the night Barry Gibson was killed; she was shagging your boss Ibrahim Benzar, at the Willow Room Hotel.'

Seeing red Bentley reared up. 'Fuck off! That was a one off. You're just trying to wind me up.'

'If that's what you want to believe, it's up to you. Sit down! We need something concrete about the theft of the Staffordshire Hoard?' Blake said.

'Benzar uses this ginger guy, a real geek who sorts out his computer tech stuff. One day I was loading stock onto the shelves upstairs in the Black Sea Mini-Market, when I heard a noise coming from behind the shelves. It freaked me out at first. Then I noticed some kind of secret entrance in the plasterboard, like a hidden room. I realised it was Leonard Vale's voice, he was talking to someone on his mobile so I quietly lifted down a couple of shrink wrapped cartons of stock, stuck my ear to the wall and listened. He was talking about knocking out the cameras at the Potteries Museum. At first I didn't understand until he said will Charlie be okay on his own. Later that day the boss sent me to fill up cheap vodka into branded bottles at his flat. Whilst there I snooped about, and found a Staffordshire Hoard guide in a clear wallet. He'd put sticky notes on certain pages, and there was a map of the inside of the Museum, and another of the surrounding streets. It was like one of those heist blueprints.'

'My, my, you are a sneaky bugger Mr Bentley.' Blake said.

'Now we're getting somewhere.' Murphy said. 'And this Leonard Vale helped Benzar?'

'Who else is involved?'

'How do you mean?'

'Stop mucking about?' Blake scolded. 'This type of job is complex. It needed meticulous planning and a team of professionals to pull it off.'

'Okay. There were other blokes.'

'Names?'

'Benzar's been knocking about with a guy called Charlie Bullard quite a bit.'

Murphy took the name down in his notebook.

'What can you tell us about him?'

'He's done time years ago.'

'Any idea what for?'

'Heard he was a bank robber in the eighties.'

'We'll get that checked out as soon as we get back the station.'

'Who else?'

'Malcolm Preston?'

'Benzar's accountant?' Blake raised an eyebrow.

'That's him.'

'Malcolm Preston's absconded; we have a warrant for his arrest. Any ideas where he might be?'

'All I know is he lives in Newcastle somewhere.'

'Is that it?' Blake asked.

'Yeah.'

'You're absolutely sure that no one else is involved?'

'I don't think so.'

'Okay, Mr Bentley that's all for now, thank you for your cooperation. We'll be in touch regarding any deal we strike up on your behalf with the CPS. However, that all depends if your intel is reliable and leads to arrests.'

CHAPTER 113

On the drive back along the A34 towards Stoke, Blake instructed Murphy to call the office manager to do a PNC check on Charlie Bullard and Leonard Vale, but his mobile was busy so he texted him.

'What do you reckon on Bentley's intel?'

'Hard to say. We'll know more once we've interviewed those two. Can't see him requesting a visit unless his info's reliable,' Blake said, overtaking a white van.

'Maybe, but he knows wasting police time will add extra to his sentence. Thing is, he's given us key suspects in the Staffordshire Hoard case and we need to act sharpish before they leg it, that is if they've not already shot through. It's attracting a ton of media attention so Coleman's likely to allocate a big team.'

Murphy's mobile rang. 'Nick?'

'I've just done a PNC on the two names; both of them have previous. Bullard did two five-year sentences for his part in numerous armed robberies during the eighties. Vale on the other hand has no convictions in the UK, but, get this, he's been done for hacking in the US, and spent three years in prison over there.'

'Thanks for the head's up, Nick. Good work. We'll be back in the next twenty minutes.'

When they arrived at the station, Nick Pemberton was sticking pictures of the four suspects onto the white board. He'd assembled everyone for an emergency briefing on the Staffordshire Hoard case.

Blake entered the room followed by DS Murphy and addressed the team. 'Listen up, everyone? This morning we interviewed Carl Bentley in Stafford Prison. Not that you'll need reminding – we recently put him away for possession with intent to supply. Sadly we didn't have enough to charge him with Barry Gibson's murder.

'Anyway, I'll get to the point. In hope of a reduced sentence, Bentley has given us the names of the gang he claims pulled off the Staffordshire Hoard robbery. As you're aware the media are all over this, so we need to act immediately. According to Bentley's intel, there's four specific suspects: Ibrahim Benzar's the orchestrator; Charlie Bullard's a convicted bank robber; Leonard Vale is a techy; and Malcolm Preston is Benzar's bent accountant.

'As you know we tried to arrest and question Malcolm Preston earlier in the week. Unfortunately he'd already absconded. The stolen vehicle he used was later found dumped in Tesco's car park. All our colleagues across the UK have been alerted. If he's still in the country, it's only a matter of time before he surfaces.'

Blake thanked Nick Pemberton for getting the case props up so quickly before passing the baton over to him.

'We set up a trace on Malcolm Preston's credit and debit cards, mobile phones, and e-mail accounts, but he's used none of them yet. He's probably using cash and communicating with a burner or public phones. Either way the clever bastard has gone to ground. DS Jamieson, can you put pressure on his wife, take a look at her banking activity and phone records for the last week, and see if there's any communication with hubby, or suspicious transactions?'

Blake looked at Murphy. 'DS Murphy, I'm tasking you with establishing links between Charlie Bullard, Leonard Vale, Ibrahim Benzar and his brother.'

'We don't know the whereabouts of Yusuf Benzar.'

'I know, but the fact these nasty bastards abducted my daughter and used her to facilitate his escape shows he must've been integral to their plans.' He looked at Evans. 'PC Evans, can you check airline records to find out if any of the gang were on flights out of the UK recently?'

'DS Moore?'

'Boss.'

'Organise transport for two teams and another couple of PCs to join us straight after this briefing. Bullard and Vale are about to get a surprise visit. According to council tax records, they both occupy addresses we've been given.'

'OK, will do.'

Blake glanced across the room at the most inexperienced member of the team. His face blushed as all eyes scanned him. 'DC Longsdon?'

'Sir?'

'Hop along the road to the Potteries Museum. First, speak to the manager about their security system again, then have another chat with the staff about the robbery. Shake the tree; see if anyone gets rattled. These high-profile robberies usually involve an insider.'

'OK, sir.'

'Don't forget your handcuffs and taser,' Murphy teased, 'it could turn nasty.'

Laughter spread through the team of officers present, which only embarrassed Longsdon more.

'On second thoughts, help PC Evans with the airline trace, then both of you go together. It'll be more productive that way. We'll reconvene after lunch for progress on these lines of enquiry.'

CHAPTER 114

Blake stood in his stab vest facing the front door of Charlie Bullard's council flat in Hanley. Luckily for them there was one entry and exit point, apart from the windows at the rear, which were three storeys up, overlooking two 1950s' tower blocks.

He politely pressed the bell for a minute, mindful of police budgets since they were now responsible for the cost of replacement doors. There was no answer.

'POLICE, OPEN UP!'

Another minute passed, but there was still no reply so he ordered PC Davis to open it with the big yellow key. The frame splintered and capitulated on the third pounding.

'POLICE! POLICE!' DS Jamieson shouted before barging into the hallway. He went flying over a small trolley case. A familiar, maroon-coloured, UK passport book, with a boarding pass slotted inside it, skidded across the soiled grey carpet tiles.

Jamieson climbed to his feet. 'Looks like he's off on holiday, chief.'

'Not anymore.'

'What time's the flight?'

'Seven-thirty tonight from Manchester, arrives in Malaga at ten,' he said, after checking it.

'Costa del Crime. Pretty unoriginal.'

Spreading out, each officer took a room whilst Blake and Jamieson stood in what appeared to be a makeshift lounge with a strange assortment of seating, a large red three-seat chesterfield, and four non-matching fold-up garden chairs.

Moments later, cries of 'all clear!' echoed round the flat.

Blake addressed his team as they gathered in the tatty kitchen. 'Charlie Bullard seems to have a lot of seats for a bloke who lives on his own. He's definitely had some kind of party or meeting recently.'

Then they heard the unmistakable muffled sound of someone holding their nose to prevent a sneeze.

'Over there!' Blake pointed to a small plastic bifold door about four foot tall, drawn across its frame. Blake nodded at PC Davis warily. He withdrew his pepper spray and yanked the door back with his free hand to reveal a pair of trainers poking through a mop and several coats hanging on hooks.

'Come out, Mr Bullard.' Blake smirked as he glanced at the other officers who were now sniggering.

The silver-haired con disentangled himself, stooped to avoid bumping his head, and climbed out of the boiler room.

'You didn't think we'd leave without you, did you, Mr Bullard?'

With a look of disbelief, he shrugged his shoulders and stood there like a rabbit in the headlights, wondering how the bloody hell they'd got onto him.

'Charlie Bullard, as a result of a tip-off we received, I'm arresting you on suspicion of being involved in the theft of the Staffordshire Hoard. You do not have to say anything.' Blake continued to read his rights.

'This is bullshit. You've got no proof!'

'We'll go over the finer details back at the station. Cuff him, PC Davis.'

Blake grabbed a ten-inch tablet from off the kitchen worktop. 'Tech forensics will take a look at this. Get him back to the station, whilst DS Jamieson and I wait for SOCO to sweep his gaff.'

Unlike the usual lengthy property search, wading through every manner of detritus, this one took literally thirty minutes flat. The sheer lack of belongings gave new meaning to the word minimal. They found a Dominion credit card. The fact it was taped under the inner sole of a shoe, in his case, was highly suggestive.

Fifteen minutes later, across the other side of the city, the second team of officers led by DS John Murphy drew up outside Leonard Vale's address, an Edwardian terraced house in Burslem.

Like the first raid, the officers weren't met by a welcoming tenant voluntarily opening his door, only this time it took longer to gain access to the property because of a five-lever lock, and three brass slide bolts, which the hulking PC Haynes demolished with exacting sledgehammer blows, to the rallying cry of: 'POLICE!'

DS Murphy galloped upstairs like a man half his age, closely followed by Haynes. Darting from room to room, he felt slightly breathless, another indicator he needed to cut back on the burgers and get in shape.

'All clear upstairs!' he shouted from the landing.

Moments later one of the officers bawled from downstairs. 'Suspect located!'

Leonard Vale had literally been caught with his trousers down, perched red faced on the throne in the bathroom. The five policemen gawped through the open doorway, hands over their noses gagging at the stench.

'Piss off!' Vale shouted.

DS Murphy shielded his nose. 'Leonard Vale, as a result of information we've received, I'm arresting you on suspicion of involvement in the theft of the Staffordshire Hoard. PC Haynes, handcuff him.'

'I'm not touching him until he's washed his hands.'

'We'll give you two minutes to get washed up and your trousers on.'

Devastated, Vale bawled at them. 'Bastards!'

Before they could close the door, the ginger geek scrambled his jeans back up without wiping his backside, revealing his oversized manhood surrounded by a mass of orange fuzz.

'Check this guy out. The smelly-arsed bugger's not going in my van!' Haynes moaned.

Unable to resist the urge to ridicule him further, Murphy pitched in. 'It's true what they say then?'

'What's that?' Haynes asked.

Murphy gave him a cocky wink. 'Geeks have big dicks.'

The five officers exchanged looks and burst into laughter; it made a refreshing change from some of the nasties they encountered during domestic raids.

A further search of the property turned up a credit card buried in a bag of sugar, and eight-thousand in used fifties and twenties stuffed in an envelope, hidden inside a book. Not the sort of mullah you'd expect someone who'd been unemployed for years to have.

Amongst Vale's fiction novels stacked on a bookcase in the living room, they found copies of Security and Surveillance magazines, and several guidebooks on computer hacking. Hidden inside an old PC casing, they found an A4 folder containing sheets of specifications of a security system, with lots of highlighted paragraphs and side notes. Murphy guessed this would match the museum's cameras and software. Again, highly suggestive!

Dropping the credit card into an evidence bag, Murphy quizzed Vale. 'Where does a bloke on the dole get eight grand from? Not looking good, Leonard.'

'That's my life savings, you bastard!'

'Yeah, right, and my other car is a gold-plated Bentley. Just thought I'd come work in the old Vectra today.'

As PC Haynes locked Vale in the prison van, Murphy called DI Blake.

'Result, Tom. How did you get on?'

'Charlie Bullard's in custody.'

'We're on our way back with the other suspect now.'

CHAPTER 115

They planned to question the experienced con first, allowing him limited time to get his house in order. Blake was stood in the corridor outside interview room one, holding two coffees, when DS Murphy arrived.

'I'm bloody parched,' he said, taking one of the coffees from his boss.

They entered the room, relieving PC Moore of babysitting duties. Pungent odours of aftershave mixed with deodorant exuded from the silver-haired 55-year-old, who sat in a black shirt and bleached jeans, nervously scratching his nicotine-stained moustache. His solicitor sat giraffe-straight, clipboard and pen at the ready next to him.

'Just to inform you, Mr Bullard, this interview will be recorded.' Blake pressed the red button on the tape machine.

'So, Mr Bullard, we've received information claiming you were involved in the recent theft of the Staffordshire Hoard. What do you have to say about that?

'Don't know, maybe some scrote's gotta grudge.'

'In different circumstances that may be the case but our info comes from a reliable source, and given your previous string of armed robbery convictions during the eighties, you fit the profile.'

'That's bollocks. Check my record; I've stayed out of trouble for years?'

'I'm afraid it doesn't work like that,' Blake continued. Just because you haven't been arrested for a while is irrelevant. Do you own a ten-inch tablet?'

The suspect leaned in to his solicitor for guidance. After a moment's pause, he said, 'No.'

'Most people think that once they've deleted files they disappear forever; thankfully for us that's not the case. Your tablet's been fast tracked by forensics.'

Bullard's face drained of colour. 'Deleted files, what are you on about?'

'I'll repeat the question, do you own a ten-inch tablet?'

He scratched his moustache nervously whilst consulting the solicitor. 'It's not mine.'

'Whose is it then?'

'My sister's lad's.'

'Can he confirm this?'

'Yes.'

'We'll need a number to contact him?'

'No chance, he's only fourteen.'

'OK, what do you use the tablet for?'

'Searching stuff online and watching old movies.'

Blake continued to probe. 'Such as?'

'Same sort of thing as anybody else.'

'Not very convincing answers, are they, Mr Bullard?'

Blake prompted DS Murphy to retrieve the suspect's tablet from his leather document wallet. 'For the benefit of the tape, DS Murphy is showing Mr Bullard a tablet recovered from his flat in Hanley. Do you recognise the tablet, Mr Bullard?'

'Yeah.'

DS Murphy tapped the screen, opening a slide show of digital photos of the Staffordshire Hoard. 'Can you explain these pictures?' Blake asked.

Bullard sighed and looked at his solicitor. After a moment's consult, he spewed, 'Must be the sister's lad doing a school project. They're always doing stuff about history.'

'You can't be serious?' Murphy chipped in sceptically.

Even his solicitor looked amazed at the absurd comment.

'Thee million quid's worth of rare Saxon gold is stolen from the Potteries Museum and we arrest a convicted bank robber possessing a tablet containing hundreds of images of the same gold, a week after it was discovered missing.'

'What are the chances of that, boss?'

'Pretty slim I'd say, DS Murphy.'

'I'm inclined to agree.'

Blake shot the suspect a stern look. 'Mr Bullard, stop wasting our time? Just after your arrest SOCO swept your flat, so think carefully about anything you say regarding evidence they've found.'

He protested. 'You can't do that without a search warrant?'

'I know; that's why we obtained one this morning.'

Bryant Preston gave his client a nod. 'I'm afraid so, Charles.'

Blake continued. 'Have you contacted Ibrahim Benzar recently?'

'Who?'

Blake pulled a face. 'Your boss! Stop pissing us around?'

'Don't know him.'

'You sure about that?'

'Yeah.'

'That's not true. Our source informed us you've been seen with Ibrahim Benzar on numerous occasions recently. What's your relationship with him?'

Still in denial, Bullard said, 'I told you, I don't know him.'

At that moment, Blake's mobile rang. 'Hello.'

'Boss,' PC Evans animated, 'we've questioned several museum staff. Interestingly the caretaker handed his notice in a few days after the robbery.'

'Do we have an address for him?'

'Yeah.'

'Hold on a min?' Not wanting to alert Bullard, he winked at DS Murphy, stopped the tape, and left the interview room to continue the conversation further down the corridor.

'How long has he worked there?'

'Twenty years apparently.'

'Even more interesting, just before the robbery he had outside help from an employment agency. According to the security guards, he's been moaning for years about backache and money troubles.'

'Sounds like he could be our inside man. Great work, PC Evans. If you've finished gathering intel, you and DC Moore come back in. We need to bring the caretaker in for questioning.'

'Will do, sir.'

Blake returned to the interview room with a smug grin. 'Well, Mr Bullard, new evidence has come to light so we can put you on a back burner for now,' he said, staring at him, looking for signs of worry. 'DS Murphy, escort Mr Bullard back to his cell.'

He picked up his notes and headed back towards the incident room.

CHAPTER 116

DS Murphy looked a touch sweaty from his jaunt down the cell block.

'How did Bullard react to the news of new evidence?' Blake asked him.

'Can't really say. He's hard to read. Typical experienced con. He knows we're onto him, so he's spinning it out, playing the system.'

'Most definitely.'

Murphy moaned. 'I reckon that solicitor's bloody dodgy. He's representing Leonard Vale as well; crafty bastard knows we can't interview both of them at the same time.'

'Limited evidence, though John, apart from Bentley's say-so, pictures on the tablet, and association. Not heard anything else from SOCO yet. Shouldn't be too hard to find stuff in his flat; it was practically an empty squat.'

'Didn't they lift any prints from the cabinets the gold was stolen was from?' Murphy asked.

'Nothing, apart from chemical-spray residue off the glass. No trace fibres at all. Professional job. Must have used forensic suits.'

'What about the replicas?'

'The Hoard curator said they fooled everyone. If the gold cleaning schedule wasn't due it could have been months before the theft was discovered,' Blake remarked.

'You have to admire their ingenuity. Where the bloody hell did they get replicas made?'

'I can't imagine it was in the UK. According to the art forgery specialist DS Jamieson spoke to a couple of days ago, it's likely they were done in an either Morocco, Turkey, China or India, which all have specialists who'll do anything for the right price.'

Looking at the white board Murphy offered an opinion. 'I don't know, things are shaping up now, albeit by association. The Benzar brothers organised this job… I'd put money on it. Brink's-Mat Charlie's the tools man on the ground. You've read his record. He's a team player… knocked off everything from high-class jewellers in Knightsbridge to security-firm wage vans in Essex. Most of his known associates are dead or still inside. Besides, London firms rarely step outside their borders.'

Blake stood up and drew connecting lines between photos of the Benzar brothers, Charlie Bullard and Leonard Vale on the white board. At the end of the row, he sketched a crude character outline and wrote 'caretaker' in red capitals. 'He's the missing link. This guy is the key to it all. Caretakers generally have unlimited access. They'll have offered him an obscene amount of money; this was his retirement fund.'

'DC Moore is calling the agency to get the name of who they sent to the museum.'

PC Evans wandered in looking rather pleased, followed by DC Moore.

'Great timing. I'm tasking you both with bringing in this caretaker for questioning. Here's the address,' Blake said, handing over an orange sticky note.'

DC Moore protested. 'What now, sir? I'm starving.'

Handing her a fiver reward, Blake said, 'Casey, get a couple of pasties on your way to Fenton.'

'Thanks very much, sir, but we'll be OK.' As the words left her mouth, DC Moore bit his bottom lip and shot her an angry stare.

'Bloody hell,' Murphy jibed, 'we used to work sixteen hour shifts on chocolate bars, fags and coffee when I was your age.'

CHAPTER 117

DS Murphy had already run a PNC check on the caretaker before he was due to arrive at the station for questioning. Apart from a driving misdemeanour, resulting in a £50 fine in 1994, he was completely clean. Both he and DI Blake hoped this suspect would provide enough intelligence to make arrests, but they wanted to be sure. Like a plate spinning act they needed to give equal attention to each suspect. Both Charlie Bullard and Leonard Vale had provided questionable alibis, but they'd gathered limited evidence. The plan was to pressure the caretaker into a confession; he'd never been arrested before, and, although his solicitor would guide him, unlike a career criminal he'd be disorientated and in a state of shock.

DS Jamieson entered Blake's office holding a couple of A4 sheets. 'Boss, I've just had work-supply agency on the phone. Turns out the temp they sent to the museum was specifically requested by the caretaker.'

'Really! Now there's a coincidence.'

'That's what I thought. Apparently the temp is called "Brian Calcot", and he only registered with them couple weeks before. Even better, they've emailed a photo and a mobile number,' he said, passing over printouts.

Blake scrutinised them. 'Is it me or does this look like Charlie Bullard with a beard?'

'Shit, yeah, I've only just printed it.'

'Do a check on the mobile number and get onto the network for triangulation; even if he's used a burner we should be able to get a GPS location. Great work, Roger. We're interviewing the caretaker soon as Evans and Moore bring him in.'

CHAPTER 118

Twenty minutes later, PC Evans and DC Moore knocked on the door of a late Victorian terraced house in Etruscan Street, Fenton. A portly lady in her mid-sixties, wearing a checked apron and fur-trimmed slippers answered.

'Hello, Mrs Mitchell? PC Evans and DC Moore from Staffordshire Police. Is your husband home?'

'Our Arthur? No, why?'

Evans continued. 'Can we step inside? We think he can help us with our enquiries.'

'What enquiries?' she said, ushering them into the front room with a mantelpiece covered in Royal Doulton figures.

'Until recently he was the caretaker at the Potteries Museum, is that correct?'

'Yeah, been there years.'

'I'm sure you'll have heard in the news about the theft of The Staffordshire Hoard from the museum recently?'

'Arthur mentioned it, but I don't see what it's got to do with him? He dunna work there any more, sick of 'em. Putting on a willing horse, they were. He's gotta bad back, you know. Years of mauling and humping stuff about.'

'Why did he hand his notice in so suddenly?' DC Moore asked her.

'Like I said, his back's killing him… sits with a hot water bottle on it all night. He's had enough.'

'What about his pension?'

'Never paid into it, couldn't afford to. He'll be drawing his state pension in a couple of years.'

'Do you know where your husband is now? We'd like to speak to him.'

'He's down the allotment.'

'Where's that, Mrs Mitchell?'

'If you go out of here, turn left and walk along the street until you get to an alleyway on your right; it's down there. He'll be there until teatime.'

'Thank you for your cooperation.'

PC Evans and DC Moore paced up and down an overgrown privet hedge in search of an entrance, eventually finding an old shed door screwed to a post with rusting strap hinges. A bolt on a length of string inserted through the Hasp & Staple held it shut. Moore removed it and they stepped inside, scanning the ramshackle greenhouses and odd-looking sheds in every shade of green and brown, littering an allotment covering about an acre.

'Where should we start?' Evans said.

'Ask that bloke over there?' Moore replied, pointing to an old chap in a tweed cap and wellies, turning soil over with a fork.

'Excuse me, sir, can you show us Arthur Mitchell's allotment?'

Startled to see two police officers, he pointed towards the bottom. 'See that duck egg-coloured shed? That's his patch.'

'Thank you.'

After a few minutes of navigating the broken-slab path winding through the allotment, they reached Mitchell's shed. Peering through the window they saw an array of garden tools hanging neatly on the wooden framework, and some kind of expensive-looking petrol machinery with the words Honda Lawn King down the side, but no sign of the caretaker.

They were just about to look inside when DC Moore nudged Evans and nodded towards a thin stream of smoke rising above the roof from the other side. They found Arthur Mitchell perched in a deck chair puffing on a pipe, reading the *Evening Sentinel.*

'Mr Mitchell?'

'Bloody hell! You nearly gave me a heart attack!' he said, fumbling the newspaper and rising to his feet.

'That's an expensive-looking lawnmower you've got in there?' DC Moore said, trying to unsettle him.

'It's a rotavator. Anyway, how's that your business?'

Keeping him on the back foot, Evans said, 'Earlier today we talked to Potteries Museum staff regarding the Staffordshire Hoard theft. Can you accompany us to the station to answer a few routine questions concerning this?'

As she spoke, Moore quickly did an online search on his phone. The Honda D26R Rotavator retailed at eight hundred quid.

'I don't work there any more,' he said abruptly.

'Yes, we know. The manager said you handed your notice in rather suddenly.'

'What's this got to do with me?'

'PC Evans just told you… this is a high-profile robbery case receiving worldwide media coverage,' Moore said, piling on the pressure.

'Like I told you, I don't work there.'

Moore emphasised the point. 'Look, Mr Mitchell, we'd appreciate your cooperation, but if needs be we'll arrest you. You don't want that, do you?'

'OK, just give me a minute to put things away,' he said reluctantly, knocking his pipe out on a large sandstone rock.

Judging by his evasive manner, and the look of sheer dread on Mitchell's face, he was definitely hiding something. The acquisition of a brand-new rotavator only added further suspicion.

On the way back to the station, Arthur Mitchell never uttered a word, but sat gazing in disbelief out of the window.

Still wearing muddy green wellingtons, Arthur Mitchell fidgeted nervously in his chair. His legal aid looked straight out of law school. A petite, pretty young solicitor in her mid-twenties, with long, flowing red hair tied in a ponytail.

Blake took a back seat as DS Murphy led the interview.

'So Mr Mitchell, PC Evans has already explained we're questioning all the museum staff about the theft of the Staffordshire Hoard. In cases such as this we need to establish everyone's movements before and after the robbery. The real gold was discovered to have been switched for replicas by the Hoard curator on the twenty-ninth of June. From the intelligence we've gathered we believe the robbery took place within a two-week time frame, just before that date. During that period did you notice anything out of the ordinary?'

'Like what?'

'Anyone acting suspicious around the collection, such as museum visitors, or staff taking a lot of pictures, or asking unusual questions regarding security that sort of thing.'

'No, I spent most of my time behind the scenes. The Hoard host and security take turns monitoring the Mead Hall, so they'd know.'

'We've already questioned them and drawn a blank.'

'Explain what your daily duties included?'

'I was just a dogsbody, opening doors moving stuff around, unblocking sinks and the odd bit of painting.'

'We've been informed you employed a temp from the work-supply agency on the eighteenth and nineteenth of June? Can you confirm this?'

Turning pale, he swallowed hard, arms crossing his stomach in a protective huddle.

'Can you answer the question please, Mr Mitchell?'

Avoiding eye contact, he said yes in a barely audible tone.

Murphy glanced at Blake; they could both see his brow perspiring. He was on the ropes, exposed and vulnerable and they'd only just started.

'The agency told us you asked for this temp specifically,' he said, showing him the A4 sheet with Brian Calcot's picture on it, who they suspected was Charlie Bullard. 'Is this the man who helped you?'

Sensing there was no way of avoiding the question he glanced at his solicitor for support. She nodded.

'No comment.'

'Mr Mitchell? I'll tell you our theory. Big robberies such as this need inside information, and an inside man. You were approached by Ibrahim Benzar to help get Brian Calcot – who we believe to be Charlie Bullard – behind the scenes, to rob the place. I can tell you now we have Charlie Bullard and a known associate, Mr Leonard Vale, in custody. Mr Bullard is a convicted bank robber. Believe me, it's only a matter of time before he names you in return for a lighter sentence. Get in first before it's too late.'

'How much did they pay you?'

'No comment.'

'Mr Mitchell? No comments are frowned upon by the judicial system. If you're found guilty of committing a crime, it will only increase any custodial sentence dished out to you. I suggest you cooperate.'

Blake bolstered his sergeant. 'Our experts have analysed CCTV covering the eighteenth and nineteenth of June and identified suspicious activity on the footage involving Mr Bullard leaving the museum. Furthermore the timelines have been tampered with; an attempt to edit out the robbery.'

Like a drowning man clinging to floating debris, he anxiously looked at his solicitor to throw him a lifeline. She made a brief note on her folio then requested the interview be stopped, to consult her client.

Twenty minutes later the solicitor returned with the caretaker dragging himself behind, looking mortified at the prospect of spending time in prison.

'Gentlemen, taking into consideration it's his first offence, my client would like to confess in return for a lighter sentence. We need assurances that this will be given serious consideration by the CPS.'

Biting down on a smile, Blake glanced at DS Murphy who was also controlling the temptation to voice a premature result.

Blake replied. 'Initially I'm saying yes, we'll see what we can do, but I need confirmation from my chief inspector. Bear with me a minute while I call him.' He left the room and speed dialled Colonel Mustard. 'Sir, I need your permission on a deal that's being offered by a key suspect's defence lawyer in the Staffordshire Hoard case?'

'Do we have enough evidence to convict the perpetrators?' Coleman cautioned.

'Very close, sir. The museum caretaker was the inside man; he's just about to spill the names of two other gang members, who, as you know, we also have in custody.'

'As long as you can assure me you've dotted all the I's. We need more than sixteen grand and the tablet containing images of the gold.'

'Sir, earlier Peter Jeffries over at Video and Audio Forensics confirmed the museum's CCTV has been tampered with. We've recovered two company credit cards from each of the suspect's properties. Both are linked to the same British public company, with a Cayman Island bank account. Very dodgy! The Cyber Crimes unit told me the minimum deposit for this bank is a million pounds. Considering one of the suspects was on three hundred quid a week, and the other two have been on the dole for years, barring a lottery win it's safe to say it's them.'

'Loud and clear, Tom, you have my permission. We can deal with any CPS bullshit as and when.'

The museum caretaker named both Charlie Bullard and Leonard Vale and was formally charged. Leonard Vale finally caved in once the Dominion credit card and museum's security system documents were produced. He recalled most of the story with surprising clarity. The planning and intricacy of the whole job astounded the detectives. The Hoard replicas were particularly impressive; sadly their value a mere fraction of the originals. DI Blake already knew this from his illicit US trade, which filled him with thoughts of self-loathing when contemplating what had happened. Aware that his desire to confess and share the burden might eventually get the better of him, he refocused on the matter in hand.

Whilst they were close to getting a result, there were still too many loose ends to be satisfied with the current arrests.

The fact that the Benzar brothers and their dodgy accountant were on the run meant there was still plenty to do. Waiting for Interpol to grind into action annoyed the shit out of Blake.

CHAPTER 119

'That's fantastic!' Chief Inspector Coleman said to a senior Met officer, after hearing the news that the accountant Malcolm Preston had been arrested. Joint cooperation between county police forces and the Metropolitan had worked out perfectly on this occasion.

They'd apprehended Preston whilst doing a dawn raid on the premises of a known forger, who'd been under surveillance for months. Preston was caught trying to buy a fake passport and flagged up on PNC as wanted by Staff's constabulary. A prison van containing the suspect had just passed Birmingham, and, traffic permitting, would be there in the next hour.

'The Met are ferrying Malcolm Preston back up to Stoke as we speak. This case is shaping up nicely.'

'That is good news. The accountant gives us four out of the six-man gang, although it's worth bearing in mind we've only charged three of them so far, sir.'

'Any news on the Benzar brothers?' Coleman asked.

'Not really. Interpol have issued a Code Red – persons wanted for arrest and extradition – but there have been no confirmed sightings yet. At a guess I'd say they were long gone.'

'Maybe the accountant will provide some intel on their location?' Coleman said.

Blake was sceptical. 'Possibly. We've been tracking their bank accounts, mobile phones and email, but as you can imagine, sir, these are well-informed career criminals, It's doubtful they'd be naive enough to use any of them.'

'Anything more on the credit cards found on the suspects in custody?' Coleman asked.

'Tech forensics are still looking into it. As I mentioned to you on the phone, sir, we know they relate to a bank in the Cayman Islands. But it's difficult to get information from these institutions – everything is tied up in red tape and client confidentiality clauses.'

'Even if the accountant proves a tough nut; at least we've charged Vale and Bullard.'

'The caretaker has named them both in his confession, but at this stage it's his word against theirs, and may not hold up to scrutiny from the defence.'

'Right. We need to go in hard on the accountant. I'll put in an application for the extension as a contingency. Let me know as soon as you begin his interview?'

'Will do, sir,' Blake said, as he watched Coleman march stiff as a crane out of his office.

Immediately after this exchange, the duty sergeant booked Malcolm Preston in, and received two evidence bags containing a wad of cash, a Dominion credit card, a wallet, an Android mobile and a three-pack of ribbed condoms. They ushered him to interview room three. Judging by his dishevelled appearance, he'd been slumming around cash-only B&Bs.

His navy suit was badly creased, and his thinning grey hair shone under the light; it needed shampooing. His horn-rimmed glasses magnified red under-eye rings. B.O. exuded from his direction and hung in the air like an abandoned trainer in a gym changing room. Subsequently the redhead solicitor representing him and Arthur Mitchell sat slightly further away from her client than was necessary.

Blake gave the suspect a telling look. 'Mr Preston, I hope our colleagues at the Met have been treating you well?'

The accountant shrugged his shoulders nonchalantly.

'So,' Blake continued, 'can you tell us why you absconded when we paid you a visit at your offices in Hanley on the sixteenth of June?'

He was suddenly tense. 'I didn't abscond; I went to visit friends in London,' he said, like a naughty child unable to accept responsibility for his actions.

'You told one of my female PCs that you'd be in for the rest of the afternoon over the phone. When we arrived your office door was locked. In a subsequent search we discovered you'd escaped through the loft space and exited the building via the rear fire escape and stolen Roy Cooper's old Fiat Panda. The vehicle was recovered from Tesco's car park in Hanley later that day. Can you confirm this?'

'No comment,' he said, realising he'd been duped and his lie was exposed.

Blake showed Preston a report from the Met. 'This states you were picked up by the Met, whilst trying to obtain a false passport from a well-known forger. Unlucky for you he'd been under observation for months, and you were caught in the crossfire.'

'No comment.'

'No luggage was found in your possession. Do you normally visit friends without a change of clothes?'

'I left my case at the B&B.'

'And where would that be?'

Preston hesitated. 'Some dive near Euston station, can't remember the name.'

'For the benefit of the tape, I'm showing Mr Preston two evidence bags. One contains twenty thousand pounds in used twenties and fifty pound notes and a Dominion credit card. Mr Preston, we have two other suspects in custody who've also been found in possession of Dominion credit cards in the name of Colonial Ltd. Our tech team have traced these cards to an offshore company account in the Cayman Islands. This investigation is ongoing but so far the bank has identified you as the company secretary, and told us that Leonard Vale, Charlie Bullard and Ibrahim Benzar form the board of directors. What do you have to say about that?'

'Colonial Ltd is a legitimate investment company with a portfolio of businesses,' he protested.

'I can imagine it is, and those businesses belong to Mr Ibrahim Benzar who is wanted for organising the theft of Staffordshire Hoard from the Potteries Museum. You're his accountant, money-launderer extraordinaire. Do you know Mr Benzar's whereabouts?'

'No.'

DS Murphy interrupted. 'Two of the board members are penniless unemployed convicted criminals. It's extremely unlikely that Leonard Vale and Charles Bullard have any money to invest; they are in fact bogus directors. Colonial Ltd is simply a conduit to launder illegal funds from the theft.'

'That's a serious accusation,' Preston responded with attitude. 'Where's your evidence?'

'We have a signed confession from the museum caretaker, Mr Arthur Mitchell – Charles Bullard, Leonard Vale and Ibrahim Benzar are all involved in the theft of the Staffordshire Hoard. We have CCTV evidence from the museum, and Colonial Ltd's balance sheet reads three million. Mr Benzar's businesses have a total value of four hundred and fifty thousand, including assets. Clearly that's bad maths. As the company secretary, can you explain these figures?'

'No comment.'

'Mr Preston, sooner or later you will have to talk to us. We will sit here all night if need be.'

'No comment.'

'Mr Preston, you realise that no comment responses aren't really acceptable any more; they'll only go against you in court,' Blake said, glancing at DS Murphy, signalling a baton pass and a change of tack in their good-cop/bad-cop routine.

'We know Ibrahim Benzar often uses the threat of violence to manipulate people into doing what he wants. You've been his accountant for over five years, during that period has he ever threatened you or your family?'

'No, I just do his company accounts.'

'I'll ask you again, where is he?'

'I don't know!'

'I'm afraid I don't believe you. Our team of experts have analysed your accountancy records, which show during the recession you lost virtually all your clients, leaving you bankrupt. Before that point your annual salary was around a hundred thousand a year. In desperation you took on Mr Benzar's accounts. Over time he manipulated you to launder money and assets in return for under-the-counter payments. It's classic carrot-and-stick behaviour.'

'That's not true. I have records that prove Mr Benzar's accounts were accurately submitted to the Inland Revenue without question.'

'Oh, come on. You know through lack of manpower HM Customs only investigate obvious tax avoidance cases. You may have submitted them, but don't take us for fools. In twenty-fourteen, his bar, gym and mini-mart's combined turnover was three hundred thousand. After tax and costs, he made a profit of a hundred and twenty-five thousand. We found forty thousand in used notes in his brother's safe; no doubt there's a lot more stashed elsewhere. Benzar paid you twelve thousand to compile those accounts, and since you only have one other client who pays you three thousand a year, you're blatantly living way beyond your means.'

'What's that supposed to mean?' Preston said defensively.

'Do we need to spell it out? You drive an S-Class Mercedes, worth sixty-seven grand; your house in Newcastle is mortgaged for three hundred and thirty thousand; your bank records show luxury holidays in Greece twice a year. Fifteen grand doesn't even cover the annual mortgage repayments. You have no legal sources of income to sustain this lifestyle. Benzar has you by the balls. Your whole world will collapse if you don't comply. Under his instruction you used your professional knowledge to set up a complex offshore company to launder several million pounds obtained from the sale of the Staffordshire Hoard. The bogus board are members of the gang who stole it. I'll ask you again… where is he?'

Horrified at hearing the undeniable truth, he shot his solicitor a worried glance. She nodded soberly in agreement with the detectives.

Strained by the interrogation, he murmured, 'What are my options?'

Blake delivered his shrewd summary like a judge. 'If you cooperate with us, the court will be more lenient when passing sentence. From what we can see you were under a lot of pressure; concerned about your safety and that of your family. However, this does not excuse your highly criminal actions. Your plight could have been avoided if you'd come to the police prior to the robbery taking place. Instead you put personal gain and wealth before your liberty. If you can help us identify the buyer, the whereabouts of Ibrahim Benzar, and most of the funds can be recovered, it will help your defence team to negotiate the best deal they can.'

His solicitor stopped the interview and spoke with her despairing client.

Blake assumed she wanted to consult with him regarding his plea.

CHAPTER 120

Later that day, DI Blake stood confidently next to his chief inspector at the front of the station's Major Incident room, and addressed all officers involved in the Staffordshire Hoard case.

'Great news, everyone. As you all know, yesterday DS Murphy and myself were summoned to Stafford Prison by Carl Bentley – recently arrested on suspicion of the murder of Barry Gibson, but due to lack of evidence charged with conspiracy to supply class A drugs. During that interview, Bentley provided key intelligence relating to the theft of the Staffordshire Hoard. He gave us the names of the gang members involved in the robbery. This morning we arrested and detained Charles Bullard and Leonard Vale,' he said, pointing to their pictures on the white board.

'We recovered evidence from both their properties, which includes: a tablet PC, loaded with high-resolution images of the Staffordshire Hoard, an A4 folder containing sheets of specifications of the museum's security system, with lots of highlighted paragraphs and notes, sixteen-thousand in used notes, and two suspicious-looking credit cards in the name of a company called Colonial Ltd. Our computer tech team has now traced these to a dodgy offshore account in the Cayman Islands, which initially made little sense. That was until DS Jamieson spoke to the bank who informed him the minimum deposit for this type of company account is a million quid. Further probing shows this account's balance sheet reads three million quid. Alarm bells rang because both Vale and Bullard are registered as company directors, which is highly suspicious considering they're both unemployed ex-cons.' He glanced at his folio notes. 'Through great detective work, PC Evans and DC Moore uncovered a major-lead. I'll let Casey explain further,' he said, giving PC Evans the nod.

With all eyes on her, her cheeks reddened. 'Whilst DC Moore and I were questioning the museum staff, it transpired that the caretaker, Mr Arthur Mitchell, handed his notice in two days after the Hoard was discovered missing. DI Blake tasked us to bring him in for questioning.' She puffed her chest proudly.

'Thank you, PC Evans,' Blake continued. 'DS Murphy and I have since interviewed Mr Mitchell, and he's confessed to being the inside man, naming both Charles Bullard and Leonard Vale in the hope of a more lenient sentence. Another person of interest is Malcolm Preston, Ibrahim Benzar's accountant. We believe Benzar organised the robbery. Unfortunately it appears he's fled the country. Interpol have issued a Code Red for his arrest and extradition. I'll let DS Murphy tell you the other good news.'

Murphy cleared his throat. 'Whilst raiding the premises of a London forger, the Metropolitan Police caught Malcolm Preston buying a fake passport. He's since been transferred to us. They found twenty thousand pounds in used notes and another Colonial Ltd credit card, linked to the same Cayman Islands bank account as Bullard and Vale. During his interview, DI Blake and I confronted him with this evidence and asked him to produce legal documentation to validate his sources of income. Backed into a corner, he eventually caved in.'

'Has Preston told you where Ibrahim Benzar is?' DS Jamieson interrupted.

'I'm afraid not, Roger.'

'What about his brother?' Jamieson added.

'It's possible they're hiding out together, but we have no intelligence on this. We know they have family connections in Turkey,' Blake said.

'Do you think we'll get them, sir?' DS Moore chipped in.

'Hard to say. Interpol issues notices and those get circulated between EU countries. We can also make use of the Schengen Agreement if need be. That means if the Benzar brothers are spotted in any of the participating countries, we'd be allowed to set up surveillance and extradition. That side of the investigation will continue.'

'Let's hope it's on Paradise Island, boss,' Roger Jamieson jested, 'I could do with a good holiday.'

'Couldn't we all, DS Jamieson,' said the Chief Inspector to a round of laughter.

'I'd just like thank you all of you for your hard work on this case,' Blake said. 'Everyone's put the hours in, which has led to four of the six-man gang being charged with robbery and the black market sale of the Staffordshire Hoard worth three-point-three million, which is still yet to be recovered. This side of the investigation is ongoing and the museum has offered a reward of forty thousand pounds for information leading to its return. No doubt this will generate a lot of media attention, considering how high-profile the case is. On the plus side, the gang's Cayman Island bank account funds of three million have been placed on hold with a view to confiscation using the Proceeds of Crime Act. If no one has anything else to add, that concludes today's briefing.'

As the CID team noisily left the incident room, DS Murphy approached Blake.

'Tom, I can't help but feel this is unfinished business. It really pisses me off those Turkish brothers are on their jollies with a million quid, especially after what they did to Isabel. Where are they?'

'Listen, mate, no one's more frigged off than me, but that won't find them, will it? It's only a matter of time before they slip up. That kind of money leaves traces. The forty-grand reward will level the playing field. Once their names are bandied about by the media, every two-bit con they've shafted will try to stake a claim. Remember Ibrahim Benzar still has three businesses in town. He's got to get in touch with somebody sooner or later about maintaining them, and, when he does, we'll be onto him. We've informed all his staff to notify us when he does.'

CHAPTER 121

'They've all been arrested. You'd better pack a bag, it's only a matter of time before...?'

He couldn't help but overhear the panic in Dominika Connor's voice as she sat in the office behind the bar of the White Horse pub, door ajar. The bar was empty and he assumed Connor's Polish wife would notice a customer, but she didn't, and continued her conversation on the landline.

'Darryl owes him fifteen grand, if this goes bad he gets half the pub. That bastard Benzar will ruin us,' she continued to gossip like a fool, until the entrance doors clanked, and two regulars entered the pub. Dominika looked nervously through the door and abruptly ended the conversation. She came out of the office to serve them, still not realising the man sat at the end of the bar had overheard her.

'Hi. What can I get you?' she said nervously after the regulars sat down with their pints.

'You okay, Dominika? Looking worried.' the man asked her.

'Just had some bad news, that's all,' she said, giving nothing away.

'Sorry to hear that?'

'I'd rather not talk about it?'

'Fair enough.'

'What you having?' She asked, her Polish accent still hard to shake off completely.

'Just a double whisky. Been doing a bit of shopping and fancied a quick one,' the man could tell Dominika was in no mood to converse. His timing was uncanny, and the vital information he'd just overheard meant he needed to act. He sank the whisky in one shot, said goodbye, and left.

CHAPTER 122

After cruising along the sun-drenched rocky Malaga coastline, the yacht with Ibrahim Benzar and Katrina Osborne on board arrived in Rabat Port, Morocco.

They disembarked and taxied to a luxury five-star hotel overlooking the Atlantic Ocean. The beautiful Sultan Oasis looked like a Moorish Castle nestled amongst the palms. The scent of its olive orchards and aromatic herb garden carried on the ocean breeze and wafted around the horizon pool. Guests could take their meals anywhere, all of which were prepared by a top Parisian chef using organic vegetables from the hotel's irrigated walled garden.

Whilst Kat was out browsing a craft market she'd spotted on a patch of scrubland behind the hotel, Ibrahim sat quietly celebrating his newly acquired wealth in a large wingback chair in the hotel's library bar. Puffing away on a hundred dollar King of Denmark cigar, he was blissfully unaware of the situation back in the UK. That was until his mobile rang.

'Where the god damn hell are you?' the Collector bawled in his ear. 'Been trying to get hold of ya for days!'

'Since we pulled the job off I've taken time out cruising to Morocco. Poor signal most of the time.'

'Morocco! Are you fuckin' crazy? It's all over CNN and your BBC World News. Are you blind, man?'

'What is?'

'The police have captured your crew and seized three million. Seems one of your so-called trusted partners is a god damn pigeon. They're onto you; your names are plastered all over the media. There's a forty-K reward for info leading to the recovery of my beautiful Hoard,' the Collector said furiously.

A sudden wave of nausea came over Ibrahim. 'Fuck!'

'Exactly! A hell of a shitstorm is heading your way.'

'Are you alone?'

'No, with a woman.'

'Does she know?'

'Of course not. What do you suggest?' Ibrahim asked.

'I hope you retained plenty of dead presidents, cause you sure going to need 'em. You can't go back to the UK; they'll hunt you down like a deer in the crosshairs. Do any of your crew know about me?'

'Only that I referred to you as the Collector.'

'You sure?'

'Yeah.'

'I suggest you check out the news online and keep a low profile. Better tell the woman now rather than later. I'm distancing myself from this, before the feds smother me like a pox. When I hear more, I'll be in touch via this channel.'

'This isn't happening. I've got three businesses in the UK. Who will take charge? Yusuf's exiled in India. What a fucking nightmare!'

'You need a plan, and quick. I gotta go.'

The line went dead. Numb with shock, he stubbed the cigar and headed back to the room to contemplate his next move.

Fifteen minutes later, Kat slipped her key in the studded oak door of their harem suite. Benzar sat on a lounger on the panoramic balcony overlooking the ocean, head in hands. The soaring heat bounced off the glass balustrade and dissipated in the air, making the distant horizon as hazy as his thoughts.

'What's wrong, babe?'

He was seething. Rising to his feet, he slammed his fist on the table. 'Fuck! I have something to tell you.'

'What's happened?'

'Promise you'll listen before kicking off?'

'I'll try to.'

'I had it all planned. This shouldn't be happening. It took months. When I find out who the grass is, he's a fucking dead man. I'll cut his throat and feed him to the rats!'

'Just tell me what you're ranting on about?'

'Where do you think all this comes from?'

'I don't understand?'

'The yacht!' he bawled. 'The villa in Ibiza, the champagne… everything!'

'Don't shout at me, I've had enough of that shit from Carl. I don't know… money from your bar?'

'That place takes about seven grand a week,' he sneered, 'and the bastard tax man robs me. We pulled off a big job worth a few million quid.'

She shot him a worried look. 'What job? You're not making any sense, Ibrahim. Stop it, you're scaring me now!'

'We robbed the Staffordshire Hoard from the museum in Hanley and sold it to order for five million.'

'Are you winding me up?'

'No. If I go back, they'll arrest me straight away.'

'You bastard! What am I supposed to do now? You've dropped me right in the shit? The police will think I'm involved,' she said, tears rolling down her cheeks, leaving visible lines in her blusher.

'You're in the clear.'

'How do you work that out?'

'Because it's the truth.'

'Yes, but you're on the frigging run, a wanted man, and I'm with you. How's that going to look? Like I was in on it.'

'You can leave any time. The police don't know you're here.'

'What if they check passenger records. They'll see I went to Ibiza.'

'Why would they do that? All they know is we shagged at the hotel back in Hanley; we're not connected apart from that. You flew from Manchester on your own; I flew to Turkey, then on to Ibiza. I booked the villa and yacht under a false name. They have nothing.'

'I need a drink.' She slammed the balcony door and stormed back into the suite towards the mini bar. She took out a two-fifty mil bottle of Chardonnay, and downed it in one gulp. In a rage she slung the empty against the bathroom wall. Glass shattered across the stone floor tiles.

Attempting to keep the uproar private. Benzar followed her in and closed the door behind him. 'Katrina! You're mad at me, I get it, but we need to talk about this. You think I'm not pissed off? If I go back, they'll lock me up, understand that?'

'Of course I bloody do.'

'Calm down, you're stressing me. I have nearly half a million with me,' he said, lowering his voice.

'Where?'

'Some on the boat, some in the hotel safe and in my case.'

'This gets worse. What if we're arrested with all that money?'

'It's Africa. European police have no jurisdiction here. Besides, no one knows where I am.'

'Where does that leave me?'

'I don't know. Maybe we could make a life in Morocco? Five hundred thousand would last forever out here. We could buy a place and travel around. One thing is for sure, I'm not doing any more prison, no fucking way.'

'You're insane!'

Livid, she opened another bottle from the fridge and strode across the room out onto the balcony, trying to comprehend the bombshell he'd just dropped. Gazing out across the Atlantic, it dawned on her how elation could easily turn into despair. She'd travelled to paradise and through no fault of her own ended up in a hellish state of limbo. God, her life was a disaster. No job, an ex-boyfriend in prison for dealing, and the looming prospect of being homeless. She had no direction or sense of purpose any more.

Ibrahim's voice dragged her back into the cold light of day. 'I know this seems like a nightmare, but I have to think hard about my next move. I need your support. Arguing only makes things worse. This could be a new start for both of us,' he said, not quite believing it himself.

Kat stood motionless, watching a small boat cross the vast ocean. It dipped and rocked struggling against the Atlantic waves, but somehow managing to plough a steady course toward Rabat Port. If something so small could master the might of the sea, maybe there was hope for them after all? Maybe being exiled in Morocco could work. This was fate. She had strong feelings for Ibrahim. They wouldn't have to worry about money, and life could be simpler if they could make it work. But the big question was, could they really spend the rest of their lives looking over their shoulders.

CHAPTER 123

It was another searing hot day in Mumbai. Traffic pollution hung in the air like a heavy fog over the sprawling Bollywood city, on India's west coast. Huge cranes pitched next to skyscrapers in varying stages of construction, hugged the coastline and dominated the skyline. The Bandra-Worli cable-stayed bridge floated across the ocean connecting central Mumbai with its western suburbs. Yusuf Benzar had waded through the concrete jungle of stray dogs, peasants and construction workers and successfully completed what he'd been tasked. The gold replicas entered the UK and fulfilled their temporary purpose and his brother paid him four hundred thousand into an Indian bank; the other half million was due later in the week.

He now had two options; stay in India and make a go of it, or return to Europe to face a catalogue of criminal charges, and years inside.

Not much of a choice… rather a forced decision, with the scales weighing heavily in favour of staying in India.

During the time he'd been there, he'd had first-hand experience of extreme poverty. The street children in particular caught him by surprise. Back home he selfishly considered his own needs, and excessive use of cocaine distorted his perception of the world. Seeing children dying of starvation on the TV paled compared to being there. On the sixth day, a painfully skinny girl, around eight years old was killed. The taxi that hit her outside Yusuf's apartment hotel didn't even stop. When it happened, he was about to cross the road. Her tiny body slipped away in his arms. Mournfully he remembered her pretty smile as she'd sat begging outside the reception since his arrival. Each day he'd given her a few rupees; in return she'd polished the city's dust from his loafers and blessed him with a small clutch of wild flowers. Their seemingly insignificant interaction now had a profound effect on him. Drug and alcohol free, he felt empathy and deep regret about the way his life had turned out. He held her until the ambulance siren was close by, before retreating into the shadows of the alley opposite, in fear of being questioned by the authorities.

That night he dragged himself towards the river, sat under the stars and openly wept. A brother and sister no older than twelve, sleeping on the quayside, overheard and comforted him. Like an epiphany, this simple act of kindness changed the direction of his future.

The following morning he found an Internet café and spent hours scouring online for charities that helped Mumbai's poor and desolate children. In the afternoon, he paced the streets purposefully holding a sheet of notepaper with their addresses and mobiles on it. Fifty grand could bring hope to at least some of the impoverished.

CHAPTER 124

Seventeen hours a day in his cell hammered home the magnitude of his desperation. The thought of spending another twenty years for murder, on top of the four he'd already been given for dealing class A, cut through Carl Bentley's soul like a white-hot blade. He'd been such an idiot to grass on Benzar. Far too many scumbags, with connections inside, and he'd played it like a real novice. Some bastard must have grassed on him, done a deal with Benzar. How else had they have found out? No one else knew.

He dearly missed the simple things he'd taken for granted: being able to hop across the pub for a beer, watch Stoke on TV, ride across the roaches on his scooter gazing at the barren Moors. But most of all he missed Kat, inhaling her intoxicating scent, her beautiful blue eyes and forgiving smile. The thought of never holding her close again destroyed him. He'd treated her badly over the last couple years and deeply regretted it. Depressingly, his incarceration meant there'd be no chance of reconciliation. It wasn't as if he could write to her, plead for forgiveness. For starters he didn't know where she was, or, even more painfully, who she was with.

His short time in prison had been horrendous. He'd been kicked, punched and received a ton of verbal from a small group of inmates intent on bullying newcomers. Most of his stuff had been stolen, including his toothbrush and toiletries.

Lying in darkness, staring at the faint glow of the moon through the tiny barred windows, every sound amplified in his head: prisoners arguing, taking drugs, having sex… it made him shudder.

The nights were an eternal hell… an emotional roller coaster of anxiety and fear of the unknown. Faces came out of the blackness, twisting his perception of reality with hallucinogenic visions. A deep depression had veiled him since his arrest, and he couldn't see any way out. His serotonin levels were depleted, afflicting him with a myriad of disturbing withdrawal symptoms from years of dope and ecstasy consumption.

Before prison he feared no man, and would take most on in a scrap, but witnessing the slashing of another prisoner's throat in the showers two days earlier tormented him. He'd only closed his eyes to wash out shampoo, no more than thirty seconds. When he opened them the victim clung desperately to a gaping ear-to-ear slash as blood sprayed with force from both his jugular veins, all over Bentley. There was nothing he could do but stare in horror as the man shook violently and crashed to the floor in a deluge of his own blood. It had dominated his nightmares ever since.

Within seconds he was cuffed and pinned naked to the tiles by four prison guards staring accusingly at his flannel draped over the camera lens, and his yellow toothbrush blade discarded in the corner by the murderer.

He knew it was only a matter of time before retribution for grassing up Ibrahim Benzar was doled out. If he couldn't prove his innocence of this horrendous killing, he'd rot in this hell-hole until he was a decrepit pensioner, if he wasn't killed first – a thought that chilled him to the bone. Staring into the darkness of his cell, hope ebbed away. Without rational consideration, he ripped the blanket of his mattress and rolled it tightly into a rope.

CHAPTER 125

Officers were called out to a gang-related fight on the Townmore Estate; apparently a turf war dispute over drugs. Unfortunately because of an accident on Collmore, the road leading into the estate, most of the rival gang members fled the scene, but officers managed to arrest one of the offenders, and he was waiting in interview room three.

Jayland Russell had only been released from prison a few days ago after serving a four-year stretch for a series of aggravated burglaries and heroin dealing.

Unfortunately, it was a well-known fact that some jobless prisoners ended up dealing again. A combination of operation Nemesis and Yusuf Benzar's supply chain disruption had meant there was a drought in Stoke-on-the Trent area.

Jayland Russell's neck was encircled with gang tattoos and his shaved head resembled that of a mummified skull, bearing several nasty scars from a life of crime and violence. His ashen skin was taut like a drum around sunken eye sockets and his pupils were tiny dots in the centre of luminous blue retinas, like a Husky's eyes. But under all that pain and ego he still desired freedom, which meant he would consider grassing on rival gang members in return for a more lenient sentence. His parole officer informed them he was on a recovery program. But judging by his demeanour and scratching, he was still using. Could they really believe anything he said?

DS Murphy studied him for a few seconds. 'What's this about, Jayland? Fighting in the streets? Your knife has been sent off to forensics.'

'This kind of behaviour is in breach of your parole. We have a witness who saw you slashing out at two rival gang members. They saw everything. You could have killed someone.'

'Doze bastards are on my turf man.'

'So, you're dealing again?'

'Na man, I'm clean. They'ze just disrespecting me, cause I's on parole. Taking the piss ya know, trying to goad me into going back inside. Fucking warned Dem off man. They'ze setting me up.'

Murphy almost felt sorry for him. What chance did he really have? A heroin addict fresh out of jail with no job prospects; he was doomed.

'So what are we going to do with you Mr Russell?'

He shrugged his shoulders and sighed deeply.

'Because it's not looking good; you've been caught using an illegal weapon in public, whilst on parole.'

Russell looked concerned. 'The shank ain't mine?'

'That's rather irrelevant now. It doesn't matter whose blade it is; you were the one using it to threaten others.'

'Yeah, but I found it in some bushes on da canal, man; it'd been dumped.'

This peaked Blake interest, 'When was this?'

'Can't be exact man my memory is shit, boss.'

Not surprising Blake thought. Smack had probably destroyed what brains he'd got left.

'Try to think; it could be important, especially if the weapon has been used in a crime.'

Russell leaned his head back, and closed his eyes.

Blake could almost hear the cogs slowly clunking into self-preservation mode.

'Yeah, I remember now. I was in the park with a few bros having a smoke when we heard loadza sirens going off up-town. It was a Friday night.'

'Which Friday? Think, Jayland?'

He sucked his teeth. 'Not sure, man.'

'Was it more than a week ago?'

'Er… yeah. That's it man. I heard one of da bros talking about a murder in a pub the next day. That's what all da fuss must've been about.'

Blake shot DS Murphy a look of amazement. 'What time did you find this knife?'

'I was off home down canal, when I tripped over summet. Fell in the bushes. When I came to it was going light, that's when I saw da shank. Got loads of nettle stings getting it man, all up me arm.'

'And your mates will confirm all of this? We'll need names so we can speak to them?'

'What's the big deal with the shank, boss?' Russell said.

Surprised and excited Blake terminated the interview for a comfort break.

'This could be the breakthrough we need in the Gibson murder case. Can we get the forensics fast tracked on the blade?' Blake asked optimistically, standing a few feet along the corridor from interview room three.

'Would have thought so. Do you want me to get onto them, boss?' Murphy said.

'Straight away. I need to have a word with the Chief Inspector about this.'

'You really think it could be the murder weapon?'

'If Jayland Russell's timing is right I think it's a possibility. Besides, we've got nothing else apart from four suspects and circumstantial at the minute, so it's definitely worth pursuing.

'Have you seen pictures of the knife yet, boss?'

'Not yet, he was only brought in hour ago. I'm off to the evidence store to take a look, before it goes off to forensics.'

CHAPTER 126

He sat in his sanctuary reading the front pages of the *Evening Sentinel.*

"Staffordshire Hoard Heist an inside job"

Robbers broke into the Potteries Museum and Art Gallery in Stoke-on-Trent, undetected and covertly switched the Staffordshire Hoard for replicas, and then stole the 3000-piece original collection worth 3.3 million. In a brief statement, Hanley CID, located within a hundred yards of the museum said this was an inside job that involved an ingenious plan designed to delay the discovery of the theft. Currently they have several people believed to be involved with the theft in custody helping with their enquiries. Two other key suspects, brothers Ibrahim and Yusuf Benzar, are believed to be the organisers of the robbery. Their whereabouts are unknown, and police will release a further statement soon. The museum has offered a reward of £40,000 for information leading to the arrest of the Benzar brothers. Anyone with information related to the robbery can call: 0800 555 122

He couldn't help feeling smug after pulling the hundred-grand double-cross on Benzar. The arrogant bastard thought because he put money into his business, he could take the piss; skimming profits each year. The word *reward* jumped off the page: possibly a way of killing two birds with one stone. Get rid of that parasite, and land an easy forty grand. If only he knew Benzar's whereabouts. Where would a career criminal like him go? Back home to Turkey? Too obvious, even those dumb plods would know that. For now this would have to go on the back burner, he thought.

CHAPTER 127

Blake had only just finished his initial interview with Jayland Russell when DC Longsdon bowled into his office looking rather pleased with himself.

'Sir, we've received a tip off from a shopkeeper. His wife saw Grant Bolton's mugshot on the online *Sentinel.* Apparently he'd bought food supplies, cans of larger, and almost cleared their stock of rolling tobacco from their remote shop on Blackshaw Moor yesterday,' he said.

'Really, that's great news.' The Gibson murder case had been problematic from the beginning, and even now Blake was still sceptical, but this new intel seemed like progress. If they could get Grant Bolton into custody, they'd have a fighting chance of unravelling the events leading up to the murder.

Blake picked the phone up and called NPAS, to arrange another helicopter search of the moorlands and surrounding area. So, he was right the first time, he thought.

'*Got something, over! Station base unit one.*' the helicopter camera-man proclaimed through the monitor's speakers.

Blake had just returned from the coffee machine. He placed his cup on the desk, and watched nervously as the helicopter camera zoomed in on what looked like a group of travellers' caravans, parked in a clearing beside a large pine wood forest just off the road.

'*Ground unit one; we'll continue to circle, can you go in to investigate?*'

'*Roger over; will do.*'

Blake watched in anticipation, as a dog unit van and two police cars shot down the narrow country lane, and veered right into what looked like a dirt access road, leading into the clearing.

All six officers exited their vehicles at the same time and approached the caravans. Just as they were about to confront the occupants, a figure shot out of the closest van to the trees and disappeared.

'*Switching to thermal image camera. Suspect running through densely forested area to our left. Over. Directing ground teams to move in and apprehend.*'

Blake followed the tiny white figure as it fled through the trees. Could this be Grant Bolton? He sincerely hoped so, for his sake.

'*Team closing in on suspect, over.*' the cameraman updated him.

He became tense as the six police officers led by the dog unit moved closer to the suspect. Then it was all over.

'*Suspect apprehended, circling the area one more time. Awaiting further instructions from SIO and ground team, over.*'

Blake rose from his seat and punched the air.

CHAPTER 128

Just over an hour and a half later DS Murphy and Blake sat in interview room three staring across the table at Grant Bolton, who judging by his appearance had been roughing it for the last few days. His jeans and boots were mud stained from the pursuit through the forest, and he'd grown a short beard.

'Why did you run when we first tried to question you in Tunstall High Street? Clearly you're hiding something?' Blake got straight to the point.

Bolton shook his head. 'You wouldn't understand.'

'Try me?'

Bolton glanced at his lawyer who gave him the nod.

'I was scared.'

'Of what exactly?'

'That you'd fit me up for the Gibson murder.'

'You can't be serious. We don't fit people up.' Blake made air commas.

'Yeah right.'

'We have witnesses who saw you arguing with Barry Gibson not long before he was murdered, in the White Horse gents.'

'That doesn't mean I killed him.' Bolton said in defence.

'Well, the fact you ran is highly suspicious. So, let's hear what you have to say. It's your chance to set the record straight.' Blake said.

He looked to the solicitor again. 'You know I've got a record, for ABH. I just thought you'd look at that and try to pin this on me. So, I legged it. Thing is I can't hack any more prison time, it would kill me. Been suffering with post-traumatic ever since last time. My head's a bit mashed.' Bolton said.

'I see. And have you had this confirmed by a doctor.'

'Yeah, it's on my medical records. Been on Fluoxetine ever since.'

'Fair enough, but *if* you didn't kill Barry Gibson, surely it makes sense to be eliminated from the enquiry?'

'I don't trust the police.'

Blake changed tack. 'Do you know the victim?'

'No.' Bolton said nervously.

'I'm afraid you're bullshitting us. We have evidence that shows you do.'

'What evidence?'

'DS Murphy, show Mr Bolton the photographs.' Blake said.

'We know from this, and several others like it, you worked on the kilns of the William Adams pottery firm alongside Barry Gibson between 1988 and 1993.'

The colour drained from Bolton's face.

'Why did you lie about knowing him?' Blake asked.

Given the evidence Bolton knew it would be hard to dodge. 'I was trying to score from him. Not the sort of thing you advertise, is it?' Bolton lied. He didn't want them to find out about his brother's beating at the hands of Gibson. He wouldn't have bought pills from that tosser, he hated him. Initially when they worked together on the kilns, being three years younger than Gibson, he'd looked up to him, but as time passed he began to dislike the skinhead's antagonistic mannerisms.

'So, you're saying Barry Gibson was a dealer?'

'Yeah.'

'Speaking of dealers, do you know someone called Stomper?'

'No.' Bolton said without hesitation.

'You sure about that?'

'Yeah.'

'What exactly where you buying from Barry Gibson?'

'Kilnee's,' Bolton kept up the pretence.

'And those are?' Blake knew, but wanted Bolton to confirm it.

'E's.'

'We'll be checking your mobile records to see when you called him?'

'It's pay-as- you- go.'

Blake tried not to show his disappointment. 'How many did you buy?'

'None, that's why he wound me up. Idiot arranged to meet us. Said he had loads of pills, then when we turned up he'd already sold them all.'

'And your mates will confirm this, will they?'

'Yeah defo.' he said, knowing they'd back him up, and with Gibson dead there was no proof to say otherwise. Besides he was a dealer.

'So, what about the beer spilling incident witnesses saw?'

'Oh, that happened after I'd had words with him earlier. Some dick head shoved into my back, and I spilt a bit of Stella down his top. That's when he started mouthing off and the landlord interrupted. It was no big deal, just a bit of banter really.'

'I'm afraid I have to disagree. One of the older regulars is on record saying he had to stand between you, to stop things from escalating into a full-blown fight.'

'That doesn't mean I killed him though?'

'Yes, but the fact you'd already had an argument with him, earlier in the evening, shows the animosity and intent on your part.'

'He was asking for it!' Bolton raised his voice.

'So, you butted him in the gents: but you didn't expect him to slip over and end up unconscious? That's when you realised if he came around he could dob you in to us, so you killed him.'

'I'm telling you now, apart from the verbal, I never laid a finger on him,' Bolton protested.

Seeing Bolton back himself into a corner the solicitor interrupted. 'Can I have a minute with my client please?'

'You've got five minutes, to go over the case notes again.' Blake said standing, as he and DS Murphy made their way to the door.

'My client stands by his earlier statement that he *did not* murder Barry Gibson. The evidence you have is purely circumstantial. So, unless you can produce forensics linking him to the actual murder, I suggest you release him?' Bolton's solicitor said.

Blake glared at him. 'Well, I'm afraid we beg to differ on that point. Not only was Mr Bolton seen arguing with the victim in the White Horse; his fingerprints were found at the crime scene, and he arranged to meet him to buy drugs on the day he was murdered. Add to that, he resisted arrest, then absconded, and denied knowing the victim, clearly shows he's withholding information from us. Until we find out why, he'll remain in custody.'

'As you now know, Mr Bolton suffers with PTSD, therefore it would be detrimental to his health to keep him locked up for longer than necessary,' the solicitor glanced at Bolton who was sweating profusely and becoming agitated, as if he was re-experiencing a traumatic event.

'Given his condition has only just been disclosed, until we've looked at his medical records, he'll remain in custody.'

'Very well Inspector, I can see you won't be persuaded, but it's on your head. Look at him, it's obvious he's not reacting well to the situation?'

The thought of spending up to forty eight hours in custody increased Bolton's anxiety even further, and he flipped out. Rising to his feet his anger quickly escalated. He slammed both fists on the table, knocking half-full plastic cups of tea all over it and onto DS Murphy's trousers. Blake hit the panic button on the wall. Within seconds, three uniformed officers barged into the room and assisted the detectives in restraining the giant, as his solicitor cowered in the corner, clutching his briefcase like a frightened puppy.

'Get him back to his cell, and call the duty doctor; looks like he needs something to calm his nerves.' Blake shouted to DS Murphy, as they bundled Bolton back down the corridor towards the cell blocks.

CHAPTER 129

'Put it this way, I know whose bringing gear into Stoke, man; big amounts, it's well on the money; straight from the horses.' Jayland Russell informed Blake.

'By that I take it you mean you know the source?'

'Bang on.' he said mimicking a pistol with two fingers.'

'I see. You've just done four years for aggravated burglary and dealing. I can't promise anything, but we can speak to the CPS. If your info's reliable, you might get less than twelve months, or even a suspended sentence, just depends on how they see it. How does that sound?' Blake said glancing at his notes?

'Yeah mega man, I'll buy that all day long. It'll get those skanks off my back for a while.'

'Okay here's how it works. You read these terms and conditions, accept them, and sign the exchange of information confidentiality form witnessed by us and countersigned in the presence of the Chief Inspector. Then if your info is on the money like you say, the deals done.' Blake said, handing over the contract.

Russell looked at them for confirmation. 'Twelve months, or a suspended you reckon, defo man?'

Blake confirmed. 'Thereabouts, yes.'

After moments contemplation he opened up. 'Prisoners swap shit. Right? One night after lights out I was spilling to this guy about smashing this bloke with his own bat. Prick chased me out of his drum. Anyways this guy spills about how some nasty Turkish supplier from Stoke cut him outa the game because he refused to supply this mad skinhead with any more Kilnee's; crazy bastard been selling them to teenagers, and a sixteen year old girl died. Guy said the Turk set him up. Got someone to break in his drum, and plant loads of extra gear all over the place, even in his scooter. He got this bird he was shagging to grass on him to the old bill. She put him in da frame for a murder in town, but turns out you lot had shit all on him. That's why he was doin the stretch; possession with intent.'

Blake felt a cold shiver, as all the ducks lined up inside his head. Could Russell's cell mate have supplied Barry Gibson with the ecstasy that killed the girl, maybe he murdered Gibson after all? 'Just to be clear, you mean ecstasy, embossed with a bottle kiln logo?'

'Dats da one.'

'And this guy was dealing for a Turkish supplier? A player, you say?' Blake asked him.

'Yeah.'

'What's this guy's name?'

Russell sucked his teeth again. 'Ah no man, that would make me a grass.'

'Hate to state the obvious but, isn't that what you're doing now. Grassing? Besides, we can easily check prison records.'

Russell frowned. 'Suppose but, I ain't given no names up.'

'I'm afraid to say if you want to cut a deal with the CPS, we need names, so we can investigate properly. What's this prisoner's name?' He wanted to hear Russell say it.

'Said his name was Stomper, but his real name Carl Bentley.'

Blake looked surprised. So, Carl Bentley was Stomper. It seriously annoyed him why they hadn't made the connection before. In hindsight it seemed, Tracy Gibson's confession about Barry's drug use linked him to Carl Bentley: who probably supplied Barry with ecstasy on the night he was murdered. With both men being dead, they'd never know for sure, he thought. He couldn't help feeling sorry for that poor bastard Bentley. Had they known about the drugs plant sooner he would have got a lesser sentence, but there was no way they could have predicted he'd be accused of murdering a fellow inmate.

'Who's the Turkish supplier?' Blake asked, already knowing the answer.

'A geezer called Benzar, that's all I know I swear boss.'

'And you'd be prepared to testify this in Court?'

'You never said nutting about no Court!'

'I'm afraid so, its clause ten on the forms you've just signed. Unfortunately, as things stand it's your word against the perpetrators.'

'Fuck, that's bad man. I'd be a grass; those maniacs will come for me.'

'It's the only way. We can get you moved and in a protection program, or if you do get a custodial, vulnerable prisoners' wing, segregated from other inmates. What do you think, do we have a deal?'

'I'm not sure now. Fucking Courts!' He shuddered.

'We'd push for a suspended sentence,' Murphy enticed.

'Yeah but I'd be marked.'

'As I said, we can offer you protection.'

Seeing despondency and hesitation in his eyes, Blake proffered him an ultimatum.

'We'll go for a coffee, give you a chance to mull it over, but we need to know in the next fifteen minutes or the deals off?'

'Fuck! OK Mr Five-O, I'm hearing ya.' he mocked.

CHAPTER 130

'John, the knife Jayland Russell found turns out to be a drop point blade; just as the pathologist described. The forensics picked up microscopic traces of blood under the rubber handle; Barry Gibson's. The prints and DNA, excluding Russell's belong to Dave Millburn, the boss of M8 security. We're going to arrest him now.' Blake said confidently down the phone.

Two teams left the station, sirens blaring as they pulled onto the ring road. One headed towards M8's office, the other bound for his home address.

Blake had a suspicion that Millburn wouldn't be in his office and he was right. His gold Lexus was parked in the drive, as the two police cars screeched to a halt outside his home.

Blake stood leaning against the car in his stab vest. 'You cover the rear entrance. If that gate's locked, kick it through?' he said addressing PC Haynes, pointing to a five feet high wood panelled gate leading into what looked like the backyard. 'Go! POLICE, POLICE OPEN UP!' He banged on the door, but there was no reply. He tried the handle, it was locked. He nodded to Davis.

He launched the big red key just above the chrome handle. The locking edge of the dark wood effect, PVC door cracked, leaving the handle swinging from its thin bolts. Davis shoulder-barged his way in, closely followed by Blake and DS Murphy, with DC Longsdon following up the rear.

'Spread out, living room and kitchen?' Blake signalled, just about to tackle the stairs.

He and DS Murphy charged towards the landing above.

'Bathroom clear!' Murphy shouted from the end of the landing.

'Bedrooms clear!' Blake shouted, stuffing what looked like a car hire dispatch form into his trouser pocket, whilst looking out the window into the back garden, which led out onto rough fields loosely scattered with mongrel horses, in all shades of brown and white.

'All clear!' came the rallying cry from downstairs.

'Bollocks!' they'd missed him. Blake groaned, banging his fist into the windowsill in frustration. Then from the corner of his eye, he saw something move in the leylandii trees clustered together to form a high hedge, separating Millburn's garden from the fields, 'The back garden now, he's hiding in the sodding trees. DC Longsdon, you and Haynes stay here and search the place for incriminating evidence.'

The other four officers stormed out of the unlocked kitchen door and ran towards the trees.

'Nothing here sir,' PC Davis said separating the dense branches with his hands.

'Through there! The bastard is legging it across the fields,' Blake bawled, watching the figure of Dave Millburn disappear a couple of hundred yards into the distance, through a hole where the greenery had died back. He jumped over the small fence separating Millburn's garden from next door, opened the gate leading onto the field, and gave pursuit, closely followed by his team. The horses scattered, running wildly towards their makeshift stables at the bottom end, as Millburn showed no signs of stopping.

He looked to be heading towards a large cast-iron waste pipe crossing the River Trent.

'Anyone know what's the other side of the river?' Blake shouted. Murphy had already capitulated and stood bent over, hands on his knees gasping for air, in the middle of the field.

'More fields by the looks of it,' PC Davis said, drawing level with Blake.

They watched Millburn clamber up the concrete cube the pipe exited from, and navigate his way around the spiked fan shaped iron bars, designed to stop kids using the pipe for a bridge. Wobbling, he ran across like a tightropist. Blake tossed his tie into the grass and followed.

'Careful sir, it could be slippy,' Davis shouted as he reached the middle, stopped and just about managed to stay on.

By this time Millburn had disappeared over a small grassy embankment, but Blake wasn't defeated yet. Finding renewed energy, he continued to chase him across what looked like the remains of an industrial site. Millburn darted through a door-less entrance, into an old outbuilding. Visions of the Grant Bolton pursuit flashed through his mind. He knelt down and picked up a rusty iron bar lying on the concrete before entering. At the doorway he stopped and cautiously scanned left and right into what looked like an old storage facility. Half the roof tiles were missing and trees grew out of the guttering. Millburn stood motionless in the far corner, hiding in the shadows.

Blake was rooted to the spot, dizzy from the chase. 'The games up Dave, you've got nowhere to run, and two of my officers will be here any second. It's over,' he said pacing towards him, lowering the bar to his side, attempting to appear less threatening.

As Blake got closer Millburn reached inside his trouser pocket and withdrew a small knife from its scabbard. Back arched, legs spread, he held the blade out to his side ready to attack.

'Fuck off pig! Let me pass, or you'll get it!' Millburn threatened, moving within five feet of Blake.

Blake stared him down, adrenaline surging through his veins. Images of the Miami Beach fight flashed through his mind. 'Do you really want another death on your conscience?' he said, raising the bar to show he'd fight back.

'What you talking about?'

'We know you battered, then murdered Barry Gibson, with a knife.'

Millburn's hand shook. 'What knife? This is bullshit.'

Blake edged back, 'The one sitting in a bag, in our evidence store, back at the station. Traces of Gibson's blood are on it, and your DNA is all over the handle.'

Millburn took a swipe. Blake jumped further back, his grip tightened on the bar.

Beads of sweat ran down his face. 'Put the knife down, now!' he demanded, wondering what was delaying his backup team.

Millburn's eyes fixed on the bar. He stiffened, and then charged. Blake swung the bar, just missing his face by a few inches.

Millburn stepped back, changed the knife to his other hand, attempting to trick Blake. He lunged at him again. Blake swung the steel bar and slammed it hard across his wrist. He screamed out in pain as his radius bone snapped and forced its way through his skin. Blood spurted from the gaping wound, his hand hung limp, inches away from the knife. Still wielding the bar like a knight's sword, Blake whacked him in the ribs. Millburn crashed to the ground in a heap, and rolled around crying out in agony holding onto his mangled wrist.

CHAPTER 131

Back at the station Blake opened the tap fully, and doused his face with cold water. Shaking his head he stared into the mirror above the sink. God, he looked like shit: his Oxford Blue shirt missing the top three buttons, moons of sweat under each arm, and his hand throbbed from wielding the heavy iron bar. He knew there'd be repercussions for breaking Millburn's wrist. Modern policing was far too politically correct these days. He'd seen it on many occasions; scumbags trying to sue the police, claiming unnecessary heavy handedness whilst being arrested. On this occasion his actions were justified; after all, the murdering bastard was trying stick him with a knife. Surely any judge would override a defence barrister on this point?

Dave Millburn had been taken to A&E to get his wrist set and plastered. But, make no mistake, soon as his cocktail of painkillers kicked in, they be up there to fetch him. He had the full backing of his chief inspector. The murdering bastard had led them a merry dance for nearly three weeks.

His phone rang. It was DC Longsdon, 'Sir, we're still at Dave Millburn's. His loft has been converted into some kind of gun workshop.'

'Gun workshop?' Blake said, confused.

'I'm no expert but, there's a long bench fitted with what looks like a bullet press. There's a few plastic tubs filled with bullet shells fixed to the wall, and a heavy duty steel cabinet about four feet high. I'd put money on there being firearms inside it. Also, not sure if this is relevant but there's a black balaclava in a desk drawer. It was on top of a Navy Seal survival guide book. Maybe he's some kind of masked robber.'

Blake was astonished at the revelation. 'Jesus, I never saw that coming. We need to get a forensics team down there, and a ballistics specialist to take a look at everything. Great work. Get the place taped off I'm sending more officers down to help; sounds bloody dangerous. I'll get onto them right now.' Shocked, he ended the call and immediately called the Chief Inspector.

CHAPTER 132

The truth usually had a habit of slowly emerging through the mire of lies and misdirection, but there was no denying it often felt like they had to climb mountains to get at it, Blake thought, sitting next to DS Murphy in interview room one. Dave Millburn sat on the opposite side of the table cradling his plastered wrist like a wounded soldier.

Judging by the seriousness of the murder allegation, Blake was expecting this to be a no comment interview. It took him by surprise when Millburn began to open up.

'Mr Millburn, I'm going to ask you to account for a number of facts relating to the murder of Barry Gibson in the White Horse pub on Friday the 5th of June. Avoiding the questions or failing to answer them honestly may go against you in court. Do you understand that?'

Millburn nodded.

'Can you speak for the tape please?'

'Yes, I understand.'

'Can you account for your whereabouts between ten and eleven p.m. on that night?'

'What kind of daft question is that? You know where I was because you questioned me.'

Blake shook his head disapprovingly, 'We questioned you after the time-line I just mentioned,' he said glancing at his notes. 'Can you reconfirm what your association with Barry Gibson is?'

'Like I told you before, I only knew him years ago through work?'

Blake continued. 'After the fight between you and Mr Gibson why didn't you call an ambulance and inform anyone? You may have been able to save his life.'

'Save that murdering sex case's life, are you joking? If you'd done your job properly, the filthy bastard would still be alive, banged up in prison, with all the other nonces.'

'What do you mean by that?'

'You should have arrested him for the attempted rape of Lucy Barnes, and supplying dodgy E's that killed a 16-year-old from the Heath Hayes estate,' Millburn ranted, 'that fucker was evil, he got my first girlfriend addicted to heroin, in the late eighties.'

'What happened to her?'

'I don't know; she left Stoke and I never saw her again.'

'Sounds like it upset you?'

'It did, she was a lovely girl before that scum infected her.'

'So, beside your ex-girlfriend's unfortunate experience, you're saying that Barry Gibson supplied the ecstasy which killed Katey Hayder in January this year, and he tried to rape a fourteen year old named Lucy Barnes?' He remembered the Katey Hayder case, but Lucy Barnes didn't ring any bells. If there was any truth in this, it looked like Jayland Russell's intel about Barry Gibson dealing for Carl Bentley was spot on. 'I can assure you we'll look into those allegations.'

DS Murphy took down both names on his pad.

'Yeah, course you will.' Millburn said.

'Do you have any proof to back them up?' Blake was interested in finding out more. Millburn's foolish outburst clearly looked like his motive.

'He groped women, and young girls. If you gave him half a chance he'd have raped them. He was a vile predator. No one will mourn his death.'

'Seems like you had quite a grudge against him?'

'Yeah, me and everyone else.'

'Dave, can you account for Barry Gibson's blood being present on exhibit D1; a three inch long drop point survival knife, found discarded in bushes on the towpath of Caldon Canal, Shelton?' Blake said, sliding an A4 print across the table: his bombshell disclosure.

'My client won't answer that,' his solicitor interrupted.

Millburn's openness suddenly disappeared, 'No comment.' His head dropped, and for the first time he looked anxious.

'Can you provide us with an innocent reason why your DNA would be on the knife handle?'

Again, the solicitor objected, raising his hand.

'No comment,' Millburn replied.

'It was you on the CCTV images we distributed to the public; wasn't it Mr Millburn?'

'You can't prove that?'

'You're right, we can't, however what we can prove is your DNA and fingerprints are all over the murder weapon. The only other prints on the knife are the persons who found it. And they have a rock solid alibi for the night of the murder. Unlike you Dave; who we can place at the crime scene.'

'You know why I was in the pub that night.'

'Yes, but you used Darryl Connor's, and Nathan Dukes' stupidity to create subterfuge. The fact they paddled all over the crime scene, made it very difficult for our SOCO team to pinpoint the DNA of the murderer. It's no coincidence you made a point of not entering the gents in front of both of them. The waters were muddied even further, because all three of you, along with god knows how many punters, used the toilets that evening.'

'You almost got away with it until the knife turned up. Lucky for us the person who found it barely touched it. Your finger prints remained all over it. Combine that with the presence of the victim's blood, and we have strong evidence to charge you for murder. The forensic analysis revealed sweat secreted from your palms transferred to the handle, but it was underneath the victim's blood. So, when you forced the blade into Barry Gibson's brain, the spatter pattern indicates you killed him. Even though, you wiped it clean, on his polo shirt!' Blake stated confidently. 'Furthermore, we have proof you broke into the Furlong Social Club in Baptist Road in Burslem; late in the evening on the ninth of this month?'

'What the hell are you talking about?' Millburn protested.

'Initially we couldn't get anyone out to the break-in, as it seemed a relatively non-related minor crime; that was until one of my DCs pointed out what was stolen; photographs taken in 1991 at the William Adams pottery factory. Among those pics were group shots of Nathan Dukes, Darryl Connor, Barry Gibson, Grant Bolton, Stomper; aka Carl Bentley, and you!' Blake laid them out on the table.

Millburn looked devastated.

He continued. 'Unfortunately this information didn't come to light until days after the break-in. I sent a SOCO to dust for prints, but he didn't find any, which bought you some time. However, after the person in possession of your knife was arrested, I decided to get another forensic sweep of the scene. Guess what? The bin men didn't dispose of every bit of cabinet glass you broke. Three or four shards from one of the cabinets were lodged in the bottom of a dirty wheelie bin. Those contained microscopic samples of your DNA, in the form of saliva. The kind expelled when coughing, or sneezing, SOCO inform me.'

Millburn's face suddenly turned white as a sheet.

Blake's mobile rang, interrupting the interview. It was a Fia Riley from forensics. 'Excuse me for a moment; I need to take this.'

Out in the corridor Blake finally got the news he needed. 'And it's a definite match then?'

'No mistake, it's his blood.' Fia Riley confirmed.

'That's fantastic news, thank you.'

Due to an oversight, forensics had only gone over all three suspects' cars a few days after the murder, but drew a blank. But, the car hire form Blake found on Millburn's spare bedroom window sill turned out to be vital evidence. Dave Millburn's Lexus was in the garage for almost a week. So on that fateful night he drove to Hanley in a courtesy vehicle. Blake got the vehicle identified from its registration, and had it brought in for a forensics examination, an hour before Millburn was interviewed. Fia had just confirmed she'd discovered microscopic traces of Barry Gibson's blood, transferred from Millburn's boots onto the driver's side floor carpet, and since the car hadn't been hired out after Millburn, due to clutch problems, the evidence was conclusive.

He was just about to go back in to carry on interrogating Millburn when his phone rang again.

'You found anything else?' Blake asked DC Longsdon.

'Forensics have been here about an hour now. A couple of guys from ballistics cut the lock off the gun cabinet with a nifty tool. They've taken the weapons and bullets away for analysis, DC Longsdon said. Guess what else was in the cabinet?' he continued.

'The suspense is killing me,' Blake joked.'

'A hundred grand in used notes.'

'Seriously?'

'Straight up, boss.'

'Looks like Millburn is involved in more than just running the doors up town. That's another feather in your cap. The Chief Inspector will be ecstatic. Good work.'

'Feather in my cap, not sure I follow sir?'

'It's just an old saying. Don't worry about it. How much longer do you think you'll be?'

'At a guess I'd say another hour maximum, forensics have only got another couple of rooms left to do.'

'OK, I'll speak to you when you get back,' Blake ended the call.

CHAPTER 133

Blake returned to the interview room and started the tape rolling again.

'Mr Millburn, I've just spoken to one of my detective constables on the phone. It seems your house is the gift that keeps giving. How long have you owned rifles?'

Judging by the disillusioned look on his face this line of questioning clearly rattled him.

Millburn's solicitor shook his head, but he knew the game was up.

'A few years.'

'What do you use them for?' Blake continued.

'Hunting. I go on deer stalking trips to Scotland several times a year.' he said convincingly.

'And you have proof to back this up.'

'Yeah. Got receipts and pictures.'

'What, of dead deer?' Even though Millburn was looking at a murder charge, Blake thought he'd indulge him, knowing how much people liked to talk about their hobbies. Perhaps he would inadvertently reveal something else, he thought.

'Yeah, among other things.'

'Like what?'

'Highland scenery, game shooting and things like that.'

'At this point we only have your word for it, and until we've seen those receipts and pictures, thc rifles will be treated as highly dangerous, unlicenced weapons, and added to your murder charge. Furthermore, my officers also discovered a *hundred thousand* pounds in used notes inside a bag in your locked gun cabinet. Can you explain where that came from, and how you obtained it?'

'No comment.'

Blake continued, 'You do realise, if you can't provide evidence that the money was legally obtained, it will be confiscated under the proceeds of crime act?'

Millburn looked horrified at the prospect of losing his massive Hoard ransom money.

The following morning Blake fetched Dave Millburn before the duty sergeant, confident all the evidence they'd gathered the previous day was more than enough to charge him with possession of unlicenced weapons, money laundering and most importantly murder. Standing there anxiously holding his broken wrist, Millburn looked devastated.

'David Millburn you're charged with the following offences. On the 5th of June in Hanley, Stoke-on-Trent, Staffordshire, you murdered Barry Gibson contrary to common law. You're also being charged with two counts of possession of firearms without a licence, and the hundred thousand pounds in used notes found at your property, will be confiscated under the proceeds of crime act. Do you understand these charges?' Blake said.

Millburn grunted acceptance.

CHAPTER 134

'Roger, good to see you. Come in,' Tom Blake said, welcoming DS Jamieson, who was fashionably late to the soirée at his home. 'Everyone's through there.' He gestured toward the open-plan lounge-kitchen as Jamieson passed him a bottle of Merlot.

'Cheers, boss.'

On the way through the lounge, he greeted DC Moore who sat on the sofa staring at PC Evans. She was standing in the kitchen, flicking the tops off bottles of Cobra in tight, leather, skinny jeans.

'Beer, Roger?' she asked.

'Love one.'

The hulking figure of PC Davis obscured Nick Pemberton who was talking to DC Chris Longsdon and Langford Gelder. Isabel perched on one of the Spitalfield barstools leaning on the granite worktop, next to Sue Collins. Both of them listened intently to Blake's neighbour, Robert Taylor, as he recited old police anecdotes to her father and DS Murphy.

Collins nudged Isabel and whispered how rugged and well-heeled the six foot 64-year-old was. From titbits of gossip she'd picked up off her dad, the 48-year-old singleton often scared blokes off with her direct approach. The only males in her life were two cherished tortoiseshell cats from a local rescue centre.

'He's a lovely bloke, likes a few whiskies though.'

'Is he an alco? It's common in retired officers, you know?'

Isabel laughed. 'No! Purely medicinal, Dad says.'

'Ah, I see. A male thing, then?'

'Yeah, he calls round at least once a week for a tipple with Dad.'

'For old-school police banter, no doubt?'

'Something like that.'

'Anyway, how you feeling?'

'Great, thanks.'

'You've had a pretty rough time recently. We've all been rooting for you at the station. Understandably, your dad's been worried out of his mind,' Collins said, expressing sympathy for her ordeal.

Isabel gave her an uneasy smile. 'It's been hard, but I'm through the worst of it. I'd rather not talk about it, if you don't mind?'

Realising she didn't know the girl well enough, Collins apologised. 'Sorry, love. I won't mention it again. Scout's honour.'

Blake tapped a spoon against his pint glass. 'Can I interest anyone in a glass of red?'

'Not for me. Thanks, Tom. Still got beer,' PC Davis said.

'I'm OK yet, boss,' DS Jamieson replied.

'I'll have one, sir,' Evans said.

'And me?' Nick Pemberton chipped in.

'Oh, y… yes, please,' Sue Collins said, almost slipping off her stool, holding out a shaky glass for a top up.

'Whoa! Steady on, Sue!' DS Murphy shouted across the kitchen, unwittingly drawing everyone's attention to the family liaison officer who had been first to arrive and appeared well oiled. DS Moore, DC Longsdon and PC Davis couldn't help sniggering at her public pants-down moment.

With their glasses charged, Blake put his arm around Isabel, raised his glass and proposed a toast. 'To my brave, wonderful daughter, Isabel!'

The group moved to the centre of the kitchen and chinked glasses. 'To Isabel!'

Her dad embraced her.

Weepy eyed, she blushed.

CHAPTER 135

Around 10.30 p.m., DS Murphy and DS Jamieson bungled a rather worse-for-wear Sue Collins into a taxi, accompanied by DC Moore who was under strict instructions to get her home safely and tucked into bed.

Before they could shut the cab door, PC Davis stood in the light cast from the hallway onto the gravel and teased, 'Don't get any funny ideas either; she's far too pissed!!' The three of them roared as the taxi pulled away, with DC Moore hanging out the opposite rear window giving them the middle finger.

'You're a wicked bastard, Davis,' Jamieson said.

'I'm only pulling his leg.'

Murphy frowned. 'He wouldn't, would he?'

'Wouldn't put it past him. You know what they say about the quiet ones,' Davis said.

Jamieson added. 'He'd never live it down. The lads at the station would crucify him.'

Returning to the house they gathered back in the kitchen. Isabel had gone to bed. Langford Gelder and DC Chris Longsdon sat in the lounge drinking coffee, waiting for their taxi to arrive.

After they'd left, Blake pulled out a bottle of vintage single malt. He poured a two-finger slug for each of his remaining colleagues as they discussed Barry Gibson's murder and the Staffordshire Hoard heist.

'Do you reckon Dave Millburn will get life then?' Robert Taylor asked Blake.

'That's what we're pushing the CPS for.'

'Such a devious psychopath.'

'You're not kidding. The military grade rifles and bullet-making equipment we found in his loft show what a dangerous individual he is. He claims his arsenal was used purely for hunting trips to Scotland: legal deer shooting. When we looked into his bank accounts, we found five payments to a small deer management company, who provide deerstalking holidays in the Highlands.

'Sounds pretty barbaric?' Taylor said.

'Apparently, it's all legal and above board. Unlike Millburn's rifles, which aren't even registered; and the fact that bills for each trip include the hire of stalker rifles, shows he has an alternative use for them. Quite what that is, we've yet to establish, but I'll leave that to your imagination.'

'Bloody hell! You reckon he could be a contract killer?' Jamieson asked.

'It's possible, but hard to prove because he made his own bullets. Ballistics informed me no two would be the same, and they've yet to find the jigs that made them, just shell casings. The fact Millburn had a hundred grand stashed in a locked gun cabinet in his loft, is hugely suggestive. So far we've been unable to trace where he got it from, but it definitely wasn't by legal means.'

'Sounds like a Hollywood script,' Taylor shuddered.

Blake continued his narrative. 'Jayland Russell's arrest was a massive stroke of luck. I'm convinced if we hadn't found the murder weapon with Barry Gibson's blood, and Millburn's DNA on it, we wouldn't have caught him, because I probably wouldn't have got the second forensic sweep of the Furlong Social Club in Burslem. That's where we discovered his DNA on some broken glass.'

'Usually, if you put enough effort into a case something always turns up. But on this occasion I'd say you were very lucky,' Taylor agreed with Blake.

'That's the way it goes sometimes, it would be unrealistic to think we can solve every crime. The Staffordshire Hoard case is a prime example.'

'No sign of the Saxon Gold yet then, fellas?' Robert Taylor asked.

'Afraid not,' Murphy replied. 'They must have sold it, but to whom remains a mystery.'

'I reckon it was stolen to order. It's not like they could knock it out piece by piece on eBay,' PC Davis joked.

'That's one theory,' Blake informed them. 'But according to Colin Jacobs, who's head of the Specialist Art and Antique Bureau, most stolen antiquities are taken by criminals intent on selling them back to the market, although everything reported stolen ends up on the Art Loss Register, making it virtually impossible for it to be sold back to the legitimate market.'

'So, how do they flog it then?' Pemberton asked.

Blake continued his attempt to steer them in a certain direction. 'Jacobs reckons organised criminals often use artefacts as currency, to pay off debts or as collateral to finance deals. In some cases they've even returned the goods and collected the reward, which is ridiculous when you think about it.' Deep down he had suspicions the American he'd encountered in Miami was probably the buyer.

'Like kidnap and ransom?' PC Davis said, realising too late that it was a touchy subject considering what recently happened to Isabel.

'Yeah, same principle,' replied Blake.

'The Cayman Island account balance tallies roughly with the Hoard's value.' Nick Pemberton said.

'Truth is, we'll never know for sure,' Blake said. 'Hopefully the gold will be recovered, but I wouldn't bank on it. According to the Art Loss Register, recovery rate is only fifteen per cent. It's a bloody shame considering the history involved.'

'And a real blow to local tourism,' Rob Taylor added.

'We could debate about it all night. Don't know about you, fellas, but I'm off to get some sleep. Early morning start tomorrow, John, on a missing persons case that came in yesterday,' Blake said, collecting their empty glasses and placing them in the sink ready for washing.

Twenty minutes later another taxi arrived and ferried the merry crew home as Rob Taylor stumbled to his bungalow next door.

In bed Blake stared into the darkness contemplating the events of the past few weeks. He felt mentally and physically drained. Thank god Isabel was on the mend; her strength increased each day. Upon reflection things hadn't turned out too badly. The overwhelming kindness of donations to her JustGiving page restored his faith in humanity. But the reality was, without fencing off two pieces of stolen Hoard for forty-five grand in America, the outcome may have been very different.

The conclusion to the Staffordshire Hoard and Barry Gibson murder cases didn't leave him satisfied, but he knew through experience acceptance was all part of the job. Dwelling on it wouldn't change anything.

Besides, he didn't want to rock the boat unnecessarily, for fear of exposing what happened in Miami. God forbid. That genie would hopefully stay in its bottle.

CHAPTER 136

The following morning Blake woke earlier than planned due to a drink-induced headache, so decided to let Isabel lie in whilst he took an early breakfast. There were oatcakes in the freezer, a block of mature cheddar in the fridge, and an unopened pack of Lavazza Grand Filtro coffee waiting to be sampled. He wrapped himself in his towelling dressing gown, and padded into the bathroom, ran the waterfall tap, and doused his face in cold water.

At the bottom of the stairs, the *Daily Mail* poked out of the letterbox. As he extracted it, a small brown manila envelope, stiffened with cardboard, slipped onto the mat. Still not fully awake he scraped it up and headed for the kitchen.

Dropping the newspaper and envelope on the kitchen table, he filled the kettle and set it to boil. Minutes later the wonderful aroma of freeze-dried coffee filled the room. While it brewed, he fished oatcakes, cheese and bacon from the fridge and made them up and grilled them.

Morning rituals completed, he perched on a stool at the breakfast bar and tucked in whilst glancing at the headline news on the front page of the *Mail.* Nothing but the usual depressing stories regarding corrupt government officials. Turning the page a suspicious death report piqued his interest. Halfway down his eyes widened. Dropping his half-eaten oatcake onto the plate, he felt a sudden coldness spread through his body.

Suspicious deaths. Bodies found at remote Shetland farm named!

Orkney Isle police are making house-to-house enquiries regarding the discovery of four male bodies, two of which were found by ramblers at a remote farm overlooking Pegal Bay. The walkers called on the farm to top up their water bottles and discovered an overwhelming smell of gas when they opened the kitchen door. Concerned, they called the police immediately, who arrived fifteen minutes later, entered the property and found two local men; one slumped across the sofa, the other in an armchair. Both were dead. They traced the source of the gas leak; an old cooker had been left on. The deceased are brothers – Fraser and Bryce Kennan – who were local wool farmers.

Officers performed an extensive search of the property and its outbuildings and discovered the bodies of two black males of African origin in an industrial log furnace.

The police have been able to identify them through bus passes found in their jeans pockets. Jozef and Frederick Simbala were illegal immigrants hailing from the Midlands city of Stoke-on-Trent in England. Police are still investigating why they were so far north of the border. In a statement to the press, DCI Burrel of Kirkwell Police, said:

'The pathologist's assessment is that the Simbala brothers both died from single gunshot wounds to their heads, but no weapon has been recovered from the crime scene, which bears the hallmarks of a contract killing. The Kennan brothers had consumed a high level of alcohol and it's thought they may have fallen asleep and been slowly gassed to death before they had a chance to dispose of the bodies.

'Anyone with information regarding this crime can call Crimestoppers on: 0800 555 122.'

Like a match illuminating the depths of his brain, the haze cleared. Once they'd liaised with the Orkney Force, the bus passes should point to an address in Stoke-on-Trent. If they could link that to Ibrahim Benzar the association might provide vital evidence linking him to Isabel's abduction, and the contract killer who took out the Simbala brothers: who he suspected was Dave Millburn. It wasn't a huge leap of faith. However, locating Ibrahim Benzar would take time and wasn't guaranteed. Millburn was looking at life inside for Barry Gibson's murder. Hopefully, the bullets embedded in the Simbala's brains could be linked to him.

He finished the oatcake, folded the paper and put it on top of his leather folio, ready to take to work. Hurriedly he opened the manila envelope and emptied its contents onto the granite worktop.

He gulped nervously staring at a collection of twelve compromising photographs taken in Miami, ranging from him counting $45,000 in the American's Corvette, to passing the envelope under the table in the diner. Horrified, he scrambled them into rows of three and sat staring at them like a bewildered rabbit in headlights. Clearly this damning evidence proved his stateside encounter wasn't covert after all. The devious bastards had used him as a pawn in their audacious heist of the largest Saxon gold ever found, although admittedly Yusuf Benzar's arrest was down to his own sheer stupidity, rather than by design, leaving the gang limited choices regarding his participation.

The key question was, would those pair of killer shadow thieves ever be found? This would play heavy on his mind. Worst of all, if the photographs ever fell into the wrong hands his career would be over and he'd potentially face a custodial sentence!

The note read:

Just a little insurance policy in case you decide to inform anyone about our settlement. Have a nice day.

Worrying about it wouldn't change anything. He now knew how the Hoard heist was planned, but his daughter being knocked down may have been the reckless act of one of Ibrahim Benzar's foot soldiers disobeying him. Ironically, if it hadn't been for her accident, and the brain scans, Isabel's tumour may not have been discovered until it was too late. For that at least he was grateful. Moving forward, he just wanted to spend a meaningful life with her and get his police career back on track. Methodical detective work helped by a dose of karma might one day bring the Benzar brothers to book.

THE END

Printed in Poland
by Amazon Fulfillment
Poland Sp. z o.o., Wrocław